THE MISTR

Greece and Turkey, the gate
astern world, the cradle of so much history, the fount of so
ıany ideas, are full of places we all know and love.

is here that, back in the fourteenth and early fifteenth
enturies, a great struggle took place between the Byzantine
mpire, the remnant of the once great Roman empire, and
ıe powerful Ottoman Turks, the Islamic force rising from
ıe Anatolian plains.

onstantinople had a famous harbour for the safety of its
hips and formidable walls and Byzantium had great armies.
he finest of its warriors were the Varangian Guards, elite
ghters who had originally come to Constantinople from
ngland as refugees from the Norman Conquest. One of
ıese Varangians, whose destiny is to save the Byzantine
mpire, is the hero of THE MISTRA CHRONICLES.

BOOK ONE

THE WALLS OF BYZANTIUM

BOOK TWO

THE TOWERS OF SAMARCAND

BOOK THREE

THE LION OF MISTRA

Praise for

The Mistra Chronicles

'A stirring tale of the struggle for Byzantium. Heneage brings to life both the tragedy and the heroism' *Tom Holland*

'One hell of a fine book. Fascinating historical mysteries and vivid colourful characters. It's a page-turner fast enough to make its own breeze' *Conn Iggulden*

'A compelling narrative of intrigue, love and war' *Bookseller*

'An electrifying historical novel that will keep you awake deep into the night' *Good Book Guide*

'James loves history and communicates that love with enthusiasm, bathing us in an era and world that I didn't know much about. The insights into the Turks' Islamic culture are fascinating . . . Enough excitement and riveting history to keep me going through to the end and enough loose ends and intrigue for me to eagerly anticipate what lies ahead' *Bookbag*

'A thoroughly enjoyable book that takes you on a very interesting journey through the 15th Century battles between the great states of the times, the Christian world and Islam. Add in a hero, romance, intrigue, plots, murder, betrayal, a hidden treasure and a writing style that is a mixture of history book and romantic novel and you're left with a book you just don't want to put down . . .' *Army Rumour Service*

'Like all the best first volumes, it ends in a cliffhanger that will leave you panting for the next installment . . .' *We Love This Book*

THE MISTRA CHRONICLES

JAMES HENEAGE

THE TOWERS OF SAMARCAND

HERON
BOOKS

First published in Great Britain in 2014 by Heron Books
This paperback edition published in 2015 by Heron Books
an imprint of

Quercus Publishing Ltd
Carmelite House
50 Victoria Embankment
London EC4Y 0DZ

An Hachette UK company

A CIP catalogue record for this book is available
from the British Library

PB ISBN 978 1 78206 118 2
EBOOK ISBN 978 1 78206 117 5

10 9 8 7 6 5 4 3 2 1

Typeset by Ellipsis Digital Limited, Glasgow

Printed and bound in Great Britain by Clays Ltd, St Ives plc

To my mother and father

CONTENTS

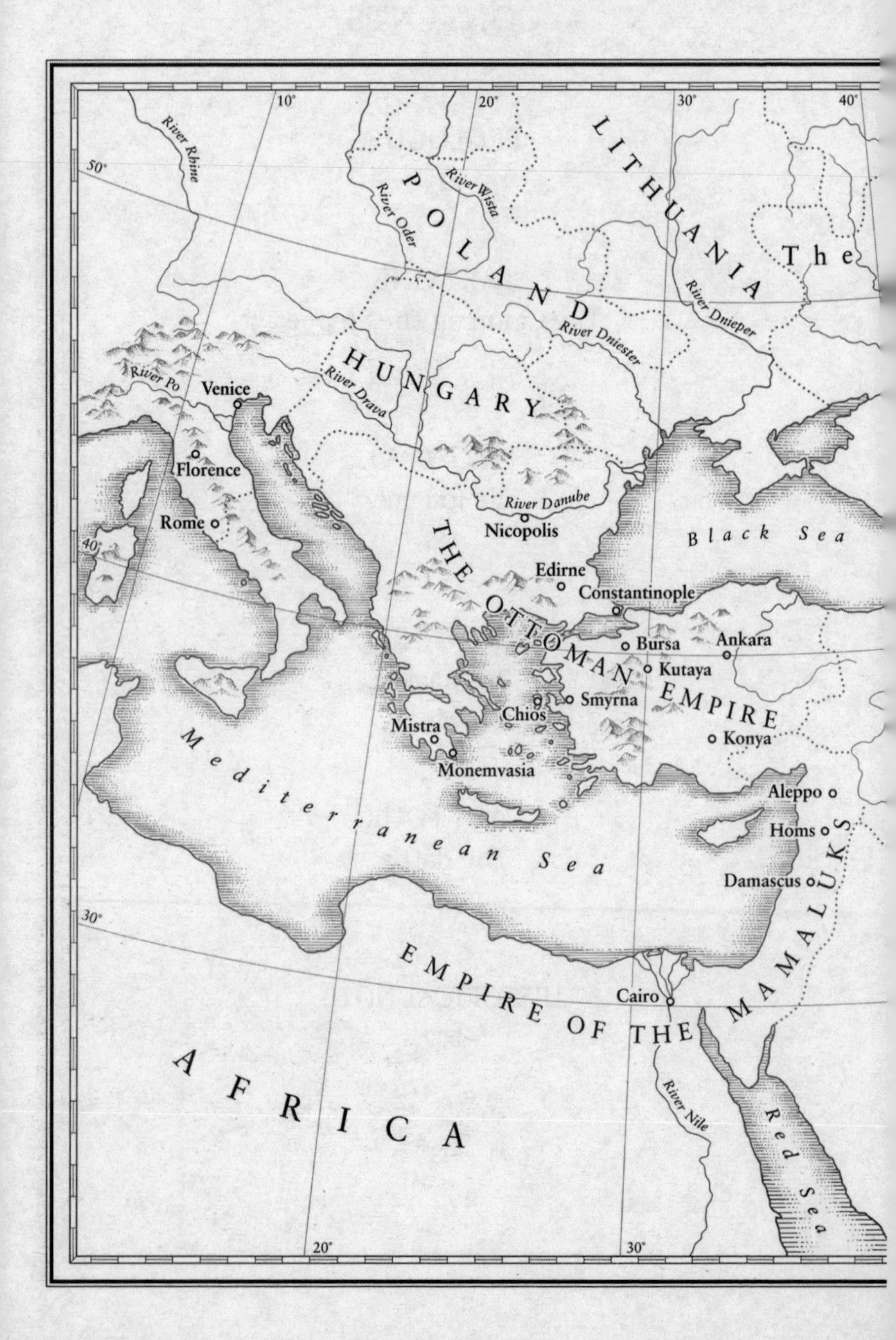
10°
20°
30°
40°
50°
40°
30°
20°
30°
River Rhine
River Oder
River Wista
POLAND
LITHUANIA
The
River Dnieper
River Dniester
HUNGARY
River Drava
River Po
Venice
Florence
Rome
River Danube
Nicopolis
Black Sea
THE OTTOMAN EMPIRE
Edirne
Constantinople
Bursa
Ankara
Kutaya
Smyrna
Chios
Konya
Mistra
Monemvasia
Aleppo
Homs
Damascus
Mediterranean Sea
EMPIRE OF THE MAMALUKS
Cairo
River Nile
Red Sea
AFRICA

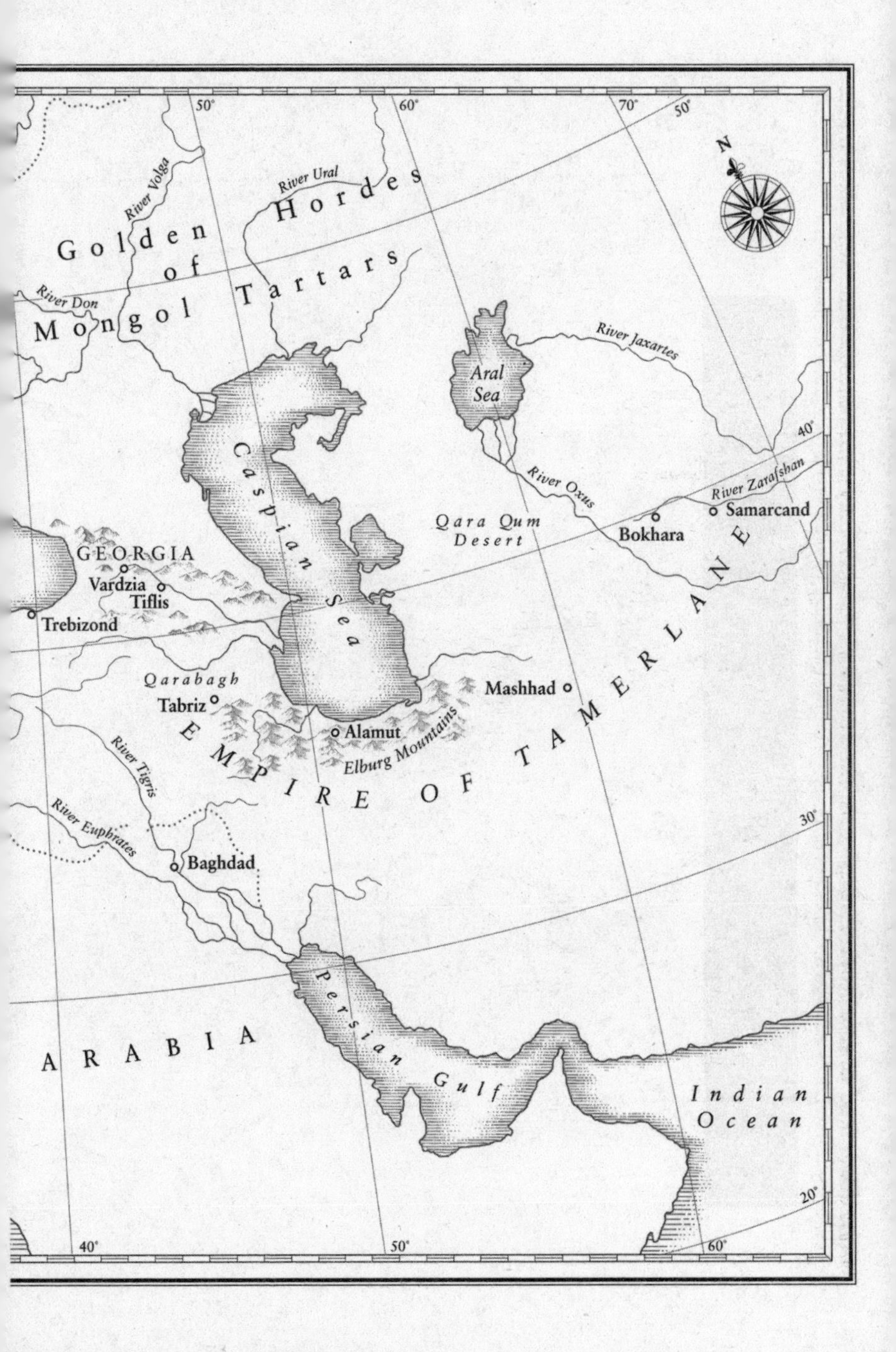

Golden Hordes of Mongol Tartars
River Volga
River Ural
River Don
River Jaxartes
Aral Sea
Caspian Sea
River Oxus
River Zarafshan
Qara Qum Desert
Samarcand
Bokhara
GEORGIA
Vardzia
Tiflis
Trebizond
Qarabagh
Tabriz
Mashhad
Alamut
Elburg Mountains
EMPIRE OF TAMERLANE
River Tigris
River Euphrates
Baghdad
ARABIA
Persian Gulf
Indian Ocean
N
50°
60°
70°
50°
40°
30°
20°
40°
50°
60°

PROLOGUE

CONSTANTINOPLE, WINTER 1396

A party of five stood on the hill of Kosmidion overlooking the city of Constantinople: the Sultan Bayezid, his three sons and the Grand Vizier, all cloaked and furred against the winter wind that swept in from the Bosporus. They held cloths to their faces.

The rain had stopped at last and a sudden shaft of sunlight ignited the spearheads on the city walls. There were pitifully few these days. Constantinople, the last gem in the empty crown of Byzantium, was a place of fields and orchards and churches whose domes no longer wore the gold to ignite.

A few of the city's garrison had emerged in sortie the night before and now stood behind, spread-eagled in crucifixion as their saviour had been, the stench of their decay all around. Bayezid spoke through his mask.

'We need cannon.'

The Ottoman Sultan had been known as Yildirim in his youth: 'Thunderbolt'. He was fourth in the line of Osman and had astonished the world by the speed of his campaigns to quell the *gazi* tribes of Anatolia and stretch his empire to the banks of the Danube. Now he was a man addicted to wine and sugar whose size of turban mirrored the size of his belly. His heir, Suleyman, stood on one side and his second son, Mehmed, on the other. They were as different as their mothers: Suleyman tall and pointed of nose and beard, Mehmed smaller, his gazi roots there in a face as flat as the steppe. Bayezid's third son, Musa, stood a little behind and was yet to be bearded. The brothers hated each other.

Suleyman patted his horse, flicking water from its mane. 'We need cannon of a size not yet created, Father,' he said. He raised his hand to the city beneath them. 'Behold the strongest walls in the world. We can throw a million men at them and they'll not break. We need cannon big enough to smash them, and they're made in Venice.'

A drumbeat sounded from somewhere distant. Half-naked men worked to its tempo, hauling forward the trebuchets, mangonels and other machines of war that would wreak what havoc they could until the cannon arrived. In front stretched the open wound of the Ottoman siege lines, livid with newly dug earth. A lot had been accomplished in the two months since this army had marched away to Nicopolis.

Nicopolis.

The flower of Christendom had come west, jousting and drinking its way to do battle with Bayezid on the Danube. It was, they said, an army that could hold up the sky with its lances. But the sky had come down on its boasting and ten thousand Christian corpses lay on the field of Nicopolis. The victory had been Bayezid's and it had sent shock waves through the courts of Europe. He had boasted: *I will water my horses at the altar of St Peter's in Rome*, and before him was the only thing that stood in his way: the walls of Constantinople.

Constantinople: the second city of seven hills to serve as

capital of the two-thousand-year Empire of the *Rhomaioi*. Once it had been the meeting place of the world, the gilded bridge between Christian West and the lands of the Prophet, the Dar ul-Islam. Now the empress's jewels lay in pawn in Venice and her city hid behind its colossal walls beneath the early darkness of an iron sky.

A rainbow had appeared above the city, a curve of colour, heaven's favour poured into its battered chalice on earth.

Bayezid looked up and then turned to his sons. 'The sickle of Islam poised,' he said. 'When do we get our cannon, Prince Suleyman? We can't wait for Venice.'

Mehmed edged his horse closer to his father's. He spoke across him. 'Didn't you say there were cannon in Mistra, Brother?' he asked.

Suleyman frowned. 'Only small ones. Not big enough.'

'Yet cannon, nonetheless,' said Bayezid, remembering. He looked at his heir. 'You will bring them.'

Suleyman opened his mouth to protest. This siege was where he belonged. It was to be his triumph.

But there are other things to bring from Mistra.

The woman who'd sworn to submit to him was in Mistra and it was time for her to be returned to him.

'I'll go to Mistra,' Suleyman said.

PART ONE

THE CAMP ON THE STEPPE

CHAPTER ONE

GERMIYAN BEYLIK, ANATOLIA, WINTER 1396

The first snows came as the old man turned to leave; great balls of it as big as babies' fists that stuck to his beard like dough.

Omar, the holy man from Konya, had brought Luke Magoris to the forty or so *ger*s that made up this Germiyan camp far out on the steppe. Around them was distance with no horizon. The snow had turned the landscape into a limitless white without shape or feature that somewhere, far away, became the sky. For Luke, a boy born into the bustle of a little city on the edge of the sea, it was beyond comprehension.

Their reception had been as cold as the weather. The business at the monastery had delayed them and made the tribe late in moving to their winter pastures. And the snows were early this year. Luke looked around him at the sullen faces.

'They don't want me here, Omar. Look at them.'

The old man looked up at the sky through crinkled eyes, then back at Luke, wiping snow from his lips.

'These are good people, Luke,' he said. 'Their movement makes them honest. "A little rivulet which is moving continually does not become defiled." There is truth in that.'

'Who said that?'

'The poet Rumi. The saint of Konya, where I must now go. The saint calls and I'm not good in tents.'

'But how do I talk to them?'

'You learn their language, Luke. You learn to ride and shoot like a nomad, like a Mongol.' He turned his horse, stopped and looked back at Luke, his fist on his saddle. 'Like Tamerlane.'

Then he was gone.

Two men approached dressed in coats with fur linings and embroidered hems and looked similar enough to be related. Father and son, Luke guessed, and the leaders of this camp. They stopped in front of Luke. The older man spoke, turned and walked away; the younger stayed. He pushed Luke to his knees in the snow. Stepping closer, he lifted Luke's chin and spat. He jabbed his chest with his finger. 'Gomil.'

Gomil.

The first night was the worst. Long after they'd eaten, the ger was still dense with smoke and Luke's eyes stung. He wiped them with the back of his hand and looked down at the sword hilt resting across his chest, its dragon eyes staring back into his. Six hours had passed since Omar had ridden away, leaving him only this sword and a line from Rumi. He'd never felt so alone.

He'd dined in miserable silence, six wary eyes watching him through the gloom. They belonged to the family with whom he was to live: Torguk, his wife Berta, who suckled a child at her breast, and their daughter Arkal, her crippled foot tucked beneath the folds of her *deel*.

They'd fed him the thick mutton stew that would be their diet until the tribe's sheep were too few for slaughter. He'd watched them suck the meat from the bones and wash it down with soured mare's milk. And when he'd finally lain down to sleep, the smell of mutton and putrid milk had punctured the membrane of his dreams.

Now he lay awake and thought of his home in Monemvasia. He saw it from afar, perched on its fist of rock thrown out into the Mirtoon Sea. He saw its narrow, climbing streets, cobbles wet with the tread of a sixteen-year-old boy come in from the sea. Was it only four years since he'd left? He thought of Mistra, where he'd never been: sixty miles distant from Monemvasia yet so different: a place of church and ceremony where the Despot ruled amongst the saints. Two cities side by side. Two destinies: love and duty, Anna and Tamerlane.

And a plan.

Plethon's plan, his destiny: to bring Tamerlane west to fight Bayezid. To bring one monster to kill another. He closed his eyes and there was Anna. He'd last seen her standing before him as he knelt beneath Suleyman's sword on the bloody field of Nicopolis. A whisper.

Are you with Suleyman?

Sleep drifted in like a mist and the whisper rose to the crash of a storm at sea. He was in waves bigger than continents, waves that hid the sky. He saw a rain-lashed jetty and a giant swinging an axe until the axe fell. He saw Anna being dragged down that jetty. Away from him.

Are you with Suleyman now?

The next morning Luke was shaken awake by the girl Arkal. She watched him shyly through her dirt and handed him a cup of salted tea. The salt stung his blasted lips. For a long moment they looked at each other. Luke put down the cup.

'Luke,' he said, pointing at himself. 'My name is Luke.'

The girl was perhaps twelve. A row of yellow teeth appeared. 'Lug.'

There was a grunt from above. Torguk was standing there. He clapped his hands and gestured to the door. They were to leave at once and there was work to do. Immediately they set about clearing out the stove, pallets, carpets and everything else from the ger before stripping the felt from its sides and collapsing the trellised willow frame on to which it was tied. Outside were large wagons to pull the tribe's belongings and larger ones on which tents had been erected for carrying the sick, pregnant and old, and for the tribe to sleep in at night.

Around the camp, fires smouldered, turning the snow into a steaming paste in which the children played until they saw Luke. Then they formed a circle to watch the tall, fair stranger as he worked, at first silent and awed, then nudgingly braver until one of them darted forward to touch his hair. Arkal limped over to shoo them away and when Luke smiled at her, she darkened in pleasure.

The young men of the tribe went from ger to ger helping to dismantle them but one they left alone. It was on the outskirts of the camp and smaller than the others. Outside it stood poles on which horse hides hung beneath animal skulls. Bones lay in the snow around them. As Luke watched, the tent door opened and an old man came out, leaning on a stick. He was dressed in a filthy deel and snakes of matted hair fell to his waist. A young girl emerged wearing skins but with bare arms and legs. Her hair was long and dirty but she was tall and had some grace. Luke couldn't see her face but, as she straightened, he knew that she was looking at him. He turned away.

*

When the camp finally moved, it travelled as fast as the oxen were able to pull the wagons. On the first two days, they ground their way across the steppe and the wind blew more fiercely and the sallies of snow grew bolder. Everyone but Luke was either riding inside the gers on the wagons or on a horse. On the third day, they came across a caravan: four hundred camels making their knock-kneed way towards the warmer climes of the Levant. They stopped and talked to merchants who'd come from Bursa and had a funny tale to tell. One of the merchants opened his mouth wide to show a grey substance that filled the holes in his teeth and the gazis gasped in wonder. Then the business of trade took over and the Germiyans swapped mohair wool and bales of felt for silk and other comforts that would make life more bearable in the terrible months to come.

Luke watched it all and, for the first time in a week, smiled.

A funny tale.

It was a fortnight ago that he'd seen his friends at Bursa: Dimitri, the seller of mastic to fill men's teeth, and Benedo Barbi, engineer to kings, popes and the Genoese *signori* of Chios, an island they called Scio.

That night he dreamt of Chios. He dreamt of Fiorenza, Princess of Trebizond, wife to Marchese Longo, Lord of Chios, who some said was the most beautiful woman in the world. He saw her lying beneath him, her buttercup hair splayed out across grass littered with flowers and shiny with evening dew. He saw her drawing him down.

You can, Luke. And you must.

The following day, Luke tried to ride. Gomil had assembled a party to hunt marmot with hawks. As it was leaving, Luke saw the chief's son stop suddenly and turn, staring hard at the horizon, his head tilted as if listening. Then, with dizzying speed, he drew his bow and released two arrows. He looked out beneath his hand and gave a grunt of pleasure. Luke judged it a good moment and he approached Gomil's stirrup and gestured to a horse. But Gomil spat into the snow and cantered away.

That evening they fed on lynx as well as marmot and, since the night held no snow, sat outside around a fire, and the men passed the airag and sang and the women looked at Luke and giggled. In the firelight, Luke studied the faces around him, faces creased by hard weather, chins bright with airag and bubbles of *koumis* on their lips. What had Omar said?

These are good people, Luke. Their movement makes them honest.

Luke looked at Gomil. Was he honest? He was certainly drunk.

At length the women and children began to drift away to find space within the tents. The chief rose and yawned and left and the rest of the men closed in around the fire and searched the cauldrons for old bones to suck on. A new sack of airag was brought, which they up-ended and splashed on to their faces. Some had passed out, some were speechless with the drink, some argued. Luke sat a little apart.

Gomil rose to his feet and fell. There was laughter and he scowled and tried again, his hand gripping a shoulder. His eyes were fixed on Luke and the fire caught their hooded malevolence. He muttered something and staggered over, lifting his feet with exaggerated care. He stopped, swayed and drew back his foot for the kick. But Luke was quick and not drunk. He rolled easily to the side and Gomil's foot swung through air and he fell again, this time hard.

Gomil swore, got to his knees and reached over to draw a burning branch from the fire. Then he lunged. Luke rolled again, feeling the heat on his back as the wood broke against the ground, sending a shower of cinders into the night. One of the men shouted something and Gomil screamed abuse at him. Now he was standing and Luke was on his knees, looking around for a weapon. He was too far from the fire.

There was another shout. Luke looked over to see the chief standing there, clutching a skin to his shoulders. He barked something and his son sat heavily on the ground, shaking his head. Luke didn't wait for more. He got to his feet and turned to find his tent.

She was standing behind him. Half in the shadows, her hair over her eyes like a veil. Staring at him. The girl in the skins.

Who are you?

The snow began to fall in earnest the following day and the horses hung their heads against its driving force and men made cowls of their furs and shrank their airag heads into their shoulders. Luke climbed aboard a wagon until pulled off by a passing rider. The wind was relentless and made his eyes stream with tears that ran down his cheeks and froze on his lips. He thought of Chios and summer evenings and the sound of cicadas and the comfort of friendship and shared language. He thought of Anna and the warmth of two naked bodies in a cave.

He looked at the ponies around him. They were tough, shaggy creatures with long hair and stubborn mouths. He'd never seen their like before. Would he be able to talk to them as he could to other horses, as he did to Eskalon? He closed his eyes and Eskalon's big head was there before him, those intelligent eyes looking into his, understanding.

Where are you now, old friend?

*

That night the storm grew in strength and buffeted the walls of the big ger in which he lay beneath furs, barely able to move amidst the mass of people. The wagon beneath them groaned in the onslaught and men moaned in their sleep. The smoke from the single stove hung heavy above the stench of flesh. Luke lay awake and thought of the horses outside leaning against each other for protection, their coats stiff with snow, their eyes closed, their patience endless.

The door to the ger moved. Someone was trying to enter. Heads turned and people sat up. A child screamed. A demon was forcing its way inside.

The door opened and the girl stood in its frame covered in a single, stiff sheet of felt. She looked into the tent and her eyes were dull with cold and pleading. She was seeking shelter from the storm. Luke sat up.

Who are you?

Gomil rose and lifted an arm. A boot thudded against the door frame, then another. A third hit her on the side of the head and she lifted her arm to protect herself. She glanced around the tent and there was fear in the look and blood next to the bruise on her cheek. She found Luke and, for a second, held his gaze. Then she backed away, pulling the door shut behind her.

Luke got up and picked up a wolf skin, ignoring the cries of those who'd lain beneath. He stumbled to the door and pulled it open and the savagery of the night outside almost flung him back inside. He could see nothing beyond a swirling darkness that tore at his hair and clothes. He turned back and grabbed a torch from the wall, shielding its flame with his body. He moved out into the night, pulling the door shut. He turned his head to left and right and called and felt the sound thrown back at him on the wind. He jumped from the wagon into the snow and called again. There was no answer.

He heard a sound to his right. He felt his way along the side of the wagon, the torch held close within his cloak, the wolf skin balled against his stomach. Every step was a fight to stay upright. He stumbled against something, something alive and huddled against a wheel, something that moved quickly away when he leant forward to touch it. He bent and felt the tangled hair of the girl, crusted with snow. He moved his torch from within his cloak and, in its scattered light, he saw her.

A bare arm circled the neck of a horse. In her other hand was a knife. There was a cut in the skin of the animal's neck where she'd opened a vein and blood ran from the corners of her lips. Luke recoiled. He pushed the skin at her and it was snatched from his hand. He looked again but there was nothing there. Nothing. She'd vanished into the storm.

A week later, they arrived, quite suddenly, at the valley. For the first time in weeks, Luke saw trees climbing the slopes up to the jagged teeth of an escarpment that ran as a high ridge on either side. Below the trees were fields, thick with snow, some of which had the shapes of old walls around them.

Further on, they met another valley that ran across theirs. A little river ran through it, outcrops of snow coasting on its currents like driftwood. They stopped to let the horses drink. Dried milk curds were produced from pockets and passed around and the men's faces curved into smiles as they chewed. Luke looked around for the girl. There was no sign of her.

Soon they were on their way again and the going was easier. The men leant from their saddles to laugh while women climbed down from the wagons to walk with their children.

The horses held their heads a little higher and the jangle of harness told of a journey's end.

By the afternoon, they had reached a flat piece of ground where the river broke into separate paths that gurgled their way around islands on which large birds stood on one leg watching them. The men dismounted and looked around at the snow and filled their water bottles from the river, sweeping aside the ice with their hands.

Luke helped Arkal lift the bales of felt from the wagons and stretch out the frame of the ger. Together, they unrolled the layered felt and wrapped it around the latticed wall, securing it in place with ropes. The work was done in silence broken only by the barked command of Berta. The little boy helped by clearing snow from the ground and dragging the wooden flooring from the wagons. Occasionally he stopped to wipe his nose on the felt.

In less than an hour, the ger was up and Luke was helping Berta to hang the wooden door on its frame. Arkal had brought rugs from the horses and was arranging them on the floor. Then the sleeping pallets were brought in and the animal pelts, and after that came an old wooden chest and a range and utensils for making food. Soon the smell of cooking wafted up into the dusk and the tribe congratulated each other that another trek to their winter pastures had been made in safety.

Luke saw it all and felt a sense of foreboding. Winter was on its way and he was a stranger in a strange land among people who didn't want him.

CHAPTER TWO

MISTRA, NEW YEAR 1397

Snow usually covered only the head and shoulders of Mount Taygetos. That year it came down from the mountain and into the Vale of Sparta and the wolves came with it. At night, the mothers of Mistra would put palms to their children's ears to shut out their howling. Some said that the Milingoi would follow, that starving savages in animal skins would soon be climbing the city walls.

Inside the city, the streets were treacherous. People slid their way down to break the ice on wellheads and a donkey carrying food up to the citadel turned cartwheels. Monks prodded the ground of their little gardens for survivors and every morning the Despot checked the city's stores for grain.

Anna Laskaris was just thankful that the snow would keep away the Turks.

From the balcony of the Laskaris house, she looked out over the Vale of Sparta and saw fields without movement, a frozen landscape of suspended windmills and skeletal trees. Birds screeched their hunger in a sky of hard blue and columns of smoke rose from the hearths of a hundred farmsteads. Anna remembered when it had been filled by a Turkish army, fifty thousand strong. She'd been fifteen then.

She looked down at the tall cedar tree in the courtyard and saw a girl of seventeen standing beneath it waiting for her father to ride through the gate with the boy who was to be her husband: Damian Mamonas. She saw herself then, unruly red hair as defiant as the mood beneath it, ready to do her duty by this marriage, to do it for Mistra, for Byzantium.

She watched a small bird, yellow and blue on its wings, swoop down to land on a stone engraved with a name and a date.

Alexis.

It was the stone from which her brother had mounted his horse for the last time, engraved by their father after his only son's death. Alexis had fought and died trying to keep Mistra free. She was destined, instead, to marry for the Empire. First Damian. Now Suleyman. And not Luke.

She heard a sound behind her and turned. Her mother, Maria, was standing in the open doorway. She seemed much smaller these days.

'You were looking at the tree, remembering when he came to get you.'

'Yes, I was thinking about Alexis.'

Maria was silent for a while, then she said, without emotion, 'You will be leaving soon.'

'Why so?'

'Because Suleyman will come for you shortly.' She paused. 'Will you marry him?'

Anna drew apart. She studied her mother, marvelling at her calm. 'If I must, yes. The Empire requires it.'

Maria let out a long sigh. 'First a husband, then a son. Now a daughter. The Empire is demanding.'

Anna remembered Zoe's words in the chapel. *This empire that devours its children.* She had been right.

'You could come and live with me. I'll look after you.'

But her mother shook her head. 'No. I'll stay here. Mistra is my home.'

Anna hugged her. 'And mine. I don't want to leave.'

The Emperor Constantine had, ten centuries earlier, decreed that the Christian Christmas should be celebrated on the twenty-fifth day of December and that year in Mistra, Christmas Day and the twelve to Epiphany were a time of untrammelled celebration. The philosopher Plethon was there for the festivities, enlisting the services of Anna, some shepherds and the repaired donkey to stage a nativity play, written and narrated by himself. The Patriarch found himself playing Joseph.

'They do it in Italy,' Plethon explained to the Despot, adjusting his toga and smoothing it over his belly. 'Some saint from Assisi came up with the idea and it's caught on. We need to learn Catholic ways if we're to unite our Church with theirs.'

The Despot sighed and nodded. It was all part of Plethon's second plan. The union of the Eastern Church with the Church of Rome so that the Pope would sanction a crusade to lift the siege of Constantinople: the second plan to save what was left of the Empire of Byzantium.

If Luke fails in the first plan: to bring Tamerlane to fight Bayezid.

Plethon's play was a success. Staged in front of a roaring fire on New Year's Day, it was set to a score written by the Despoena Bartolomea. Afterwards, the party went on until the pages were asleep on their feet.

Omar came to visit but wouldn't say where he'd been. He

was scarred and tired, too tired even to prevent Plethon volunteering him as a magus. When they weren't rehearsing, the two men spent long hours talking alone. The engineer Benedo Barbi arrived one day from Chios, summoned to hoist angels on pulleys up to Plethon's strange heaven.

Christmas came and went in the little city on the hill and the new year brought new foreboding. Spring would arrive soon and surely the Turks would come then. After all, there was little to stop Bayezid now. At Nicopolis, four months ago, he'd defeated the best that Christendom could send against him and, to make the point more keenly, had had two thousand knights executed on the field of battle. If it hadn't been for Prince Yakub of the Germiyans, Luke would have been among them.

Now it was February and a brilliant sun shone down upon Mistra, making the eaves of the Metropolitan and, beneath them, the nose of St Demetrius, drip with equal purpose. People looked out from the city walls and saw the glint of metal in the distance.

The Turks had come.

Anna was upstairs in the palace with the Despot, Plethon and the man who had succeeded her father as Protostrator, Michael Frangopoulos.

'It's Suleyman, lord,' Frangopoulos was saying, turning from the messenger, 'but his army's not large. Perhaps ten thousand.'

Plethon nodded. 'All that can be spared from Constantinople, I imagine. Enough to take our little city.'

The siege of Constantinople had been resumed as soon as the Ottoman army had returned from Nicopolis. Bayezid had entrusted it to his heir, Suleyman, who knew that his best chance of success lay in cannon cast in the foundries of Venice.

'So why has he come?' asked the Despot.

Anna knew. 'He has come for me,' she said quietly. She was standing at a window looking down across the plain, her back to the gathering and her long hair falling to her waist. She turned and two green eyes, pooled with sadness, settled on her ruler. 'He's come to take me back to Constantinople so that he can marry me in the Church of Hagia Sophia once the cannon arrive and the city has fallen and the church has become a mosque. He's come for me. And Zoe.'

Zoe Mamonas, daughter to the Archon of Monemvasia and twin sister to the man to whom Anna was still married. She shuddered. She looked down at hands that were as pale as milk-gourd and found them still.

'Don't worry. I've always known I'd have to go. I'd just hoped for a little longer.' It had been an impossible dream: waiting in Mistra until Luke returned with Tamerlane. He wouldn't return from such a task. She turned to Plethon. 'He will want Zoe as well. Will you release her?'

Plethon nodded. 'What choice do we have?'

'She tried to bury me alive and her father is helping the Turks get cannon from Venice.' She paused. 'But you're right, philosopher. What choice do any of us have?'

She lowered her head and Plethon took her arm.

'Where is he?' she asked softly, turning. 'Can I at least know that before I go?'

Plethon looked at her for a long time. 'Luke is with nomads, Anna. Learning their ways. Preparing for Tamerlane.'

'Does he have friends?'

Plethon nodded slowly. 'There is someone. A girl. She will be his friend.'

Anna frowned. Something cold had entered her spine.

What girl?

'I should get ready,' she said.

The Ottoman army that Anna, Plethon and Zoe rode out to meet was indeed much smaller than the one brought by Suleyman five years ago. Anna had tried to bring help from Monemvasia, but Suleyman had found her outside the city and ridden with her on his saddle right up to the walls. He'd threatened to kill her unless the city surrendered. She'd defied Suleyman and in return he'd fallen in love with her.

Now she saw him ahead of her, mounted on the same stallion, black as night, with its horned head and coat of mail down to its hooves. He was wearing gold armour and a tall helmet from whose top sprouted silk in flower. On either side of him were two of his bodyguard, one holding the Horsehairs, one the green flag of the prophet. Beside them stood the rest of the Kapikulu, his household cavalry drawn from the conquered nations of Christendom and now slaves to Islam. They held pennanted lances and had wings on their backs. Behind, formed up in crescent, was the army: janissary *ortas* in the centre and *sipahi* knights from Rumelia and Anatolia on either wing. It was, as usual, silent as the breeze.

Anna glanced at Zoe. She was looking straight ahead and her eyes were bright as diamonds beneath the fox fur, pulled down to cover her ears. Her head was tilted to one side and the tip of her nose was a pinker olive than the rest of her flawless face. Her breath came in little mists from lips curved into the smallest of smiles.

Plethon turned to her and said: 'We are releasing you, Zoe, in the hope that you and your father might prove more loyal to your empire in future. Mistra needs your father's wealth and talent more than Bayezid does.'

Zoe smiled and shook her head, still looking ahead. 'You are releasing me because you have no alternative, old man.' She paused. 'My father is interested in trade and trade has no loyalties. As usual, you deceive yourself.'

Plethon was forty and didn't consider himself old. But it was true: whatever Zoe's crimes, they'd had no option but to obey Suleyman's instruction to deliver Anna and his mistress to him without delay. He said: 'If you harm one hair of Anna's head, we will find you and kill you.'

Zoe laughed. 'Harm her? Why would I do that? She will be company for me when I visit the harem.' She looked across at Anna. 'If she's not too tired, that is.'

Anna looked ahead at the man waiting. Suleyman had watched only her as they'd ridden across and was not smiling. At Nicopolis, she'd promised to submit to him. But she'd run away instead.

'You have kept me waiting,' he said as the three of them approached. 'Four months, in fact. I've been waiting four months for you to return from your father's funeral. As you said you would.'

Anna didn't reply. She looked into his eyes and saw the pride, the arrogance, the hurt.

'So, in the end, I came to get you.'

Still Anna said nothing. She sat on her horse and looked at him. Suleyman had changed. There was a new, brittle quality to his voice.

He turned to Plethon. 'I want whatever cannon you have in the city.'

Plethon shook his head. 'I regret we have never had cannon,

lord. You may send men in to scour the walls and armouries. We have no cannon of any size.'

Suleyman knew this to be true. But then that was not why he was there. Someone spoke to his front.

'Is there no greeting for me, lord?'

Suleyman's beard lifted in smile. His messenger had demanded two women be delivered to him and he'd greeted one but not the other. 'But of course,' he said, bowing from the saddle. 'We have much to discuss.'

The discussion that took place later was conducted on the bed in Suleyman's tent. On entering, Zoe had seen a large stove with a chimney that disappeared through the roof. Its doors were open and the scented heat made beads of sweat gather quickly at her temples. In the middle was a bed with the skins of antelopes upon it. The only other objects were a table with a jug and two cups and a basin of petalled water. Towels were draped over its side.

Zoe began to undress while Suleyman poured the wine. One took longer than the other since Suleyman had not greeted her out on the plain and could wait. At last she was lying naked on the bed, her body the colour of honey in the firelight, her long hair spread across the pillows.

'It's been some time,' she murmured, her fingers tracing their way from her breasts to the triangle of hair between her legs. 'You've looked forward to it?'

Suleyman's face was half in shadow so that only a part of his smile was visible. There was no sound beyond her breathing and the smell was of sandalwood. 'Of course.'

In fact Suleyman had looked forward more to seeing Anna, however unreciprocated the pleasure would be. But there was no doubt that Zoe's body gave him satisfaction beyond anything derived from the harem.

Zoe said: 'Come here.'

She had opened her legs and her fingers were deep inside the space between. Suleyman emptied his cup, rose and removed his mail. He wore a simple caftan of silk beneath. He took off the caftan, walked over to the bed and lay down beside her.

'Now,' said Zoe, 'we will discuss.'

The first discussion involved few words and went on for an hour. At its end, they both lay staring up at the roof of the tent, enjoying the feel of sweat upon their skin and the smell of consummation all around them. They were thinking of different things: Suleyman, a siege; Zoe, what had been different about this lovemaking. It was certainly different, containing a desperation that could not just be explained by the passage of time. Suleyman had changed. She rose from the bed and walked over to the basin, splashing water over her face and drying it with a towel. 'Tell me about your father,' she said, returning the towel to the basin.

Suleyman yawned. 'My father? Why do you want to know?' He paused. 'He is mad.'

'Madder than before?'

'Madder. He's been getting letters. From Tamerlane.'

Zoe considered this. Bayezid's obsession with Tamerlane had been there before she'd left for Mistra. The world did not seem big enough for both of them. 'What do the letters say?'

Suleyman rolled on to his side, watching her. 'They taunt him, call him vassal. Sometimes in verse. They're quite funny.'

Zoe walked over and sat next to him on the bed. She put her

hand to his cheek, stroking his beard with the backs of her fingers. 'And you? How does he treat you?'

Suleyman looked down at his hands. 'He hardly talks to me any more, just Mehmed, even Musa, and they tell him to lift the siege and go east to prepare for Tamerlane. Bring the Khanates of the Black and White Sheep on to our side.'

'Which makes sense.'

Suleyman stiffened. He turned his head away from her so that her hand fell to the pillow. 'Not to me. My future depends on my taking Constantinople. You know that.' He paused and stared ahead, his face a frown. He said: 'If we go east, it will be because Constantinople hasn't fallen. Mehmed will inherit this empire and I will go to the bowstring.'

Zoe brought both her hands to her lap. She sat up, her back straight. 'So you must take Constantinople. Where are the cannon?'

'Still in Venice. There are delays.'

'Such as them splitting in the cast? I think Plethon has been there with money.' She paused. 'What about Chios? When the time is right, you could take Chios and give it to Venice. You know how much they want the alum trade.'

'I'd have to wait for my father to go away. He's forbidden any further attacks.'

Bayezid's teeth were graced with the same fillings that Luke's tribe had seen in the caravan, provided only by the mastic of Chios. The island owed its continuing freedom to the Sultan's toothache. She leant towards him. 'If you don't take Chios soon, it'll be impregnable. They're building more maze villages.'

'Your spy told you this?'

Zoe nodded. 'If you take it quickly, with your soldiers rather than the corsairs, Bayezid need never know. What does he care if it's run by Venetians or Genoese as long as he gets his mastic?'

The Prince thought, fleetingly, of how he'd missed her. She rose and walked over to the table with the wine. She poured them both a cup and gave one to Suleyman. She took a sip of her own. It was warm from the fire. 'And I have another plan. You know about the Varangian treasure that was said to be buried somewhere in Mistra?'

Suleyman lifted the cup to his lips. His eyes were alert.

'Well, I found it and I don't think it's treasure. Well, not gold or jewels anyway. Something far more valuable. Something that might persuade Emperor Manuel to surrender Constantinople.'

Suleyman's eyes were bright above the rim of the cup. He swallowed the wine slowly and leant over the bed to put the cup on the carpet. 'Why do you think that?'

'Because it is a single casket and the casket is not large.'

'So what do you think it is?'

'I don't know. But Plethon does and he thinks it important enough to save an empire. Or destroy it.' She paused. 'And Anna knows where it is because she reburied it with him.'

Suleyman rolled on to his back. He sighed. 'She wouldn't tell me.'

'Not under torture?' Zoe asked softly. 'I think she would.'

Suleyman didn't reply. He was looking straight up at the ceiling of the tent and his eyes were unblinking. Zoe sat down again on the bed. 'I think she would talk under torture,' she murmured. 'What do you care more about: her or Constantinople? Her or the bowstring?'

Suleyman sat up and swung his legs over the side of the bed, his back to Zoe. He sank his head into his hands, running his long hair through his fingers. She could see his shoulders moving in time with his breathing. She moved across the bed slowly until she was holding him from behind, her breasts pressed to his spine, her arms circling his forearms.

'You couldn't do it, could you,' she said quietly. It wasn't a question. 'Even for Constantinople. Even for your life.'

Suleyman was sitting very still, his shoulders the only part of him moving. He was staring into the shadows of the tent. They were both silent for a long time, both acknowledging new boundaries, new vulnerabilities.

'There is another way,' she said.

He didn't reply.

She moved to sit beside him, no longer a lover, now a friend. 'Luke. She would tell you if you threatened Luke.'

'But I don't know where he is. Only Yakub knows and some Venetians who are now dead.'

She took his hand. 'I could find him. Di Vetriano recruited Karamanids to help him take the monastery The Karamanid lands are next to Yakub's Germiyans'. The Karamanids might know something.'

Now Suleyman turned to her. 'You would go there?'

Zoe nodded. 'And bring him back.' She paused. 'For you.'

'And your price?'

She squeezed his hand and then brought it slowly to her lips. 'There is no price, lord. I want you to win.'

CHAPTER THREE

ANATOLIA, SPRING 1397

After six months with the tribe, Luke had learnt their language but still hadn't got on a horse. Gomil had seen to that.

The chief's son hated Luke for many reasons. He hated him for helping Shulen. He hated him for humiliating him by the fire. Most of all he hated him for being there at all. Luke's presence in the camp pointed to a plan that faced east, to an alliance with Tamerlane. Gomil wanted the tribe to look west, to march with Bayezid into the Christian heartland of Europe.

Early on, he'd seen Luke's ways with horses; how he could talk to them, be understood by them. He saw how Luke loved them above all things and decided that his punishment would be to be removed from them. His father had given him Luke to train. He hadn't said how.

Over the winter months, life in the camp was pared down to the necessities for survival. In the early days, when the sun still had some pale energy, the meat from animals was pegged out to dry and huge vats of ewes' or mares' milk boiled to extract butter and the rock-hard curds that would keep through the cold days and be turned into yogurt. Cured meat and millet meal were stored inside the gers alongside piles of dried cow dung and sheep pellets for fuel.

Afterwards Luke would remember it as a sort of hibernation where all activity was rationed, directed solely to the task of staying alive. He spent much of the time sitting with Arkal in the ger, where the light through the horn of the smoke hole disfigured all that it touched. At first, Arkal just stared at him. Then, by degrees, she began to talk to him. Then to teach him.

First, she taught him the words to describe the pale cocoon of their existence. *Khana* was the wooden lattice, and she stretched her thin arm out to touch it, on to which the *isegei*, or felt, was attached; the poles in the ceiling above were *uni* and the smoke hole, which could be opened and closed by these pulley ropes, was the *toghona*.

When the snow paused, they went outside and he learnt the words for the trees that bunched on the valley sides like teeth, for the freezing river below them and the snow all around. She limped over to the giant open sheds that stretched between poles, pulling his sleeve as they went. She told him about the sheep and cattle and goats that lived there. She pointed high, high into the sky, to describe the clouds and wind that moved them and the black birds that were flung about on its currents.

By now he knew that the strange girl who'd sought shelter from the storm had survived. Her ger had been erected away from the others with the same horsehides and skulls surrounding it like hunched spectres. She never appeared but the old man did, usually to scavenge amongst the bones left outside doors or to gather water from the river. Luke wanted to know about them but Arkal scowled and tapped her head to say they were mad and dragged him away to show him other things.

And so Luke learnt to speak their language, thankful for

the gift that Fiorenza had said was the most remarkable she'd seen. He learnt simple words at first and some names. The chief was called Etabul, his son Gomil. The mad man had no name but he was the shaman who would enter trances to connect the tribe to their ancestors and the old, old gods of the wind and steppe that they'd not quite forgotten in the onslaught of Islam. The girl was called Shulen and might be his daughter and was a witch. It was said that she had the art of healing although few dared approach her for she was unclean and evil spirits walked at her side.

Arkal told him that Gomil was the best archer and bowman in the tribe but that he was a proud and violent man. He'd gone with Yakub to fight for Bayezid at Nicopolis where the tribe had lost many men. He'd returned from the battle full of hate for the infidel West, repeating again and again Bayezid's threat to water his horses at the altar of St Peter's in Rome. But his father had shaken his head and talked of Tamerlane and now this infidel, Lug, was living among them. She told him that Gomil hated him entirely.

Arkal became his friend, shy at first then firmer than granite. Luke told her about himself, how he was a Varangian and how Varangians had once been numbered in their thousands, an imperial guard to an emperor that ruled in Europe and Asia. Now they were few and there was little of the Empire left to rule. He didn't tell her of the treasure but then what was there to tell? Only Plethon and Anna knew where it was. What it was.

As the weeks dragged on and the air turned colder and great drifts of snow piled high against the gers, holding their doors closed fast, the life of the tribe became confined to the tent. Luke came to understand that the ger was a place of individual territories: the right side for the men, their bows and dogs; the left for the women, the children and the cooking. The hearth was a sacred place where the family spirits dwelt and where no one should tread, positioned such that the noonday sun would strike it daily through the toghona. Luke understood the importance of these rules as the weeks became months and the space inside the tent grew smaller by the day.

Then the first murmur of spring arrived on the breeze. The sun came out and washed over the snow like Cypriot wine and men and women emerged from their tents blinking and rubbing their eyes. Children ran down to the river to break the ice and plunge into its icy torrent. Women joined them to wash away the dirt of weeks and the men checked the horses which, to Luke's astonishment, had almost all survived.

But it didn't last. After a few hours, clouds hurried in to mask the soft heat of the sun and an icy wind came down the valley from the north, shaking snow from the trees. Soon people retreated back to the warmth and doors were pulled shut.

Another storm hit them that night and the gers trembled and rattled beneath its assault. Great forks of lightning fractured the dark and thunder shook the earth, making Berta and Arkal cling to each other with every crash. The boy rose from his pallet and stood there, shaking with fear. He turned to his mother and, in his rush to be with her, tripped and fell headlong into the fire.

At first, no one was quite sure what had happened. Then lightning lit up the tent and the boy was crouching there, his face a contortion of burns, his mouth open, too shocked to scream. Torguk leapt from his pallet and rushed for the bucket of water, hurling it at the boy while Berta thrashed at his smoking clothes. Then he screamed.

Arkal was shouting at Luke and gesturing to the door. 'Take

him to the shaman's daughter! My father is too frightened. *Go!*'

Luke lifted the boy in his arms as Arkal opened the door. However he held him, he seemed to touch a burnt part of the body and the boy writhed and clawed and bit to be free. Outside the tent, the air was a confusion of snow and flying debris. Luke hunched his big frame into a shield for the child, turning his back to the wind and moving slowly towards where he thought the shaman's tent stood.

'*Shulen!*'

The wind picked up the shout and scattered it into a thousand fragments.

'*Shulen! Where are you?*'

He could hardly see anything in the darkness and the snow was in his eyes, blinding him. He opened his mouth to yell again. In an instant, his mouth was full of freezing water, choking him. The boy beneath him was no longer struggling. Perhaps he was dead.

A flash of lightning lit the world around him. He thought he saw skull-poles away to his right. He lurched forward, pulling his cloak over the boy and feeling the heat of terrible burns against his arms.

'*Shulen!*' he screamed into the night, wiping the snow from his eyes with the rim of his cloak.

He stumbled against the side of a tent, feeling rope against the side of his arm. The boy was shaking in his arms and Luke felt warm vomit wash down his forearm. The boy was alive.

'*Shulen!*'

He didn't even know if she would help. She was an outcast, a pariah, a witch. He'd never heard her speak more than a word at a time.

Why should she help him?

His elbow hit something upright and wooden; a door. He threw his weight against it.

He fell into the tent, landing on his elbows to protect the child. He looked up, shaking his head to clear the snow from his face and hair. Someone was standing above him who was tall and slender and free of dirt. She was dressed in a white caftan that fell from the contours of her body like rain.

Shulen.

Luke looked around him in astonishment. The ger was small and its walls were covered in the skins of different animals. It was tidy and warm and at its centre stood a brazier that threw a scattered light on to everything around. To one side was a low bed and on it lay the old man. Low sounds came from his lips like a chant.

'The boy needs you,' said Luke as he laid the frozen body on to the soft pelt. 'They say you can heal.' He looked at her but her face was empty of emotion. 'Can you help him?'

He leant towards her but she recoiled like a snake. She bared her teeth and growled and her hands came up, her fingers splayed like claws.

'Shulen . . .'

She hissed something and swayed back and forth on her heels as if preparing to strike. She pointed at the door.

'The boy will die . . .'

She sprang forward and pulled the door open. The storm rushed in, lifting the skins from the walls and scattering coals from the fire across the carpet. The air smelt of burnt wool. Luke looked desperately at the girl. Her eyes were entirely white.

She will keep him.

He looked back at the boy. He'd stopped moving. There was no time to waste. Luke stumbled out into the night and heard the thud of slammed wood behind. He looked about him but could see nothing. There was no light beyond an occasional spasm from the sky. He sat on the ground and gathered his cloak around him. What should he do? He couldn't go back to Torguk and Berta, having left their son to the mercy of the witch. And Shulen would rather the boy froze to death than let Luke stay in her tent. He had no option but to wait. But to wait here meant death: his joints were already stiffening in the cold.

The door opened and he felt heat against his back. He turned to see two skins flung in his direction. He rose quickly but the door shut and her name died on his lips. He picked up the furs and wrapped them around him as tightly as his numbed hands would allow.

Later, Luke tried to remember how long he'd lain outside the shaman's ger that night. It could have been one hour or six. All he remembered was the cold: the cold that seemed to freeze the very blood in his veins. The throbbing agony of frostbite in his fingers and toes made him cry out at first, made him dream of plunging them into the hot embers of Shulen's fire. But soon his head cleared, the messages of pain freezing on their journey to his mind. He tried to fight the drift into nothingness that stole up his body like a vine; tried to conjure back the pain that might keep him alive. But the tide was too strong and he felt an overwhelming longing for sleep, for the oblivion that would finish it all. His last thought was of someone far away.

Anna.

But it wasn't Anna that looked down on him when he awoke some time later. He was inside the shaman's tent and he was warm and his naked body was touched by fine fur and the air around him was heavy with the scent of herbs.

Shulen was kneeling on the rug beside him and the fire was behind her so that he could not see her face. She was completely still and the caftan hung from her shoulders without moving. He could see dark shadows below small breasts. He wondered if she was even breathing. Held between her hands was a small earthenware bowl, steaming.

Luke raised himself to his elbow and tried to say something but no sound came from his mouth. The storm outside seemed to have blown itself out and he glanced up at the toghona and could see no glimmer of dawn beyond it. He looked around the tent and saw the boy lying next to the man on the bed. He saw the rise and fall of his little chest, the even breathing of a child in the peace of sleep.

Then he remembered the night and a pain so great that he'd never believed he would be free of it. He stretched his fingers, then his toes. They were there and warm and he could feel the texture of the fur and wondered why he'd never marvelled at its softness before.

He tried to speak again but a wave of dizziness rippled over him and his eyelids grew heavy and the smell of herbs made him weak with longing. He lay his head back down on the fur and imagined himself upon the back of Eskalon, his face pressed to the warm muscle of the horse's neck, a wind scented with Greece in his nose and in his hair. He was falling asleep again and he didn't want to. There was so much that was new here . . . so much he didn't understand. He had to talk to Shulen.

Shulen.

He opened his eyes and she had gone. His eyes travelled the tent walls, roving over the skins and furs and, below them, the trays of dried herbs, neatly lined in rows. She was not there.

She had disappeared.

CHAPTER FOUR

CHIOS, SPRING 1397

On the island of Chios, Fiorenza, Princess of Trebizond, was standing on the balcony of her home at Sklavia beneath a sky of piercing blue flecked with gossamer clouds. She was awaiting her husband's return.

She was dressed for a summer's day in a chemise of finest lawn; her hair was gathered to her head and she had woven flowers of the season into the golden ball. Eight months of pregnancy were behind her and she carried what was in front with precision, her fingers entwined across her belly like a belt. She knew that thirty-two was old for childbirth so she ate ginger comfits and took no chances with the heir to Marchese Longo.

But the days were tedious and she had Lara to thank in making them less so. Since her marriage to Dimitri, the girl had become her friend. Fiorenza knew a great deal about healing oils and Lara, through her husband, knew everything about mastic. Chios was full of snakes and together they'd worked to produce an antidote for every one of their poisons. They were nearly finished.

She'd been looking out for Marchese Longo to the south,

for him riding up from the village of Mesta, which she'd been told had been attacked by corsairs. Her usual calm was breezed with uncertainty. The dogs could feel it. Longo's two hounds, one black, one white, sat watching her with their heads on one side and their ears hooped in question. They moved from shade to shade. Occasionally one would whine.

It was early in the day and a plate of something lay untouched on the table beside her. She looked down at it and saw water pooled like mercury in a lettuce leaf. There was rain still in the pergola'd vine above, the same rain she'd heard outside her window in the hour before dawn. She'd been awoken by a kick and had lain on her side, hoping for more kicks but feeling instead the nudge of unease.

She turned and walked over to the other side of the balcony, the dogs following her. On this side, she could see over the terraces of gardens, vineyards and citrus groves to the broad plain of the Kambos below where the families of the *campagna* enjoyed their estates. It was a landscape criss-crossed with walls and irrigation channels and in between sat the mansions of rich men surrounded by the red earth that fed and irrigated them. She remembered that Luke had a house there somewhere and tried to think where.

Luke.

Was it really only eight months that he'd been gone? She looked down at the road that wound its way up to the gates of the Sklavia estate and remembered watching him ride up it two years before, remembered the first mumbled greeting on the steps to the terrace. And she remembered a golden time of only him when she'd taught a Greek boy of no learning but infinite talent to become a man capable of anything.

A donkey brayed in the orchards below and the bell tower

next to their little church sounded the hour. A light wind carried the sounds to her with the smell of newly cut grass. A butterfly hovered over a bush to her front and she remembered others in a valley where Luke's learning had reached its fulfilment. She looked down at the curve of her belly.

You will be tall. Like him.

Since the sinking by storm, a year past, of most of the ships blockading it, Chios had not seen the Turks. What was left of the Ottoman fleet sat in the Propontis facing the walls of Constantinople and not even Venice's Arsenale could build ships quickly enough for it to blockade Chios as well. And anyway, Bayezid had forbidden it.

As a result, the campagna grew richer. The Genoese joint stock company that leased Chios from the Empire of Byzantium was in the business of alum, mined across the straits in Phocaea, and alum was achieving record prices in the markets of the West. Their mastic was doing even better. Uniquely grown in the south of the island, Dimitri's miracle was filling teeth, softened by sugar, from London to Baghdad. The harem in Edirne was buying it by the shipload to sweeten breath held in nightly anticipation of a visit by the Sultan. And, by a curious irony, that part of the mastic profit belonging to the campagna's youngest partner, Luke Magoris, was being spent by Plethon at the Arsenale on bribes to delay the cannon intended for Suleyman's siege.

All of which explained why Marchese Longo Giustiniani, acknowledged leader of the campagna, was looking the right way down the barrel of a gun. It had been filled with grapeshot and was aimed at the thickest group of Turks in the square in front of them. Fired at this range, it would be lethal.

He was standing next to the engineer Benedo Barbi in the village of Mesta. The village was strewn with Turkish dead, their faces blistered by boiling water, their bodies punctured by crossbow bolts shot from above. At every turn in the village, at every bridge or balcony, at every dead end, the Turks had been hit by missiles fired from places they couldn't get to. And every time they'd broken down a door, it was to find no access to the *pounti* above. When they'd staggered outside, it was to see men escape across roofs. This wasn't fighting; it was a fiendish game. And it was a game they were losing.

'Well, he was wrong about that,' Longo whispered.

'Wrong? Who was wrong?' asked the engineer.

'Luke,' replied Longo. 'He told me they'd never reach the tower.'

Barbi grunted. It was evening, and the heat of the day had passed but he was still uncomfortable. His armour was biting into his shoulders. 'They're not supposed to be here at all. I thought that had been the price of Dimitri filling the Sultan's teeth with mastic.'

Longo shrugged. 'Well, it may not be Bayezid giving the orders. Prince Suleyman is running the siege at Constantinople. Perhaps these are his men.'

Barbi wiped his brow. He didn't much care whose soldiers these were. 'When can we fire?'

'When they've all come into the square.' Longo turned to the gunner behind him. 'You fire and we'll rush them. Then reload and fire at any that come to their aid.'

'There are no Greeks there?' asked Gabriele Adorno, oldest of the signori.

Longo shook his head. 'Every man, woman and child of the

village is inside that tower, Gabriele. They're on the upper level where the Turks can't get to them.'

It was two years since Luke had shown Longo his idea for villages that were also many-levelled mazes. Now there were five such villages in construction among the mastic groves of the south and Mesta was almost complete. The village was a labyrinth with a tower at its centre and every villager could reach the tower without his feet touching the ground.

I have much to thank Luke for.

But this was worrying. These men had landed at the new port of Limenas, arriving in ten huge galleys and, thought Longo, must number well over a thousand men. Looking at them now, he could see that they were different from those that had come before. These were not casual raiders. These were a disciplined force obeying orders from mounted knights that looked to him a lot like sipahis. These were the Sultan's forces.

Or Suleyman's.

The engineer beside him spat. 'We might clear them out this time,' he said morosely, 'but what about next? And what if they bring cannon?'

It was what Longo had been thinking. But that was the future. For now they had to throw these Turks out of Mesta.

Marchese Longo knew about fighting. As a young man, he'd learnt the art of war from one of the greatest *condottiere* of the day, Gian Galeazzo Visconti, fighting against the forces of Padua. Now Visconti was Duke of Milan and still friend to Longo. It was he who had sent the ribaudequins. These, and Barbi's flame-throwers, were what he was relying on.

The engineer had recently rediscovered how to make Greek fire, an art that had been thought lost to the Byzantines. He'd used it to help Luke escape from the assassin at the monastery of Battal Gazi, where Omar had been tortured by Venetians. Now it was time to use it to defend Chios.

'Now!'

The fuse was lit, the little cannon threw out death and the nozzles of three canisters spewed forth the flames of hell. The distance was less than a hundred feet and the grapeshot and fire tore into the Turkish ranks, throwing them against the tower walls and turning men into fireballs.

Then the Genoese charged. They were no more than fifty strong but well armed and had the advantage of surprise. They fell upon the Turks, hacking and stabbing and finding the gaps in their smoking armour into which to plunge their steel.

'Retreat!' yelled a sipahi knight. 'Get back to the boats!'

The Turks began to withdraw to the side of the square. By now the cannon was reloaded and another hail of metal drove into their ranks, shattering mail and armour like glass. More men went down and the cobbles were slippery with their blood. On the walkways that connected the tower to the surrounding streets, men were now running to take up positions ahead of the fleeing Turks.

'Lord Longo!'

The shout came from the top of the tower and Marchese looked up. 'Dimitri! Is everyone safe?'

The Greek was standing on the battlements, a crossbow in his hand. His face was black and his shirt stained with blood. He was grinning. 'All safe.'

Longo ran to a corner of the tower from where he could see the Turks streaming into the empty side streets beyond. Then there was a flash as the first of the villagers' booby traps ignited. Screams echoed through the alleyways, adding to the confusion. It seemed that death was all around them.

But there was one street that the villagers had left clear: one street, narrow and endlessly cornered, in which the villagers had posted no men in the bridges and walkways above.

It was the street that led out of the village and back to the boats.

Later, when the Turks had left, Longo sat with Barbi, Dimitri and the rest of the signori in the little square, talking and drinking iced Chian wine. A light rain had just fallen, leaving as quickly as it had arrived, doing nothing to wash away the blood on the ground around them. At least the bodies had been removed.

'Sit still,' Longo was saying to the engineer whose arm he was bandaging. 'I bet you wish you'd never returned from Mistra.' A vessel containing a compound of mastic, vinegar and rosemary stood on the table beside them.

'It's just a graze,' said Barbi 'You wouldn't have noticed it if I hadn't taken off my armour.'

Longo ignored him and turned to Dimitri. 'What are our dead?' he asked.

'No dead, lord,' said the Greek, wiping the sweat from his eyes. 'Only a dozen or so wounded, including the poor engineer here.' He paused to scowl at Barbi, whom he'd warned a thousand times not to join battle. He was too valuable alive.

'And them?' enquired Zacco Banca. He was cleaning blood from his armour which, like the rest of the signori, had the Giustiniani arms emblazoned on its cuirass. 'How many did they lose?'

'We've not counted yet, lord. But it must be at least two hundred.'

Longo knew he should look happier at the news. After all,

the village had proved itself. But he couldn't rejoice amidst the cries of agony that rose from the streets around him. And the Turks would come again.

'They'll come again,' he said.

Barbi turned to him. 'Once they've taken Constantinople, yes, they'll come. And they'll bring their Venetian cannon.' He paused. 'Which is why I'm going there.'

'To Venice?'

'No, to Constantinople. Once I get word that the cannon have arrived, I'm going there to destroy them. So is Dimitri.'

Longo frowned. 'But why? It's not our battle.'

'It's everyone's battle, all of us,' said Dimitri quietly, leaning forward to help tie the bandage.

Longo changed the subject. 'Did they do much damage?' he asked.

Dimitri shook his head. 'They burnt a warehouse in Lemnos and a few fields between there and here. But the village survives and we still have the mastic stored in the tower.'

They were all three silent after that, half listening to the celebrations around them. The Turks had sailed away and the day belonged to the men and women of Chios. The villagers had uncorked wine and some were already drunk. Every so often, a scream of pain rose above the laughter.

'Should we stop that?' asked Longo, looking out into the maze of streets.

It was Lara who answered. Lara, whom Dimitri had brought to the island and who was now his wife. Lara, who, with Fiorenza, had confounded the island's snakes. She'd brought a torch to help with the dressing of Barbi's wound. Now she doused it in the ground, turned to Longo and spoke softly. 'Lord, these people have lost their children to slavery at the hands of those men. I doubt you could stop it even if you wanted to.'

Marchese thought of Dimitri and Lara's child that was on its way. He looked down at the gentle curve of her belly and then up at the new day. He thought of Fiorenza. He should get back to her.

He rose and turned to Dimitri. 'We have a traitor on this island, my friend. The Turks knew when to attack and where. We only just arrived in time.'

Towards evening, Fiorenza was still watching from the balcony at Sklavia when she saw two riders coming quickly across the fields, chased by horses without riders. She shielded her eyes from the sun. In five minutes they were there, Longo in her arms and Barbi bowing awkwardly behind him. They were wearing armour and their faces were streaked with black.

'Thank God,' she said, pulling away. 'We were worried.'

'We?' asked Longo.

'Me, the dogs, Giovanni. He'd stopped kicking.' She brought her hands to her middle. 'There, he's started again. He knows you're safe.

She had started calling the child inside her Giovanni, certain that it was a boy. Longo, less certain, smiled and put his hands over hers.

Fiorenza brought his hands to her lips. 'Was it very fierce?' She remembered Barbi and turned to him. 'Did we lose many?'

'None, lady,' replied Barbi. 'The village worked. We have Luke to thank.'

'And you,' said Longo, turning to the engineer. The dogs were now sitting on either side of him, looking up with devotion. He held a dog's ear in each hand. 'After all, you built them.'

'But it was Luke's design, Luke's dream.' Barbi glanced at Fiorenza. 'We just interpreted it.'

Fiorenza thought back to the *kendos*, the celebration of the mastic harvest beside the sea where Luke had had the dream that had brought forth the villages. Her hand went back to her belly. 'You must be tired and hungry.'

Much later, when they'd eaten and drunk and washed away the worst of the dirt, they talked about Barbi's visit to Mistra. Fiorenza asked: 'Is she very beautiful?'

The engineer smiled as he thought of Anna. 'She's nearly as beautiful as you, lady. She has red hair and green eyes and a face that might launch a thousand ships if they hadn't already been put out for you.'

Fiorenza threw back her head and laughed. She'd never heard Barbi speak more than a sentence, certainly not one like that. 'She's clearly turned your head, engineer. Suddenly you're a poet!'

Longo leant forward. 'Unfortunately she's turned Prince Suleyman's as well. There's some story of him meeting her when he first took an army to Mistra five years ago. He is infatuated with her and returned with another army soon after Benedo left. She's in Edirne now.'

'Does Luke know?'

Barbi shook his head. 'I doubt it. It's probably better that way.'

Fiorenza picked up her glass. Inside was iced water flavoured with lime. She took a sip and put the glass down with care. She turned to Barbi. 'Does Luke know about me?' She reached over and took her husband's hand. 'About *us*?'

'That you're with child? Yes, Dimitri told him at Bursa.' Barbi paused. 'He was overwhelmed.'

'As are we,' laughed Longo. 'It's a miracle, nothing less.'

Barbi said, 'He told us about Nicopolis as well. He didn't betray the Christian army. He tried to save it. Plethon confirmed it in Mistra.'

Longo smiled. 'I never thought that he did. He is a member of the campagna and therefore a man of honour.'

Fiorenza asked, 'What happened after Nicopolis?'

Barbi stretched his legs. He was tired and wanted to go to bed. 'You heard about the slaughter of the French knights? That Luke and his three friends survived because a gazi chief pointed out that the Holy Book forbids the execution of prisoners below a certain age?'

She nodded.

'Well, after that he was sent to live amongst the tribes in the chief's *beylik*. He's there now. And he survived a Venetian assassination attempt on the way.'

Fiorenza looked up quickly. She was frowning. 'Venetian?'

'A man called di Vetriano whom I'd already met in Alexandria. A poisonous species. He's dead now.'

She asked, 'Why did he want to kill Luke?'

Barbi's eyes still stung from the soot. He put his fingers to them, massaging the lids. 'The Serenissima seemed to have got it into its head that mastic could cure the plague and that Luke knew the compound that would do it.' He paused. 'It can't of course, any more than it can fix dye. People are getting over-excited.'

Fiorenza had gone very quiet. The frown was still on her brow and she appeared to be thinking hard. She didn't react when Barbi asked leave to retire. Longo smiled. 'Benedo, my wife is distracted. Of course you must go to bed.'

The engineer rose, bowed, and removed himself from the terrace.

Longo rose and looked down at his wife. 'I should follow him.' He paused. 'You were thinking of the Venetians?'

Fiorenza nodded slowly. 'I was thinking that they seem to spread their malice everywhere.'

Longo yawned. 'Well, the Turks certainly knew where to go tonight. They landed at Limenas and marched straight to Mesta.'

'You still suspect the Medici agent?'

The Medici bankers of Florence had lent the campagna the money to build the maze-villages. Most of it had been repaid. Longo inclined his head. 'There's no reason for Tommaso Bardolli to be still on this island; the bank has no office here. And the Medici are friends with Venice. They've lent them the money to re-equip the Arsenale to build ships and cannon for the Turk.'

Fiorenza nodded. 'And I'm told Bardolli spends much of his time riding around the south of the island.'

Longo yawned again. 'In six months we'll have enough money to repay the full loan,' he said. 'I'll go to Florence then and ask for Signor Bardolli to be given a new posting.'

'No,' said Fiorenza. 'I should go since I arranged the loan. In six months, God willing, I will be well enough to travel.'

Marchese Longo might have argued the point had not exhaustion broken over him so that he had to put his hand out to the balustrade. Anyway, six months was a long way away.

After Giovanni has come into our world.

Some time later, in Bayezid's capital of Edirne, when the harem was awakening from its afternoon rest and applying mastic to its many mouths and the fires were being lit in the palace kitchens, Zoe was sitting beneath an orange tree in a little courtyard outside the harem walls. Fruit hung above her head like planets. She was thinking about Luke.

She'd not seen him since before Nicopolis, almost a year ago. She knew that he was somewhere in Yakub's beylik and had a plan for discovering where. But was she bringing him back for Suleyman or for herself? She frowned.

For Suleyman, of course.

Surely, whatever attachment had come from growing up with Luke in Monemvasia had disappeared, if it could ever be said to have existed. He'd been her servant, after all. And it had surely vanished, at least on his part, when she'd lied about Damian's accident all those years back. Did she mind? Why *was* she bringing him back?

For me?

She heard someone clear their throat behind her and turned. Pavlos Mamonas was standing there, more supplicant than father. He was dressed, as always, in Venetian black, and wore long riding boots turned down at the top. His hair was darker than she'd remembered it and she wondered, fleetingly, if he'd resorted to dye. He held his hat in his hands.

'I'm not disturbing you?'

Zoe would have preferred some warning. 'Of course not, Father. Come and sit.'

Pavlos Mamonas sat. He put his hat on his knees and looked at his daughter. 'You look well. Mistra suited you?'

Zoe turned to him, irritated. 'I was imprisoned. It was tolerable.'

'Why were you there at all?'

This was why she'd have liked some notice. She thought hard.

'To accompany Anna to her father's funeral. Someone from our family had to go and it was hardly going to be Damian.'

Father and daughter were silent, both contemplating the feebleness of the lie. Pavlos said: 'You have some influence over Prince Suleyman.'

Zoe remained silent.

'He is not in favour.'

'Which is why you now prefer to run errands for his father?'

Zoe looked back at the tree. Pavlos Mamonas put his hand on his daughter's. 'The family is in a difficult situation, Zoe. Venice still wants Chios. Bayezid has forbidden any further attacks on the island because its mastic stops his toothache. Suleyman's last attempt was repulsed. He's unlikely to try again. Difficult.'

'So Venice gives Suleyman the cannon to take Constantinople. Byzantium falls and Suleyman gives Chios to Venice. It seems simple.'

Mamonas sighed. 'The Doge is disinclined to supply the cannon just now.'

'And Suleyman is disinclined to go back to Chios.' She paused. 'Again, difficult.'

Zoe looked down at her father's hand still covering hers and removed it. Then she stood and walked over to a column as if a message had appeared on its fluted sides. She looked up at it. 'Father, why should I help you?'

Pavlos Mamonas shook his head slowly. 'Zoe, your brother . . .'

'My brother is more competent drunk than sober.'

Her father remained silent. Zoe was stroking a ridge in the pillar with her fingertips. She said, 'If Suleyman gets Chios for Venice against his father's wishes, it will be risky for him . . . for me. I'll want a reward appropriate to the risk.'

Pavlos waited. He was watching her carefully. He wondered,

as he often did, about what might have occurred between her and the Varangian, the one he'd punished for letting the horse trample Damian. He wondered whether it was the bitter residue of loss that had created such ambition within his daughter.

Then she turned and smiled. 'Your empire. I want your empire when you die.'

CHAPTER FIVE

ANATOLIA, SPRING 1398

Luke's second spring with the tribe came in a rush. The thaw was sudden and the air crackled with storms that arrived with no warning. Feet sank to the ankle in plushy ground and the frozen river bubbled off its ice, then rose to a torrent.

The grass on the valley sides grew at a speed that astonished him. First came a brown stubble which overnight became green. Then a carpet of flowers rose from the ground, turning shy, insect-hazed heads towards the sun. At night the valley sang a strange, whispered song, lulling the tribe into sleep beneath a giant moon, poised on its rim before beginning its journey through the stars.

Every day, birds flew over in ever-larger formations: geese and duck and ptarmigan homing back to the warm lakes of the south where the carp and perch were already beginning to spawn. The air was full of the shrill cries of their travel, and the shriller cries of animal birthing. On all sides was the sound of forest awakening, of trees released from their blanket of snow, of the creak and crack of stretching limbs, the hiss of sap rising.

It was a time of birth but also a time of burial. Many of the tribe's old had died in the winter, their bodies placed out in the freezing snow. Now the dead men's horses were slain and their bodies put next to them in their graves. Their saddles, bows and bridles straddled them both, bonding man to rider in their journey into an easier world. A few of the horses had succumbed to the cold and their flesh lay drying in the sun and the wind. What couldn't be ridden or honoured would be eaten.

The tribe wouldn't move to its summer pastures out on the steppe until the birthing and the first shearing were done. Until then, the shepherds out on the hills would be midwives as well as watchmen. Luke's daily task was to carry great bales of fleece to the women, who laid them out on the felting mats, beating them hard while the children ran back and forth from the river to fetch water to sprinkle over them. Then the fleece would be layered and tied on to skins stretched between poles and thrashed until a single mat of perfectly smooth felt had been created.

It was tedious work and Luke longed to ride but Gomil had prevented his every attempt to get on a horse. Now there was an expedition gathered to hunt Chukar partridge with hawks around the southern lakes. They would bring back fish glue for the bows and goose feathers for the arrows. Gomil was to lead it. But first he had to bid farewell to his father in his ger.

Luke was helping Arkal tie her younger brother to a pony. The boy had recovered from his burns and it was time for him to learn to ride He'd be tied to the saddle until he became part of the horse; until he became a centaur.

'Lug!' shouted one of the expedition. 'Does he have a name yet?'

Luke looked around, shielding his eyes from the glare of the morning sun. The dew was still on the ground and a low mist rose around the horses as they stamped. The man was grinning.

'His name is Tsaurig,' said Luke, glancing at Arkal, 'And today's his first ride.'

'Will you teach him?'

'I will teach him. With Arkal.'

There was laughter amongst the men on horseback. 'But, Lug,' one called out, 'you cannot ride!'

Luke looked away. 'I will teach him on the rein,' he said, yanking the string too hard.

The sound of argument came from the chief's tent. The riders fell silent and Luke leant into the boy's saddle, pulling the girth tight. 'There, Tsaurig, you'll ride like your father now. And soon' – he nodded in the direction of the hunting party – 'you'll be bringing fat partridge back from the plains.'

The door of the ger flew open and Gomil strode out, his deel flying behind. He wrenched the reins of his horse from a rider and vaulted into the saddle. 'What are we waiting for?' he barked, swinging round. 'We go to Karamanid territory. So keep your bows strung.'

Luke looked across the saddle at Arkal. She shrugged. 'I heard my parents speak of it,' she whispered. 'He's been told to marry a girl from the Karamanids.'

'The *Karamanids*?' said Luke. 'But they're your enemies!'

'It's come from Yakub,' she said. 'He wants an alliance.'

'With Allaedin ali-Bey? They hate each other!'

Arkal shrugged again. 'Who can tell these things? But Gomil must go and inspect the girl and not give offence. They say she is ugly.'

Luke looked at the riders, a mass of furred flank muscle in dust shot through with sunlight. The smell of horse rose all around him. He felt bereft.

I want to ride.

Arkal was watching him. So was someone else. Luke felt it. He turned towards the shaman's tent. The girl was standing in the shade of a horsehide, her body quite still. She was watching him without expression.

Arkal spat on to the ground. 'She is no good.'

'She saved Tsaurig's life.'

The girl grimaced, shaking her head. 'The *spirits* saved my brother!' she whispered. 'She had nothing to do with it.'

Three weeks later, Gomil had still not returned and his father stood in daily vigil on the escarpment above the camp. The chief's son had taken twenty of the best warriors with him and the tribe should have left for summer pastures by now.

Luke was polishing the dragon pommel of his sword, sitting cross-legged before his ger. It was mid-afternoon but the sky was dark and bruised with storm. The animals in the pens were tense, their ears pricked and their noses lifted to the scent of danger; they sensed something coming in on the wind. Luke saw them stamp and move together, searching for the comfort of touch, the fear sweeping over them, stiffening the hair on their coats. A fleck of rain stabbed the side of his cheek. He looked up to the rolling tide of cloud and saw the the first stab of lightning break.

He glanced around. Women were gathering looms and pushing children before them into the tents. Men were checking ropes and driving pegs further into the ground.

'Lug!' Arkal shouted. Tsaurig was holding her hand, dragging her towards the safety of the ger. 'Come inside! This one will be fierce.'

Luke looked at the sky. It was almost black now and darts of rain were hitting the ground around him. He looked towards the shaman's tent and saw Shulen standing halfway up the hill behind it, staring up at a tree, arms outstretched as if in greeting. A flock of crows exploded from the tree.

Lightning struck again and the tree burst into flames, sending sparks high into the sky. She was still looking up at it, her caftan clinging to her body.

'*Shulen!*'

She was too close to the tree. Flaming debris was falling all around her.

'*Shulen!*'

She turned and stared at him.

He looked up at the tree. Bigger branches were beginning to come apart from the trunk, each a blazing torch that crashed to the ground in fountains of fire. At any moment, she would be struck. Luke ran through the gers, vaulting the ropes in his way. Then he was running up the hill. There was a crack and a branch landed next to her. The tree was going to fall. Luke reached her, and threw himself forward. They rolled together down the slope as the tree fell above them, sparks flying over the camp to land on the roofs of the tents. A dog howled and ran in circles.

Suddenly Luke was angry. 'You can speak, damn you!' he yelled at her through the rain.

She was still in his arms but her body was limp. She looked at him, a slight frown breaking the dirt on her brow. Luke saw that her skin was scorched from the heat. He turned her face to the rain and the water ran down her cheeks and through her hair. He picked her up and began to make his way down the slope, her head against his chest, her long hair heavy on his forearm. He felt the tide of her breath hot upon his skin. Lightning struck again.

Inside her tent, it was the same as before: rows and rows of herbs laid out on the ground to dry and the fire burning something scented which gave off a light smoke. The old man lay on his bed and didn't stir as they entered. Tallow candles were lit.

Luke set Shulen down on her pallet and turned to stoke the fire. He looked back. She was watching him, her head thrown to one side, hair spilt across the lynx fur like ink. Steam rose from the folds of her tunic. He studied the face that was not like other women's in the camp. It was longer, softer, more subtle, not of the steppe. He put down the iron and went over to her. He sat down and felt the fur beneath his palm. The smell of herbs and other essences seemed stronger where she lay.

'Shulen,' he said softly, 'I know that you're not the shaman's daughter. You're not his daughter and you're not of this tribe. You choose not to speak. Who are you?'

She reached out a thin hand and placed it on his forearm. The fair hair was still wet and she raked her fingers through it. She looked beyond him and smiled as if at some memory. Then her eyes came back to his.

'I am what I am,' she said. 'I am yours.'

Luke frowned. 'You're not mine and you're not theirs. Are you here to help me?'

'As you have helped me.' The hand on his forearm travelled to his shoulder. It was a caress. She traced her fingers round to the nape of his neck and, bringing his head down to hers, kissed him on the brow. It was more a breath than a kiss. 'I am yours.'

Luke closed his eyes. The smell of the herbs was overpowering, reaching into his brain. There was a humming in his ears and his skin seemed to lift from the bones beneath to be nearer to her. He was overwhelmed with longing for this thin, strange girl. He remembered another time, another place.

You can, Luke. And you must.

Fiorenza. He had been drugged then. Part of someone else's plan. Was he drugged now? He opened his eyes and pulled away. She was frowning at him, a question in her eyes.

'Is this Omar's doing?' he asked. 'Is that why I am here in this tent? Didn't he tell you about Anna? I am not yours, I'm hers.'

It was said more roughly than he meant it. But he'd so nearly succumbed, so nearly betrayed Anna a second time. He rose and shook his head to clear it. He walked to the door and heard the rain on the other side, drumming its rhythm on the wood. He glanced back. The inside of the ger was lit by lightning and it caught her eyes, illuminating them like a cat's. She wasn't just not of this tribe; she was not of this earth.

He pulled the door open and stepped outside. Rain hit his head and shoulders and he looked up at it, welcoming its force. Then he was running.

In Konya, Allaedin ali-Bey, chief of the Karamanid tribe, lay sprawled across an extravagance of cushions.

It was night and the same storm that had afflicted the Germiyans had moved south and was now poised over the city of Konya where Omar lived. Lightning strikes lit up the domes and minarets of this holiest of cities and the thunder echoed through its streets like a warning.

But no sound could distract the eight men who swirled before their ruler. Like dizzy crows, the dervishes turned and turned, their eyes closed, their long black skirts rising and falling with the motion. Their bare feet wove patterns on the patterned floor and the tall black hats on their heads remained perfectly still.

Allaedin yawned. He was a man of professed devotion but this nightly performance by Rumi's disciples was trying. It was the anniversary of the saint's death and Konya was full of earnest men making pilgrimage to his tomb. That night, Allaedin's only entertainment was in counting how many of them were asleep when lightning lit the room.

The hall itself was large and vaulted and part of the great palace built by his father. Its pillars were lit by sconced torches whose flames moved in a light draught that was all they felt of the storm outside. Between the pillars were row upon row of turbans, their colours muted in the uneven light. Beneath the turbans were men from every corner of the prophet's lands, sitting transfixed or otherwise, while the dervishes turned ecstatically for their god.

From his dais, Allaedin was watching the only man not wearing a turban. And, insolently, the man was staring back at him. He was slight of build and something told Allaedin that he was from Venice.

Venice.

The dance was reaching its climax and the viol and tambour had quickened their tempo. Another lightning strike lit up the room and Allaedin forced himself to pay attention. He was, after all, guardian of this holiest of shrines. At last it was finished and the Emir leant across to his vizier and whispered. The vizier looked towards the Venetian and rose.

Some little time later, the Venetian found himself in private audience with the ruler of the Karamanids. The room they occupied was small, pillared and richly decorated with stone arabesques. A low table of cedar inlaid with mother-of-pearl stood at its centre and on either side of it were cushioned divans. The Venetian was invited to sit.

Allaedin studied him. He was very young, barely more than a boy. He hadn't removed his hat, which was pulled low over his head. The Emir said: 'A Venetian in Konya. Are you a follower of the saint?'

The young man inclined his head. 'The saint Rumi is revered by all men of discernment.' His voice was high.

Allaedin sat back against the cushions, putting his head to one side. He took in the black doublet, expensively made and loose at the front. He took in the curve of thigh above the riding boots. 'Why do you not remove your hat in my presence?'

The Venetian brought his hands together in the sign of prayer. He dipped his forehead to his fingers. 'Forgive me, majesty. It is cold.'

'Remove it.'

The Venetian didn't move for a while. Then he slowly raised his hands and lifted the hat from his head. A cascade of black hair fell past his shoulders. Allaedin ali-Bey smiled. 'It is as I thought. You are a girl.'

Zoe tucked a stray strand of hair behind her ear and raised her head to look the Emir straight in the eye.

'You present yourself for my harem?' he asked.

Zoe thought for a moment before replying. Allaedin was middle-aged, fat and many-chinned, but she would do whatever was required. She wondered whether his tastes inclined in her direction. 'Your harem is filled with better creatures than I, lord,' she said. 'I come to you from one who would befriend you. I am a messenger.'

Allaedin ali-Bey raised his eyebrows. 'Who is this that would befriend me? The Doge?'

Zoe put her hands to her knees, in part to hide her thighs towards which the Emir's eyes kept darting. His tastes were clear. 'Not the Doge, lord. One more powerful.'

The Emir leant forward, frowning. He clicked his fingers twice and a servant appeared instantly bearing cups.

'Sherbet,' he said. 'As befits the guardian of the saint's home.' He paused. 'It is a pity this friend could not come himself. Tell me, were he here in place of you, would he perhaps prefer wine?'

Zoe smiled. 'He would. But not in the quantities enjoyed by his father.'

Allaedin smiled, his eyes narrowing with the movement of his face. He lifted the cup and drank its contents in one gulp, wiping his lips with his sleeve. Allaedin ali-Bey was a man of forty-five years, most of them spent in embellishing a talent for cunning. His beylik was the only independent kingdom left in Anatolia, the only one not to have been annexed by the Ottoman Turks. He was married to the sister of Bayezid and his watchword was caution.

'So, messenger, what does the Prince Suleyman want of me?'

Zoe brought her hands back to her lap. 'My master seeks a man. A Greek from the Despotate of Mistra. He is somewhere in the lands of the Germiyans. Your neighbours.'

Allaedin raised an eyebrow. 'He wants my help to find a *Greek*?'

Zoe remained silent. The Emir stroked his beard and gazed at the beautiful swirling script that flowed across the surface of the table. 'Why is this Greek so important to the Prince?' he asked.

'I don't know, highness. But I know that he would be grateful for his capture. Alive.'

Allaedin thought. He thought about the first, faltering steps of an alliance he'd made with his old enemy Yakub: the arrangement of a marriage between two junior kinsmen of them both, far out on the steppe. After decades of war, the Germiyans and Karamanids were going to try friendship instead. It was all part of the plan to bring Tamerlane.

Only Allaedin ali-Bey had more to lose than Yakub if he backed the wrong side: his kingdom. What harm would come from helping Suleyman?

'We do have some contact with the Germiyans, it is true,' he said slowly. He paused and looked up at the stone arching above him. His hand came up to caress the luxuriance of beard that fell in waves to the hill of his belly. 'There is a marriage.'

Zoe nodded slowly. 'I had heard as much, majesty.' She paused and looked down at the tips of her fingers. 'The girl, the bride–'

Allaedin interrupted, '–has been inspected by the man who will marry her, yes. So she may know where this tribe is now. They move, you see.' He lifted his empty cup and his thumb traced the complicated design on its side. 'The tribe has a stranger in its midst, I'm told.'

Zoe did not say anything. This was treacherous ground.

'I'm also told', continued the Emir quietly, 'that the girl is very reluctant to go into this marriage.'

They sat in silence for a while, the sound of the storm distant beyond the walls. A window rattled far above them. Zoe took a silent breath. 'Might I, perhaps, meet this reluctant bride, lord?'

CHAPTER SIX

ANATOLIA, SPRING 1398

At first Luke thought it was Gomil's party returning. The long line of riders was strung out along the escarpment, silhouetted against the red ball of the setting sun.

But there was something wrong about them. They were moving too fast and sitting low in their saddles. And they were carrying their bows as if they meant to use them. These were not men returning to their homes, this was a raiding party.

Luke was alone on the hillside, a mile down the valley. He was wearing a sheepskin deel drawn together by a belt which held no weapon. He'd been allowed to keep his sword but not remove it from the ger. Around him grazed a herd of angora goats, their bodies thin and scarred from shearing, and they fed noisily on the rich new grass. It was warm and the evening air was hazed by the flight of night insects fanning out to carouse amongst the scents left over from the day.

Luke had been preparing to drive his herd home when he'd seen the riders. Once he knew that they weren't from the camp, he collected his stick and the bundle of curds left over from lunch and ran fast down the hillside. If he could get to the stream at its bottom and use the cover of its bank, he might just reach the defile where the two valleys met before the riders got to it. Then he'd have to get a horse.

Bending double and sliding part of the way, he made it to the stream and jumped in. It was shallow and fast-moving and the pebbles beneath his feet gave no grip. The cold left him breathless and numbed to the knee. He half ran, half crawled as fast as he could and soon the junction of the two valleys came into view and the banks of the stream began to rise to form the defile.

But he'd been seen.

In his hurry, he'd slipped on a stone and landed headlong in the water. When he looked up, pushing hair from his eyes, he saw a rider a hundred paces to his front, watching him. At least he assumed that he was watching him. It was difficult to be sure for the man wore a long mask of painted wood that obscured all of his face and much of his chest. The masked man raised his bow, an arrow on its string, and pointed it directly at Luke.

Very slowly, Luke got up, his arms raised in the universal sign of submission. The rider didn't move. Luke looked hard at him. The mask was very large and the eye-slits narrow. Firing accurately would be a challenge at that range. He could either flee or advance. He didn't have much time and he wanted the horse. He began to advance.

The rider did nothing. Luke was making his task easier; the range was narrowing with every step. Luke held his head high. He was watching the horse and the horse was watching him. It was young and skittish and nervous of the currents flowing about its feet. The sudden glance of sunlight breaking on stone wasn't part of its life on the steppe. Still Luke watched it.

I, too, am afraid. I will come to you and we will master our fear together.

Their eyes were locked. The space between them was fifty paces, then forty.

But there's something I want you to do.

It was twenty paces now and still the man aimed the bow at Luke. At this range, he couldn't miss.

Now!

The horse reared. For a moment it looked as if the rider would keep to his saddle. Then it reared again and the man came down. The bow fell and its arrow glanced against a rock. Luke sprang forward as the horse scrambled to the bank, water exploding around its hooves. The rider thrashed about, trying to draw his sword, but the current was too strong and the water too cold. Then Luke was upon him and the mask had been pulled away and the man's head was between two powerful hands that were pushing it under.

The fight was short and vicious. The man was strong and wanted to live and he gripped Luke's forearms with a force that seemed beyond human. Twice his face came up, eyes bulging with defiance as he choked and bit at Luke's hands, but each time Luke forced him back beneath the water. The heaving chest rose a last time and told of lungs full of water and the man's hands fell away. Then he was still and the bubbles rose from purple lips and Luke knew that he was dead. Exhausted, he rolled away into the water.

The horse.

He looked up at the bank and the horse was there, calmly cropping the grass. Luke whistled softly. The animal raised its head, grass hanging slack from its mouth and recognition in its eye. A fly settled on its nose and was shaken away but the horse remained still. Luke rose, picked up the bow and walked unsteadily to the bank, opening and closing his fists to restore the circulation. He felt suddenly exhilarated by the prospect of climbing on to the back of this horse. Then he was beside it and his hands were deep within the thick hair of its mane and his mouth was next to its ear and the bond that was without explanation was being made. He put his foot in the stirrup and pulled himself up into the saddle.

We will master our fear together.

It was half a mile to the camp and he knew the raiders were ahead of him. He dug his heels into the horse's sides and it leapt forward, relieved to be free of the water. They found a path that ran beside the riverbank and Luke urged the horse into a canter. By now it was nearly night and the rim of the escarpment was outlined by the sun that had just gone down behind it. He reached the junction of the two valleys and turned north for the camp. Up ahead there was fire in the sky.

Luke kicked harder, breaking into a gallop even as the sides of the valley grew steeper. There were trees in front of them with a halo of light above them. Then he was in the trees and the smell of burning was among them and the sound of fighting only just beyond. He emerged from the wood and before him was chaos. Ahead were the ribbed skeletons of tents aflame and silhouettes between. Arrows flew and people were running and falling. He saw swords arc and heard the screams of men as they fell. There was an explosion of flame as a tent collapsed.

'Lug!'

It was a girl. He strained to see who but was blinded by the glare. Then he saw Arkal, hand in hand with Tsaurig, running towards him as fast as she could. The pair reached him and Arkal bent double to regain her breath. She was holding her leg, obviously in pain. Dismounting, Luke wondered fleetingly why he'd never asked her about it.

'Lug . . .' She was panting hard and the words came in spasms. 'Lug, you must not go on. They . . .' She looked behind and then up at him and there was desperation in her eyes. 'They're looking for someone . . . someone not from our tribe.'

She straightened. 'They were looking for *you*, Lug.'

Tsaurig began to cry. Big tears ran down his cheeks and pooled in the folds of his deel. He grabbed his sister's hand again.

'Where are your parents?' Luke asked softly.

The girl didn't answer.

'Arkal, are your parents alive?' he asked, taking her free hand.

Arkal shrugged. She pushed hair from her eyes. There was blood on her forehead. 'Lug, why do they want you?'

'I don't know,' he said. 'But I will find out. Where have they gone?'

'They have taken our horses and gone back to where they came from.'

Luke looked beyond her to the remains of the camp. The flames were dying now. There were no horses. He let go of her hand. 'Arkal, take Tsaurig into the wood and stay there until it's safe to go back. If the camp has lost its horses then I must go after them myself.'

Arkal began to protest, then slowly nodded her head. 'Be careful, Lug.' She turned and began to walk towards the trees, Tsaurig behind her. She stopped. Looking back, she asked: 'You'll come back, won't you?'

Luke smiled. 'Of course.'

Then he mounted and pulled the horse's head towards the slope. He kicked and rode up the valley's side, pausing once to see Arkal reach the wood. At the top, he reined in and looked out at the vast connected shadow of land and sky. The stars blinked and shimmered and fell like snow over the steppe. Luke patted the neck of his pony and leant down.

Which way did they go?

There was wind here, a soft, soothing thing that came from far, far away and had begun in the east. Luke lifted his head and breathed deeply. The smell of horse was faint but unmistakable.

They have gone east.

He looked again at the stars and turned his pony into the wind and pressed his heels to its sides. The land was flat and the grass new and the going easy. He rode with his head low on the animal's neck and he talked all the while as it covered the ground in its short, uneven strides.

It was halfway through the night when the raiders stopped to rest. The Germiyan horses were spread out across the plain and being herded together. Luke could see them quite clearly in the light of the moon that had risen above the mountains to the west. He dismounted and slapped his horse away and lay down on the dark side of a low hill to watch. The riders were erecting a makeshift pen around the horses, their bows slung across their shoulders. They were many miles from the camp by now, too far for anyone to reach them without horses, and they spoke in loud, excited voices.

Some of them had made a fire and food was being taken from saddlebags to cook. Luke heard song and saw the silhouette of an airag sack being passed around. He looked over to the pen where there were men posted at each corner. One of them shouted to his friends and the airag was brought over. Laughter rose into the night, the smell of spiced mutton rising with it, and drink was passed between men who laughed louder as it did its work.

Luke was cold and hungry. The ride had been fast and hard and his horse had stumbled in marmot holes towards the end. The animal was sick. He'd looked into those white-rimmed eyes and seen fever. He glanced behind him.

Stay with me, friend. We have work to do.

Much later, when the fire had died down and men were sleeping around its embers, he moved. Three of the men guarding the horses were asleep, the other mumbling to himself. He could see that all of the horses had been penned together.

That's good.

Cursing the moon, Luke began to crawl towards the horses, the tall grass covering him. The sleeping guards were snoring and the one that wasn't was sitting with his back against a post. Then his head nodded and fell forward. Luke could see a dagger glinting at his waist. The moon was still undimmed by cloud and if the man woke, Luke would die. Rising to a crouch, he waited to hear some noise within the pen before making his rush. A horse whinnied and another answered and he ran. He was as fast and silent as his Varangian father had taught him to be. Before the guard could awake, Luke had ripped the dagger from his belt and slit his throat from side to side. There was no sound beyond the slither of metal breaking skin.

Now he was moving quietly along the rope, talking and soothing as he went and looking for the signs in each horse that marked it out as leader. Luke crept up on the second guard from the side, clamped his hand over his mouth and drove the knife between his ribs. Blood splashed over his hand and the man jerked in tiny, gurgling spasms before he died. Luke wiped his hand on the ground and rolled into the pen. The horses stood around him and he looked at each in turn.

Which of you is leader?

He moved further in, the horses parting before him, puzzled, curious. Luke looked from head to head, calling softly, cajoling, seeking out the one that would persuade the others. Then he saw him. A black gelding with white socks and a lozenge on his nose. There was space around him, which meant that he was held in respect by the others. The horse looked at Luke and Luke looked back.

I know you.

He knew that he'd seen the animal before. Luke had spent as much time as he could getting to know the Germiyan horses. He'd fed them, watered them, talked to them; he'd done everything but ride them. And he'd marked this one out as special. Now, in the soft light, he looked into two big eyes with moons in them, eyes that were watching him without fear.

We know each other.

He put out his arm and touched its nose, moving the flat of his palm down to cover the nostrils. He would have the smell of horse on that hand. He moved it down to the grooved rubber of its lips, cupping its chin and lifting the head so that their noses touched. The white lozenge shone as it met the moonlight and Luke looked straight down its silver path into those big, unblinking eyes.

There is something I want you to do.

A minute later, Luke had mounted a different horse. With no saddle, he was able to lie almost flat along its back as he moved slowly through the herd, gently pushing animals out of their way. He reached the perimeter, slid to the ground and pulled up two posts, laying them flat on the ground. Then he led the horse down the side of the pen until he got to the corner and a good view of the sleeping raiders. They were lying close to the dying fire. There didn't seem to be any guards although a single horse stood in silhouette, tethered slightly apart.

Luke bent down and picked up the sack of airag. He pulled the stopper from its mouth and smelt its contents. Then he put it to his lips and drank. Fire burnt his throat and he buried his face in the pony's mane to stop himself from coughing. He mounted the horse, the airag in his hand. The landscape around the fire moved; one of the raiders was sitting up. He'd heard something. Luke saw him turn to wake others.

Now.

Luke started over the open ground and the man rose and reached for his bow. He was shouting and other heads came up. Then Luke was on top of them. He swung the airag sack twice above his head before hurling it into the fire. There was an explosion and burning debris flew into the air. A scream of pain came as a man's clothes caught light.

Luke was already backing his horse away when he felt the wind of an arrow above him. He ducked and turned the horse's head for flight. Out of the corner of his eye, he saw someone grab for the tethered horse. He kicked hard and struck the pony's flank with his fist.

He looked up at the stars and found a plough. Above it would be the North Star. The pony was moving quickly now and Luke was skirting the pen, a hundred pairs of eyes watching his progress. When he reached the place where the rope had been lowered, he saw the horses already beginning to leave the enclosure, the gelding at their head. He whistled sharply, and turned to the west. The horse neighed and broke into a trot and then a canter. Luke's heart lifted.

It's working.

He looked behind him. The horses were spreading out across

the steppe and the thunder of their two thousand hooves was like a storm rolling through the grasses. But there was a rider following him.

At first he thought it was a rogue horse that had broken free from the herd. Then he saw that there was a shape above the horse, a shape bent low for speed, a shape that included the curve of a bow. Luke looked down at his pony. It was no Eskalon. He cursed that he'd brought no bow. But then he hadn't yet learnt how to shoot from the saddle. He'd have to outride his pursuer.

The gelding. I need the gelding.

He steered his pony towards the gelding, which was now almost level with him. He looked at its gallop, its rhythm and the space between its hooves. He made the judgement.

One, two, three . . .

He'd begun the leap when his pony went down. Shot through the leg, it could do nothing but fall. It sank to the grass, twisting as it did so and bringing Luke with it. He was pinned. In seconds the herd would be on top of him. He closed his eyes and prayed.

The horses came on, jumping the obstacle one after another. Then one shied and was hit by those behind. Yet still they came on and Luke held his breath, waiting for the hooves that would trample him, feeling their thunder shake every part of his being.

Then the thunder passed and he lay beneath the rough underbelly of the horse and listened to the beat of his heart. He felt something hard digging into his side and managed to move an arm. It was the arrow.

He pulled it free and there was no sound from the horse beyond the horrid slurp of release. It was quite dead. And it was heavy. Digging his elbows into the ground, he managed to shift himself to the side of the carcass. Then, with another heave, he was free. He looked up.

There was his pursuer, pale as a ghost in the moonlight. The man was small and slight and almost entirely hidden by the monstrous mask he wore. His horse wanted to follow the herd and was straining against the rein, turning circles on the flattened grass. But the rider was out of arrows. He threw the bow to one side and drew his knife. Then he charged.

Luke waited to the last moment before throwing himself to one side. As he did so, he thrust the point of the arrow up like a dagger into the upper arm of the man. The man? The cry of pain was not that of a man; it was a boy's. And the arm glimpsed in the moonlight was hairless. The horse reared and the boy came down. Luke recovered his balance to see the horse moving away to catch the herd. He lunged for the reins and with one finger, caught them and looped them round his wrist. Then he threw himself into the saddle and kicked.

There was no time to look back. He had to catch the horses.

At the Germiyan camp, daylight brought the misery of seeing.

The light arrived slowly, creeping out from behind the stars like a jewel-thief, and the people of the camp sat around wrapped in blankets and stared silently at the ground. The only sound came from dogs that moved like servants from person to person, heads tilted in query. The gers stood charred and stripped to the bone, the ground around them black and strewn with things dragged out before the torches hit. Felt was everywhere, burnt and curled and stinking.

The camp had lost only two men but all of its horses. Those standing there now, nose to nose, belonged to Gomil's hunting party, which had just returned. They were waiting for the order to remount and follow the raiders.

Gomil was standing next to his father, who had blood on his face and a bandage around his thigh. They were talking together in low voices and Arkal was standing a little apart, listening to every word and squeezing Tsaurig's hand every time he drew breath to cry. She had found her parents alive but beyond speech. Now she wanted to know about Luke.

'The girl says that Luke went after them,' said the older man. 'One against twenty. He will die and we will be blamed.'

Gomil looked gaunt and tired. His deel was filthy. 'It is because of him that they came,' he said. 'You said it yourself: they were looking for someone not of the tribe.'

Etabul shook his head. 'They followed you to the camp,' he said. 'They wanted the horses.'

Gomil grunted. 'We should not have stopped for the night. They must have overtaken us then.'

Etabul looked up. 'Why were you so late in returning?'

'The girl would not let us go. I had agreed the marriage with her father but she kept arguing. I couldn't leave.' He looked beaten. He waved Arkal and Tsaurig away. 'Father,' he said quietly, looking over his shoulder at the waiting men, 'we can get new horses but we must get rid of the foreigner. He has brought us trouble.'

His father turned on him. 'New horses?' he asked. 'Tell me how we can get horses when we have no horses ourselves.' He stared at his son and then glanced at the men around them. His voice fell to a whisper. 'Without horses we are nothing.'

Gomil frowned. He knew it was true. A tribe with only twenty horses between them was finished. They would be forced to join a neighbouring camp, subservient to others' whims. Suddenly he felt very angry. 'It's Lug's fault,' he said.

Etabul grunted and looked up at the sky. The first rays of the sun had crested the ridge and scattered across the sky, turning cold grey into blue. Small birds left the trees behind them in clouds of tiny wingbeats. Today would be spent in planning for a desolate future. He felt drained. 'Well,' he sighed, 'at least you won't have to marry the Karamanid girl. They won't make a match with a horseless tribe, whatever Yakub wants.'

Gomil had considered this and had been surprised that relief was not among the emotions he'd felt. He'd been told by the father to look at the girl's legs. Strong legs would mean a strong, child-bearing wife. But he'd looked instead at her face.

'Was she ugly?' asked his father.

'No,' replied Gomil. 'She wasn't ugly.'

A falcon screeched and they looked up to see it soar into the rising birds and emerge with a shape between its claws. Gomil was about to whistle for its return when he heard a shout from one of the waiting hunting party. The man was pointing south along the valley. Father and son turned to look.

There were horses coming towards them. Far beyond the woods, there were horses, hundreds of them, and they had no riders. They were spread out along the valley bottom, some in the river, water splashing around their hooves. At their head was a rider, upright and waving.

'Lug,' Etabul said softly.

Now people from the camp were running, running towards the horses. Children had broken free of their parents and were skipping and jumping and clapping their hands. Even the sheep and goats had raised their heads and were calling out the news.

Etabul turned to the waiting party. 'Give me a horse,' he said.

CHAPTER SEVEN

VENICE, SUMMER 1398

Pavlos Mamonas, Archon of Monemvasia, was in the Arsenale of Venice learning about the making of cannon with his son Damian. Or, to be more accurate, they were learning about the unmaking of cannon, for the examples they were looking at had all split asunder.

They were standing in a large courtyard, high-walled, that was attached to the gun foundry. Both men had disposed of their doublets and their linen *camicie* were open to the waist and dark at the armpits. The foundry had been hot. With them was the chief gunsmith, a man called Rudi, who'd come from Ragusa on the Dalmatian coast. He was the best gunsmith outside China and also one of the richest, his salary from the Serenissima augmented by Plethon's bribes. He was explaining to Pavlos what had gone wrong.

'It's the size, master. No one has ever tried to make them this big before.'

Pavlos wiped his brow. 'So what happens?'

Rudi pointed to a long hollow frame that was lying on its side, its wood charred by heat. Next to it stood two brass bells, both cracked, and behind them their own flasks, bell-shaped.

'It happens in the flask. Bells, cannon – it's the same. We put in the clay pattern, pack the sand around it, then take it out and pour in the molten bronze.'

Pavlos had seen the crucibles suspended on chains in the foundry. Their heat was still on him.

'Once the brass has hardened,' continued Rudi, 'we break the mould and take out the barrel. But every time there are these air bubbles trapped in the metal. They make it weak.'

Pavlos looked at the man. He was dressed in a long leather apron and little else. He was as bald as a eunuch and had a face reddened by the furnace. Pavlos remembered his last visit to the Arsenale and the more complicated dress he'd been obliged to wear: the clothes of the plague doctor. For a moment he wondered whether the calm of the Doge had split like these cannon when he'd heard the news.

Mastic doesn't, after all, cure the plague.

Pavlos turned to the cask. He'd taught himself about cannon. There was too much at stake not to. 'Why not try steel then?' he asked. 'After all, it's harder.'

The gunsmith shook his head. 'Too brittle. Bronze has the malleability and is better with friction. The balls are iron now.'

'What about the pattern then?' asked Mamonas. 'I'm told they use wax in Delhi, and chase it out with the hot bronze. Would that work?'

'No I've tried that.' The gunsmith looked back at the flask lying on its side. 'The only thing to do is make the cannon walls thicker, so that the air bubbles matter less. It's what we're trying now.'

The Archon was worried. He'd promised the cannon in June and now it was August. And there was another problem.

'We need more brass. We're running out,' said Rudi.

Pavlos's head ached. He had no idea how to get brass. He glanced at his son. Damian was standing apart looking, with no interest at all, at a bell. Suddenly, Pavlos felt irritated. 'Do you have any suggestions, Damian?' he called.

His son turned and walked back to his father and the gunsmith. His limp seemed more pronounced than ever. Pavlos had heard that he'd come back to the fondaco at dawn. He could smell the wine still on his son's breath.

Damian said, 'What about iron hoops? Why not wrap them round the barrel? Wouldn't that stop it?'

Rudi was shaking his head. 'Wouldn't work. If the crack's on the inside of the barrel, the ball won't come out properly.'

Damian turned away, already bored. He walked over to where their doublets were hanging from a stave and began to put his on. Clearly he felt that the interview was over. Pavlos Mamonas looked at his back and thought of the conversation with Zoe. He'd still not decided.

He walked over to his own doublet. He looked down at its rich, patterned broadcloth, too thick for August. He didn't want to put it on. He turned to the gunsmith. 'I don't much care how you do it, but I must have cannon big enough to bring down Constantinople's walls by the end of the year.' He put an arm through a sleeve. 'If you are unable to do it, then we'll give the commission to the Hungarians. And you will have to answer to the Doge.'

Later that same day, the philosopher Plethon was half a mile away studying the workings of the Rialto. He was standing in a little square next to the rising bridge of that name. The square was bordered by cantilevered buildings – banks, insurance agencies and tax offices – above which rose the squat tower of the Church of San Giacomo with its useful clock. Plethon was looking at its face and wondering whether he had time for lunch before his meeting with the Doge.

The square was unpleasantly hot and filled with overdressed people and Plethon silently blessed the ancient connection of philosophy with toga. The air smelt badly of the fish market next door and Venice in the heat: a mix of rank canal and ranker humanity. At least the mastic had improved people's breath. The noise was appalling. Seagulls, calling above, mimicked the calls of commerce. Plethon wondered why money always had to raise its voice to be heard.

His eyes travelled from the clock face to those of a stout banker and his wife, awash with discomfort in the crowd. They were clearly a couple of some standing. She wore a high-collared *cioppa* of figured silk, decorated with the pomegranate motif. Her head was veiled and her long hair gathered in a knot beneath with a ribboned tail running down her back like a dog's lead. Her husband was top-heavy in black doublet and hose, the doublet slashed to reveal enough colour to please the dyers' guild but not so much to challenge the sumptuary laws. They were middle-aged and there was a fat son in tow.

Plethon watched the couple approach a table with weights and measures and coin on its surface. A blackboard was propped beside it with the exchange rates for the florin, *gazzetta*, *marengo* and other currencies chalked up. Next to it were other boards showing commodity prices, and Plethon saw the man stoop to the line showing Malvasia wine and take note. Then the man moved to another board on which were written the prices for metals. He spent some time looking at the price of bronze. He shook his head. Plethon walked over to them.

The man's wife saw him first and her face coloured with

alarm. Conversation with a toga'd stranger might not be helpful in their rise through society's ranks, were Venice's ruling caste ever to be opened to new families again. She tugged at her husband's sleeve.

The philosopher stopped in front of them and bowed. Straightening, he threw a fold of toga over his shoulder. He smiled. 'Georgius Gemistus at your service,' he said.

The couple blinked at him. Plethon was known but Georgius Gemistus unheard of. 'Tommasi Giacomo at yours,' said the man uneasily, bowing. 'My wife, Dominia.'

Plethon turned and bowed again. 'Forgive me. I saw you interrogate the blackboard and note down the price of Malvasia. I myself have a commission to buy the wine in bulk and thought, perhaps, you might know how I can make the transaction?'

Giacomo thawed slightly. 'I am factor to the family that makes it,' he said. 'Their fondaco is nearby. We can talk there.'

Plethon shook his head. 'Sadly, I am to meet elsewhere. But, tell me, would that be the Mamonas family of Monemvasia?'

Giacomo smiled. He was nearly as proud of his position as his wife and he hoped they were being overheard. His wife raised a warning finger to the boy who'd begun to whine. 'The same. And you are from?'

'Mistra and Chios. I have houses in both,' said Plethon, without a blush.

Giacono had interlocked his fingers and begun to rub his palms against each other. 'Would your transaction be in cash or in kind, sir?'

Chios might mean mastic and the market was short of mastic.

'In kind. But not mastic. I have copper. And tin from Cornwall. Some of it mixed. The best.'

Bronze.

The factor lowered his voice and glanced around. He drew Plethon to one side. 'What makes you think my master has need of such metals?'

There was the sound of a slap and the boy began to cry. The factor ignored it. Plethon frowned.

'But', went on the factor hurriedly, his voice low, 'it is possible that the Arsenale . . .'

Plethon nodded. 'Is your master in Venice?'

The factor looked uncomfortable. He'd had strict instructions to say nothing of his master's movements, not even that he was in the city. But this Greek had bronze. He looked around him and lowered his voice still further. 'It is possible that he might be in Venice. And he might be able to talk for the Serenissima on the subject of . . . *metals*. He acts for them in other areas.'

'I would want an exclusive. The status of sole provider for three months. It would be reflected in the price.'

For someone revolted by trade, Plethon had mastered its language surprisingly well. He sounded convincing. The fat man nodded and glanced back at the blackboard. The price was its highest yet. He pressed his hands together. 'I will do what I can. You would meet with him?'

Plethon shook his head. 'No, it is better that this transaction is done through intermediaries. The quantities are considerable.'

A light veil of sweat now covered the man's face. He could no more conceal his excitement than his wife could prevent the child from now giving voice.

Twenty minutes later, Plethon was humming as he crossed the Piazza San Marco on his way to meet the Doge. If anything, the day was even hotter and the crowds had abandoned the square to the pigeons, men in black clinging to its shadowed sides like bats. The philosopher was too absorbed in thought even to shake his customary fist at the bronze horses of the cathedral.

He was wondering whether the ruse would really work. He'd used some of the considerable funds that Luke was amassing in Chios to bribe miners of copper and tin. He'd asked them to create a flawed alloy, one that a colluding gunsmith could make use of. The idea of the exclusive had come to him at the Rialto.

Three more months of delay. It all helps.

Plethon was humming so hard that he didn't hear the request from the two *excusati* guarding the entrance to the Doge's palace. He found himself facing a cross of tasselled halberds. 'Ah yes. Georgius Gemistus Plethon. I am expected.'

The halberds rose and he entered a large courtyard with an imposing staircase that led up to a loggia. Men in long scarlet robes were walking down it – men of the Grand Council. With them, and in deep conversation, were a covey of cardinals. Red and purple, a pope's ransom in dye flowed towards him down the marble steps. Two cardinals known to Plethon stopped to talk. Their news from the meeting was not encouraging.

Not long after, Plethon was standing in the Scudo Room where the coat of arms of Antonio Venier, Doge of Venice hung. Unlike Pavlos Mamonas, he'd only met this man before within the confines of his palace. He bowed.

Venier said, 'You will have been trampled by prelates on your way up. And the cardinals are not light.'

Plethon liked Venier for his ruthless pragmatism. There was never any skirmish to their conversation. 'Weighted with disappointment it seemed, magnificence,' he replied.

The Doge went over to an open window and looked down into

the courtyard. The buzz of conversation below rose as a faint music. 'Yes,' he murmured. 'Still . . .' He turned and looked at Plethon. There was silence between the two men, broken only by the tide of Plethon's breathing. The steps had been many and steep. 'They want me to stop building things for the Turks.'

'And the Grand Council?'

'To build faster, of course. They worry about our alum not getting past Constantinople because of the blockade. And they worry about Genoa.'

'Genoa?'

The Doge turned back to the window. In its frame, he looked like the study of a man bent under the burden of age and cynicism. A little wind ruffled his unruly beard and he put his hand to it. 'They worry that if we don't help the Turk, Genoa will, and all the gains of the last many years will be wasted. Genoa controls the alum from Chios, as you know.'

Plethon asked: 'May I sit?'

Since he'd been doge, this question had seldom been put to Venier but he covered his surprise well. Plethon was already seated at the long table when he came over to join him. 'Wine? We have it from Monemvasia. Iced.'

Plethon shook his head. The Venetians were said to strengthen their wine in negotiations and he was tired from the heat. He asked: 'You've heard of the French writer Gautier de Coincy? The one who wrote of the Virgin's miracles?'

The Doge was pouring himself wine and nodding. He hadn't heard of the writer.

'Then you will know that there is one in which she rescues a man who makes a bargain with Mephistopheles. The Devil makes him rich and powerful and comes to collect his debt: the man's soul.' He paused. 'The Virgin intercedes.'

The Doge saw where this was leading. He said: 'You speak of Venice and the Turk. There is a difference.'

Plethon waited.

'The difference here is that the debt is the other way round. We've sold to them and not vice versa.'

'It is immaterial,' said Plethon. 'You've made a pact with that which will destroy you. Eventually.'

The Doge sipped his wine and winced as ice touched a hole in his teeth. 'We disagree. The Turk will need trade to pay for his empire. We will provide it.'

Both men looked at each other for a while. Both were as clever as their beards were long. There was mutual respect. 'Anyway,' said the Doge, 'the Serenissima has been excommunicated before. I'll have friends below. We can toast together.'

Plethon smiled again. He rose from the table and walked to stand beneath the Venier coat of arms. 'You would give the Turk the Middle Sea for fifty years of gain. No more dreams of *Mare Nostrum*. What will future Veniers make of you?'

The Doge shrugged. 'We Venetians live on water, Plethon. What could be more unstable than that? We move with the tide.'

Plethon looked up at the shield for a long time before speaking again. He did not turn round. 'I have two strategies for stopping the Turk from taking all of Christendom. The first is to bring Tamerlane to fight Bayezid.'

Venier shook his head. 'He won't come,' he said. 'We have agents in the court in Samarcand. He's more interested in China.' He reached for his wine. 'They tell me he is obsessed with reuniting the four Khanates under one Mongol rule. He's done three: Chagatai, Persia and the Golden Horde. Now he's just got the empire won by Kublai Khan to conquer: China.

Anyway, Tamerlane might not beat him. Bayezid's never lost a battle.' He smiled. 'What is your second?'

'To forge a union of the Churches which will enable the Pope to send another crusade before the Turk is too strong and it's too late.'

'But we are blessed with two Popes. Which is it to be, Rome's or Avignon's?'

'They can be reunited.'

The Doge looked sceptical. 'How?'

'Incentive,' said the philosopher. 'I want to talk to men who see advantage in a single Curia. The Medici, for instance. I would like you to arrange a meeting.'

The Doge frowned. 'The Catholic Church has been in schism for decades and many reputations have been lost in the attempt to reconcile it. Why will the Medici want to risk theirs?'

'Because they've already started. They are grooming Baldassare Cossa for the task. Why else have they bought him his cardinal's hat? They want the banking of a single Curia. Think of the revenues from all those sees.'

'But what about the two Popes?'

'Ah,' replied Plethon, leaning forward and dropping his voice to the conspiratorial. 'For them I have the ultimate incentive.'

'Which is more money? Plethon, something has been puzzling me. Where is all this money coming from? We have the Empress's jewels here in pawn.'

Plethon nodded. 'We have new money.'

'You've found your treasure?'

Plethon blinked. Was there anything this man didn't know? 'Possibly. But if I had, it would provide a different kind of incentive, one much more persuasive than money,' he said. 'No, this money comes from Chios.'

'From Chios?' Venier paused. 'Now, here is irony. Chios is Suleyman's bait to get us to build cannon for him and it's also the source of your bribes to prevent it. The island is busy.' He paused. 'Wouldn't it be simpler for you just to give Chios to us?'

Plethon shook his head. 'We do not abandon our friends so easily.' He looked hard at the other man. 'Anyway, now you know that mastic doesn't cure the plague, why is it still important? Is it just to deny Genoa?'

The Doge shook his head. 'No, pleasant though it is to deny anything to Genoa. We want Chios because, with it and the trade from Trebizond, we'd have the monopoly for alum. We could price as we wish.'

Plethon considered this. At Christmas, Benedo Barbi had told him that the thriving market for alum and mastic, as well as the Medici loan, had built new villages to strengthen the island's defence. He'd heard that the last Turkish assault had been disastrous.

He said: 'You know, of course, that Bayezid has forbidden further attacks on Chios? After the failure of the last one, I doubt Suleyman will have the nerve to try again. I suspect that is why you allow me to go on bribing your man from Ragusa.'

The Doge looked up. 'You are a cynic, Plethon. But you may judge for yourself how hard I might find it to continue blocking the cannon if Chios once more came into play. The signori of Venice are much taken with the prospect of the alum monopoly.' He paused. 'There is also the question of which Mamonas to deal with. The father is understandably cautious, given the Sultan's injunction. The daughter, who is Suleyman's lover, is more reckless.'

Plethon looked down at his hands. He was suddenly very tired. He began the business of gathering the folds of his toga.

He looked up. There was a smile hidden somewhere deep within the bush of beard across from him. The Doge leant forward.

'Don't worry, Plethon,' he said, sotto voce, 'I'll let you go on bribing my gunsmith a little while longer. We Venetians are, after all, Christians.' He paused. 'And I'll see what can be done about a meeting with de' Medici.'

CHAPTER EIGHT

ANATOLIA, SUMMER 1398

The days were long and full of dust. Every day, a relentless sun blazed down on the scorched grass of the steppe from the same indigo sky and the rivers began to run dry. It was poor grazing for the herds and the animals had to be taken further and further to find food.

Vast game drives were organised with local tribes across the steppe. Three camps beat the animals to a killing ground in the hills where a fourth would be waiting in ambush among the juniper trees, their bows poised.

There were snakes everywhere. Careless children were bitten and one died. Shulen was out daily with her forked stick, silently looking for them around the camp and bringing them back to make antidotes from their poison. Their patterned skins hung like sullen bunting outside her tent. Luke had not spoken to her since the storm.

He was as happy as he'd ever been in his life. As his reward for saving the tribe's horses, he'd been given one. By day, he rode where he wanted and thrilled to the challenge of mastering this small, quick animal that could turn on a florin and show bursts of speed beyond anything he'd seen. He taught himself to ride with his legs, to command with his knees, to understand this tough little cousin of Eskalon as once he'd understood Eskalon.

At night, he ate mutton beneath the stars and drank airag. In the early hours, he'd lie awake and listen to the wind outside singing its same, whispered song of distance and freedom. The sound of the camp awakening would comfort him as his mother Rachel had once done in Monemvasia and he'd watch the gathering light seep through the roof above him and think of the day to come. He was, bit by bit, becoming a gazi.

Gomil was his only worry. Luke could feel him watching his every move, the heat of his rage on his neck as he mounted every horse and pulled every rein. He saw how Gomil's hatred for him was turning into something worse.

One morning, Torguk was waiting for him outside his tent, his daughter Arkal standing next to him.

'Lug,' he said as Luke emerged from the ger to wash, 'I have something for you.'

He was standing awkwardly, his deel wrapped close against the morning chill and his hat in his hands. Arkal was holding something wrapped in lynx-skin and tied up with horsehair. She was flushed with the anticipation of giving pleasure and hopped from good leg to bad.

'Here!' said Arkal, thrusting the present into Luke's arms. 'Open it.'

Luke glanced down at the parcel. He heard a shout to his right and looked up to see Tsaurig running towards them, rubbing sleep from his eyes. Arkal frowned.

'Open it!' she commanded, patting the skin.

Luke sat on the ground, shooing away a dog that had come to investigate. He drew his knife, cut the horsehair and opened the skin. Inside was a bow. It was about the length of Luke's outstretched arm and its limbs were bent into two deep and graceful curves that ended in ears of horn, angled forward. Its outside was covered in birch bark and had been oiled to a dark and stubbled sheen. It smelt strongly of fish. It was beautiful.

'Torguk,' said Luke softly, 'no.'

Luke knew this bow. Ever since the expedition had returned last year from the southern lakes, Torguk had been working on it. He'd taken two lengths of well-grained maple, steamed them into shape and joined them to a belly of cow-horn, using sinew and glue made from the swim bladders of perch. Luke had watched him score the horn and wooden stave before adding the fish glue and binding them tightly together with waxed intestine. Then he'd watched him set aside the bow for the year it would take for the glue to fully cure, taking it out from time to time to admire it and test its strength and flexibility. It was, as he'd often told him, the best bow he'd ever made. Now Luke had it in his hands and was staring at the man who had made it.

'Torguk,' he said, 'I can't.'

'Lug,' replied the man gruffly, not looking at him, 'you have saved my family and my tribe. It's not much in return.'

Arkal stopped hopping and now stepped forward and pushed the bow further up Luke's arms. 'Take it, Lug,' she said quietly. 'It will make him happy.'

Luke picked it up by its middle, feeling the ribs of hardened sinew beneath his palm. He lifted it and turned it into the light of the new day. The sun threw its first rays high into a violet sky and the curve of the bow glowed in its light.

'It's perfect, Torguk.'

'Then you'll take it?' He looked up from his boots, his wide face wreathed in smile.

'I will take it, Torguk,' said Luke, 'but only on one condition. That it is you who teaches me to use it.'

And so Luke's teaching began and never were teacher and pupil better suited. In his time, Torguk had been not just the tribe's best bowyer and fletcher but also its best shot. In the annual gatherings of the tribes, no man had yet to beat the Mongol archer Esukhei's distance of 335 *ald*, but Torguk had come close. And at 40 ald, he could hit an acorn.

Every morning, Luke would awake at dawn to the banging of his ger door and find Arkal outside it, grinning above a bowl of hot gruel. He would eat and wash and dress and tie up his hair. He'd then strap thick hides to the inside of his legs to stop the chafing of a day in the saddle. Soon afterwards, he'd be riding with Torguk by his side and Arkal not far behind, galloping and whooping over the steppe to the place of his morning lesson.

Torguk began by getting Luke to practise again and again the drawing of the bow until he was able to pull it as far back as his chest and then past his ear. Because Luke was strong, he learnt quickly and what would have taken some men a year took Luke less than a month. Torguk taught him to shoot high into the air and judge, to a distance of three ald, where the arrow would land. Then he taught him how to fire with accuracy, how to keep both eyes open in the aim and to see the target not the arrow, even when it was too distant to see.

Torguk would carry a target on these rides, a piece of wood with something drawn on its front by Arkal, quite often Tsaurig's face. These got smaller as the days went on and still Luke hit them. He was a Varangian. He had the blood of men who fought for a living in his veins and he'd spent much of his childhood being trained in the use of arms. He took to this new weapon quickly and with a skill that astonished his teacher.

And Arkal sat on her little pony, watching and smiling and glowing with pride for them both.

Soon Luke was shooting at Arkal's funny faces from the saddle, gripping and steering the pony with his knees while he drew the bow, aimed and fired. The experienced gazi warrior could fire twelve arrows in a minute, the thumb-draw critical to the feat. Within a month, Luke had mastered the thumb-draw and was firing ten. He could fire at the trot, at the gallop and behind him like the Parthians.

One day, when the three of them were resting beneath the shade of their hobbled horses, Torguk paid Luke his first compliment. 'I have never taught anyone better,' he said, smiling, cutting a ball of dried curd in two with his knife. 'You have great talent.'

'Better than Gomil,' giggled Arkal, her mouth full of bread.

Luke reached for the gourd of water. The sun was high in the sky but the leather was still cool to the touch. 'Torguk, it's the bow that is good,' he said. 'It's better than any weapon I've ever used. In Greece, we have a longbow, over six feet in length and made from a single piece of yew. It came over from a country called *England*, the land of my ancestors. Their archers are trained to draw them from childhood, but their bow is not as good as yours.'

Torguk nodded. He'd heard of the English longbow. 'Perhaps that's why we win our battles,' he said equably. 'Gomil thinks so.'

Luke thought of a battle at a place called Nicopolis and of the rain of arrows that had fallen on the lumbering knights of Burgundy. He thought of a hillside strewn with the flower of Western chivalry. This, thought Luke, was a new kind of warfare, one that was faster, more flexible and, in their pride and stupidity, the Princes of Christendom had not understood it. Nor, it seemed, did they know how to stop it. Luke fingered the goose feathers of the arrow in his lap. He decided to change the subject.

'When do we move to our winter pastures, Torguk?' he asked, putting the arrow back in its quiver.

'Earlier than last year, I hope.' Torguk broke off some bread. 'Soon after Gomil's bride arrives, I should think.'

The tribe had been waiting for her to arrive for the past week. She was late and some thought it rude, possibly deliberately so. The marriage was not popular in the camp.

'Perhaps she is there now,' he said, rising stiffly to his feet. 'We should return.'

It was the smell of roasting mutton that told them that Gomil's bride had arrived, and they lifted their heads to it in pleasure. The sun was low in the sky and poppy-red and touched by wisps of broken cloud.

There was a light canopy of smoke above the gers that spoke of a feast in preparation and birds of prey circled high above it in hope. As they drew closer, they saw that a second pen, safely distant from the camp, now contained horses.

They rode in and it was Berta they saw first: Berta washed and shiny-skinned in the deel she wore to Friday prayers. She gestured to them to dismount. 'Quick!' she hissed, holding Torguk's stirrup as he climbed down. 'The woman has arrived and we are to feast at sundown. You stink of horse.'

'Does she have a name?' asked her husband, tethering his horse to a post.

His wife was now fussing over Arkal, looking with disapproval at the matted mess of her hair. 'Of course she has a name!' she retorted. 'Her name is Khalun.'

'Is she pretty?' asked Arkal.

'Pretty enough,' said her mother. 'But she's not happy. I've never seen such a face!'

Then Luke saw Gomil and he, too, looked far from happy. Dressed in his best deel and wearing high boots of red leather, the chief's son was standing outside his tent staring at a new ger that had been erected outside the camp and around which stood about a dozen supercilious camels. There were garlands of flowers hanging around the tent door. Gomil's hands were behind his back. Torguk spat.

'This match is a mistake, Lug,' he said quietly. 'Karamanids feasting at our fire? I never heard of such a thing!'

They weren't to see the Karaminids until night had fallen and the tribe had gathered around a huge fire. As was usual, the men sat on one side, the women across from them. Luke, with his intermediate status, sat with the children in between. This gave him the advantage of having Arkal close to his ear to explain what was happening.

Several spits had been erected next to the fire and the sheep were being slowly turned and sprinkled with herbs and oils by women who sat back on their heels and used their free hand to swat away the insects of dusk. The smells of mutton and sage and oregano and rosemary hung in the still air and overwhelmed the familiar stench of the camp. Dogs, tied to the ropes of tents, barked and whined but the people were silent in expectation.

Then there was the sound of bells, tiny bells shaken by women's fingers, and into the light of the fire wobbled a richly harnessed camel. Behind it came a little tented cart. Leading the camel was a small boy of perhaps fourteen, who threw dark looks to left and right as he walked. He had a jewelled dagger tucked into his belt. Around the camel and cart were perhaps a dozen women of all ages.

'The bride's eldest brother,' whispered Arkal, 'and her mother, sisters and aunts. They don't look happy.'

They did not. The women had put up a kind of keening which Luke had last heard at a burial. Each of them wore a shawl and a cape that covered most of their faces and they carried bells at the end of heavily ringed fingers. Even the dogs fell quiet. 'Where is the bride?' he asked.

'In the cart,' replied Arkal. 'Gomil will draw back the curtains when she comes to him.'

Luke glanced over to where Gomil sat on a vast cushion, a shawl over his shoulders. On one side of him Etabul was sipping a cup of airag and smiling grimly between sips. The gold of the little cup caught the firelight as his hand rose and fell. On Gomil's other side was an empty cushion with what looked like lavender scattered across it.

The camel stopped outside the ring of people and sank to its knees while the women untied the garlanded harness. Then the animal rose and was led away and six women took up the shafts and began to pull the cart inside the circle and round to where Gomil sat. They set it down and the bride's brother placed a set of steps before it.

Luke saw Etabul glance over to Gomil and apply his fly whisk to his son's ribs. Gomil stood and straightened his turban and walked over to the tent. He lifted an arm and drew aside the curtain. A hush fell over the gathering and hundreds of eyes strained for the first glimpse of the Karamanid bride. But nothing happened.

There was a long, silent wait. Then a deep sigh came from inside the tent and an arm appeared, laden with gold and silver bands that met percussively. Next, a slippered foot emerged slowly to feel for the first step. This was not a bride hurrying to reacquaint herself with her betrothed.

Khalun was heard before she was seen. The chimes of a hundred tiny things of metal told that she was on the move. After the arm and ankle came the rest of her body and it was covered from head to shoulder by a glittering shawl. Her face was veiled and gave little away as to her beauty. Attached to her cape were miniature shapes hung from threads.

'She's frightened,' Arkal whispered.

Luke considered this. He saw Khalun led to the cushion and seated. She turned away from her bridegroom. 'She doesn't look very frightened,' he whispered back. 'She just looks cross.'

'No, she's frightened,' insisted his neighbour. 'Look at all the amulets.'

They were indeed many. From her headdress were suspended tiny silver plates of different sizes with writing on them. There were beads shaped like eyes and what looked like a pig's tooth. Arkal nudged him. 'See the pouch sewn into her cape?'

Luke narrowed his eyes for better focus. Something had been thrown on to the fire that made it dance higher. It was difficult to see anything for the flames.

'There is a pouch in her cape. It will have salt in it. It's there to ward off evil, like the amulets. She thinks we're evil and she's frightened.'

Luke wondered what she might feel like when she met Shulen. In fact, where was Shulen? He looked along the faces of the rows of seated women. She wasn't among them. He looked back to Gomil and his bride. Gomil was helping her remove her shawl. Beneath it was a long, sleeveless robe of the brightest red.

'Red for good fortune,' said Arkal. 'Now they will exchange shawls.'

But Luke had seen something else. The arm that had emerged from the shawl was graceful and strong, its flawless skin glowing in the firelight. Except that it wasn't flawless. On the upper arm was a scar which was jagged and savage and which had been made, quite recently, by a pointed weapon. Luke frowned.

Arkal continued, 'They'll do one more thing and then they'll eat, but not for too long. Remember the wedding is tomorrow and tomorrow night is the main feast.'

'What is the final thing they'll do?' Luke asked.

'Show us her face,' answered Arkal. 'Of course, Gomil has already seen it but we haven't. He'll remove her veil to show us his bride. Look, he's doing it now.'

Khalun's veil had disguised her anger. But then, as Gomil removed her cape and unhooked the side of her veil, her mood was there for all to see. Her face was a scowl. She was not many years older than Arkal but her features were more formed. She was dark, with long waves of hair that fell past her shoulders to her breasts. She held her head high and the eyes above her small, straight nose were defiant. She looked around with contempt at the rows of people staring at her.

Then her eyes met Luke's.

At first she looked surprised and her head tilted to one side. Then she remembered something and for the first time there was doubt in those eyes. They widened and held his for longer than was correct.

I know you.

Luke felt the colour rise in his face. He was the first to look away and when he did he saw at once that Gomil was watching him. Luke wanted to shout out: *It's not what you think.*

But he knew that it wasn't just Gomil who was staring at him. He turned his head slowly, willing it round, and as he did so, the fire leapt up, as if hit by wind, and sparks flew into the night.

Shulen.

She was standing quite far behind the seated women and he wouldn't have seen her if the fire had not risen. She was wearing white and there was a bird of some species on her arm. It was not a hawk. Then she was gone.

Arkal was speaking to him. 'Why did she stare at you like that, Lug?' she whispered.

'Who?'

'Khalun. Who else?' she hissed. 'You must have seen how she stared at you.'

Luke said nothing. He was not thinking of Khalun.

'Gomil saw it too,' continued the girl. 'He looked as if he would kill you.'

Luke looked back at Gomil and Khalun. A change seemed to have come over her and the new shawl sat on lowered shoulders. Now she had turned to her betrothed and was talking. She even smiled.

Others must have seen it too for the mood of the feast relaxed. Khalun's sisters and aunts took their cue from the bride and began to talk to their neighbours and toast their health with cups of mare's milk sweetened with honey. But Luke could neither eat nor drink. His mind had drifted back to a night on the steppe, to a chase which had ended with a single rider, a boy he'd thought, whom he'd stabbed with an arrow.

Whom he'd stabbed with an arrow in the upper arm.

Much, much later, Luke lay alone in his ger and stared up at the circle of pale moonlight that hung above him like a shield. He was wondering what he should do.

There was no noise from the camp outside, beyond the sound of animals and the occasional cry of a child. The wind was light on the steppe and its caress was a low, whispered lament. The fire had long since died and the shadows that had danced across the walls of his tent had died with it. Luke's head was cradled in his hands, alive with thought. It had been an evening of revelation.

Soon after Khalun's unveiling, the food had been served. Great hunks of mutton were hacked from the spits and placed on wooden platters with wild carrots and bread. Chins and beards soon shone with grease below smiles that broadened as the airag was passed. Arkal chattered to him of marriage and child-bearing and her readiness for both and he'd half listened and thought of what he'd learnt.

It was Khalun behind the mask.

He heard movement outside his door. A dog probably.

But why? Did they just come for our horses because theirs were sick? Or were they looking for me?

He heard the sound again. It was close to the door. If it was a dog, it was a large one. He felt for his sword and brought it beneath the skin covering him.

Why would the Karamanids attack the people they had just agreed a marriage alliance with?

But if there was an answer to that question, he'd not find it that night. Better to consider what to do now.

Etabul. I must tell Etabul.

The sound again. This time he knew that it was human. He rose silently from his pallet and tiptoed to the door, his breath suspended. He held the sword tight in his hand, the dragon head staring up at him.

Whoever it was, was standing on the other side of the door, waiting for something. Luke inched his hand along the inside until he found the catch, drawing it back silently. Then he pulled the door open suddenly and stepped backwards, his sword at the ready. Standing there was Khalun's brother and he looked terrified. Luke lowered the sword. 'What do you want?' he asked quietly.

The boy didn't answer. He was staring at the dragon head. The moon was large behind him and he looked younger than his years.

'Who sent you? Khalun?'

The boy nodded. Luke stepped away from the door and gestured for him to enter. The boy shook his head.

'Do you speak?' asked Luke.

The boy could speak. 'Come.'

'No,' said Luke.

The boy looked nervously around the camp. It was empty; everyone was asleep, many comatose from the drink. A loud snore from the adjacent ger punctured the silence. 'My sister wants you to come.'

'Why?'

The boy didn't answer the question. He glanced again at Luke's sword. 'It is safe. Bring your sword if you wish to.'

'I asked you why she wanted to see me,' said Luke.

The boy shrugged. 'I don't know.'

'Then I will not come.' Luke began to close the door of his tent. The boy put out his hand.

'Wait.' He looked around again. 'My sister . . .' he whispered, 'my sister wants to speak of who was looking for you.'

'Who was looking for me? When?'

'When she came to take your horses,' said the boy.

Luke looked at the youth. There were sparse hairs above his lip and on his chin that stood out in the moonlight. He had sallow, greasy skin and his nose was pockmarked. His voice was recently broken. 'How do I know it isn't a trap?' he asked. 'It would suit your sister to have me dead.'

'If it's a trap, then bring your sword.'

Luke was thinking hard. The only retinue of Khalun's he'd seen had been female, apart from the brother. And if she had information about who'd been looking for him that night, he needed to know it. He could always take the sword.

I need to know who's looking for me.

'I'll come,' he said.

He regretted that decision within a minute of entering Khalun's ger.

He'd expected the brother to remain. But the moment that Luke's foot had settled on the carpet, he heard the click of the door closing behind him. It left him in almost total darkness and he wondered if he was alone. He drew his sword from his belt.

'Khalun?' he asked into the blackness, turning slowly.

There was no answer beyond the faint rustle of clothing somewhere to his front. He considered escape but knew that the door was locked behind him. He peered around him and realised that there was, after all, some light in the tent. There was the faintest glow coming from a level lower than himself and, as his eyes adjusted, he saw that it came from a candle beneath a shade of horn. Beside it was a figure.

'Are you going to kill me with that sword?'

Luke didn't reply.

'I don't think I have much to fear from you. If you'd wanted to kill me, you could have done it on the steppe. Why didn't you?'

Luke lowered the weapon and looked around the tent. 'Because I needed your horse,' he replied. 'Are we alone?'

'We are alone,' answered Khalun and she moved towards the candle, lifting off the horn shade with her shawl. 'See for yourself.'

Luke looked around the tent and saw that they were indeed alone. Apart from the two of them, the tent contained a bed, a low table of carob wood and a metal vase set with yellow coins of jasper, which held a variety of dried grasses.

Khalun was now visible. She was standing on a dead leopard whose head she was stroking with her bare foot. She was dressed in the same red dress that she'd worn at the feast but now the buttons at its front were undone and the shawl on her shoulders open. Luke glanced down at the curve of her breasts and the shadow in between. He cleared his throat. 'I shouldn't be here,' he said. 'It's dangerous for both of us. Your brother said that you had something to tell me.'

Khalun laughed. She put the shade back over the candle so that it was almost dark again inside the tent. She'd used the shawl to hold the shade but now she let it slide from her shoulders to the ground. She lowered herself on to the leopard skin.

'Will you sit?' she asked.

There was something strange in her voice. The words were

too joined, almost slurred. Luke didn't answer. There was nowhere to sit but the carpet.

'Well, at least put down that sword,' she said softly. 'Can you see the table? Put your sword there. Then we can talk.'

Luke walked slowly over to the table and put down his weapon. He smelt lavender and something else. Airag. She had been drinking.

'Say what you want to say to me and then I'll leave,' he said.

'So soon?' She paused and he heard the sound of drink being swallowed. She spoke again. 'Why are you so frightened? Is it because you're alone in a dark tent with a woman promised to another man?'

Luke didn't answer.

'Gomil didn't like the way you looked at me tonight. He thinks you desire me. Do you desire me?'

Luke had had enough. He turned.

'Surely you will want to know why I attacked the camp?' she asked quickly.

Luke stopped. The girl was no more than five paces from him and he could hear her breathing.

'Well, I'll tell you anyway,' she said. 'I did it to get out of marrying Gomil. No one was meant to die.'

'But they did,' said Luke.

'Yes, they did,' she said flatly. 'That was not my fault. We were joined by others. Men I didn't know who came out of the darkness at the last moment. They didn't want the horses, they wanted something else.'

'Me?'

'Yes.'

The tent was very quiet. He could feel the dark eyes upon him. She laughed softly in the darkness. He heard the movement of clothes. He heard something tear. 'How did it feel?' she asked softly.

Luke knew what she meant. He couldn't speak.

'How did it *feel*', she said again, 'to put that arrow into my arm?'

The shape in front of him moved. The body was raised at the hip. He knew what she was doing. He stepped backwards. Towards the door. He heard the call of an owl outside, heard another answer. He'd not heard an owl in the camp before.

Luke peered into the darkness. He knew she was naked on the rug. She laughed.

'Come to me.'

He turned towards the door. He needed a weapon. He ran forward to the table and seized the sword. Then she screamed. Luke turned and saw the door thrown open and the glare of torches outside. There were the shadows of men at the entrance. And then one stepped in.

It was Gomil. Gomil with a sword in one hand and a torch in the other. Behind him was Khalun's brother.

A trap.

The torch lit up the tent. It lit the table and the vase upon it. It lit the dull eyes of the leopard and the soft curves of the woman lying naked upon it. And it flashed upon the blade in Luke's hand.

'Kill him!' screamed Khalun.

Gomil was still drunk but he moved quickly. He lunged at Luke with his sword and almost hit him. He recovered his balance and threw the torch out through the open door. The air was thick with the smell of airag. It was dark and the space within the tent was confined. Luke glanced towards the entrance and saw men still there.

'Gomil,' he said, 'I have not touched her.'

But the chief's son wasn't listening. With a roar, he kicked over the table, scattering the candle and the grasses across the carpets. He had been waiting for this moment. He sprang forward, aiming his sword at Luke's heart. Luke sidestepped, parrying the thrust with his own and pushing his assailant away. Gomil fell and his head hit the table hard.

Khalun screamed again. Gomil rose, put his palm to his temple and wiped the blood from his eyes. He shook his head.

Luke tried again. 'Gomil, I am not your enemy.'

But he *was* Gomil's enemy. For two years Luke had humiliated him by his very presence in the camp. Gomil licked blood from his lips, turned his head and spat. When he looked back, there was murder in his eyes. He lifted his sword and charged.

Luke was ready for him. He ducked beneath the first swipe and parried the second. Then, as Gomil raised his arm to deliver the third, Luke struck. It was an upward thrust aimed at the belly but at the last moment Gomil tried to turn. The blade entered the heart. Gomil was dead.

There was a sound behind him and Luke turned. Etabul was standing in the doorway, his sword drawn. He looked dishevelled. 'What have you done?'

On the floor of the ger, amidst the broken table and scattered candles, lay Gomil: an island of spent flesh in a sea of blood. Khalun was the first to speak. 'He tried to rape me.' She pointed at Luke, pulling the shawl up her body with her other hand. 'He killed Gomil.'

Etabul was staring at the body of his son, the sword slack in his hand. A slight frown contoured his brow. His eyes were blank. 'What have you done?' This time it was a whisper.

Luke was shaking his head. He couldn't speak. The girl

shrieked, 'Look at the sword. Look at the sack of airag. He made me drink it.'

For a moment Luke was in another place at another time. He was in a palace in Monemvasia standing before its archon and another girl was telling lies that would change his life. Now it was Khalun and she was shouting at Etabul. 'What are you waiting for? Why don't you kill him?'

Etabul didn't move. For a long time he looked at the girl and then at the sack of airag and the candle on the floor, and he looked at the red robe strewn across the rug which had been ripped at the front. Finally, his gaze travelled to Luke. 'You killed my son.'

Luke began to speak but Etabul raised his hand and turned to the men behind him. 'Bring him.'

Luke waited until he was through the door, a guard on either side, one carrying his sword. There was a crowd of people around the entrance, some with torches. He tried to remember which of the two horse pens was nearer.

He struck to left and right with elbow and fist, bringing both men down. He picked up his sword, lowered his head and charged in the direction of the nearest pen. People scattered as he came, falling over each other. Then he was there and over the fence and a knot of mane was in his hand and he was vaulting on to a back that was already moving. There were shouts behind him and the hiss of an arrow. He was bent over the pony's neck, his mouth as close to the ear as he could make it. Then he was jumping the fence and before him were gers and open country and escape. He dug his heels into the sides of the horse beneath him.

So it was that Luke found himself riding towards the dazzle of a rising sun, alone and with no idea where he was going.

The steppe was turning to furred gold and dew was rising in the finest of mists that hung above it like incense. The calls of carrion birds were loud above him as they began their search for what hadn't survived the night. Hills rose in the distance.

He'd ridden hard at first, assuming pursuit, but none had come. He'd stopped in the darkness again and again, turning his head to listen for the sound of hooves on the hard ground. There'd been none. By dawn he knew he wasn't being followed. But where to go now?

East. To Tamerlane. But first, some answers.

Once again he stopped his horse and turned in the saddle. He'd heard something. There was a cloud of dust in the distance. Someone was following him.

He wondered if he should ride on for the hills, to find the cover of trees. But if his pursuers meant him harm, why had they alerted him? Besides, it was at least a day's ride to the hills. Luke saw that it was just one person riding towards him. He wondered why he'd ever imagined that she wouldn't come.

Shulen.

She rode up to him, her little pony turning as she hauled on the reins. She was dressed for a long ride, with chaps strapped to her bare legs and provisions behind her on her saddle.

For a while they sat on their horses and just looked at each other. Then Luke spoke. 'Are you finally going to speak to me?'

Her face remained impassive. She looked from him to the distant hills and then up at the sun. 'Where were you thinking of going?' she asked.

Luke looked around him at the emptiness that was the steppe. A light wind blew dust into the furred gold that hovered above it. Faraway, a bird called. Further, there might be answers.

'To Yakub. I'm going to Kutahya.'

CHAPTER NINE

EDIRNE, AUTUMN 1398

The season was changing from yellow to gold and Anna was taking her ease among falling leaves in the harem garden of the palace at Edirne. It was almost two years since she'd come here and the passage of time had been made bearable by the discovery of new friends. She was with them now, watching a strange animal that had the mouth of a camel, the body of a horse and the eyelashes of a courtesan. Its forelegs were longer than its hind and its hooves were like a bullock's. Its belly was white and its body gold and covered by large white rings. But those were not its most extraordinary feature.

'The neck!' cried Angelina, leaning over the pavilion's balustrade, her hand to her mouth. 'Have you ever seen anything like it?'

Maria thought that she had. 'I saw it in a book once,' she said, coming to lean beside her. 'In Trebizond. A book of wonders. It's called a *jornufa* and it eats only leaves.'

'Or birds perhaps,' laughed Anna, joining them. 'Look at it nuzzling the cages in those trees. The poor things are terrified!'

The animal had ambled slowly to the wall of the harem garden, undisturbed by the giggling concubines who crowded as close as they dared. It had begun to pull branches from a tall tree on the other side of the wall and the caged birds were screaming their alarm.

'Where has it come from?' asked Maria.

Anna looked at the men trying to guide its progress with bamboo poles. It was early in the evening and the waning sun shimmered in the yellow folds of their pyjamas and turbans. Their black skins shone with exertion.

'The Sultan in Cairo,' she said with confidence. 'The Mamluk Sultan has sent it as a gift to Bayezid. The jornufa must come from Africa.'

There was another shriek, this time from the bathing pool where other girls had been playing with a ball. The jornufa was approaching them.

'It wants to drink!' laughed Angelina, clapping her hands together. 'Now we'll see its face!'

The animal stopped by the side of the pool, its smile reflected among the lily pads and apples. The harem girls were lying naked on the grass, helpless with laughter.

'Its horns! Look at its horns!' cried Maria, moving to get a better view. 'Like a young stag's!' She looked beyond the pool. 'Speaking of which, where are the deer?'

The deer were cowering in a group against the far wall, necks erect and ears twitching with bewilderment. Above them was the balcony of the Valide Sultan, Gülçiçek, a woman bitter with age and spite who hated Anna with every nerve in her withered being. It was said that she was sick and Anna hoped, with all her heart, that she was close to death. Already, in her absence, the heady scent of rebellion was in the harem air. Anna had not seen her for weeks: not since the old witch had had her bed dragged on to her balcony to watch the punishment meted out to two Circassian girls. They had been caught in lesbian embrace – understandable given the Sultan's indifference – and the Chief Eunuch had had them flogged.

Since then, Anna had taken charge and decided that the regime should be relaxed. Away had gone Gülçiçek's word games and in had come games in the pool, races through the gardens and the rare sound of laughter.

'He's smiling!' whispered Angelina, leaning to Anna's ear and pointing, not at the jornufa, but at the Chief Eunuch. 'He's actually smiling. I never thought I'd see that!'

Neither did Anna. But then everything was so new suddenly. Angelina and Maria, for example. Captured at the field of Nicopolis, the two girls had been brought to the harem and, such was their beauty, Gülçiçek had had them instantly locked away. Angelina was the illegitimate daughter of King Sigismund of Hungary and her sixteen-year-old looks were famous throughout Europe. Maria was older, fair and from Trebizond, a niece of the Emperor, and no one knew why she'd been at Nicopolis at all. Anna was grateful to them both. Angelina had brought laughter and an indifference to protocol. Maria had brought oils.

'What have you anointed me with, Maria?' she asked, turning to the Greek. 'I smell like a Persian whore.'

Maria smiled. 'Many things. But mainly musk from Silingui, mixed with camphor and a little rhubarb.'

'And it's the musk that smells so?'

'It is,' replied Maria. 'The Arabs will tell you that it's among the scents that the blessed will breathe in heaven, along with Persian rose, basil from Samarcand, citron from Tapurastan, violets from Isfahan, saffron from Qom, water lilies from Sharvan, aloes from India and amber from Sikhr.'

'So many!' cried Angelina. 'How will they manage their doe-eyed virgins in such a heady mix?'

'Ah,' replied Maria, lowering her voice, 'musk is used for many things. The Chinese believe it to be an aphrodisiac. So perhaps they will manage.'

Anna asked: 'Who taught you, Maria?'

'I was taught by a cousin. She was the most beautiful creature I've ever seen. And she knew about every potion there is to make, especially love potions.' She paused. 'She eloped with a Venetian.'

There was noise from the other end of the garden where a gate led through to the main part of the palace. Two eunuchs with scimitars had hauled themselves to their feet and were adjusting their turbans. The Chief Eunuch was gesturing towards the jornufa.

'This might be Suleyman,' said Anna. 'Do you want to go?'

Angelina squeezed her hand. 'I am the daughter of the King of Hungary.' She smiled. 'I am not daunted by eldest sons.'

'He might prefer you,' said Anna, looking towards the gate.

'Over you? No, he's in love.'

It was Suleyman. He strode through the gate, stopped to look at the jornufa, and then shouted something at the eunuchs. The girls around the pool had seized their clothes and were already making their way to another gate. Suleyman marched through the fruit trees with his eyes fixed on the chiosk. Then he was standing at the top of the steps, breathing deeply.

Anna studied him with calm. He was the opposite of Luke. He was tall and wiry with a dark, high-ridged face that ended in a beard of pointed precision. Luke was fair and generous in face and dimension. She'd hardly seen the Prince since he'd come to get her from Mistra. They said that he never left the siege, determined to do what no ruler of the House of Osman had yet been able to do: pluck the Red Apple from the tree of Byzantium.

'I thought you said that you would never enter these walls again,' he said, glancing at the two strangers before making the smallest of bows to Anna.

Anna rose from the bench. 'Lord, may I present my friends to you?'

'No,' said Suleyman. 'I wish to talk to you alone.'

In Kutahya, the stench of the Porsuk River reached over the walls and into every room of Yakub's home. The palace had been built by his father, another Yakub, and sat on high ground. The river, since it was the height of summer, was low and the carcasses of fish and other animals littered its steep banks. Where there wasn't death, there were chimney stacks built into the banks. Kutahya was expanding fast and its brick-kilns were working at full blast.

The smell of rotting fish and lime came in with the wind. It wafted in past the ruins of the Byzantine castle, past the domes and minarets of the city, past the pyred cremations of herbs that lined the palace walls. When it became unbearable, Yakub would leave the audience hall to receive visitors amongst the lemons and flowers of the little orchard surrounding the carp pools.

He was there now, dressed for the hunt with his high boots tided with dust and his shirt open to the waist. He was in a less-than-congenial mood. He'd spent the morning chasing boar and jackal in the hills to the north of the city and had not wanted to stop. Next to him sat a mastiff and greyhound, both silver-collared.

'You're supposed to be elsewhere,' he growled. He was

crouched by the side of the lake, throwing bread to the carp. He looked up.

Luke had changed since he'd last seen him after Nicopolis. He was thinner and his hair and beard longer. Both were bleached by the sun and his face bore the mark of the steppe: wind-blown and sun-blasted. It was as it should be, he thought. Luke looked like a gazi or, given his height, perhaps two.

Yakub picked up an arrow and began to wipe its head with a cloth. 'Poison for the boar. Did you know that your emperor John Komnenos scratched himself on one of these and died?'

Luke didn't answer.

'Or that the Emperor Basil got his belt caught in an antler and was dragged for a mile to his death?' He paused and looked up. 'We have to hope that this emperor is less careless in the hunt. You do not like his plan?'

Luke shook his head. 'It's Plethon's plan. I don't understand it.'

Yakub's hand went into his pocket and emerged with a biscuit. He broke it in two and gave a piece to each dog, patting both heads. 'What's there to understand? You learn how to ride and fight like a Mongol, then bring Tamerlane to fight Bayezid. That's the plan. That's all there ever was.'

'Except that it isn't working. Gomil wouldn't let me ride and now I've killed him.'

Yakub nodded slowly. 'I'd heard. But perhaps it's for the good. Tamerlane is finally on the move and it's time for you to go east. If the world thinks you dead, you'll get there quicker.'

'But it wasn't me that died.'

'Yes it was. You were executed for killing Gomil. If there's no Luke, there's no one to pursue. We'll spread the news and you can go east without further delay.'

Suddenly Luke was angry. He'd spent two years in this man's beylik and nearly died. He said: 'I am not going anywhere until I've seen Anna.'

Yakub stopped wiping the arrow. Then he began again, more slowly. His voice was low. 'Tamerlane is on the move. He wants to go to China. He must be persuaded otherwise.'

Luke said: 'By me? Why not you, Yakub?' There was silence while both men stared at each other. Luke continued. 'You speak for the gazi tribes, I don't.'

Yakub shook his head. 'Tamerlane will not be persuaded by reason, only by someone he trusts.'

'And why will he trust me?'

Yakub shrugged. 'Because you are a warrior prince with a talent for making horses do what you want. It has already been seen at the camp.'

'But I can't speak for the gazi tribes who Tamerlane will need to defeat Bayezid. Only you can do that. Will you come with me?'

'I will come with you as far as Tabriz. Bayezid wants me to go and talk to Qara Yusuf, chief of the Qara Qoyunlu, who rules from there. He wants to strengthen his borders with an alliance. I can't go further without Bayezid suspecting.'

'But I can because I'm dead.' Luke paused. He looked down at his hands. 'Yakub, I want to do what is best for my empire. But what about Constantinople? Can't I be of help there?'

'Constantinople is not your concern.'

Luke shook his head. 'The city needs good engineers with good weapons and the money to make them. I have all three.'

Yakub scratched his chin. There was thick stubble beneath the curve of his moustache and the sound reached across the silence. The sun dappled the orchard grass around them and felt warm on his neck.

'You can best serve your empire by going to Tamerlane. Now tell me what you need to go without further delay.'

Luke thought for a while. Then he said: 'I want to see Anna, here, before I go. And I want my Varangian friends to join me for the journey.'

Yakub raised an eyebrow. 'You're making conditions?'

'Yes I am.'

Yakub glowered at him. Then he shrugged. 'The girl who brought you here, Shulen. She will travel east with you. She will help you.'

Luke remembered a time in a tent not long ago. He'd thought her a creature of Omar. Was she obeying Yakub instead? They'd hardly spoken on the fast ride to Kutahya.

'She has already tried to help me. I don't want that kind of help.'

Yakub's face darkened. 'She will go east with you. It is *my* condition.'

'For seeing Anna?'

'For seeing Anna.'

At that moment, Anna and Suleyman were watching the backs of Angelina and Maria as they walked away from the chiosk. 'Do you know who they are?' Anna asked, sitting again.

'Do I care?' asked the Prince.

'Both are royal. They deserved some manners.'

Suleyman shrugged. 'The King of Hungary is about to be a vassal and Trebizond will fall when we sneeze in its direction. I will expend manners where they are useful.'

The Prince walked over to the balcony and looked out. By

now the jornufa had been led to the gate and there appeared to be debate as to how to get it to the other side. The deer were gingerly reoccupying the garden and one had even approached the bathing pool and was nibbling at an apple. The sun was low in the sky and little fingers of shadow were reaching towards Mecca. Suleyman joined his hands before him. He seemed irritated.

'Is it your grandmother?' Anna asked. 'They say she's very ill.'

'Which should please you,' said the Prince, addressing the garden.

Anna glanced up. 'She wishes me harm. And the harem is a better place without her.'

The Prince turned. 'Are you practising to be Valide?' he asked unpleasantly. 'Soon the birds will be free too.'

Anna looked away. She could hear the sound of deer nearby cropping grass. The evening was very still. Suleyman turned his back on the garden and folded his arms. He was wearing a tunic of dark blue damask embroidered with gold peacocks' fans. The collar was lifted so that his long hair was splayed across his shoulders like a fan.

'Luke Magoris is dead,' he said.

Anna felt the sudden beat of a drum close to her heart. Four words. She blinked once. Twice. She looked away. The jornufa was being pushed through the gate now, its neck roped low by a minder. Soon they would be alone. She couldn't hear anything except for a ringing in her ears.

A lie. It's a lie.

'He tried to rape the bride of the chief's son, then killed him.' Suleyman was watching her closely. 'He was killed trying to escape. Yakub has just delivered the news.'

Relief. *Rape. Luke? No.*

Anna forced herself to look at Suleyman. It was a lie and it was clumsy. No. She felt herself recovering, her mind re-engaging. The lie had been told by Yakub so it was important. Somehow.

A lie for a purpose. I must lie too.

'It was following a banquet. He must have been drunk.' Suleyman shrugged. 'Anyway, he's dead. You can get the annulment of your marriage to Damian Mamonas. There is nothing to stop it now.'

Anna nodded slowly. The jornufa had left the garden and they were alone with caged birds in faraway trees and a smell of jasmine. 'The Patriarch will need to be persuaded that my marriage to Damian was not consummated.' Suleyman was watching her from beneath those hooded eyelids. She continued: 'He will need to see me in person. I will have to enter Constantinople.'

Suleyman walked over and sat beside her on the bench. He took her hand and it was a dead thing without bone. He looked down at it. He'd arrived expecting resistance and there'd been none. She seemed more docile than he'd ever seen her. 'I had thought as much. Yakub has offered to take you into the city as guard.' He paused. 'We will be married there,' he said, his voice softer. 'We'll be married in Constantinople once it falls. Which it will, soon.'

Anna turned to look at him and saw the uncertainty spread like a map across his features, invading every line and contour of his face. She felt a sudden onrush of pity. She lifted her hand and brought her fingertips to his cheek, tracing the high ridge of bone that divided it. He looked up and grasped her hand and kissed it again and again until she pulled it away. Then he took her face between his palms and forced it up and his lips came down to hers and what had begun in Anna as pity was quickly turning to something else. She pulled away.

'No,' she said, wiping her lips. 'No, not now. Not yet.'

Suleyman was breathing hard, his nostrils moving. He looked away. 'Of course,' he said quietly. 'You are in mourning.'

Anna felt her heart beating loud enough to be heard. She was not in mourning because Luke was not dead. She was as sure of it as she was that there was a message in the news. They were silent for a while, both looking ahead, no part of them touching the other. Then Anna said: 'The Varangians. Their friend is dead and I have agreed to the annulment. They must be released from their oath to Bayezid and allowed to go home.'

Suleyman frowned. There had always been conditions. Was this all part of it, part of why he loved this woman with fire for hair and jewels for eyes?

'Very well.'

Watching the scene from the balcony of a bedroom that wasn't hers was the Valide Sultan Gülçiçek. She was propped up on a bed and sitting on it with her was her son, the Sultan Bayezid. The bed was pulled back so that it couldn't be seen from below. A sunshade was above them, its shadow not deep enough for her liking. But it was only Bayezid, her first-born, who was close enough to see the mark of death upon her. And smell her smell.

They had enjoyed the jornufa but were finding what had followed more interesting. They couldn't hear anything of what was being said but Suleyman's gestures required little explanation.

‘My grandson is in love,’ murmured Gülçiçek. Beside her was a cup of sherbet with a straw. She extended a brittle arm to it. Bayezid leant over to the cup and lifted it. He sucked up some of the sherbet before passing it to her.

‘I must be one of the few people safe from your poison, Mother,’ he said, wiping his lips with the side of her sheet.

Gülçiçek coughed and grimaced. The pain in her stomach was worse. She ignored the comment and closed her eyes. ‘He is in love and he is angry. Why is he angry, Bayezid?’

Her voice was little above a whisper and held a rattle somewhere deep within it. Speaking more than a sentence was tiring. Bayezid sighed and looked around for wine. There was none. The Sultan stood. ‘He is angry because he cannot get his way. It was always the same.’

‘Constantinople?’

The Sultan nodded. ‘I won’t storm it without a breach in the walls. I’m waiting for cannon to do it. From Venice.’

Gülçiçek would have spat if she’d been able. Venice was *Shatan*.

‘And he’s angry because I listen to Mehmed more than him these days.’ Bayezid paused. ‘He’s afraid.’

‘And he’s right to be,’ whispered the Valide Sultan. ‘You sent your own brother to the bowstring when you ascended the throne. Why not kill a son?’

Bayezid considered this. Was he strong enough to kill Suleyman? The truth was that he too was afraid. Suleyman had support at the court, the Grand Vizier for one. He turned. ‘He wants to kill me, Mother.’

Gülçiçek nodded, her eyes still closed. ‘I know.’

Gülçiçek knew most things about her son and those around him. Her tentacles were long and many, and one had been smacked away by this young Byzantine girl with whom her grandson was in love. She hated Anna for the love bestowed on her by her grandson. She hated her for daring not to reciprocate it. She hated her for usurping her in the harem and for her own powerlessness to do anything about it. Her hatred for Anna was infinite.

But there was another Greek girl on whom Suleyman was slaking his lust, a dark girl much more to her liking. She sensed that her grandson was more afraid than Bayezid knew and that this girl was becoming more and more important to him, a refuge as much as a lover. She would prefer to see *her* marry Suleyman.

But how to bring it about?

They were both silent for a while, both listening to their own breathing, both knowing where this conversation was meant to lead. Finally Gülçiçek said, 'I won't do it. He is my grandson.'

'It's either him or me.'

Gülçiçek shook her head slowly against the pillows. 'No, there is another way. The girl.'

'What girl?'

'The red-haired one he's in love with. The one down there.'

'What good would it do to kill her?'

Gülçiçek took in air. Talking was hard. She signalled to Bayezid to help her sit higher on the pillows.

'It would either send him mad,' she continued, the message coming in rasps, 'in which case you would have reason to kill him, or it would make him see sense, in which case you wouldn't have to. She is a large part of the reason that he's so obsessed with taking Constantinople.'

Bayezid considered this. 'How would you do it?'

'I would do business with Shatan,' she replied. 'I would send someone to Venice.' She yawned. The opiates were beginning to have their effect.

'Whom would you send?'

But she was asleep.

At the other end of the palace, in a dormitory adjacent to the Throne Room, three Varangian Guards were taking their ease.

Matthew, Nikolas and Arcadius were Luke's closest friends, raised with him in Monemvasia and the sons of Varangians, as he was. They'd been with him at Nicopolis and had managed to escape as he had. Now they were Varangian Guards in the service of Bayezid: tall, fair-haired adornments to the Sultan's throne. Hostages in all but name.

In the two years that they'd passed in Edirne, they'd seen emirs and sheikhs, beys and pashas bend the knee to find some favour from this man who won his battles. And they'd seen Princes from the Kingdoms of Christendom arrive to find out if Yildirim had really meant it when he'd said that he'd water his horses at St Peter's in Rome.

The three had just come in from displaying their skill with the axe to a delegation from Dulkadir. They were still dressed in their gold, scaled armour and blue *chlamys* cloaks and their *distralia* were leaning against a wall, each blade polished to a blinding sheen. They were lying on beds, too tired to speak.

Which was how Anna found them.

To begin with they didn't see her because their eyes were closed. She paused in the doorway to study each of them: Matthew, as fair as Luke and almost his build; Nikolas with his pointed good looks and eyes, even when shut, arced with laughter; Arcadius bigger than all of them. She thought they looked much older than when she'd last seen them.

'I've found your treasure,' she said.

Six eyes opened. 'Anna!'

Then they were on their feet and smiling and inviting her to sit on the remaining couch. They offered her wine, which she took. They'd not seen her during their time in Edirne.

'Yes,' she said, 'I found it with Plethon. It's extraordinary.'

'And you can't tell us what it is.' This was Matthew.

Anna smiled. 'No, I can't tell you. But it's not gold. Something better. Something that might, perhaps, still save our empire. And I've brought your freedom.'

'Our freedom?' Matthew had come to sit beside her. 'We're free to leave?'

Anna nodded. 'Free to leave. Free to go and join Luke. He needs you.' She paused. 'And you must take Eskalon.'

Eskalon. The horse that Luke had made his own. It was stabled at the palace and had been Suleyman's gift to Anna. Matthew had cared for it, finding in those deep brown eyes some memory of his closest friend. He missed Luke with an intensity that surprised him.

'Where do we go?' he asked

'First to Constantinople. Yakub is to take me in to see the Patriarch. I'm to get an annulment. I think Yakub will tell you where to go next.'

Matthew frowned. 'An annulment to marry Suleyman. Was this the price of our freedom, Anna?'

Anna didn't reply. She looked down at her hands, remembering a kiss that she hadn't hated. Suleyman's taste was still on her lips. She turned to Nikolas, who was sitting on the adjacent bed. 'They will tell you that Luke is dead,' she said. 'Suleyman believes he was killed after committing rape. Does that sound like Luke?'

Matthew had taken her arm. 'If he's not dead, then why must you marry Suleyman? Why get the annulment?'

When she turned back, there were tears in her eyes. 'Because it's the plan,' she said. 'If Luke is following it, then so must we. We are not free.'

Matthew looked hard at her. There was something new and unrecognisable in her eyes. He thought suddenly of a night of wind and rain when he'd stood beside Luke on a jetty and faced the soldiers of the Mamonas family, Damian sitting on a rock, laughing. He remembered her dragged back along the jetty while Luke sailed out into a storm. 'How do you know that Luke is still alive? He may not have raped, but that doesn't mean that he's alive.'

'He is,' she said. 'I have been to Eskalon and looked into his eyes. Luke is alive.'

CHAPTER TEN

MONEMVASIA, AUTUMN 1398

It was evening and Pavlos Mamonas was standing on the battlements of the citadel high on the Goulas of Monemvasia looking out across the bay. The first darts of rain had flown in on a rising wind and he couldn't see much beyond the vague outline of hills on the mainland. Beyond them lay vineyards, mile upon mile of red earth and vine that was now heavy with Malvasia grape. His grape. Could it be harvested in this weather?

The truth was that he didn't much mind. The wine was, by now, only a small part of the Mamonas fortune. It was the Mamonas Bank on the Rialto that made the greatest profits, and it was the earnings from supplying Venetian cannon and ships to the Turks that had furnished the capital to establish it. He smiled.

But that's not the biggest prize.

The biggest prize of all was alum. Only two mines provided the vital fixative for the dyeing industry of Florence and the Low Countries and both were in Ottoman hands. What Pavlos Mamonas really wanted was the monopoly in alum. And the man who would give it to him was Bayezid.

He closed his eyes against the rain and moved along the battlements, opening them again when he faced the bridge that joined the island to the mainland. Below were the wharves and jetties and a hundred ships at anchor that bobbed in the sea like apples. Here the drop from the balcony was sheer and he thought of the sea pounding the rocks below, trying to claw this stubborn rock back into its depths. He heard the screech of a cat and, somewhere beyond, a church bell sounding the hour, the noise rising and falling with the wind. He breathed in the smell of salt and decay and turned to look over the Goulas plateau. Beneath the citadel stood the new barracks of the janissaries next to their little mosque. Birds blew like paper around its minaret, white as snow against the bruised sky. The Turks had brought the Mamonas family back to their city and had stayed to guard them from its hostile citizens. He looked at the two big city cisterns next to it. How clever, he thought, for the Turks to control the city's water supply.

Water. Mamonas. You control both.

He frowned. These days, Pavlos Mamonas did not much like to be in Monemvasia. The citizens hated him for bringing the Turks and he'd left Damian to run the family business there, an easy enough task since it could run itself. He'd come today to meet with his son and tell him some news. But Damian wasn't there and the palace servants had looked at their feet when asked where he might be found. But Pavlos knew: in a tavern or brothel. And this was his heir.

Now it was evening and he was getting impatient. He was tired and he wanted to eat. Most of all, he wanted to get this encounter over. Where was Damian?

There was a noise from behind and he turned. Damian was leaning against the battlements, his shirt unbuttoned and his long black hair covering half his face. Pavlos could just make out the scar that ran across his cheek below an eye that was trying to focus on him. It was the scar from the accident with the horse.

The accident that started all this.

'You're drunk.'

Damian shrugged. He pushed himself up from the wall and began to button up his shirt. He had difficulty with the buttons. He gave up and pushed his hair from his face. 'I thought you didn't like this place.'

Pavlos Mamonas's frown deepened. The truth was that he loved this place. Monemvasia was where he'd been born, its labyrinth of streets where he'd grown up. He loved this little city on the edge of the sea: its endless rhythm of tide and trade; its smells and echoes; its many, many cats. He thought suddenly of Damian as a boy, unscarred and without limp, high on his shoulders, fistfuls of hair in his hands, watching the Mamonas ships come in.

Before the accident.

Six years. It was six years ago that the Varangian's son had pushed Damian in front of the thrashing hooves of a horse. They'd told him that Luke Magoris had a gift with horses. He had, but he'd used it to save himself. Now Magoris was dead, his cowardly, raping evil expunged from the earth. At least that was something. He looked out into the gathering night and thought of what to say.

Damian spoke again, the words sliding together. 'Have you come to watch the harvest, Father? Are you worried that I might miss a grape?'

Pavlos remained silent. The rain was coming in harder and he could feel its chill through the cloak. He heard Damian move, stumble, curse. Was it the leg? Then his son was beside him, looking out to where he looked. Pavlos could smell the wine on his breath.

Damian asked: 'Why are you here?'

Pavlos closed his eyes. It was finally to be done. He hated it with every nerve in his being but it had to be done. Finally. Now.

'I have come to a decision. You will not inherit,' he said quietly. 'The Mamonas bank, estates, studs . . . everything we own will go to your sister when I am gone.'

Damian didn't move. He continued to stare into the night, the wind lifting his hair. Pavlos heard him release a long, slow breath as if something deep inside was escaping. He glanced across. Was it rain or tears that ran down his son's cheeks? He looked back at the dark.

'You will be provided for. There will be some part of the business you can run. There will be no shame.'

He heard movement beside him and saw that Damian was slowly shaking his head. 'No shame.' It was a whisper.

Pavlos Mamonas straightened. He'd said it and it was right. His son was a whoring, hopeless drunk. He couldn't run his own life, let alone others'. He'd had his chance at marriage and he'd failed in that. He'd had his chance abroad. He was beyond redemption. It was right.

So why do I feel it isn't?

He knew the answer: Zoe and the deal they'd made for Chios. Was he sacrificing his son's future for a business transaction? No. He could smell the wine, hear the laboured breaths. It was right. He realised that Damian was watching him.

'Have you changed your will?'

'Not yet. I wanted to talk to you first. It will be done tomorrow. You will witness it.'

Damian had looked away and was shaking his head again.

Pavlos opened his mouth to speak but no words came out. Damian's hand was at his throat. In his other hand was a dagger. Damian hissed: 'No shame. Is that what you said, Father? No shame?'

Pavlos was pressed against the battlements, his back stabbed by stone. His son was strong and not as drunk as he'd thought. 'Damian . . .' he whispered.

'What do you know about shame, Father? When have *you* had to limp your way across the Piazza San Marco with Venetians sniggering into their sleeves? When have *you* had to suffer the pity of whores? When have you felt shame, Father?'

Pavlos was being pushed towards the open crenellation, beneath which was a drop of two hundred feet. Damian's hand was tight around his neck and he could feel the point of the dagger in his side. He looked up into the rain. Damian's face was close to his and his wine-breath hot on his chin. He was nearing the opening, the point when there'd be nothing between him and the rocks.

'Damian . . . listen.'

But Damian was listening only to the ringing fury in his ears. For six years, this man whom he'd loved beyond reason had looked at him with disappointment, then contempt. For six years he'd felt the growing tide of failure wash over him, drown him. Yes, slowly, inexorably drown him. Now this.

He said: 'You've not made the will, Father.' His fingers dug into his father's throat. 'So if you die, there'll be no will.' The dagger moved upwards, towards the heart. 'There'll be no *shame.*'

Then Pavlos felt emptiness behind his right shoulder. Air. Below were rocks and sea. Far, far below.

'There will be no *shame*, Father.' Damian was drawing back for a final push or stab, his eyes half curtained by hair, his teeth set.

The wall was now only supporting half of Pavlos's back. He could feel himself losing balance, the rain against the small of his back. He was thinking hard.

He'll push, not stab. He'll not want the wound.

Pavlos knew what he must do. And he knew he had to do it now, before it was too late. But it must be finely judged. Too much and his son would fall. He shifted his foot and kicked at where he knew his son's lameness lay. With a howl, Damian lurched over, his hand seeking a wall where there was none. Pavlos turned to catch him before he fell but his hand caught in his cloak.

'Damian!'

His son was suspended above the crenellation, clawing the air. Throwing aside the cloak, Pavlos reached out to take his hand. But the hand he held for an instant was slick with rain. It slipped out of his and the body beyond it fell.

Damian's scream followed him on to the rocks below.

In Venice, Zoe stopped suddenly. She'd heard a scream. She looked around her. The street was empty. The scream had been far away. Far, far away. She frowned, then shrugged. There were screams everywhere. Venice was in carnival. Venice was always in carnival.

Carnevale, farewell to meat. Officially, it was the last chance for scandal to run amok before Lent. But, these days, it took any excuse and tonight the city was full of masks.

Zoe, disguised behind her own *bauta*, had escaped the throng watching the fireworks launched from the Rialto Bridge. She hadn't been among Tommasi Giacomo's party in the Mamonas *barche* since she was in Venice incognito. She had, however, seen the size of the jewel nestled between his wife's breasts. She'd like to review the factor's books when she returned in a more official capacity.

As the Mamonas heir.

She wondered, fleetingly, how her twin brother would receive the news.

She was making her way through back streets towards the Jewish Quarter and there was little traffic abroad, the Jews finding themselves, more often than not, the target of Christian revelry at Carnival time. She passed a couple engaged in masked copulation in an alcove, the woman's skirts lifted and her hands clutching Moors' heads on the doors against which her bottom slapped. Otherwise she saw nothing but beasts. Carrying her torch high, she saw animals emerge suddenly from the dark. Lions, gorgons, gryphons and hippogryphs came at her from walls and doorways. All around her was the drip, drip, drip of water, the melancholy music of this city of 130 islands and that many churches, this place of secrets, whispers and shadows.

A face loomed out on her right, an old woman with a cup, her grin uneven and dripping water, her eyes sightless.

Gülçiçek.

Zoe would not forget that meeting as long as she lived. No ocean of potions could save the terrible ravages of that face, no mountain of mastic could sweeten the breath of the awful creature that had sat propped up in her bed and talked of terrible things.

Zoe had sat across from her, forcing herself to study the abnormal as if it were normal, forcing herself not to run, retching, from the room. The Valide Sultan had told her what she wanted; what they both wanted: Anna dead. She'd told her of her fondness for her grandson Suleyman and of her determination that he succeed his father to the throne. She'd told her of her understanding that he might want a Greek wife. After all, she herself was Greek.

But not Anna.

She'd said it was her wish that someone more suitable should marry Suleyman and bear his Greek heirs. Someone who would have her confidence . . . and that of Bayezid.

Zoe had felt giddy as she considered what she was hearing. She could have everything. The hand of the greatest ruler on earth as well as the Mamonas fortune. And it would happen. It would happen because Anna would die slowly, giving her time still to bring back Luke to witness it. And, with Luke, she'd get the treasure too. She hadn't been deceived any more than Anna by the news of his death and there was someone she knew in Venice who would bring him back for her: di Vetriano's younger brother. She'd already made enquiries and knew that there was enough hatred there to suit her purpose.

But the poisoning would have to be done so carefully, the perfect poison found. That's why she was in Venice.

For many years, Bayezid's mother had tried to forestall the process of ageing by application of the *teriaca* compound, a mix of powdered viper, crushed stag's testicles, unicorn horn and forty other ingredients that was made only in Venice. The *teriacanto* she was visiting was not only the best but also one that made poison as well. Behind a panel in his pharmacy lay his *sala dei veleni,* the room where he put the powdered viper to other uses beyond teriaca. It was here that he drowned a hundred living scorpions in a vat of olive oil to make his *olio di scorpioni,* where he milked the fangs of serpents to make poison. He was a master of his art and the rulers of the western world, both temporal and spiritual, beat a path to his door. Usually by proxy.

Now Zoe's torch shone upon a window of leaded glass through which light could be seen. She knew she was in the right place because the air smelt of sulphur and the door had a viper's head to knock by. She pulled her hood around her mask and lifted her torch to the viper. But before she could knock, the door opened.

The Jew was bent so low that she didn't see his face as she entered. When he rose again, she nearly cried out for there was hardly a line on that skin. Closing the door, the man led her through the pharmacy and into his sala dei veleni, where a fire burned in the grate and the shelves on the walls were lined with glass and ceramic jars, each labelled. Beneath the shelves were benches and in front of them a strange confusion of vessels and tubes and receptacles in which coloured liquids were in motion. On a table sat a mortar, pestle and large set of scales, its pillar shaped as a serpent. Beside the scales was a small bottle, unlabelled, which contained a clear liquid, and beside it was a single sheet of parchment. Beneath the table were latticed containers full of snakes that made no noise but glistened as they moved. There was no light in the room except that bestowed by fire.

'Sit, please,' said the Jew, indicating a chair before the fire. 'Forgive the darkness. I am engaged in the *sublimation* process by which coarse elements become noble. Light disturbs it.'

The man spoke in a whisper and Zoe felt it unlikely that his voice was ever raised above it. Was it the result of a life spent with snakes? She took a deep breath and glanced up at the ceiling. Low beams, blackened by fire, bore down on the room. She very much wanted to be outside again. She looked at him. 'You received the message?'

'That your patron wanted something . . . unusual? Yes, madonna. It was passed to me.'

Zoe waited while the man sat down opposite her. Lit by the fire, his unlined face was almost a child's. 'She will pay well.'

The man smiled, a horrid motion. It occurred to Zoe that he was already half-snake.

'It is not the money, madonna,' he whispered. 'What I do is an art that has taken eighty years to perfect.'

Eighty? Zoe looked at the unlined face and felt sick. She held her hands tight to her lap.

'But the commission is not without its fascination,' he continued. 'To create something that works so slowly, so *implacably*, that it is untraceable? Now that is a challenge.'

'Can it be done?'

The man smiled again and raised his head. Zoe saw with horror that his lips were wet. 'Everything can be done, madonna,' he said. 'I have something prepared. It has the viper for its base but I've added the juice of many other reptiles, most from an island in the Greek seas. The compound has an ingredient that releases the poison very slowly. It is flavourless and without smell. And it dries in an instant.'

'Dries?'

The Jew rose from his chair and went over to the table. He picked up the little bottle, removed the stopper and poured a small part of its contents on to the parchment. He brought the parchment over to Zoe.

'Invisible.'

He showed it to Zoe, then lifted it to his nose, his nostrils dilating. He closed his eyes.

'Odourless, and . . .' A long tongue darted from his moistened lips. '. . . tasteless.'

Zoe recoiled.

The Jew smiled. 'It is as I said: it works slowly. The amount I have ingested will do me no harm. But over weeks, every day . . .' He put the bottle and parchment down on the table and sat again. 'Does the victim read?'

Zoe was startled. The question seemed irrelevant.

The Jew continued: 'Books. Does she read books?' He paused. 'I assumed her to be educated.'

Zoe nodded. 'Yes, she reads. Whatever she can.'

'And a favourite book?'

Zoe considered this. Of course. There was the book she'd given to her: the book about the Emperor Alexios. 'Yes. There is a book.'

'Good. Then you will coat the top corner of each page with this liquid. She will lick her fingers to turn the pages.'

Zoe looked at the tiny bottle. It looked like water and yet it would kill. Slowly, steadily it would kill. Anna would read, sicken, take to her bed and read again.

It was perfect.

CHAPTER ELEVEN

ANATOLIA, AUTUMN 1398

Anna set off for Constantinople a week after agreeing with Suleyman to go in and get the annulment, riding through the Ottoman lines with Yakub and a gazi guard. Yakub had come to the siege from Kutahya to discuss with Bayezid and his sons how best to secure the eastern borders against Tamerlane. He'd offered to take Anna into the city and, while there, to learn what he could about any Karamanid alliance with Byzantium.

The Turks had been busy since their return from Nicopolis and two siege lines ran from the hill of Kosmidion down to the Propontis. New trenches had been dug, wicker palisades erected and a mineshaft built for a tunnel that was inexorably worming its way to the city walls. They saw cradles prepared for the cannon, swing doors to their front and buffers behind for the recoil. Balls of iron were stacked next to the cradles and the ground around cleared against fire. As they rode, Yakub explained why it had been necessary to pretend that Luke had died.

'It would have broken the Karamanid alliance. And if Suleyman thinks him dead, no one will be looking for him.'

Anna shook her head. 'Zoe won't have believed it,' she said. 'She knows Luke better than that.'

They rode under the Golden Gate at sundown, its towers throwing long shadows to the east. This had once been the meeting place of nations and the gate through which trumpet-borne armies had marched to do the Emperor's bidding. Now, grass grew between broken stones and its giant doors, scorched by fire, opened on to a landscape of fields.

Anna was shocked. 'Where are all the people?' she asked, shielding her eyes.

Yakub shrugged. He hadn't been inside the city before. 'They say that Constantinople is a shadow of what it was,' he said. 'Those who remain live in the centre. But at least they can feed themselves.'

They rode on through field upon furrowed field, the occasional church tower a reminder of this city's stubborn religion. Anna saw it all and thought of Mistra where the streets jostled with the traffic of human interchange. She thought of the noise that assaulted the Laskaris house from dawn to dusk: the sound of argument and laughter and trade and cats that got in the way. Here there was silence broken only by the call of birds.

They arrived at the inner wall where Yakub's gazis were obliged to wait until Anna had finished her business with the Patriarch. Yakub's loyalties were known to Manuel, Plethon and a few others in the Byzantine court. But while in Constantinople, his men would be treated as the enemy.

From there, Anna and Yakub were taken straight to the Blachernae Palace, a city in miniature of halls and towers that rose in tiered landcape to look out over the calm waters of the Golden Horn. There were gardens between, some of which held orchards, others turned over to the plough. They walked down marbled corridors until they arrived at the throne room.

Inside were the Emperor Manuel, Empress Helena Dragaš and Plethon, seated around a table with a map pinned down by goblets of wine. Two gigantic jewels rested on its surface.

'Anna!' Plethon rose and came forward to take her in his arms, a kiss for each cheek. Manuel did the same while the Empress rose to greet Yakub, then returned to the map. She was a woman of compact middle age whose beauty had settled with ease upon the changes wrought by time. She had known Anna from birth.

Now she turned from the map to Anna and said: 'The jewels are placed on Samarcand and Constantinople. Which do you think is false?'

Anna smiled. 'The one on Samarcand, highness.'

The Empress nodded. 'Of course. The city is new and of no substance, like the jewel. The real one is in pawn at Venice.'

'Where we should place a turd,' said Plethon.

'Plethon!' The Emperor was half smiling as he turned back to Anna. 'We were discussing Tamerlane's next move, which seems certain to be China. Oh, and Plethon's plan for Mistra: a kingdom built on Spartan lines with elders at the top of Mount Taygetos. Ridiculous.'

'He would have us all wearing togas,' said Helena to Anna. 'Did you know that he doesn't believe in God?'

Anna tried to look shocked. The Emperor spoke again. 'Which I suppose makes his plan for unifying the two Churches easier to attempt. He has no conscience.' He turned to the philosopher. 'But the people of Constantinople do.' He moved to a chair and sat. 'Anyway, we're not here to discuss that. Yakub, what is the plan?'

Yakub explained that Anna had four days' grace to get her annulment. It had been put about that the Patriarch was busy in retreat and she'd need the time. Then he told Plethon of Luke's demand.

'Anna ride to Kutahya?' Plethon spread his hands, his voice enormous. 'But she'll need wings to be back in four days.'

Anna, still dizzy at the news, said: 'How do I get there?'

'You leave disguised as one of my gazis. You get through the Turkish lines. Then you ride to Kutahya with the Varangians. They've been told where to meet you.' Yakub turned to the Emperor. 'Did you know the Turks are tunnelling, highness?'

Manuel nodded. 'We need a good engineer.'

'Which Luke says he can provide,' said Yakub. 'One who'll bring you Greek fire too. He's called Benedo Barbi and he lives on Chios.'

Plethon was humming softly, pretending to look at the map. Then he turned to Anna, taking something from the folds of his toga.

'I want you to give this to him,' he said.

Anna was far ahead of the Varangians, but then she was riding Eskalon. It was over twenty hours since she'd left Constantinople, dressed and bearded as a gazi, to meet the three of them at the agreed place. Since then, they'd stopped twice to change horses. Or the Varangians had.

At first, they'd sped towards Bursa through forests thick with pine and chestnut whose smell flavoured the air. At night, tree-eyes stared out from either side and wolves' howling lifted the horses' ears. They travelled a wide stone road that had seen the armies of Xerxes, Alexander, Pompey and a hundred others tramp its surface. It was worn and smooth with age and had milestones at its edge.

As Bursa approached, the country opened and a watery sun

shone down on fields shorn like sheep, stubble steaming. It was a rich land, well tended by the sipahi and *akritoi* farmers who lived side by side: Turkish and Greek frontiersmen who preferred to forget old allegiances to gather in the harvest.

Matthew said aloud what they'd all been thinking. He was riding by Anna's side. 'Will Tamerlane be any better?'

The two of them had been talking, snatching conversation above the pounding of the hooves. Matthew had told her of what they'd seen at Edirne, of the power struggle that gripped the palace: Suleyman wanting to go west, his brother Mehmed wanting to turn east before it was too late. He'd told her of Bayezid and the toothache that had once governed the Sultan's mood but had disappeared with Dimitri's mastic. He told her how they'd missed Luke. Arcadius had fallen ill, first with a cold and then with fever. Both Matthew and Nikolas had been worried for their friend until the news of joining Luke had seemed to cure him. Finally they'd talked of Tamerlane.

Now Anna was riding out of the hills north of Kutahya towards Luke. She'd be there within the hour. It was very dark and the world was full of sound and smell: the panting of exhausted horses, the smell of night dew and horse sweat. She was far ahead of the Varangians, which was as well: she was too nervous to speak. She thought of a recent kiss from a man she was obliged to marry soon. She thought of another in a cave in Monemvasia that had led to other, wonderful things.

What would he say to her? Had he summoned her to tell her that he'd changed his mind, that he'd come back with her? But according to Yakub, he was just changing the plan and seeing her was part of it. She reached down to check that the box was still safe in the pouch around her waist.

As she approached the city gates, she slowed to let the

Varangians ride beside her. There were men on horses with torches, little pools of light lighting their faces. Eskalon neighed and tossed his head. He was there.

Luke.

He was seated on a horse that looked too small for him so that his legs hung well below its belly. His hair was longer than she'd remembered it and his face more gaunt. He was dressed in gazi skins and had his dragon sword tucked into a wide belt. He held his torch high.

The Varangians slowed their horses as they saw him too, leaving Anna to go on alone. Luke passed his torch to another and trotted forward. When their horses were side by side, Luke looked up at Anna, putting out his hand to touch her face. His fingers met her cheek.

He said: 'They told me you'd be bearded.'

'I shaved for you.'

There was a snort and Anna's horse raised its head with a suddenness that made the other start. Luke leant forward to pat the big head that was turned to him.

'Eskalon!' Luke stared into eyes that were oracles.

'I saw you in them,' Anna murmured, rubbing her nose. She'd taken the hand that wasn't stroking Eskalon's neck. 'You were there when they told me you were dead. Is it only me that sees things in them?'

Luke smiled. 'I see different people. Sometimes Plethon.'

'Whom you seem to be defying. Leave the horse and kiss me.'

And he did. The kiss went on for a long time until interrupted by a cough. Matthew had come forward on foot, leading his horse by the rein. He said: 'We only have two hours.'

Luke leapt down from the saddle. 'Matthew!' He threw his arms around his friend and hugged him hard. He whispered into his hair: 'I can't do it without you. You'll come with me?'

Matthew nodded. 'We all will. It's why we're here.'

Then there were others in the embrace. Arcadius and Nikolas had dismounted and come to join them and they were all boys again, four heads together, arms intertwined, the world within warmer than the world without. Anna watched them and heard the laughter and felt the deep, deep friendship that might just make a difference on the journey east. She leant forward to pat Eskalon. She whispered: 'Look after him.'

When the friends had separated and Luke had taken Eskalon's rein in one hand and her hand in the other, the five of them went into the city, passing the tents of those who'd come too late to be let in and the hovels of those who would never be let in. They walked up through sleeping streets, their tread loud on the cobbles. A few sleepy eyes watched them pass, curious to see such tall, fair men in their city. Some of the oldest remembered when they'd seen them before, when the double-headed eagle of Byzantium had flown from Kutahya's walls, when the mosques had been churches and hadn't had towers from whose tops men sang.

It was the hour before dawn and the smell of baking bread was in the air. The night was still and the stench of the river far away. The Varangians quickened their pace as the palace came into view.

Matthew said: 'We'll see you later.'

When they'd left, Luke turned to Anna. 'We'll go to the harem. There's someone I want you to meet.'

Anna knew who it would be, warned by Yakub that she'd be there. They entered the Gate of Felicity and walked across gardens taking shape in the first light of dawn, scattered with animals sleeping. The air smelt of grass and rotting leaves. A peacock shrieked and Anna wondered.

Who is she?

Then they were there. They walked through a low arch and into an audience chamber with thick oak beams and a fire in the grate. There were candles on the walls and their light was unmoving. Apart from the woman waiting for them, they were alone.

'Anna, this is Shulen.'

Anna had her hood over her head, but seeing Shulen standing there with her long black hair free, she lowered it. The girl before her was younger and thinner than her and had a beauty that was more animal than human. Her eyes never left Anna's as she approached.

'Shulen. You have helped Luke. Thank you.'

Anna took her hand, then kissed her. Despite the heat of the room, Shulen's cheek was cold. She didn't reply.

Anna said: 'You must have had a difficult journey.' She paused, suddenly awkward. 'Will you return to the camp?'

Shulen's eyes stayed on hers and were the only things that spoke. Anna was shocked to see what they said.

He may not always be yours.

'Shulen is coming east with us,' Luke said.

Anna was about to ask why. She bit her lip. 'That will be good.' She turned to Luke. 'I have messages for you. Are we to have time alone?'

Behind her, Shulen moved and when Anna turned back, she'd gone.

'Who is she?' she asked.

'I don't know. Yakub says she's important.' He paused. 'You

have not come to talk about her.'

Anna hesitated. Then she said: 'I've come because you summoned me.' She came towards him and was in his arms again. They kissed and she made him kneel before her. She put her forehead down to his, her eyes on his and her arms around his neck. 'I've come to persuade you to come back with me.'

'You know I can't.'

She moved her arms so that her hands were interlinked behind his neck. She pressed in with her palms. 'Yes you can. We both know that your journey east can have three outcomes: you'll be sent back; you'll bring Tamerlane to fight Bayezid; you'll be killed. None of them are good.'

'Which is worst?'

She didn't bother to answer. Instead she said: 'Plethon thinks that bringing Tamerlane will save the Empire. But what if Tamerlane takes Constantinople instead of Suleyman? As his wife, I can perhaps control Suleyman. But Tamerlane? He'd slaughter every living thing within its walls. He always does.'

Luke felt the shock. She'd said three words that had the power to upset his world, and she'd said them so calmly.

As his wife.

He took a deep breath. He'd not wanted to talk about anything except how much he loved her. Now there was this marriage.

'You don't have to marry him.'

Anna kissed him then, for much longer. Her lips brushed his nose. She whispered into his ear: 'Come back with me and I won't.'

Luke drew back. He rose and walked to a curtain, parting it to sit in the alcove behind. The stone was cold against the back of his leg and there was a faint draught from the window. He looked down into his lap where his hands were joined. 'We both go to places neither of us want to go to. Yet not going would be with us for the rest of our lives.' He looked up. His voice was soft. 'Anna, for whatever reason, we both feel compelled to serve this empire and have to hope that there is some reward for it all.' He smiled then. 'It is our destiny, Anna, isn't it?'.

It was a question in need of an answer. She nodded slowly. They could spend the short time left arguing or making love. She rose. 'I've brought you something.' She reached into her pocket and brought out the box. She walked over to the alcove and put it in his lap. He opened it. In it was a gold ring without jewel or ornament. It shone dully in the candlelight as Luke took it out of the box.

'What is it?'

There was a stillness in the room that perhaps they hadn't noticed before. All sound seemed sucked into the words they were speaking.

'It's from the treasure,' she said. 'Plethon wants you to keep it.'

Luke studied the ring for a long time, turning it slowly in the light. It was very old and had some inscription on its surface – nothing he could read.

'I will take it with me,' he said. He put it on his third finger and held it up. 'It even fits.'

Anna took his hand and brought it to her lips. 'Never take it off,' she said. Then she remembered something. 'No, only take it off if you ever stop loving me. Will you promise?'

Luke smiled. 'I promise.'

PART TWO

THE JOURNEY

CHAPTER TWELVE

ANATOLIA, SPRING 1399

Surely it was a joke.

In strict translation from the Arabic, *Ablah* meant 'perfectly formed', but the camel beneath Luke was anything but that. It wasn't so much the hump or even the supercilious face, which were much like any other camel's. It was Ablah's walk. It was distinctly uneven. Could it be, he wondered, that he was riding a camel whose left legs were shorter than its right?

It was now the fifteenth day since the caravan had left Yakub's capital of Kutahya to go east across the steppe. For Luke, they'd been fifteen days of torture. What made it worse was the sight of his beloved Eskalon tethered behind, looking at him in relentless puzzlement. But Yakub had been firm: if he and his friends were to pass themselves off as servants to the merchant Abdul-Hafiz and his daughter Fatimah, then they must ride camels. And Eskalon, meanwhile, was to be a handsome horse for sale.

He'd spent the winter in Kutahya with his friends in great comfort. Yakub's palace was spacious and draped in silk and they'd slept on scented goose-down and awoken each day to lutes and good food and fountains that played on to lily-pads.

The Germiyan capital was a busy trading centre on the road to the east, full of noise and colour and the flash of coin changing hands. Outside it, the beylik was mainly steppe and sky and passing caravan. Inside, it was a place where nations met and bartered. For Luke, each day had been another day of renewed friendship with his Varangian brothers and with Eskalon. They'd spent hours together in the saddle hunting or racing, Luke teaching them to ride and shoot like gazis. At night, they'd talk of what was to come and not always fall quickly into sleep.

Now they were on their way: the four of them, Shulen and Yakub. The gazi chief would accompany them as far as Tabriz where he was to treat with Qara Yusuf, Lord of the Black Sheep tribe, on behalf of his master, Bayezid.

Luke looked back towards where Shulen rode the Bactrian cousin to Ablah, a curtained howdah affixed to the space between its two humps in which she could rhythmically recline. Her only gripe was that she couldn't see the world outside.

And the world outside was fair. Spring had come early to the steppe and the only hint of winter lay atop the peaks of mountains far to the south. The grasses were green and scattered with iris and poppy and the few trees they met oozed new sap from trunks scraped clean by deer. It was a land of lake and plateau and few towns or villages, of skies as big and as blue as oceans. It was a land in movement. The rivers they met were full and fierce and leaping with fish to be speared and cooked later in camel-milk. Goats and sheep were everywhere, herded by boys who smiled, beneath hands, up at the long, long thread of camels swaying their measured way across the endless steppe.

Luke turned to look at the line of camels, perhaps five hundred of them, stretching into the distance. Each was roped to the one in front and collected in files of eight, their puller at their head. On either side of them merchants, herders, cooks, musicians, storytellers, snake charmers, guards and everything else that made up this nomadic circus walked or rode. And next to them ran the dogs that would protect their camps at night. For fifteen days they'd stopped only to sleep and pray.

He drew up beside Abdul-Hafiz. The merchant was riding a horse largely smothered by the many folds of his cotton *thoub*. Without the garment he would have been large; with it, he was colossal. Luke knew that he came from Andalucía in Spain but had not been home for many years. This caravan, one of many he owned, had started in Bursa and was bound, via Kutahya, for Samarcand.

'Master,' began Luke, using the term agreed, 'how is it that a camel with legs of unequal length can be called Ablah? Is it a joke?'

Abdul-Hafiz looked at Luke, then Yakub, and grinned between the shores of his explosive beard. His teeth were not of the same white as his thoub. 'Call it what you will, my boy,' he replied amicably. 'Do you have a better name?'

Luke did. It had been given him by a man who had lied to him. 'Aatirah?'

The merchant's grin widened and he looked across at the camel. The cavernous laugh that had rumbled up and down the caravan for two weeks was rising from its depths.

'Your camel is well known to shit often and everywhere, Luke. Its dung alone is enough to cook our food every night. Your camel stinks.'

Yakub leant across from his saddle as the merchant exploded in laughter. 'Aatirah means fragrant, Luke.'

Luke nodded, patting the animal's neck. He'd stay with

Ablah. 'When do we reach the border?' he asked.

'We reach the lands of the Qara Koyunlu tomorrow,' said the fat merchant, wiping the last tear from his eye. 'Tonight we stop at a caravanserai.'

In fact they had yet to stop at a caravanserai since their route had been unusual. Among the many nations represented in the caravan there were merchants from Venice who traded in horses. They had wanted to travel due east to the beylik of Dulkadir, which was famed for its stallions, and Yakub had agreed since it had given him a chance to look in on its ruler, Nasredin Mehmed, whose daughter Emine was being considered as a match for the Sultan's second son, Mehmed.

'You want to watch your horse,' said Abdul-Hafiz, jabbing his thumb in the direction of Eskalon. 'I've seen the Venetians looking at it.'

Luke looked back at Eskalon.

'And I would never trust a Venetian,' continued the merchant. He winked and tapped the side of his nose. 'Dark people who live on water.'

There was a shout from in front of them and a message was passed from puller to puller. A man pointed to the west where a long haze of grey hung on the horizon. Ablah stopped suddenly, snarled and buried her nose in the grass. Abdul-Hafiz glanced down at the camel. '*Waa faqri*,' he muttered. Then he heaved himself up to stand in his stirrups, shielding his eyes with his big hand. 'A sandstorm is coming. We need to get to the caravanserai.'

That night, the four Varangians, Shulen and Abdul-Hafiz sat around a fire within the walls of the caravanserai listening to the wind moaning outside. They were in a vast open courtyard, surrounded by stables and storerooms, with towers at its corners where soldiers crouched beneath ramparts. It was a place of roasting mutton and refuge.

They had hurried inside just as the wind had begun to hurl the debris of the steppe against its walls and the merchants had gone to the little mosque to give thanks to Allah. The camels had been led to the warehouses and the Varangians had wandered through the halls to watch the wares being laid out for checking.

It seemed as if an ark had parked at this oasis and disgorged a version of everything that was precious from the world outside. There was ceramics and glass from Venice, sable and fox-fur from the lands of the Golden Horde, jewelled ostrich eggs cradled all the way from Addis Ababa and damasks from Cyprus, finer than any Luke had seen on Chios. Later, they sat around a fire with Abdul-Hafiz and talked of trade.

The merchant drew the world he'd travelled on a stone using a piece of chalk. Then, winking at Luke and dabbing the rolls of his glistening chins with a handkerchief, he drew what looked like the veins of a leaf inside the boundaries of his world.

'I call it the Silk Road,' he said, 'but it's not a single road and it carries more than silk. It is said that the road began when the wife of the Yellow Emperor watched a cocoon fall from a mulberry tree into her tea and unravel before her very eyes. Soon the Romans wanted silk for their togas and the road ran all the way from Chang'an to Rome, which they called Daqin: six thousand miles to the west, or two years' travel.'

He paused and his fat finger hovered closer to the map. 'Rich cities sprang up along the way, cities like Palmyra which were built on oases and could tax merchants for water and safety. Between them were built caravanserai twenty miles apart which was the distance a camel could walk in a day.'

Abdul-Hafiz pointed to the arteries spreading out from the spine. 'But soon the road had many branches. Ivory and gold came up from Africa and frankincense from the sands of Arabia. And from India' – he paused to wipe his brow with his hand – 'came wonderful things. Pearls as white as snow from the Kingdom of Maabar. They fish for them there in the seas south of Bettala where the Brahmin priests are said to hypnotise the sharks for one-twentieth part of their value.'

The fat man chuckled at the thought. He looked up to see Arcadius frowning. 'You don't believe me?' he asked, pointing his stick. 'My family has been travelling this road since the birth of Allah. There is nothing we haven't seen.'

'Please, Abdul-Hafiz,' said Luke, 'please continue.'

The merchant looked around and, satisfied that his audience was rapt, went on. 'Yes, from India. Wonderful things. The King of Ceylon owned a ruby as big as a man's fist without a single flaw. Kublai Khan offered him the value of a city but he wouldn't sell. My father once saw a diamond like this' – he made a circle between his thumb and forefinger – 'which came from the Hindoo Kingdom of Mutifili on the Coromandel coast. They use eagles there to find them, throwing meat into gorges so that they swoop down and swallow them. Then they pick them out of their shit. Ha!'

Shulen's finger was tracing the route, the back of her hand soft in the firelight, her eyes aglow. 'And what would you see?' she murmured. 'What would you see on this Silk Road?'

Abdul-Hafiz smiled, scratching his beard with the end of the stick and waving away a spark from his cheek. He seemed to Luke like a fat camel in the firelight: the same lazy hooded eyes and crooked smile. He wondered if that happened, over time, to all caravan merchants.

'You would see great cities,' murmured the merchant. 'Like Tabriz in Persia, where we will arrive before the next moon.'

Matthew leant forward to look at the stone. 'And after Tabriz?'

'After Tabriz, more cities of a size and wealth unimaginable to you from the West. Damascus, Baghdad, Bokhara, Samarcand. And huge rivers like the Oxus that take a day to cross. And then there are the deserts. You know what Taklamakan means? The desert east of Kashgar?' He paused. 'It means *go in and you'll never come out*. It is a desert of ghosts.'

The Varangians looked at each other.

'Oh, and the fierce animals,' he continued, warming to the theme. 'I shouldn't forget the lions and leopards, and the wolves in the wild Alburz Mountains. We lose many camels along the way. Even good Muslims sometimes.'

'And bandits?' asked Nikolas, his eyes wide. 'Are there robbers along the way?'

The merchant shook his head. 'No. That's one good thing about the Mongols,' he replied. 'Genghis and his sons made the trade routes safe. They even exterminated the assassins from the lands east of Tabriz who used to fall on caravans from their mountain castles, fired up by that *hashish* they smoked.' He paused. 'They say that a virgin can travel from Tabriz to Chang'an carrying a ruby on a golden plate and not be molested.'

'But before Tabriz?'

'Before Tabriz we will be travelling through the lands of the Qara Qoyunlu, which were overrun by Tamerlane ten years ago. Now they've been taken back by Qara Yusuf and there is less order. But our caravan is large. We'll be safe until Samarcand.'

They were silent for a while and let their various thoughts

rise into the night where the wind gathered them up and carried them away along the road to the land of the Ming. Luke looked down at the sword in his lap. He hadn't thought it prudent to carry it on the ride and even now, only the hilt could be seen. The dragon eyes glowed up into his. There was a cough behind them.

An old man was watching them from the shadows. He was short and neat in every visible respect. His eyes were part of a smile that began in the creased curve of his bearded chin. He seemed happy to see them.

'Abdul-Hafiz, *salaam*,' said the man, stepping forward. 'Don't you recognise me?'

The merchant stood and held out his arms: 'Ibn Khaldun!' he exclaimed, his smile a melon slice. 'You are here!'

'Apparently so,' agreed the man, moving into the embrace. 'I join you yet again. The conversation is irresistible.'

The merchant threw back his head and laughed, his many chins jostling with pleasure.

'And your friends?' asked the stranger.

'Ah yes . . .' The merchant turned and glared at the Varangians who were still seated. He held out his hand to Shulen. 'Yes. Well, I don't believe I ever told you that I had a daughter.' Abdul-Hafiz indicated Shulen, who had covered her face with her veil. 'May I present to you the Lady Fatimah?'

Ibn Khaldun looked amazed. 'Well now, how long have we known each other?' he asked, bowing deeply in the direction of Shulen, his hands pressed together. 'And in all that time you have never mentioned a daughter. Allah forgive you for such modesty! Does your wife know of this lady?'

The fat merchant looked uncomfortable. 'My wife glories in our daughter, of course,' he said, spreading his hands. 'But I fear that now Fatimah must depart with her servants.' He had turned to the four friends and begun a series of minute jerks of the head.

But Ibn Khaldun was not finished. 'Please,' he said, lowering his voice, 'I was listening to your conversation. It was not the talk of master to servants. I would like to meet these friends of yours.'

Abdul-Hafiz looked around. He put his lips to the ear of the smaller man. 'You have seen Yakub?'

'It was he who sent me over,' whispered Ibn Khaldun.

Luke had read Ibn Khaldun's work on Chios. Now he stepped forward and took the man's hand in his. 'Ibn Khaldun,' he said, 'we are honoured to greet you. Please join us.' He gestured towards the fire. 'May I present my friends Matthew, Nikolas and Arcadius? We are all sons of Varangians who used to guard the Archon at Monemvasia. And this is Shulen, not related to Abdul-Hafiz.'

Ibn Khaldun smiled again, the deep lines of his face curving to frame a mouth uncluttered by teeth. 'Varangians from Monemvasia?' he asked. 'I'd heard of you from Plethon.' He sat and looked around. 'We have mutual friends in Plethon and Omar. Like them, I'm a thinker, interested, above all, in history. I'm engaged in a great project: a history of the world.' He paused. 'I live in Cairo where, until recently, I was Kadi to the Mamluk Sultan Barquq.'

Luke was staring at him, entranced.

'So why am I here?' he asked. 'The Sultan of Egypt fears that Temur, whom you call Tamerlane, may be bringing his hordes west. I am interested in an alliance between the Mamluks, the Turks and the Qara Qoyunlu, who some call the Black Sheep. Yakub knows this.'

The man was seated on a folding chair of wood and canvas

and his thin ankles were thrust forward to the fire. He wore embroidered slippers lined with squirrel fur with ends that curled. Above, he wore a thoub tied at the waist with a crimson sash. This was a fastidious man who felt the chill. He placed his hands on the arms of his chair and leaned forward over the stone.

'Now, let's see,' he murmured, taking the chalk from the merchant and beginning to draw. 'This must be China, this India and up here, the land of the Golden Horde. Down here' – he was drawing a coastline – 'is Africa. The Portuguese are finding more to the south every year.' He looked up at the merchant. 'Not good news for you, my friend, who does so well from this land route.'

Abdul-Hafiz frowned.

Ibn Khaldun continued. 'Over here is Constantinople where your silk road ends and beyond are the Christian Kings. These are not rich or populous lands.' Now Ibn Khaldun looked up at Luke. 'Do you know what the largest city in Christendom is, my friend?'

Luke shook his head.

'Paris,' he answered. 'Ninety thousand people. Tabriz itself has a population of a million and its annual revenues exceed those of the King of France. One street in Cairo contains more people than the city of Florence and the number of ships that dock at its Nile port is three times the number in Venice, Genoa and Ancona combined.'

Luke shifted his sword and leant forward to put a log on the fire. 'But what has this to do with Tamerlane?'

Ibn Khaldun folded his arms on his lap. 'The question everyone is asking is: will he come west? His obsession is the building of Samarcand. He needs money to do it and there is more money in the east than the west.'

Luke asked: 'So why do you fear him coming west?'

'Well now,' Khaldun replied, 'Barquq managed to execute the Mongol envoys sent to him last year, one of whom was related to Temur himself. Very unfortunate.'

'So you think he'll punish the Mamluks?' asked Abdul-Hafiz, his jowls alive with concern. 'What then would stop him sweeping across the Maghreb? Soon he would be at the Alhambra!' His huge torso quivered at the thought and he spat unhappily to his side.

There was movement from outside the circle. It was Yakub. He was carrying a jug. 'I bought wine from the Venetians,' he said, looking at Luke. 'They said it comes from your home.' Yakub had a stool with him which he set down next to Ibn Khaldun. He poured himself a cup and passed the jug to Luke. The rich smell of Malvasia filled Luke's nostrils and memory rose with the smell. He passed it to Matthew without pouring. He asked: 'Is Tamerlane as bad as his forefathers?'

'That's the problem,' Ibn Khaldun replied. 'They're not his forefathers. Temur was born into the Barlas tribe, a minor clan in the lands of the Chagatai. His claim to kinship with Genghis Khan is through his wife Bibi Khanum, the widow of his old rival Husayn. She is a princess of the royal line. Temur does not like not being of direct descent.'

'So what does that mean?'

'It means', Khaldun answered, 'that Temur's overriding ambition is to unite the four kingdoms that were once the Khan Empire. He has already brought together the Chagatai Khanate, the northern kingdom of the Golden Horde and the Ilkhanate of Persia. There's one left to do and it is the most difficult and Temur is an old man, over sixty.'

'Which is China?' asked Arcadius.

'Which is China, yes: the vast Yuan Empire created by the greatest of Genghis's grandsons, Kublai Khan. Kublai's reign was a time of prosperity for China but his successors were dissipated and the last of them taxed his people cruelly to fund his debauchery. Then a peasant leader called Chu Yuan-chang gathered the people in revolt and threw out the tyrant, establishing himself as the first Emperor of a new dynasty, the Ming. He holds the throne still, but is old. I believe Temur is waiting for him to die.'

'So he'll invade China?' asked Luke.

'Ultimately, but it'll be no easy task. The Chinese have over a million men under arms and have cannon and countless other machines of destruction. Indeed, they invented the powder that fires them all. Any campaign against the Mamluks will just be to fill in time before an assault on China.'

'Which makes sense,' said Luke, thinking back to his time in the Germiyan camp. 'Temur knows that he has to keep the tribes occupied or they will fight between themselves.'

Ibn Khaldun nodded. 'And there's another reason for attacking the Mamluks: revenge. It was the Mamluk Sultan Baybars that inflicted the only defeat ever suffered by the Mongols. A century and a half ago, he destroyed Hulagu's army after the rape of Baghdad and so turned back the Mongol hordes.'

Abdul-Hafiz was sitting very still, his eyes wide open with fear. He was running his tongue over his bulbous lips as if considering for a moment the possibility of wine passing between them.

'He must be stopped,' he said in a barely audible voice. 'This is the Devil, Shatan sent to earth. This is the end of the world.'

No one spoke. Perhaps it was. A vast army come up from hell to kill everything that stood in its path. An army of Shatan.

Luke reached down and curled his fingers round the hilt of the dragon sword. He glanced at Matthew and knew they were thinking the same thing.

Are we mad?

There was a shout from the other end of the courtyard. Food was being served and a stream of hungry people poured from the dormitories.

'We should go,' said Abdul-Hafiz, patting his stomach, 'or there'll be nothing left.'

At the other end of the courtyard, away from the clamour of food served, sat the Venetians, who were eating their own. Cloaked, hatted and booted in black, they looked like a group of sextons peering into a grave. They were talking about the Chinese merchants who were also part of the caravan and their whispers did not escape their circle.

'Ten lengths?' whispered one.

'That's what they said. Or gestured, anyway. They want it for breeding.'

For a thousand years and more, Chinese merchants had been travelling west to find the best horses in the world. Once, these had come from the Fergana Valley, east of Samarcand, whose horses, the Tang had believed, were bred from dragons and sweated blood. Then they'd bought *kuluk* horses from Khota that could run forty miles without stopping. Now they wanted Arab stallions and those from Al-Andalus where the Carthusians had blended blood to such effect. Eskalon was from the Maghreb, bred by Berbers. He was a blend of Arab and

Spanish blood and it showed in his colour and bearing. Perhaps the Chinese had seen this.

'And they will pay ten lengths of silk?' asked the first Venetian. 'For one horse?'

The other nodded and leant forward over the fire. 'Raw silk.'

The first whistled quietly through his teeth. That was a lot for one horse.

'So how do we do it? The fat merchant's daughter won't sell to the Chinese and she won't sell to us either. I've asked her.'

At that point, one of the four, who had yet to speak, turned from the fire to look across the courtyard to where the merchant had sat before the call to food. Only the gazi remained there now, sitting hunched on his stool staring hard into the flames. The Venetian was a young man, previously unknown to the others, trading Malvasia wine for the Mamonas family, some of which he'd just sold to the gazi. He'd come from Venice and his name was di Vetriano.

'I think he's Greek,' he said.

'The horse?'

'No, the servant. The servant that leads the horse. He has a sword.' He paused and looked round at them. 'The lady's servants are all Greeks and they want us to believe they're Arabs.'

The Venetians were silent for a while, each evaluating this new evidence. One of them looked up from the fire. 'They're spies?'

The young man nodded. 'The Greeks want to ally themselves with Tamerlane against the Turk. They want him to come west to fight Bayezid.'

'So they go to Samarcand?'

'Or Sultaniya. They may want to meet Tamerlane's son, Miran

Shah, who is viceroy there. But they'll have to pass through Tabriz first.'

'Where Qara Yusuf rules?'

'Where Qara Yusuf rules and might be interested to know who they are.'

The three older Venetians were silent then, thinking of the profit that could be got from a horse that became available. The youngest of them smiled into his wine.

CHAPTER THIRTEEN

TABRIZ, SUMMER 1399

The city of Tabriz had not had walls since Tamerlane had sacked it eight years before and the green haze of its orchard suburbs could be seen from afar. It was built in a high valley between two ridges of hills, those to the south capped with snow. The caravan road approached it up a gentle slope that rose from the northern shores of Lake Orumiyeh.

'A thousand concubines and enough gold to sink a fleet of junks,' said Yakub as he rode up beside Luke. They were skirting the salt-crusted rocks at the lake's edge and the gazi was pointing his whip across its waters.

'The island of Shahi, where Hulagu was buried,' he explained. 'He sleeps there with his harem. Only they were alive when they entered the tomb.'

Luke looked across at the dim outline of a mausoleum. There were birds rising from the lake's surface in a riot of beating wings, the early sun on their backs and golden circles of water spreading beneath their feet. There was a smell of salt in the air.

'Did Hulagu sack Tabriz?' he asked.

'Yes, but not badly. And it's now busier than ever with the northern road closed.'

Luke knew about this from Ibn Khaldun. A decade ago, Tamerlane had fought a long and bloody winter war against his erstwhile ally Toktamish in the north. He was leader of the Golden Horde and had invaded Tamerlane's empire in the middle of winter. Tamerlane had driven him back into his own lands, finally cornering him in the snowy wastes of Russia. Now the northern trade route was closed and merchants had to come south to Tabriz and Sultaniya to exchange their wares. For Tamerlane, this meant more to tax and more money to lavish on his beloved Samarcand.

Two hours later they were weaving their way through streets thronged with stalls selling the produce of every continent. Luke was dazzled by the scale and noise of the place. It was beyond anything he'd seen, an endless warren of streets opening into huge squares, each with its own fountain. Next to this, Monemvasia was a village.

'Where does all the water come from?' he shouted into Ibn Khaldun's ear. They had dismounted now and were threading their way through a crush of jostling people. Luke was leading Eskalon and water was running through channels on either side of the street, some of it splashing against the horse's hooves.

Ibn Khaldun pointed at the pavings below him. 'From down there,' he replied. 'The Persians built underground pipes that bring water down from the mountains. In the summer they put ice in the fountains and leave vessels by their sides. I've seen it.'

They passed a jewellers' bazaar where a group of women were admiring slave girls displaying necklaces and bracelets for sale. A row of Jewish merchants sat behind with long beards and prayer beads. They came into wide square paved with white stone with pebbles between. The buildings around it were a mixture of mosques, caravanserais and madrassahs. At its centre stood an enormous juniper tree, a hundred feet tall, beneath which old men sat on benches and talked.

Luke pointed to the roof of the madrassah. 'Yakub, do you see those men?'

The gazi came up to his side and squinted into the sun. 'What of them?' he asked. 'Don't point.'

'They've been watching us. I would swear it.'

'Then don't look up. We should separate. Where are your friends?'

Luke thought of weapons. He had his sword wrapped in a cloak on Eskalon's back and Torguk's bow tied to the saddle. It would take time to reach them. 'They're ahead. With Shulen and the camels.'

'We need to keep distance between us. Slow down.'

Up ahead, Shulen was walking between Nikolas and Arcadius. She'd seen that all the other women of the city wore long white headdresses with a veil of black horsehair covering their faces. She stood out.

'Arcadius,' she whispered. 'See if you can buy me a veil somewhere. One like the other women are wearing.'

Arcadius nodded and began to move away. Then Matthew saw something.

'Wait!' he hissed.

There were men approaching them through the crowd. Armed men in mail. 'Are we surrounded?'

'It looks like it. What do we do?'

They had formed a little triangle by now, with Shulen inside it. Matthew had drawn his sword. It was the only one they had between them. The soldiers were getting closer, pushing aside men and women as they came. Nikolas spoke.

'Well, we're not going to win. We've got one sword and they've got two each.'

Matthew didn't agree. 'We can get past them. If we all rush in the same direction, we can break through. Shulen, take my hand. The rest of you, on my count.'

The Varangians readied themselves to charge. They were unarmed but they were strong and they were light. And there were many people about.

'One . . .'

The soldier in front lifted a bow. There was an arrow on its string.

'*Now!*'

They charged, Matthew in front. The soldier with the bow went down as his head drove into his midriff. A woman in front of him screamed.

'Follow me!' he yelled, lifting his sword.

People were falling over each other to get out of the way. A stall selling bolts of cotton collapsed and a Persian merchant screamed abuse. A money changer was hit on the head by an awning as it fell. It was chaos.

They'd reached the opening to a street too narrow for stalls. It was blocked by a donkey whose cargo of raw silk was being unloaded. Matthew smacked his blade against the animal's rump and it shrieked and started down the alley. A fat merchant came to his door and tried to hold on to Shulen as she passed. She kicked him in the shins and he sank, howling, to his knees.

'Run!' Matthew yelled.

But Shulen had tripped. Her hand slipped from his and he looked back to see her on the ground with Nikolas trying to help her up. Now there was a soldier at the head of the street and he was calling for others to join him.

Matthew turned to see the other end of the alley blocked by men with swords. Shulen had risen to her feet but was clearly in pain. They were trapped.

'Great idea,' said Nikolas. 'The charge. That worked.'

The night they spent in the pit was a night spent in hell.

Marched from the street of their arrest, the three Varangians were disarmed and thrown into a place of darkness: a darkness so complete that they could only find each other by sound or touch. They wondered what other creatures shared the cell with them. There was breathing and scratching all around them that could have been rats or a chained lunatic. The smell was overwhelming. The stench of centuries of excrement and dead vermin had entered the ancient stone and now filled their noses, their mouths, their minds. It was a path into madness. Matthew hoped that Shulen was being held somewhere better than this.

They'd already guessed that their captor was Qara Yusuf, Lord of the Qara Qoyunlu. But why he should want to imprison them they had no idea. Nor did they know who had betrayed them or whether Luke and the others had managed to escape.

Answers came at dawn. Just when Matthew had managed to subside into sleep, a shaft of light from above awoke him. A ladder was handed down, and in their blindness it took some time for the Varangians to climb it. When they had, they were led down a narrow street towards a large blue-domed building, which they took to be the palace. Then they were searched twice, bound by the wrists and taken into an anteroom on the far side of which were two tall doors through which came muffled conversation.

'What do we say?' hissed Nikolas, turning to Matthew.

'We tell them that we're Greeks trying to find a better life out east. We tell them that we were at Nicopolis and can see that the days of the Empire are numbered.'

'But why were we in disguise?'

Matthew's hands were bound tightly behind his back and his shoulders had begun to hurt. 'We're in disguise because otherwise the caravan wouldn't have taken us,' he answered. It sounded feeble. 'Just leave it to me. I'll think of something.'

Then the doors were pushed open to reveal an ornate hall of some size. It was a throne room and it contained six people, four of whom were the Venetian merchants from the caravan. The throne, raised on a dais, held the only person seated. He was sallow of complexion and had the nomad's flat face while his groomed beard spoke of the court. His robe was a rich red and spread from the base of the throne like a bloodstain. On his fingers were many rings of different coloured stones that seemed too heavy for his hands to lift. He looked nervous. Beside him stood an old man with a long beard.

'Are these the men?' he asked. His voice was cracked and high, almost the pitch of a eunuch.

The old man beside him, who might have been the vizier, said, 'These are the Greeks, lord.'

'I thought there were four of them.'

'One is still missing, lord. He will be found.'

Qara Yusuf studied them for some time. He seemed restless, as if wanting to be somewhere else. Matthew judged him to be twenty years his senior.

'Are you Greek?'

The Varangians were kneeling on the floor, their faces flat to the marble. Matthew raised his head. 'We are Varangians, lord.'

'Varangians? From Constantinople?'

'From Mistra, lord.'

Qara Yusuf's chin was propped on his fist; a finger uncurled to stand sentinel to his lips. His eyes never ceased to move, as if ungathered thoughts lurked everywhere around him like enemies. At last they settled on Matthew.

'Mistra? Where in Mistra?'

'Monemvasia, lord.'

'Guards to the Archon Mamonas?' The Prince's eyes had darted to the Venetians, one eyebrow raised.

'Our fathers, lord,' Matthew said. 'We decided to go to Nicopolis.'

'That was foolish.'

There was an uncomfortable silence.

'We are here to find work, lord,' continued Matthew. 'We're on our way to find service in the east. There is much fighting to be done there.'

Qara Yusuf nodded. 'Indeed. But why not the west? Didn't you Varangians first come from some island in the west? Is it not said so?' He paused and leant forward. 'Why not go home?'

Matthew lifted his hands, his palms open. 'The answer is all around you, lord. Fortunes are to be made in the east, not the west.'

'So you would fight for me?'

'For you or any that would pay us well, lord. We are Varangians. It is our craft.'

The youngest Venetian coughed and stepped forward, bowing from the waist. The Emir looked at him. 'Speak.'

'If I may be permitted, highness.' Di Vetriano straightened up. 'The Serenissima is friend to the Sultan Bayezid and, like you, fears the intentions of Temur. The Greeks, on the other hand, see Temur as a saviour. These men are on their way from the Emperor in Constantinople to treat with the Mongol lord. Otherwise why the disguise?'

Qara Yusuf turned back to Matthew. 'Why the disguise, Greek? And why the lie about this "Lady Fatimah"?'

Matthew swallowed. His neck was hurting from the strain of keeping his head up and the marble was hard on his knees.

'And you may rise to answer. I can't see you properly down there.'

Matthew rose, as did his friends. He smoothed the front of his thoub, and dared to rub his knee. 'We asked the merchant Abdul-Hafiz if we might be permitted to dress as the other travellers in the caravan. We did not want to draw attention to ourselves, highness.'

Qara Yusuf's eyes continued to wander. Frowning, he turned to the vizier. 'Bring the girl.'

The vizier clapped his hands, the big doors opened and two guards entered with Shulen. She walked with her head held high and a look of impatience on her face. Her caftan was creased and she was barefoot, her feet silent against the veined marble. She stopped in front of the dais and neither bowed nor knelt. Unlike the Varangians, towards whom she did not glance, her hands were free.

'Why am I here?' she asked quietly, her eyes as steady as Yusuf's were restless. 'Why are my friends bound, highness? Are we criminals?'

Qara Yusuf answered her question with another. 'Where is the fifth member of your party, the other Varangian?'

'I don't know where he is but I hope he is safe.'

'Why are you all in disguise? Why do you claim to be what you are not?'

She did not hesitate. 'I am married to the Varangian who is

not here, lord.' She paused. 'But he is Christian and I Muslim and you will know that assassins still exist east of this city, ready to attack caravans. They are Shi'ite and do not look favourably on marriages between the faiths. It seemed prudent to be mistress and servant while we passed through their lands.'

Di Vetriano spoke. 'It is this man that leads them, lord,' he said smoothly. 'He must be found or he will go to Temur's son Miran Shah in Sultaniya.'

Qara Yusuf turned to the Varangians. He yawned. The proceedings were becoming tedious. 'I don't believe you,' he said, rising, 'and I don't want to hear any more of your lies. You will die. The girl too.' He studied Shulen for a while. 'Or you may come to my harem. It's up to you.'

Di Vetriano stepped forward. He looked agitated. 'Lord, we agreed that we were to take these prisoners back with us.'

Qara Yusuf yawned again. 'I've changed my mind. You may have their goods.'

The following morning, Matthew awoke to sunshine in his eyes and sand on his lips. There was a narrow grille at head height that ran the full length of the cell he and his friends had spent the night in. Sand was blowing through it.

'What's outside?' he asked.

'Our place of execution,' answered Arcadius, getting up from the floor. 'Come and have a look.'

Matthew rose and walked over to join him at the window. He pressed his face against the grille and felt the warmth of the sun on his skin. His last morning alive and how sweet the sunshine felt.

Outside, the world rose above them. The window was at the bottom of a wall that encircled a sanded arena, a circus of some kind. Above were tiers of stone benches that ran around until they met a pavilion where two thrones had been set beneath a purple canopy.

'Perhaps we're to face lions. I wonder where Shulen is?'

Arcadius shrugged. 'Her best hope is the harem,' he said flatly. 'I'd rather know where Luke is.'

They were all quiet after that and the only sound came from rakes smoothing the sand outside. Then the drum began. Qara Yusuf had entered the royal pavilion and behind him walked Shulen with the four Venetians. There was nobody else in the arena. Yusuf and Shulen were both dressed in robes of brilliant white, as if they were to be married.

'Looks like she agreed to the harem,' said Nikolas.

There was another beat of the drum and four men were led out, their necks joined by chains. They were old and in rags, their long hair matted with filth, and flies followed them as they shuffled. They were lined up in front of the pavilion and made to kneel. Then, as Qara Yusuf examined one of his ringed fingers, each man was seized by a soldier and his head forced back to face the sky. A man entered the arena. He was bald and muscular and had the long moustaches of the executioner. He was carrying a short dagger in his hand and he bowed low in front of the pavilion. Qara Yusuf looked up and nodded.

The man walked over to the prisoners. He tested the blade on his thumb and then, one by one, gouged the eyes from the old men's sockets. After each excision, he grabbed the victim's hair, wiped his blade on their beard and tossed their eyeball into the sand. Pinned down by the guards, the men screamed and writhed in their pain. Then they were released and stumbled around on their knees, wailing and calling out to one another while Qara Yusuf laughed his high laugh and clapped his jewelled hands.

The Varangians were too shocked to speak. Matthew looked up at Shulen. She was sitting rigidly upright, her hands folded in her lap. She looked calm, almost bored, her eyes unseeing.

'Now us, I suppose,' muttered Arcadius.

Not yet. As the blinded men were led away, a door opened in the wall and a tall man in chains entered between files of guards, each with a bow slung at the waist. He was dressed in silks of gold and he carried the Koran in his left hand. His head was held high and on it he wore an extravagant turban, from which an osprey plume rose like a geyser. Nikolas whistled.

'Who is *that*?'

The prisoner seemed indifferent to his surroundings and, arriving before the pavilion, waited a while before bowing stiffly to the man within it. Qara Yusuf leant forward over the balcony. He said something and was answered.

'The vizier,' said Matthew. 'Or he was.'

The tall man was talking now, making small gestures with his hands. But Qara Yusuf interrupted him and raised his hand. One of the soldiers stepped forward, unslinging his bow.

'Ah, the bowstring,' murmured Arcadius. 'At least it'll be quick.'

The vizier knelt on the ground and removed his turban, placing it carefully on the ground before him. Then he lifted his long white hair and held it with one hand to his head. The soldier moved to stand behind him, the bow held horizontal.

Qara Yusuf looked for a long time at the man, his face expressionless. Then he nodded. The soldier lowered the bow over the vizier's head so that its string was against his neck. Then he began to turn it, slowly at first and then more quickly.

The vizier remained upright for the first turn and the second. By the third, both hands were clawing at the bowstring, the blood running down his neck and into the folds of his gown. His white hair was no longer white and his hands were washed red to his wrists.

At last it was over. With one jerking convulsion, the tall man lifted his hands. He stayed like that for a moment, then fell forward into the sand, dead. His body was dragged from the arena.

'Now it must be us,' said Matthew.

He was right. A heavy bolt was slid back and the door pushed open. Two guards were standing there with drawn swords. The Varangians walked from the cell, up some steps and out into the arena. The first thing they saw were the circling birds. Bloodied eyeballs lay in the sand and the birds were awaiting their chance.

'Courage,' Matthew murmured. 'We are Varangians.'

He looked towards the pavilion. Qara Yusuf was watching them, an uncertain smile on his lips. A boy had entered who sat to one side waving a fan. Behind him stood the Venetians. The one called di Vetriano was frowning.

'Varangians!' shouted Qara Yusuf. 'Approach us, please.'

The guards pushed them forward until they stood directly beneath the pavilion.

'You Varangians are famous throughout the world for your skill at fighting. I would like to see it.' He raised a hand and a door opened into the arena and four men entered carrying weapons and armour. The men stopped in front of them and each laid his cargo at their feet. Then they left.

'I wonder whom we are to fight?' But Matthew knew the answer.

'Varangians!' shouted the Emir. 'You will put on the armour and fight.' He paused and his smile broadened. 'You will fight each other. One will survive and go free.'

Matthew was shaking his head before the statement was out. 'We'll not do that, lord,' he said. 'You'll have to find another way to make us die. We'll not hurt each other.'

Qara Yusuf looked surprised. He held out his hand and a man stepped from the curtain behind him and placed a dagger in it.

'No?' he asked, pointing with the dagger towards Shulen. 'Not even if I remove a finger or an ear or a nose with every blow you strike which I deem not to be genuine?' He paused and allowed the point of the knife to stroke Shulen's cheek. 'I think you'll fight.'

Matthew turned to his friends. 'It doesn't seem we have a choice.'

He began to put on the armour. He looked up at Qara Yusuf. But the emir was looking beyond him, his eyes wide.

Behind them the vast doors to the arena were slowly parting, pushed from outside. The soldiers pushing them came into view and they were not Qara Yusuf's men. They were dressed in the green of the Prophet's flag and the swirling mark of the Caliphate of Egypt was emblazoned on their fronts. There were dozens of them.

Qara Yusuf was standing now and the boy had ceased to fan him. A man appeared from the curtain behind and pushed aside the Venetians. He whispered something into the Emir's ear. Yusuf frowned, squinting into the distance, and nodded once. Then he sat down.

A horse walked into the arena.

Eskalon.

Beneath the gaudy magnificence, it was Eskalon. Beneath the

trappings, bardings and caparisons, it was Luke's magnificent horse. But it wasn't Luke on his back. Riding him was the historian Ibn Khaldun, once the Kadi of the Sultan of Egypt. And in case there was any doubt as to his status, he wore a coat of golden mail on which was emblazoned the prancing lion of Baybars. His helmet was tall, pointed and carried the long horsehair of jihad. It was an impressive sight.

On one side of him rode Yakub. He wore the furred deel of a gazi chief and had a coiled whip within his belt. On his other, rode Luke, dressed as a Varangian. His dragon sword hung at his side and Torguk's bow was on his shoulder.

The guards fanned out into the arena and now stood to attention in two lines between which the three riders slowly advanced. They arrived at the pavilion, stopped, dismounted without hurry and prostrated themselves in the sand. There was silence.

Qara Yusuf was sitting very upright, gripping the arms of his chair. 'Please arise,' he said, his eyes darting from one to the other. 'I know who you are.'

The three rose to their feet. Ibn Khaldun spoke. 'Then, highness, you will know that we are emissaries sent by two Sultans. We have letters from our masters.'

Qara Yusuf was frowning now and had lifted his wine. 'Letters that couldn't wait?' he asked, his voice higher than ever. 'Weren't you told I was busy?'

Ibn Khaldun now bowed and pressed his hands together. 'The interruption was unforgivable,' he said, 'but the men who stand charged before you are part of our retinue, as is the girl by your side.' The historian was apologetic. 'I'm afraid, highness, that you have been misinformed as to their intentions.'

Ibn Khaldun's voice was as silk drawn on silk and it caressed the air like a zephyr. He continued: 'We judged it right to force an entrance after being refused by your officials. We were keen that no embarrassment befall your person by the harming of your friends' emissaries.'

Qara Yusuf looked round at the Venetians. 'But these men said they were spies. They said they were on their way to meet Miran Shah in Sultaniya. To bring Temur to fight Bayezid.'

Ibn Khaldun's voice was a wash of silver. 'These Greeks are Varangian soldiers who have rebelled against their Byzantine masters. They are enemies to the Mamonas clan, which is a friend of Venice. The men behind you may have omitted to tell you that.'

Qara Yusuf's eyebrows were arched in surprise. He turned again to the Venetians. 'Do any of you work for the Mamonas family?' he asked.

Di Vetriano stepped forward. 'I am carrying their wine, highness, and some glass from their factory on Murano.' He paused. 'Lord, I find myself wondering why, if these men are as described, they should feel the need for disguise?'

There was a cough from the arena. Yakub had stepped forward. 'I'm not like my Arab friend here,' he said gruffly, indicating Ibn Khaldun. 'I am Yakub of the Germiyan, a blunt gazi with little education. But I speak for Bayezid and I know the Venetians.'

Qara Yusuf's eyes were everywhere.

Yakub continued: 'They build ships for my sultan because they want to add to their empire yet they try to stop an alliance between our three kingdoms because they wish to befriend Temur.' He paused. 'Only this time, their planning has been clumsy.'

The oldest Venetian had stepped to the front of the pavilion.

He was shaking when he turned to the Emir. 'That is not true, majesty. We are merchants, not politicians. We have come here to trade.'

Another official stepped forward to whisper long into the Emir's ear. Qara Yusuf listened and then nodded slowly. He rose and walked over to di Vetriano.

'You and your friends will leave my city of Tabriz this very day and will be handed over to my cousin Bayezid. And if you ever get back to Venice, you should tell your doge this: Qara Yusuf of the Black Sheep honours his friends and looks sourly upon any man who seeks to come between them.'

The oldest Venetian opened his mouth to speak but the Emir raised his hand. 'One thing more. You may leave your merchandise. It will be given to these men you have so dishonoured. Now go.'

Qara Yusuf turned back to the arena. 'Now, please, let us talk of this alliance.'

It was not until evening that Yakub emerged from his talk with Ibn Khaldun and Qara Yusuf. There was a big fire in the palace square around which three Varangians and Shulen sat and talked. He found Luke in the palace stables, grooming Eskalon.

All day Eskalon had waited patiently, tethered in the meagre shade of a juniper tree next to the palace well. Luke could only guess at the stallion's discomfort under the heavy brocades of his caparison. Meanwhile Yakub's mare had sensibly stood in his shadow. Luke had spent the day with his friends, explaining what had happened: there'd been Mamluk soldiers following the caravan all the time. Ibn Khaldun had had to wait for them to reach Tabriz before mounting the rescue.

Luke looked up as Yakub entered. He was standing by Eskalon's side and had a brush in each hand.

'How did it go?'

Yakub sat heavily on a bale of straw. He scratched the back of his head and spat into a water bucket. 'As expected. We agreed a three-way alliance against Tamerlane. Then Ibn Khaldun left and it turned into two.'

'Which means that if Tamerlane defeats the Mamluks, Qara Yusuf and you will side with him against Bayezid?'

Yakub nodded. 'If we're able to, but it'll be difficult.' He rubbed his eyes. 'My argument is with Bayezid, not Tamerlane.'

Luke knew this. Yakub had spent eight years imprisoned in Ipsala Castle after Bayezid had taken his kingdom. His beloved sister, Devlet Hatun, had been forced to marry the Sultan. He hated Bayezid with every nerve of his being.

'And if Bayezid joins forces with the Mamluks?'

Yakub grunted. It was not what he wanted to imagine. He looked up and his eye travelled along Eskalon's back. 'Your horse did well today.'

Luke smiled. He looked at Eskalon. 'Mount to the Kadi of Cairo. It'll go to his head.'

Yakub rose and went over to Eskalon, taking his mane and patting the broad plain of his neck. He turned. 'You did well too. In fact you've done well all along. You were kind to Shulen. That was good.'

Luke narrowed his eyes. 'Why?'

Yakub shrugged. 'Because she will be important. She will help you.'

'Not so far,' said Luke. 'If she hadn't hurt her ankle, my friends would have got away.' He began to brush Eskalon's withers. 'How will she help us?'

Yakub took the other brush from Luke and began on Eskalon's flank. 'Whatever you've learnt from us, you're no nomad, Luke. Nor are your friends. She is. She will understand Tamerlane better than you. And she will take you to someone.'

'Who?' Luke had stopped brushing. 'I have already told you, Yakub. I will do things *my* way from now on. Who will Shulen take me to? Is it Tamerlane's son, Miran Shah? Is that why we go to Sultaniya?'

Yakub was silent. He continued grooming the horse. Luke was watching him, his head to one side.

'Who is she, Yakub?' he asked softly. 'Who *is* Shulen? '

'Shulen is Yakub's daughter.'

They both looked up to see her standing in the doorway. The firelight was behind her and they couldn't see her face, only the silhouette of her grace and the long hair that covered it like a gossamer shawl. She was standing quite still. Luke shook his head.

Of course.

'That is why I must come with you,' she continued. 'I can speak for the gazi tribes.'

There were so many questions suddenly. She came to his aid. 'I don't know who my mother is. He won't tell me. I was put with the tribe when I was a baby, put into the care of a shaman and his wife. She taught me healing. I was given education by Omar, secretly, when he visited.' Her head moved towards Yakub. 'My father visited seldom.'

Yakub was now looking at the floor. 'It was difficult.'

Shulen's voice had dropped. 'Perhaps. Anyway, I became a woman within the tribe and the target of unwelcome attention.'

Yakub was shaking his head. 'I didn't know,' he whispered. 'Nor did Omar.'

'Because I chose not to tell him.' Shulen stepped forward into the light of the torch. She looked ethereal. 'Anyway, that is the past. My father wishes me to accompany you east.' She turned to Luke. 'I wish it too.'

Yakub had straightened. He placed the brush on a table below the saddle-rack and picked up his whip. 'I must go,' he said.

His eyes flickered between the two of them, then he turned and left. They heard his tread on the stone outside grow fainter. They were silent for a long while, standing there in the torchlight. They heard laughter from the fire. Shulen walked over to Eskalon and put her mouth to his ear. The horse moved its head fractionally to acknowledge her presence.

'Eskalon, you are more blessed than you will ever know,' she murmured. 'How have you managed to capture this elusive love? What have you done to earn it?'

Luke saw the dark beauty of this mysterious girl who'd changed from witch to companion in half a year. He looked at her thin, angled body, so different from Anna's, and at the long, long veil of hair that half covered her face and swept down to those healing hands. The only sound in the stable was the soft sweep of Eskalon's tail against his flanks.

There was a shout from outside. Abdul-Hafiz was calling for them. They left Eskalon and walked across the stable yard to where their friends sat round the fire. There was light coming from a large building with camels tethered outside it. Big bundles of merchandise, roped within leather carriers, were scattered across the ground. Luke saw Ablah looking into the distance with contempt.

'Varangians! Come out here and help with these baskets. Why must an old man do all the work?'

Luke walked over to him with Shulen. 'Where's the Venetians' cargo?' he asked.

Abdul-Hafiz pointed. 'Over there, on those camels. We haven't touched it yet. We thought there might be snakes.'

Luke said, 'We'll do it then.'

The two walked over to where a dozen camels were sitting placidly on the ground, their bundles next to them. One of them turned its head as they approached.

'I'll start at this end,' said Luke, 'and you can start at the other. We don't need a full inventory, just some idea of what they have. Most of it can go on with Abdul-Hafiz to Samarcand where he can sell it for us.'

They began their search, untying the thick ropes and laying the merchandise out on a rug. It was an hour later when they next spoke.

'Luke!' Shulen called. 'Come over here. There's something strange.'

Luke rose stiffly and went over. The ground around Shulen had piles of glassware on it. In Shulen's hand was a small rectangular box. 'Look at this.'

Luke knelt beside her and saw that the box was lined with velvet. Cradled inside it were small prisms, stacked vertically and almost flat, and some thin pieces of wood.

'What are they?' asked Luke.

Shulen was staring hard at the contents of the box and didn't answer for a while. Then she smiled and turned to Luke. There was a light in her eye. 'I don't know,' she said softly. 'But I think we'll take them with us.'

CHAPTER FOURTEEN

TABRIZ, SUMMER 1399

The Varangians, Shulen, Yakub and Ibn Khaldun left Tabriz in a fine calvacade of plumes and pennants and high-stepping Mamluk stallions. Qara Yusuf, accompanying them as far as the city gate, had the grace to apologise. He bowed to them from the saddle, placed his hand above his heart and wished on them the blessing of Allah. Then they took the road west into gazi lands.

The next morning, after a night in a caravanserai, Ibn Khaldun and Yakub departed as the first rays of sun caught the breastplates of their Egyptian bodyguard. Ibn Khaldun would return to his master in Cairo with an alliance he didn't entirely believe. Yakub would return to Bayezid in Edirne with one he didn't believe in at all.

An hour later, the Varangians and Shulen set out along the same road but soon left it and followed a lesser route back towards Astara on the shores of the Khazar Sea, some four hundred miles to the north-east. For a week, their horses carried them through desert and mountain, forest and river, night and day. They rode under merciless sun and merciful moon, bathing in the sweat of their bodies by day and cool streams at night. They talked little and slept less. And not once did any fall behind.

Late one afternoon, they stopped to look over a sea with villages scattered along its edge and tiny boats strewn across its surface.

'Tonight we eat fish,' said Luke and he turned to smile at Shulen who'd ridden up to his side.

'And then?'

Luke had produced the map drawn for him by Ibn Khaldun and was studying it. 'Then we follow the seashore until we see the Alburz Mountains rise up on our right. There we go to Sultaniya.'

'Where we become Shi'ite,' she said, smiling.

Luke smiled. 'Yes, where we become gloomy Isma'ilis and you disappear behind a veil. Where we meet Miran Shah.'

'Who is mad and dangerous.' This was Nikolas. 'Luke, can you just tell us why we want to meet a dangerous madman? Nothing too long, a summary will do.'

'Nikki, he's Tamerlane's son. They're all mad and dangerous. Anyway, it's in the future so let's not think about it. For now, let's have some fun.' He turned in his saddle. 'We've spent the week clinging to mountain paths. What say we race to that village?'

Eskalon snorted and Matthew laughed. He leant over to the horse. 'Are you too fat now from eating the kadi's food, Eskalon?' Then he lifted his heels and was gone. By the time they'd entered the village, their horses were panting like Jezebels and Matthew was triumphant. 'Too fat. Or perhaps it's the rider. They fed you too well in Kutahya, both of you.'

Shulen arrived just ahead of the other two Varangians.

'Hey!' said Arcadius, riding up to her, his brow thick with dust. 'We carry armour. You have nothing but your bedding.'

'And the Venetian glass, don't forget that,' said Shulen, leaning back on her saddle. Her face was pink and her long hair had knotted into waves across her back. Luke smiled.

You're changing.

The village they had entered was a desperate place and seemed empty of people. It was built at the point where the track they'd come down met one that followed the shore of the lake. On either side of it were dismal hovels of mud and grass and beyond them, banked in the black sand, lay broken fishing boats. Smoke drifted skyward from the roofs and the smell of cooking fish rose with it.

'Do we stay here?' asked Nikolas. 'It seems we might get fed.'

A door squeaked open and a child appeared, filthy and almost naked. Luke dismounted and reached into his saddlebag for bread. He held it out, speaking over the child. 'We mean no harm. We just want fish to fill our bread. We'll pay for it.'

A man came out holding a piece of wood. He was dressed in rags and as filthy as the child. He stood staring at Eskalon. Then he nodded.

Luke turned to the others. 'We eat fish tonight.'

So they did. Sitting around a fire made of driftwood and seaweed that bubbled and hissed as it burned, they gave bread to the villagers and got fish in return. Later, they lay beneath the stars in blankets heavy with salt and listened to the rasp of the waves on the sand and the anxious murmurings of the people who'd sheltered them. And the next morning they left before any were awake.

It took them another week to reach the Alburz Mountains. It was a week in which they galloped over sands or picked their way along cliff-top paths, trees blasted horizontal beneath them, the nests of seabirds between their roots. Always by their side was the grey expanse of the sea, rhythmic as the womb, its surface featureless except when pierced by the moon or fishing boats and the frenzied fight of their wakes.

The people of this land were strange, subdued creatures, hybrids of earth and water. They were refugees, thrown across the world by invasion to seek invisibility among the lagoons and caves of this sea. They were Armenians, Georgians, Azerbaijanis and people of other races who wanted solitude and peace and asked no questions of five travellers making their way east.

It was a week of hard riding and at night they slept deeply among barrels and nets and crabs that darted between them. They awoke stiffened by salt and cold, with the cry of birds carried loud and faint on the currents above them. Once they slept at some salt pans; they warmed themselves next to the chimneyed furnaces that made the salt, which was stacked around them in boxes: crystals winking up at the stars.

The next day they saw mermaids on the shore and swam with them for a while in the waves, stripping to their cotton shorts. But the mermaids were afraid and came to sit with Shulen on the rocks and throw shells at their suitors. And Shulen laughed and reached into her saddlebag to show them her strange Venetian glass.

At last, the Alburz Mountains rose up to the south and they turned towards them, finding a path through meadows grazed by herds of wild horses that raced beside them as they rode. Further on, the path rose gently, then steeply, into foothills covered in pine and chestnut until, above the trees, they could see mountains stretched out before them, their western slopes tinged with crimson.

Luke looked at his map. 'Tomorrow night we should reach the castle of Alamut, which is out there somewhere, about fifty miles away. There are wild tribes in those mountains and Ibn Khaldun recommended we sleep in the castle's shadow. The people don't go near it. They think it's still full of assassins.'

'So what about tonight?' asked Arcadius.

'Tonight, we find a cave.'

'Fire?'

'No fire, no cooking,' Luke said. 'From now on we must remain unseen. We will reach Sultaniya from the east, which will not be the direction anyone still looking for us will expect us to come. But it will take us another week.'

That night, lying in the darkness, Luke told them what he'd learnt from Ibn Khaldun of the man they were to meet in Sultaniya.

'He is Temur's second son. His older brother, Jahangir, died of some sickness when only twenty. Jahangir was his father's favourite: brave, good, and everything that Miran Shah isn't. And he had a beautiful wife, Khan-zada.'

Shulen said: 'Some say that it is Khan-zada who has driven Miran Shah mad. She was forced to marry him when Jahangir died and Miran Shah knows she'll never love him as she did his brother. His jealousy has driven him insane.'

Nikolas asked: 'Will we meet her?'

'I hope so,' replied Luke. 'Yakub says that she has influence over Temur.'

'Why would she have influence?' asked Matthew.

Shulen said: 'Because she was Jahangir's wife and because she is mother to Temur's favourite grandsons, Mohammed Sultan and Pir Mohammed, both of whom seem to have inherited their father's virtues. Mohammed Sultan is Temur's heir.'

Luke yawned. 'And there's another reason she has influence,' he said. 'You will remember how Ibn Khaldun said that Temur is obsessed with Genghis Khan? About how he minds not being of his line? Well, Khan-zada is of royal blood. She is the granddaughter of Uzbeg, Khan of the Golden Horde in the north.'

'Which means he'll listen to her?' asked Matthew.

There was no answer because Luke had fallen asleep.

That night they slept well and awoke glad not to have salt in their hair and the smell of fish in their nostrils. They found a waterfall and washed as best they could and filled their flasks. They ate cold mutton and biscuits before setting out into the Alburz Mountains.

The riding was hard and slow and the horses slipped on shale or stumbled through rock falls, their ears flat against their heads and their nostrils quivering with alarm. The sounds of their hooves echoed up from ravines too deep to fathom or rolled down the slopes above, and no one thought of speaking. It was a high, barren land of jagged ridges and sudden shadow and they felt no part of it.

In the afternoon, they began to descend, sparse scrub giving way to single trees, then woods which were thick and shut out the sun. The sudden gloom made the horses start and blow and they kept their reins short. Then they came out into a wide valley, terraced on either side and startlingly green. There had been people here once, many people, and their deserted villages were still scattered along its sides. Wasted fields stretched all around them. They rode in silence beside a river that twisted its way through gulleys and cataracts and opened out into deep pools where people once must have swum and washed their clothes.

'What happened here?' Arcadius was riding next to Shulen.

'The Mongols,' said Shulen. 'These were the lands of the assassins and Alamut was their stronghold. The Mongols destroyed them a century ago.'

'The assassins?'

'Later, Arcadius. Look up there.' She was pointing to a crag at the end of the valley that had come into view. 'That's it. The Eagle's Nest: Alamut.'

At first he saw only the steep sides of a mountain that rose higher than its neighbours. Then he saw that the sides became walls and the walls battlements, all brushed with the same orange of the late-evening sun. It was impossible to believe that anything could have been built on such a peak. He whistled softly.

'Impregnable.' Arcadius had reined in his horse to stare.

'Not to the Mongols,' said Luke, who had come up beside him. 'We need to get to it before dark.'

They broke into a trot and an hour later arrived at the bottom of the mountain. An old track, barely visible, rose around its side and they took it.

'We'll stop here,' said Luke. They'd found a wide-mouthed cave above the track that, with some disguise, would be invisible from either direction. It was big enough to accommodate both them and the horses. 'If we cover the entrance, we can light a fire,' he said, dismounting. 'But no cooking.'

The others climbed down from their horses and undid the saddlebags strapped to the animals' sides. They took down their bedrolls, removed the saddles and bridles and poured water into vessels for the horses. When the animals were tethered, they set off to find wood for camouflage and fuel. By the time they'd returned, it was almost dark and a half-moon was high in the sky.

When the mouth of the cave had been stopped with foliage, the fire lit and a meal eaten, they set their bedrolls against their breastplates and laid down to talk. The horses were tied at the front of the cave and would provide warning of any approach.

Arcadius said: 'Shulen, you were going to tell us of these assassins.'

She picked up a stick, turning it in her hand, before replying. 'They were an elite band of warriors, especially trained to assassinate their enemies.' She paused and smiled. 'Rather like you Varangians.'

Nikolas, who was lying next to her, his head almost touching hers, said: 'I should hope better. We were forced to leave Monemvasia, were on the losing side at Nicopolis and nearly got executed by a madman in Tabriz. The only people we might have assassinated are ourselves.'

Shulen smiled. 'Your time will come.'

Luke looked at the fine, dark beauty of this woman, no older than himself. She felt his eyes on her and turned her head to him. For a while no one spoke. Matthew looked from one to the other of them. 'The assassins?' he prompted.

'The assassins, yes.' She turned back to the fire. 'Well, they were a cult. They were Shi'ite Muslims, which means they believed that the true line of the Prophet runs from his son-in-law Ali. Most of the Shi'ites live here in Persia.'

She looked around at the faces, tired from their long ride but alert and listening. 'The assassins were founded by a man called Hasan-i Sabbah. He was born two centuries ago not far from here. He was a brilliant man: a mathematician, philosopher and alchemist. He converted to the Ismai'ili belief and gathered many disciples around him. He soon found himself on the run from the Sunni Seljuk Turks, who ruled at that time, and he came here to the Alburz Mountains where the people were Shi'ite and had long resisted the reach of the Seljuks. He saw Alamut and decided that it would be his base.'

'He laid siege to it?' asked Arcadius.

'No, he infiltrated it with his followers and they took it from within. It took him two years. Then he started the assassins.'

'What were they, these assassins?' asked Nikolas. 'What did they do?'

Shulen prodded the fire. 'They were young men recruited for their strength and intelligence. They were indoctrinated with the Ismai'ili beliefs such that they were ready to sacrifice their own lives to murder anyone they were told to. Invariably they died in the attempt.'

'Who did they kill?'

'Usually Sunnis of power and prominence. The Seljuk vizier Nizam al-Mulk was the first. They carried out their killings in public places to make their point.'

Luke pondered this. What would persuade a man to sacrifice his own life to kill another? Was that what he would do for his empire?

'It is said', she went on, 'that Hasan-i Sabbah would drug the young *fida'iyin* with hashish and that, when they'd fallen asleep, would have them taken to a beautiful garden within the castle. There they would awake to find ravishing women and all that they could want. Then Sabbah would tell them that they were in paradise and that if they wished to return to it they would have to carry out the deed assigned to them.'

Matthew spoke. 'And now?' he asked. 'What of them now?'

Shulen returned her gaze to the fire. 'Now, only their ghosts remain.' She rolled on to her back and looked up at the roof of the cave where their shadows danced. 'They were destroyed in these mountains by the Mongols. Their castles were taken, one by one, and their people massacred. That's why the valley is as it is. But there were assassins west of here by then, in Syria. They were recruited by the Mamluk Sultan Baybars to carry out killings on his behalf. It is said that the sultans in Cairo still use them, but it is only rumour.'

Shulen had moved because the smoke from the fire had begun to make her eyes sting. Now she rose. 'I am going outside. I want some air.'

The Varangians exchanged glances. Luke nodded to Matthew. He picked up his sword and said: 'I'll come with you. It's safer.'

They walked to the mouth of the cave and Luke patted Eskalon's neck while Shulen lifted aside the branches. The horse turned to him and nuzzled his shoulder.

Then they were outside among the smells of juniper and pine. They lifted their faces and saw a moon straddled by passing clouds granting light and shade to the landscape around. They walked slowly down the slope, not talking, until they came to a mound of stones, levelled at the top.

'An altar,' said Shulen, reaching out to touch its uneven sides. 'Perhaps a fire altar of Zoroaster. It's ancient.'

Luke turned back to the mountain behind them. The moon had emerged to reveal the castle above, stark against the night sky and perched beyond the reach of man. He shivered.

Shulen had turned too. 'Alamut,' she murmured.

Luke was silent, thinking of a darkness enveloping the world, of the moon's face hidden forever. He turned away from the castle and sat down, his back to the altar. An owl screeched and something wild grumbled from the woods deep in the ravine. Shulen sat next to him and took his hand.

'Are you frightened?' she asked softly.

He looked at her and all he saw were two eyes. 'Aren't you?'

The moon came back and he could see she was smiling.

'Of course. Tamerlane is a monster who kills every man, woman and child that stands in his way, yet he spares artists to create beauty.' She paused. 'I want to meet him. It's the waiting that's hardest.'

Luke nodded. He knew what she meant. 'You talked of Omar in the cave. How did he teach you?'

'He'd come to the camp, pretending to visit the shaman. That would allow us to spend hours alone together. He taught me to read and write and be curious about the world. He left me books and I learnt more.'

'And the shaman?'

'He played along, as did his wife. They were kind but pretended otherwise when we left the tent. She taught me the power of plants and herbs to heal and I came to love her in a way. She died when I was nine.'

The moonlight disappeared and Luke shivered again.

Far above them sat an empty, ruined castle from whose shadows men, masked and dressed in the black of the night, had once emerged with one ambition: to kill another man.

Silent as cats, the four assassins came down the mountain on ropes, pushing out with their feet from rock to rock as they fell. They were invisible against the slope, swathed in black robes that left only their eyes uncovered, everything hidden but the swords strapped to their backs. Their descent was fluid and effortless and had the grace of night creatures whose survival depended on their stealth.

They dropped to the ground behind Shulen and Luke without making a sound and stayed crouched and perfectly still until the landscape had taken them in. Even their breathing was controlled.

But Luke felt them. 'We are not alone,' he said softly.

Shulen looked around. 'We are alone,' she whispered. 'It's

the ghosts. Ibn Khaldun said we'd feel them. Tell me about Monemvasia.'

Luke rose and looked hard at the towering rock above. He could see nothing. He sat again. 'Monemvasia? Well, it's friendlier than this place. What would you like to know?'

'How you met Anna there. She was the child of the Protostrator, you of a Varangian Guard. How did you meet?'

Luke smiled. 'So, it's not Monemvasia that you want to know about.' He paused. 'Shulen, have you never loved?'

She was holding her shins with her forearms, chin on her knees. She was rocking slowly backwards and forwards. 'Gomil,' she said. 'But I was young and impressed by silly things. He was the chief's son. He tried to have me and shunned me when I rejected him. He hated me after that. Then you came and helped me and he hated you instead.' She turned to Luke. 'I'm in your debt.'

Luke was shaking his head. 'There's no debt,' he said quietly. 'But you can tell me the truth. Why did Yakub send you to the tribe?'

He felt her shrug beside him. 'Shame? Convenience? Who knows? Perhaps I was an embarrassment.'

The assassins remained motionless while the couple beneath them talked. Then they began to move forward at the crouch, an inch at a time, no part of their bodies making any sound. They moved when there was conversation and when the moon was hidden by cloud. When they were close enough to see that the couple's hands were joined, two of them took pads of cotton from their sleeves. The other two, with infinite care, moved their swords to their laps.

Luke stopped what he was saying and lifted his head. 'What's that smell?'

Too late. The assassins were upon them.

CHAPTER FIFTEEN

ALAMUT, SUMMER 1399

Luke awoke from the sweeping contours of sleep to the precision of shapes.

He was in the uppermost room of a tower whose circular walls rose into a dome, painted black and dotted with the white stars of a celestial map, in places joined to form zodiacal signs. Into it was cut a narrow channel, open to the sky and displaying the vivid curve of morning blue. The channel's sides were scored with minute calibrations etched in gold.

Below the dome, the walls were covered with bookcases and, between them, silk screens on which were written astronomical tables and the symbols of alchemy. There were empty sconces above the screens and congealed wax ran down their surfaces.

The floor was wooden and carpeted and supported a central round table on which stood instruments used for distillation. Against the walls were two beds, side by side, with a small table between. On one bed was Luke and on the other Shulen, both of them washed, brushed and dressed in fresh linen clothes. Luke's sword and bow were propped up against the foot of his bed. Both of them bore the scent of anointed oils.

Luke had dreamt of the Goulas of Monemvasia, of eagles

rising from nests that clung to its walls and of the narrow jumble of streets below. He'd dreamt of his mother and of kermes laid out on the balcony to dry. He awoke strangely calm and happy and beset with a raging thirst. He looked at the table to his side and saw water and cups; he drank. Beyond the table, he saw Shulen.

She was awake and watching him through waves of hair. It shone with a deep lustre that he'd not seen before and, for a moment, Luke couldn't connect it to her face and neck. She was smiling.

'Did you dream?' she whispered.

'Yes. Of strange things. And you?'

She nodded. 'We were drugged. They must have put something on those cloths they held to our mouths. Hashish, I should think.'

Hashish. Assassins.

'Were they assassins?' he asked. 'Did you see them?'

Shulen drank some water. She was lying on her side facing Luke and had her head propped up on her hand. 'No, I didn't see them. But if they were assassins, they were poor ones. We're still alive and you smell better than you have for weeks.'

It was then that they saw that they were not alone. There was a sound from the other side of the room where a woman stood by a window with her back to them. She had straightened up but did not look round. Now she spoke.

'Yes, they were assassins. And if they'd wanted to kill you, you would now be dead.'

The voice belonged to someone who had always been obeyed. There was no cadence of doubt or suggestion in it; there was just fact.

'Where are our friends?' asked Luke.

The woman did not turn. Beyond her spread the flawless sky and the tops of distant mountains. There was grass growing from the lintel outside and it moved slowly in the wind above her head. They were high up in a ruin.

'Your friends are safe. They are below.'

Luke imagined Matthew and the others anointed with healing oils and smiled. He looked up from the woman's back to the channel running through the apex of the dome, flanked by measurements like the tiny legs of a caterpillar.

'It is a quadrant. For measuring the hour of sunrise or the moment of noon.' She had turned and was looking straight at Luke and he knew immediately who she was.

'Khan-zada,' he whispered.

She gave the minutest of bows from a neck embraced by a high collar of intricate design. It was part of a simple white tunic that fell to her thighs, beneath which were black trousers of a tougher material. The tunic was frogged at its front and the trousers had leather patches on their inner sides for riding. She was wearing boots that came up to her knees.

'Where are we?' Shulen asked.

Khan-zada turned her face to the other bed and Luke was able to study it in half-profile. It was a small head which was set back on its long neck so that her nose and chin were tilted upwards. She had a wide, unlined forehead and eyebrows arched by paint above eyes that saw beyond frontiers. Her black hair was gathered in plaits upon her head and held there with enamel birds whose jewelled beaks and tails joined to encircle it in colour.

'*Aluh amu't*, the Eagle's lair. In the observatory of Hasan-i Sabbah,' she said and smiled with something near to warmth. 'You know of him?'

Shulen nodded. She was staring at the woman with fascination.

'Well, this was where he would come to measure the seasons or the distance between celestial bodies or the time of the next eclipse. The garden is still here but overgrown. And without its houris.'

Every movement this woman made was performed with care and grace and Luke saw that her head remained perfectly still when the rest of her body moved.

'And when he wasn't doing that,' she continued, 'he would be searching for the philosopher's stone or the secret of *aqua vitae*. But he was less interested in the alchemy of base metals than the alchemy of souls: in the transmutation of the mortal into the immortal.' Now she turned slowly back to Shulen and there was a question in her eyes. 'That is more interesting, don't you think?'

Shulen was transfixed. Her mouth slightly open, she was breathing quickly and there was colour in her cheeks. She said nothing.

Khan-zada had moved to the wall. 'Here are the seven planetary metals and here the four elements.' She was pointing at symbols. 'The language of alchemy.'

'And the books? Are these his books?' asked Shulen.

Khan-zada walked over to one of the cases. She pulled down a leather-bound volume, scarred with age. 'Some. And some are mine.' She was stroking the book's cover. 'I come here to read. Ptolemy, Jabir ibn Hayyan, Ibn Sina . . . many of these books came from Baghdad and Bokhara, looted by men of my race who couldn't read.' She looked up slowly from the book. 'I used to come here to dispute with scholars. Even Plethon and Omar have visited. Now I come to escape.'

'Was it you who anointed us with the oils?' asked Shulen.

'Ayurvedic oils prepared by myself,' replied Khan-zada. 'But you too are a healer. In your baggage there are many compounds that I've not seen before.'

Shulen began to say something but then changed her mind. Instead she asked: 'And the oils you gave us?'

'They helped you to rest and now they will help you to ride.'

Ride?

Luke had sat up in the bed. He saw riding clothes laid out at its end. 'To Sultaniya?'

'No, not to Sultaniya. *Away* from Sultaniya. We ride to Samarcand.' The uplifted head had moved its penetrating eyes on to Luke.

'Why not to Sultaniya? We came to meet your husband.'

'Then you are madder than he is,' she said. 'Your plans have changed.'

There was a knock on the door and two men entered. They were dressed in the loose black clothing of their kidnappers and they bowed low. They spoke from behind masked mouths in a language that Luke did not understand. Khan-zada listened to them, walked back to the window and looked out.

'They are coming,' she said quietly. 'They are perhaps four hours away. The assassins will try to delay them and one will dress himself in my clothes to be seen from the battlements, but it will only give us a few hours. We cannot wait any longer.'

Luke wanted to know more but saw that Shulen was already preparing to leave.

'Wait!' he said, louder than he'd meant. 'We were on our way to meet Prince Miran Shah in his capital and now you say we must not. I want to know why.'

Khan-zada turned slowly to look at him, mild irritation

in the pellucid eyes. 'My husband is not your best means of meeting the lord Temur,' she said quietly. 'I am.' She paused. 'My husband spends his time ingesting hashish and wine and fornicating with children of both sexes. And when he is not destroying them, he is destroying any building of beauty around him. He is eaten up with jealousy and with hatred for his own mediocrity. He is mad.'

She took a deep breath and looked from Luke to Shulen. 'All of this I could put up with. For the sake of my children, I could bear it. But I learnt that he was plotting against Temur himself. Then I knew he was mad.'

'But who is coming?' asked Luke.

The Princess raised her arched eyebrows further. 'Still the questions? His creatures are coming. They are coming because my absence has been noticed and they will know that I have come here. They will spare me but they will kill you. So we must leave. Now.'

Khan-zada, Shulen and the four Varangians came down the mountain as the assassins had done, with ropes coiled around their midriffs fed out from above. They jumped their way past caves, ledges and birds until they reached the shallower slope in front of the cave where they'd been taken. There, looking up at them in the fresh morning air, were Eskalon and the other horses, all saddled, provisioned and ready to ride.

A single assassin stood with the horses, holding them by their reins and wearing a brown deel with a green stripe at its edge. Around his neck hung a rectangular piece of iron with three circles engraved on its face.

'He will come with us,' said the Princess, untying her rope and gesturing to the man. 'He has a courier's *paizi* around his neck and is dressed as one. He will take us to the first staging post where he will subdue the guard and then stop the courier sent by Miran Shah.'

Matthew had mounted and was adjusting his stirrups. 'Why do we need to stop a courier?' he asked.

'Because', she explained, 'he will be carrying a message from Miran Shah to all staging posts telling them not to give us fresh horses on pain of death. We will need those horses if we are to escape the men who follow us.'

The assassin's head was uncovered and Luke found himself looking at a man little older than himself. He was slight of build and delicate of feature. He did not look like a killer.

'So which way do we go?'

The assassin answered in Greek. 'We go due south through the mountains until we meet the royal road. Then you go east and I stay. It is four hundred miles to Mashhad and it will take you four days. Afterwards you will cross the Kara Kum desert and reach Bokhara. After that is Samarcand.'

'*Four days?*' Nikolas looked up from examining his crossbow. 'How are we getting there, on eagles?'

The young man was unmoved. 'With the paizi you can change horses at every fifty-mile staging post, or *yam* as we call them. It is what it's for.'

'And sleep?' asked Arcadius. 'Or even food? What chance of those?'

'You will eat and sleep in the saddle. Those following you will be doing the same.' The man had mounted and begun to move down the path. It was steep and the horses could only walk it and Luke found himself at the back behind Khan-zada. There was much he still wanted to know.

'Highness,' he ventured, 'why did you go to all the trouble

of kidnapping us? Why not simply ask us to take you to Tamerlane?'

The woman did not look round immediately and he wondered if she'd heard him. Then she reined in her horse so that there was distance between her and the rider in front. 'I needed to see you.' She had not turned and her head was held as high as always. Her voice was low. 'I needed to see you to know if I could trust you. And I needed to see the girl.'

'And you couldn't do that by meeting us on the road?'

'How?' She put the question to the sky. 'How would I have met you? How would you have reacted to being stopped by a group of assassins?'

Luke saw the truth of this. But it raised another question. 'How did you know we were on our way to Miran Shah?'

She did not answer this and was silent for a long time. Luke watched her back as it moved in time with the sway of the horse. Even mounted, she had the grace of a queen. Then she asked a question of her own. 'Do you love her as much as she does you?'

Luke was still muddled by the drug and wondered how she could possibly know about Anna. Then she spoke again.

'I was watching her while you were asleep,' she said, now turning so that the piercing eyes were on his. One hand was holding her reins, the other resting on the rump of her horse. 'She didn't know I was there. I saw her look at you for an hour before you awoke.' She paused. 'You are fortunate to be so loved.'

Luke felt the familiar pang of guilt. He took his eyes from hers and began to busy himself with his bow.

'So, it is unrequited,' she said quietly and looked back to her front. 'A pity.' She kicked her horse to catch up with the others and Luke was left feeling only shame.

They had reached the bottom of the mountain now and a green valley stretched out before them, steep-sided and with a broad path at its base. Immediately they broke into a canter and Luke had to pull Eskalon back to prevent him from overtaking the others. He looked behind him. There was no sign of pursuit and he wondered how much time the assassins' deceit had bought them. At least the seven of them would be fast. The Varangians rode well and Shulen had been raised in the saddle. Khan-zada, meanwhile, looked as if she had the same control of her horse as she did over everything else.

We might just do it.

The valley led into another and the mountains on either side were falling to foothills when they saw the royal road beneath them. It was evening and the slope to their right was straddled with the long shadows of rocks scattered across its surface like embers. The horses were tired from hours without rest and their manes hung limp against their necks. They could not go much further.

The assassin, still leading, reined in his horse. 'The yam is a mile beyond the place we will join the road. I will go on alone from here. Wait until dark and then ride to join me.'

Khan-zada nodded and the man rode on down the slope.

Luke watched him go and then looked left and right along the road. It was empty. He looked at the desert beyond and saw only birds circling, black specks against a red sky. The late sun had turned the flat land into a sheet of bronze that waited, pulsing, for the cool of night. Then he saw a black shape by the side of the road. 'What is that?' he asked, pointing.

Khan-zada looked up from studying the map. 'It's a horse,' she replied. 'A dead horse.'

She went back to her map, then decided that more

explanation might be required. 'It's a courier's horse. Anyone carrying a paizi is permitted to take any horse from any person along the road if he is on Temur's business. Even members of the royal family must give up their horses. So the couriers leave their horses to die by the side of the road. It is quite usual.'

Nikolas whistled softly, looking at Luke and then Eskalon. 'We certainly needed that paizi.'

'Temur is obsessed with many things but most of all fresh news,' she continued. 'So our postal service, our *shuudan*, is the fastest in the world. It helps him rule.'

They dismounted and sat on the ground and stayed there watching the sun fall behind the hills, each occupied by their own tired thoughts. They'd given what water they had to the horses, which drank noisily and scraped their noses along the sand looking for grass. When it was nearly dark, they rose and remounted and walked down to the road and along it until the dark outline of the yam came into sight. It was a small, squat building of stone with a low chimney and beside it was a longer one that would be the stable. As they approached, they could see a light shining from within.

'Wait here,' said Luke, pulling up his horse. He'd unstrapped his bow from the saddle. 'Matthew, if it's a trap, take everyone back to the hills and find another way east.'

Shulen spoke. 'I will come with you.'

Luke looked at her and remembered Khan-zada's words. He spoke gently. 'No you won't. You will stay with Khan-zada and the others. They need you.'

Shulen began to answer but the Princess had ridden up and taken her bridle. 'Stay with us,' she said softly. 'He will be safe.'

Luke rode forward to the building and dismounted. There was no sound from within the walls. He walked up to the door with his bow, arrow pointed to the front. Slowly, using the tip of the arrow, he pushed the door open.

The assassin was seated by the fire with an old man at his feet. There was a pool of blood around the man's head and his throat was open.

'He's dead,' he said. He was turning the blade of a long knife in the firelight.

'You had to kill him?'

The man turned. His face was empty of emotion. 'It is what I do,' he said simply.

Luke stood awhile looking into the coldest eyes he'd ever seen. Then he nodded slowly and turned back to the door.

'You are the strongest of them,' said the man to his back. 'You will have to do such things if you are to survive. We are not so different, you and I. Here, take the paizi.'

Ten minutes later, they were riding different horses away from the staging post. All except Luke who was still on Eskalon and now had the paizi hanging from his neck. The assassin stood by the door to watch them go and Luke was glad to leave him behind.

As he rode, he lifted the paizi in his hand to examine it. On one side were engraved the three circles of Temur's kingdoms on earth and on the other, the outline of a fish. He pondered this. Was it, perhaps, the boast that Tamerlane laid claim to the oceans as well?

Night had fallen and for once they were thankful that the moon was only half full. It was cold and they had put on extra clothes, the Princess wearing a fur-lined hood which all but concealed her face. It was too dark to travel fast on the road and they ate a meal of bread and cheese as they bumped their way east, their horses' ears alert to the sounds of the night.

By dawn, half of them were asleep in their saddles, slumped over their horses' necks like sacks of grain; Arcadius was snoring loudly. Only Luke, Khan-zada and Shulen were awake and riding together at the front. They had not spoken for hours and Luke had slept a short while and dreamt of three Magi going west.

Now he broke the silence. 'Highness, does Temur know nothing of what his son is doing in Sultaniya?'

Khan-zada lowered the hood from her head. The sun had yet to rise before them but the night's cold was in retreat and the glow on the horizon gave the promise of warmth to come. She had removed the birds from her hair and it tumbled out like a rich carpet.

'He knows some of it,' she replied. 'But Sultaniya is a long way from Samarcand and anyone who might speak against Miran Shah is either dead or too frightened to do so. Besides, Temur is unpredictable and could easily turn on the person who told him.' She paused and smiled at him. 'We shall see.'

There was a grunt from behind them and Luke turned to see Arcadius, still snoring, slipping slowly from his horse. Luke wheeled round and pulled him up into his saddle by the collar. He looked at his friend's face, still asleep. In the half-light of the moon, he looked haggard with deep lines under his eyes. He hadn't spoken at all since leaving the yam and Luke wondered if he was sickening again. He rode back to join Khan-zada.

'Did he hurt you?' Shulen was asking the Princess as he rejoined them.

Khan-zada shook her head. 'No. But he might have soon. There was a feast. It lasted a week. He had a dish served that was first a huge horse, roasted with chestnuts and herbs. Then it was cut open and there was an antelope inside. Then the antelope was opened to reveal a calf, and inside that was a hare. He was drunk and began talking about serving up a woman slave in this way, with her foetus still within. I was disgusted and left the tent. Afterwards he was angry and I thought he might hurt me.'

Luke and Shulen looked at one another in horror.

'So you see, he is truly mad. And someone has to tell Temur.'

There was a flash of colour over the hills ahead, a thin line of cadmium that hooped quickly into a crescent and flung rays into the sky, transforming it instantly to indigo. They stopped.

'Now *that* is alchemy,' murmured Khan-zada, her face aglow. She turned to Shulen. 'Is it not?'

Shulen was looking at her with something unreadable in her eyes. '"The alchemy of souls . . . the transmutation of the mortal into the immortal." That's what you said, highness. Is it possible?'

'Immortality?' she smiled. 'Perhaps. Hasan-i Sabbah thought so.'

The road they followed was wide enough to fit half a dozen horses abreast. It followed the contour of the foothills of the Alburz Mountains so that on their left a steep slope of stone and shale rose above them and on their right the vast desert of Kavir stretched out to infinity. The cold of the night fled the instant that the sun rose and soon they were removing clothes as they rode, folding them flat to put between them and their saddles. No one spoke except Luke who, as was his custom, spoke quietly to Eskalon.

Soon the sun was high in the sky and the ground under their horses hooves seemed to beat beneath its heat. The desert beside them was a lifeless thing, its only movement the spirals of sand and scree that would rise and turn and fall back to earth. Its cracked surface spread out to a horizon blurred by distance and mirage and desert.

Luke bade farewell to Eskalon at the next staging post. The stallion was exhausted and could barely stand, but he looked at his replacement with deep suspicion.

'Hide him,' Luke said. 'If you give him to anyone, I will come back and kill you.'

For three days they rode. For three days they felt the morning sun warm their foreheads and the evening sun their backs. For three days they ate, drank and slept in the saddle, as they'd been told they would, and only paused to shit or change horses, their paiza working every time. They sped through villages and towns called Rey and Damghan. As they went further east, the people they met were fewer and poorer and numbered hardly a man among them.

They arrived in Nishapur, a walled city of cracks and empty houses. There was scaffolding everywhere but no sound of building. The water that ran in open drains by the side of the road was foul and the air stank. They wove their way through empty streets with cloths pressed to their mouths. Luke turned to Khan-zada. 'Where are all the men?'

The Princess, veiled and erect, was staring ahead as if the answer might be written somewhere above the houses. 'Taken east,' she said quietly. 'Taken in chains to build the mosques and palaces of Samarcand and Kesh. Enslaved.'

'Don't they have men there?'

'Not enough to put Temur's dreams into stone. He is making buildings bigger than anything the world has yet seen.'

She paused to pat the neck of her horse that had been startled by a flea-bitten dog. 'He wants them finished before he dies.'

Luke thought of a man with unimaginable power who still feared the neglect of future generations. He thought of a man born in a tent who knew that immortality lay in stone.

'I have seen his Summer Palace in Kesh,' she continued. 'The Ak Serai. It is magnificent and larger than anything you could ever imagine. Numberless rooms and a garden for every hour of the day. Do you know what is written above its gate?'

Luke was silent.

'"Let he who doubts my power, look upon my buildings."' She laughed then, a joyless sound, muffled by silk. 'And do you want to know the irony?' she whispered. 'They have no foundations!'

'No foundations?'

Khan-zada shook her head. 'No foundations. The man tasked with their completion is my cousin. He told me that the architects are working to an impossible timetable. They are so terrified they will not finish in time that they have built without foundations. The buildings will fall down in ten years. They had better hope that either he or they will be dead by then.'

They had reached a square where a pitiful fountain dribbled water from its spout. There were people here setting up market stalls but the produce displayed on them was thin.

'You could say', she went on, looking around her, 'that these are the lucky ones. Temur killed millions when he led his hordes this way. Ten years ago, these cities were emptied. Now they've been filled with widows and orphans from the devastated lands around.'

They left the city as fast as they could. It was a day's ride to Mashhad and Luke wanted to reach it before dark. It would be their last staging post before the Kara Kum desert and they would need to change their horses for camels to cross it.

So far, they'd seen nothing of their pursuers. They had no way of knowing how much time had been bought for them by the assassins, but it was unlikely that they'd been able to travel faster than the Varangians. Luke supposed they must be fewer by now, limited by the horses left for them at the various staging posts. He prayed none were on Eskalon.

The camels would present a problem. They couldn't cross the desert without them but anyone chasing them on horseback would catch up with them in hours. And, of course, their pursuers didn't need to cross the desert. It was time to confront these creatures of Miran Shah.

They left Mashhad at dawn in possession of a long wagon. After the horses, the camels' rolling gait seemed slow.

'Don't they go any faster?' asked Nikolas, his hand between his bottom and the cushion on which he sat.

Matthew said: 'I had no idea you were so keen to get to Tamerlane.'

The four Varangians were silent after that, each thinking of what was to come. Their task was to persuade the most dangerous man on earth to do what he didn't want to do: to come west. It seemed impossible that they'd survive such a task. Luke rode behind his three friends, watching them sway like drunks at a wedding. At least he'd come near to being a man of the steppe, while they were still fair-haired giants from the west, as alien to Tamerlane as mercy.

They came down through the mountains late in the afternoon, the black sands of the Kara Kum spread before them like a burnt offering. By evening, they'd arrived at a narrow defile with high hills on either side. They pushed the wagon on to its side and blocked the road.

'It won't fool them, but they should be riding fast enough

for it to confuse,' said Luke, wiping his brow. 'And that may be all we need.'

'How far behind are they, do you think?' asked Matthew.

Luke shrugged. 'Who knows? But the camels have slowed us down a lot.'

'We'd better get into the hills then,' Matthew said. 'We know what to do.'

They led their camels back the way they'd come and tethered them. Luke unstrapped his sword and bow and pointed them to their positions.

They were just in time. As he was arranging his arrows beside him, Luke saw a cloud of dust rise from the foothills. Half an hour later, he heard the drumming of hooves and, soon afterwards, the jingle of harness. Then they came into view. The riders were pushing their horses hard, desperate to reach their quarry before the sands of the desert engulfed them.

There were five of them. Five men only, riding without armour or anything that would slow their pursuit, five men with swords strapped to their backs and bows by their sides. They had come so close to catching them up.

Now they saw the wagon and their horses reared up as they reined them in. Luke closed his eyes for a second's relief. None of them was Eskalon. 'All right. Let's bring them down.'

Luke aimed Torguk's bow as Nikolas and Shulen did the same. Three arrows were loosed and three horses fell, bringing their riders with them. But the men were good. They jumped from their horses as they fell and took cover behind their twisting bodies. Meanwhile the two remaining riders galloped back to find cover. The three in front let fly their arrows, forcing the Varagians to duck below their rocks. The two behind dismounted and began climbing the hillside to outflank them.

But it was all too late. The men sent by Miran Shah had expected a woman and her servants. Instead they had Varangians. The men on the hillside were halfway up when Arcadius and Matthew emerged from behind their boulders and fired into them at point-blank range. The men were dead when they fell.

Meanwhile, the three in front lay with their backs exposed, not knowing the fate of their comrades. Matthew and Arcadius had time to reload and move to positions from which they could not miss.

In a minute, it was all over. Their pursuers were no longer pursuing them and the Varangians had two new horses. Already, birds were circling above the corpses and flies humming around the arrows that protruded from their bodies. There was blood on the ground and the air smelt of death. Only the desert now lay between them and Bokhara. And beyond Bokhara lay Samarcand.

But the desert ahead was three hundred miles of scalding desolation, with few staging posts and fewer oases. Travelling as fast as they were able with camels, it would take at least two weeks to cross. Luke knew that it would be their greatest challenge yet. He looked over at Arcadius, who had sat down on the ground, staring at it. His friend was sickening.

'We stop and rest here. And tonight we cook.'

CHAPTER SIXTEEN

DESERT OF KARA KUM, SUMMER 1399

Their mistake was not leaving immediately to journey on through the night.

In Mashhad, they'd bought tents to shield them from the sun and Khan-zada had warned them of the merciless heat of the Kara Kum; they should travel at night and sleep through the day. But Luke had judged Arcadius too tired to go on. So they left at dawn, the twelve humps of their six camels undulating down the last slope of the Alburz Mountains like a lumpen snake, the two horses behind. An hour later they were out in the fractured hinterland of the desert, watching lizards disappear before them and tufts of brittle grass fade to nothing. Then there was sand and stone and more sand.

At first the land was flat and hard and their camels stepped with measured ease amongst the rocks and the ride was not without comfort. But soon the landscape around them began to rise into dunes, carved to arabesques by the wind. By mid-morning, the heat was unbearable, the leather of their saddles too hot to touch. The sun above them was a pulsing furnace, different from the one that had risen that morning. This was a malignant force, a purveyor of death not a giver of life.

Luke saw Arcadius hunched over his camel's hump and called a halt. 'We'll put up the tents while we still can and rest. We move on at dusk.'

They slept fitfully in heat that was searing even in shadow. The camels sat together and yawned and grunted as they chewed their oats and Arcadius mumbled and groaned in his half-sleep. As the sun went down, they rose and ate and took down the tents and soon were on their way under a generous moon and the first pinpricks of stars.

They rode all night and grew dizzy watching the vast canvas of the heavens, connecting the stars into shapes they recognised, trying to pull patterns from the scatterings between. They didn't speak because their voices were too thin and their messages too feeble to intrude upon such majesty. Even their camels, heads high beneath the moon, confined themselves to the sounds of movement and defecation.

And as Venus rose to lead them into morning, Luke heard a faint tune. It was Khan-zada singing and her song was a sad one, a plaintive caress offered to her fellow riders that made them think of home and of loss. Luke thought of Anna and Shulen thought of Luke. But Khan-zada's song was to one who was long dead: Jahangir, whom she'd loved more than life itself.

The days and nights joined head to tail like the camels beneath them. They rose at sundown and walked or rode until dawn, when they stopped to eat and then sleep. Except that they never really slept. The heat was too great for anything more than a sort of delirium, a hybrid state between the conscious and unconscious in which they cried out to no one of things buried deep.

All the time, Arcadius grew worse. He hardly spoke at all

now and rode with his shoulders slumped, staring at the hump before him. Matthew and Nikolas took position either side of him to make sure he didn't fall. In the mornings, it became more and more difficult to persuade him to continue. His friends glanced at each other, worry in their eyes.

They travelled for a week before they came to Merv, once the largest city on earth. It had made the mistake of opening its gates to Tule, son of Genghis, who had butchered the population nearly two hundred years past. The city was a place of ghosts and Khan-zada hurried them through.

A week later, they had entered and left Chardzhou and had crossed the Amu Darya River, which the Greeks had called the Oxus, and were only days from reaching Bokhara. But Arcadius had got much worse. He was beset by tremors and headaches and would eat nothing. It was dusk when the camels put their heads into the sand.

Luke said: 'I've seen this before.'

The sandstorm was on them before they'd had time to secure the tents, the scream of the wind rushing towards them like an army of howling dead. It hit them hard and they bent double from its impact, their feet stamping for footholds. Luke had taken Shulen's hand and Matthew was trying to shield Khan-zada, his big back to the storm. Only the camels seemed likely to withstand the onslaught.

'We need to find cover!' yelled Matthew into Luke's ear.

'Yes, but where?'

'No,' shouted Khan-zada from behind, 'we must keep moving. There's no shelter and if we stay here we'll be buried alive.'

It seemed impossible but they had to do it. Staggering headfirst into the chaos, Matthew and Luke half carrying Arcadius, they led their camels and horses in a direction they hoped was east. The sand stung every part of their bodies, drilling their heads and shoulders and filling their eyes and ears and every fold of their garments. They could see nothing but the dim outlines of camel and man ahead and could hear only the roar of the storm and the snap of their garments. At last they could go no further and sat huddled behind their camels, closing their eyes against the raging world outside.

The storm continued through the night and most of the next day, and when it was over, they were buried in sand and numb with exhaustion. It had finished as suddenly as it had begun. A giant hole had opened in the ground and sucked the wind back into hell. The Varangians began to dig their way out of the sand. Luke saw that Arcadius hadn't moved.

'Matthew, help me.'

They rose and staggered over to their friend, pulling the sand from his hunched frame. His back was rising and falling. He was breathing.

Matthew lay back. 'Thank God.'

Luke lifted Arcadius's head. His face was a mask of sand, his eyes closed. He gently wiped the sand away with his sleeve. 'Arcadius?'

One eye opened. It gained focus, blinking, and recognition came into it. Arcadius smiled slowly. 'Can I have some water?'

Luke's skin was already in his hand. He lifted it to his friend's lips. 'Here. Drink.'

Arcadius drank and then let his head fall back against Luke's chest. He was already asleep. Luke lowered him slowly to the ground and rose. He walked over to sit with Shulen. 'I don't know if Arcadius can do much more.'

Khan-zada rose and came to sit next to them. She took a

small flask from her cloak. 'Give him this. It will help him go on. For a time.'

Luke took the flask and got up. He looked beyond his friends to where he expected the camels to be. Four of their six camels had gone, and both of the horses.

Nikolas said: 'It must have happened during the storm.'

Luke shook his head. 'They could be miles away by now, in any direction.'

'What were they carrying?' asked Shulen.

'That's the bad news,' said Nikolas. 'All of the food and most of the water.'

Matthew rose and went to stand by Luke. 'What are we going to live on?'

'Food is not the problem. We can kill a camel if we have to. It's the water. How much do we have left?'

Not much. Two skins, half-full, between six of them.

'How far are we from Bokhara?' asked Nikolas. 'It can't be too far.'

'If we knew where we were,' said Khan-zada, 'it would be no more than two days away. We could get there on the water we have. But the storm has forced us from the road. We don't know which way to go.' She glanced at Arcadius. 'And we have a sick friend.'

Luke had produced Ibn Khaldun's map and laid it flat on the ground. He pointed to a black square on it. 'The oasis at Bokhara is large, is it not? So a wide area around the city will be cultivated, with many villages. Even if we can't get back to the road, if we head north-east, we should get to it. We can use the stars.'

But Khan-zada was shaking her head. 'There will be no stars,' she said quietly. 'A storm such as that throws too much into the sky. It will be overcast for days.'

They were all silent for a long while, sitting in a circle in the sand. The storm had left their throats dry but no one mentioned water. Luke looked up at the leaden sky and then at the vast sea around them. There was nothing there: no hill, no tree, no blade of grass; nothing but mile after mile of black sand. And night was coming. Black on black.

'Well, we can't stay here,' he said, getting to his feet. 'The wind came from the east and I remember which direction that was. We need to move.'

Drinking a cup of water each, they tightened the remaining two camels' loads and wrapped themselves against the night cold. Luke and Khan-zada woke Arcadius and gave him water. Arcadius rose, as if in a trance, and allowed himself to be supported by Matthew and Nikolas. They put him on to one of the camels and each held an ankle either side.

They set off but the going was much harder than it had been. The sand off the road was deep and every footstep an effort. Even the camels stumbled and sank to their haunches in drifts. Later, when it was dark and there were no stars to watch over them, Luke and Shulen walked side by side.

'We can't do this, can we?' she asked quietly. 'We cannot reach Bokhara before the water runs out, can we?'

Luke said nothing. If they knew the direction to travel, then it was just possible. But they didn't. He felt her hand slide into his.

'Well, there's no one I'd rather die with,' she said.

They walked for some time in silence then, comforted by each other and the darkness around them. It was inconceivable that they could still be heading in the right direction but there was some small solace in knowing they could do nothing about it.

'If only we had a fish,' Shulen murmured.

'A fish? Why are you suddenly so particular about what you eat? Won't camel do?'

She laughed softly. 'Not that sort of fish. A lodestone.'

'A lodestone? What's a lodestone?'

'I heard of it in Konya. The Arabs call it *al-konbas.* It's a piece of metal which has special properties. If you rub a needle against it, and float the needle in water, it will point to the south.'

Luke had stopped and was staring at her in the dark. He let go of her hand.

'Why is it called a fish, Shulen?'

He heard the rustle of shoulders shrugging. 'I don't know. Perhaps the lodestone was made in the shape of a fish?'

Luke's heart was beating fast. He felt inside his thoub to where the paizi lay heavy against his chest. 'Shulen, do you have a needle?'

She was very still. 'Why? Do you have a lodestone?'

'Perhaps.' He was trying to keep his voice calm. He brought the chain of the paizi up over his head. The fish was face-up in his hand, invisible to all. 'And a candle and bowl. Do you have those?'

Khan-zada had heard them. She approached Luke and pulled something from her hair. 'Here is your needle.'

Then Shulen went to her camel's side. Her camel had been one of the two that had stayed and her baggage contained a candle and a bowl: the stuff of healing. She lit the candle and, placing the bowl on the ground, poured the precious water into it. Matthew and Nikolas had come up and the five of them knelt around it as if in prayer.

Luke turned the paizi over to show them the fish in the light of the candle. 'It would make sense, wouldn't it? I mean this must happen to couriers all the time.'

He rubbed the needle against the fish and carefully placed it into the water. Immediately it began to turn. Then it stopped. Luke gave a sigh of relief.

'I think we have our south,' he said softly.

The two women rode on a camel from then on, the bowl held by one, the candle by the other. They were two high priestesses bent over a sliver of metal, able to bestow life or death on those that followed them. Luke led them, while Matthew and Nikolas walked on either side of Arcadius, who was slumped over the second camel.

Well after the grey dawn had crept up around them, they were still moving, knowing that to stop was to risk not starting again. They had all drunk another cup and one of the skins was empty. The sky was overcast. Luke brought his camel next to the one carrying Arcadius. The big body of his friend was hardly moving.

He looked at Matthew. 'I am going to suggest we take a gamble.'

Luke turned to the two women still hunched over their little altar behind. They had erected a clumsy awning above them to shield them. He said: 'I'm sure that we strayed south in the storm. So if we aim off a bit to the north, we must hit the road.'

It made sense. The road, even covered by sand, would be faster than the open desert. They had hardly any water left and Arcadius was dying.

Shulen glanced at Arcadius and nodded. Her throat was parched and sore from the sand that she'd swallowed in the storm. She could no longer speak without pain. She looked into the bowl and pointed out their new course.

It was only an hour later that Nikolas, now in front, let out a cracked shout. His feet had made contact with something hard. They'd found the road.

They stopped to rest there, knowing that sleep would more likely come with the relief. They put up their tents and drank a single gulp of water each. Arcadius was lowered from his camel and helped to drink his. Then they lay back and tried not to think of their thirst. None of them spoke.

By evening and the time to leave, the thirst was tormenting them. There were perhaps two cups for each remaining in the skin and they did not know how far they still had to go to reach Bokhara. There was no food but it didn't matter. None of them wanted to eat for to do so would worsen their thirst. Luke sat in the sand and felt empty of strength. His head spun and there were dots in front of his eyes. He was staring at the belly of the women's camel and thinking of the water inside.

'No,' whispered Khan-zada from above. 'It will kill you.'

He squinted up at her and noticed that the pale disc of the new moon hovered above her like a halo. It was behind cloud and it was faint but it was there. It meant hope. Was the sky clearing?

He put a hand on the ground and slowly pushed himself to his feet. His three friends were still sitting and he went over to them. Two of them were staring ahead without seeing. Arcadius was lying on his back, shivering as if from a fever. Very gently, the three of them lifted their friend on to the camel.

With the veiled moon above them, they should have been able to travel faster that night. The desert around them now had substance and they could even see the outlines of dunes. But they were tired and weak and their stomachs raged with the pain of emptiness and their swollen throats made each swallow a thing of agony. Every step they took was like ten.

And Arcadius was dying.

Luke was out at the front, still leading the camel on which the two women sat above the compass. He heard a thud behind him. He stopped and turned.

Arcadius was lying on the ground with Matthew and Nikolas kneeling on either side of him. Luke dropped the rope and staggered over to them.

'What happened?'

Nikolas was shaking his head. 'I'm sorry. I fell asleep.'

Luke knelt. He looked down into Arcadius's face. It was without movement. He gently lifted his head and tried to pour water into his friend's mouth but the lips wouldn't open. He turned to Matthew. 'I think he's finished,' he whispered. He felt the tears pricking his eyeballs. 'He won't drink.'

Khan-zada and Shulen had dismounted and were now kneeling beside Luke. Shulen put her hand over his. She leant forward to look into Arcadius's face. 'It's too dark to see if he's breathing.'

Then, in an instant, it wasn't.

Arcadius's face had turned to silver and his friends looked down at its peace and then above to the sky. There were a million, million stars in a heaven that was suddenly clear. There were more stars than they'd ever seen and, sitting back on their haunches, they stared up at them.

Luke turned back to Arcadius. His friend's eyes were open.

'I'm sorry,' Arcadius said.

Luke gazed into eyes that still trusted him, eyes that knew they were looking at their final night. Tears ran down his cheeks.

Then Khan-zada was next to him. She whispered into his ear. 'Luke, look.'

He turned. She was pointing at a star brighter than the others. 'Venus,' he whispered. 'Kervan Kiran, the morning star. Arcadius, do you see it?'

But Arcadius's eyes had closed.

'No,' whispered the Princess, 'not Venus. It's the wrong direction. It's the Kalyan Minaret. It's a beacon.'

'A beacon?'

'Yes, Luke, a beacon to guide travellers into Bokhara. We have arrived.'

CHAPTER SEVENTEEN

BOKHARA, SUMMER 1399

Bokhara the Holy, with a mosque for every day of the year; Bokhara the Magnificent, second city in Temur's empire; Bokhara the giver of life, where the Prophet Job had struck his rod into the dusty ground and brought forth water.

Bokhara: the giver of life.

The Kalyan Minaret, taller than any building in the world, had, over the centuries, rescued many travellers from the desert to its west. By day, it looked down on a bulbous seascape tiled in azure and majolica and from its giddy heights muezzins fanned the flame of the city's faith. By night, it was a lighthouse.

And, like those it brought in from the desert, it was a survivor. Even Genghis Khan had spared it before trampling the pages of the Koran into the sand of the mosque beside it. Now Luke stared up at it in wonder.

It was the morning after they'd reached the city and the time in between had been spent in the deepest sleep that he could remember. They had almost crawled through the city gates and only Khan-zada, her head held high, was able to give the command that they should be taken to the Ark citadel immediately and given rooms, food and water.

Arcadius had been lifted gently from his camel and carried before them through the streets to the citadel. It was the hour after dawn and they were full of people who'd parted to let pass a man either dead or near to it. Behind him strode a woman, unveiled, recognised by some who nudged their friends to make their reverences. On one side of her was a tall, fair man with a paizi around his neck, on the other a thin beauty dressed as a man. Behind staggered two giants. It was a curious party.

The Ark citadel was a town within a city. It was a jumble of palaces, offices and mosques behind thick, sloping walls which stood like vast ochre teeth in the centre of a sanded *registan* where executions took place to drumbeats, markets rang with merchants' prices and teeth were pulled for two dirhams a tooth, or one if people could watch. Within the Ark was a hospital and it was there that Arcadius had been taken, his face ashen and his limbs without movement. He was little changed when Luke visited him the next morning. If anything, he was greyer. Luke lifted his feeble hand from the sheets.

'I failed you,' Arcadius breathed, turning to him. 'You relied on me.'

'You didn't fail me,' said Luke. 'You lived.'

Arcadius tried to smile but he was full of anger at himself. He'd not be with them when they got to Tamerlane. 'This will be the biggest game we've played yet,' he said, frowning, 'and I won't be there to play it with you.'

Luke smiled. 'There'll be plenty still to do when you join us.' He took the paizi from around his neck. 'Here, have this. You'll need it to get to us.'

Later, the rest of them prayed in a mosque built at the place where Job had stamped his rod and which Tamerlane had venerated with a new dome. They were praying to the same God in different ways and their prayers were of entreaty. They were safe for now, but their friend was not. Afterwards they sat in a square with a fountain next to a fig tree and Luke asked the question again.

'Will he live?'

There were men in white caftans who'd come with them from the hospital to pray and who sat across from them, quietly talking. Khan-zada gestured to them.

'Luke, Bokhara was the home of Ibn Sina, the greatest healer the world has ever seen. He lived here when the Samanids ruled this city four centuries ago but the doctors still practise what he taught. Arcadius will be in good hands.'

Luke looked from Khan-zada to Shulen. The women were curiously alike. Both were healers, intrigued by the alchemy of plants and oils, who'd themselves performed a curious alchemy over the past weeks. He stood. 'I'll see to the camels,' he said. 'Highness, can we send someone with a paizi back to fetch Eskalon?'

But Eskalon was already on his way.

Three Varangians, Shulen and Princess Khan-zada left Bokhara at dawn the next day, taking the road east to Samarcand. The country they rode through was Mawarannahr, the land beyond the river, a rich and fertile place full of beauty, human and otherwise. It was here that another Greek had come long ago to choose Roxanna for his wife. They rode on horses that Khan-zada had commandeered from the imperial stables, just as she'd taken clothes for herself and Shulen from the imperial wardrobes. She was, after all, Temur's daughter-in-law.

They rode down the valley of the Zarafshan, a route lined

with silver poplars beyond which stretched citrus orchards and vineyards and fields where row upon row of cotton fleece hung like iced breath amidst women bent beneath bales. It was land that drank water fed by channels, and wheels pulled by camels; a land of mixed bounty, where cattle meandered next to goats and Karakul sheep, whose infant lambs had the best wool in the world. It was a land of roadside stalls selling gigantic melons, striped like a Venetian's hose; a land of mud-baked villages and grape-juice sellers and boys with sticks; a land of turbaned men atop donkeys, legs spread out like oars. It was a land of vigour.

The road was a good one, their horses fast, and it was early evening when they came to Samarcand. Ibn Khaldun had called it the 'Mirror of the World'. But when Khan-zada reined in her mare to gaze at its beauty afloat in a distant wash of gold and blue, she murmured: 'Behold, the Garden of the Soul.'

Luke, his two friends and Shulen reined in their horses next to her and stood silent in wonder. Enormous domes, towers and minarets soared above a distant mantle of green like a magician's crown.

'Where's the army?' asked Nikolas.

Luke exchanged glances with Matthew. 'If it's not here, then it's somewhere else. My guess would be on the road to China.'

They rode on, marvelling at the scale of the city they were approaching, bigger than anything they'd ever seen. As they drew closer, they saw that it was ringed by immense gardens.

'They say he rarely goes into the city these days,' said Khan-zada as she rode up beside Luke. 'And when he does it's to throw meat and money to the masons building his wife Bibi Khanum's mosque.'

'The one without foundations?'

'Indeed,' smiled the Princess, turning to him. 'Temur belongs to the steppe. He prowls around the city, moving from garden to garden as if not trusting to touch the monuments he's creating. I'm told he's currently holding court in the Garden of Heart's Delight, which is just outside Cairo.'

'Cairo?'

'He's given all the new suburbs the names of the greatest cities on earth to prove that Samarcand is the greatest of them all. So we have Cairo, Baghdad, Damascus, Sultaniya and Delhi.'

'And is it the greatest?'

'When it's finally finished, perhaps. It's certainly had the finest artists brought in to work on it. Here you'll find the world's best architects, masons, glaziers, scientists, astronomers, calligraphers, silk-weavers . . .' She ticked them off on her fingers, one by one.

They had come to the top of a rise and beyond it was an immense walled garden with a small city of tents within it. Around the tents were meadows and trees and water with animals in between. The scent of flowers wafted up to meet them. They were looking into the Garden of Eden.

Khan-zada was pointing. 'That's Temur's tent,' she said, indicating a pavilion in the centre that was built as a castle, with turrets and battlements of silk. To either side of its entrance stood caparisoned and painted elephants with towers on their backs. 'They say he has three obsessions these days: China, Samarcand and those elephants. He got them from Delhi. He loves each and every one of them.'

Luke looked at her, remembering something. 'Tell us about Delhi.'

'Delhi?' said Khan-zada quietly. 'It was very terrible. More than a million slaughtered.'

The shock took his breath away. It was an unimaginable number. '*A million?*'

'So I'm told,' she replied. 'Temur marched an army of a hundred thousand over the mountains and up to the gates of Delhi. Nasir ud-din brought out his elephants, ninety of them with poisoned scimitars on their tusks and flame-throwers on their backs. Do you know what Temur did? He had his men dig trenches and tethered camels to the front of them with dried grass on their backs. When the elephants charged, Temur's men set light to the camels' backs and the animals rushed forward in their panic. The elephants were terrified. They turned and charged back into the Indian troops, trampling them. The battle was won.'

'What happened then?' asked Matthew.

'He entered the city in triumph and the elephants were made to kneel before him and he chose thirty for his army. Then he stayed in the city to celebrate his victory with an enormous banquet, leaving orders that his army be left out on the plain.' She paused. 'But there was an incident. His wives wished to see the city and had left the gates open. Some of Temur's army entered and began to loot. Then the whole Mongol army rushed in and so began three days of murder, rape and destruction.'

The Varangians looked down on a paradise that held, within it, a man more terrifying than any they'd heard of. None of them could find anything to say. So Khan-zada continued, nodding towards the crowds of people moving between the elephant sentinels: 'He's holding audience. We should go down and make ourselves known.'

The Varangians rode behind Khan-zada and Shulen. They were dressed as gazis and held pennanted spears aloft as would a bodyguard. Khan-zada wore a tunic of dazzling silver and had a gold band around her head while Shulen was dressed in blood-red. They looked a magnificent pair.

When they reached the gate of the garden, Khan-zada called out to the men guarding it: 'I am the Princess Khan-zada and I wish to see my father-in-law immediately.' She removed a ring from her finger and gave it to their captain. The man took it, bowed and disappeared. Luke wondered if his friends' hearts were tapping out the same frenzied tempo as his own. He wiped the palms of his hands on his deel.

Nikolas, who was by his side, whispered: 'I've just remembered something: the omen.'

'What omen?' whispered Matthew, who was on Luke's other side.

'That Temur was born with blood in his hands. Did you know that?'

Luke, looking directly ahead, whispered: 'How exactly does it help us to mention that now, Nikki?'

The Varangian shrugged. 'I just thought of it, that's all.'

Khan-zada and Shulen were looking up at the elephants. Their faces were painted in stripes of green and henna and their eyes had crude eyelashes etched like sunrises into their foreheads. They looked like elephant courtesans. The towers on their backs were of intricately carved wood and had velvet draped from their sides. Inside them musicians played.

After some time, the captain returned. He was a handsome man, now out of breath. 'The Emir is seeing the ambassadors from China and Castile, highness. He asks that you enter and await his pleasure. Your guard and the woman will remain here.'

'No, they will accompany me,' Khan-zada said in a voice that did not expect the conversation to continue. She dismounted and handed her reins to a guard. 'My guard will deliver their weapons to you and they will enter the garden behind me.'

The captain glanced at the three Varangians, seeing their long, fair hair above gazi clothes. His eyes travelled down to Luke's sword and then back to Khan-zada. 'Of course, highness.'

They walked through the gate and into the garden and soon were within the maze of lesser tents that surrounded Tamerlane's. Khan-zada walked fast, her head erect, ignoring the stares and bows of the men they passed. Then they entered Tamerlane's tent.

Inside was a universe of silk which stretched around them in imitation of the world outside. Above, it was a summer's day with feathered clouds spread across an acre of blue silk. Holding it up were tent poles the size of trees and painted as such, with green foliage spreading at their tops to support the weight of the ceiling. The tent was filled with Mongols and they parted to let Khan-zada and Shulen pass, bowing deeply as they did so. The men were short and broad and their narrow eyes narrowed further to study the tall, fair strangers that came behind.

Khan-zada led them through to the other side where the tent opened on to a garden of fruit trees and shade amidst which walked deer, peacocks and pheasants. There was a pool at its centre where lotus leaves stroked the water's surface. Carpets were spread out by its banks on which women lay against cushions. A gentle slope rose on the other side and at its top stood a wooden dais surrounded by richly dressed men and a group of boys of various ages. The dais was of carved mulberry wood and had a low rail around its sides. It was empty save for some cushions and a folding lectern bearing an open Koran. Above it was a canopy of white silk, held up by tasselled poles, on which inscriptions had been painted in the shape of birds around a ship in sail. In front of it, on a low table, was a chessboard.

Khan-zada led them to the shade of a tree where they could see without being seen. 'He has yet to arrive,' she whispered. 'But his family is here. The women on the carpets are his wives and sisters. The man next to the throne is Shahrukh, his third son who was born during a game of chess. His name means "king-knight".'

Luke looked at the chessboard. Its pieces were made of jade and exquisitely carved but there were too many of them. 'What sort of chess does he play?'

'His own kind. He's invented a new version which he calls "the Great Game". It's played with more pieces over a hundred squares. He plays it with my sons.'

'Which are your sons?'

'Next to Shahrukh.' She was pointing. 'That is Mohammed Sultan and that Pir Mohammed. Are they not handsome?'

Luke looked at the brothers. They were certainly handsome. They wore richly embroidered deels that ended above boots of red leather. Jewelled swords hung low by their sides, their scabbard tips resting on the ground. Both were bearded and had long ponytails. Mohammed Sultan was the taller and had the bearing of one who expected to rule. He held his head high like his mother.

Luke saw several younger versions beside them looking up with reverence. 'And the boys beside them, who are they?'

'His great-grandsons. The younger ones he lets read the messages from the ambassadors. You will see.'

'Who are the other men?' he asked. 'The men around the throne?'

Khan-zada raised herself on tiptoe to take them all in. Then she spoke: 'The one in the green turban is Mir Sayid Barakah, Temur's spiritual adviser; on his right is his greatest general Burunduk and beside him the genius Omar Aqta. He is the court calligrapher and five years ago he set all of the Koran on to a signet ring and gave it to Temur. Is that not wonderful? The others are astronomers, scholars, generals and viziers. I forget their names.'

Luke touched the ring on his own finger, feeling the tiny indentation of script beneath his thumb. He wondered again why Plethon had given it to him.

A silence fell upon the garden broken only by the peacocks. Heads had turned towards the other side of the garden where another tent opened on to it. Then there were two drumbeats and everyone fell to their knees.

Eight men of identical height appeared carrying between them a carpet. On it sat an old man and, beside him, a monumental turban. The garden had gone very still and the carpet seemed to float the distance to the throne. Then, on a nod, the old man was lowered on to the dais and the cushions, lectern and turban set beside him.

Temur, Sword of Islam, Lord of the Celestial Conjunction, Conqueror of the World, was among them.

Tamerlane.

At last.

Luke stared at the man. He stared at a face that was scarred by time and battle and burnt by countless seasons. He looked into cold, milky eyes, half-closed beneath eyebrows thickened with paint, which stared straight ahead of him. He looked at a beard that was cut short and streaked with grey and stood proud from a neck knotted with ancient muscle. He looked at shoulders that were broad, at immense forearms, spotted with age, that bulged forth from his tunic. Here, before him, was the terror of the world and he was old and nearly blind.

Tamerlane lay back against the cushions, his hands folded at his groin. On his fingers were rings, one larger than the rest.

'Is he blind?' whispered Luke.

Khan-zada nodded. 'Almost. But you'll see him look often at that ring. When it clouds, he believes that the man before him is telling lies.'

Luke looked at the ring, a colossal amethyst that rested in Tamerlane's lap like a giant tear.

Tamerlane was dressed in a long belted tunic with short sleeves and peacock fans traced in silk across its red surface. He wore a cloak swept over his shoulders that was clasped at the neck with the three circles of his earthly kingdoms worked in gold. On his head was a domed crown from which sprang a horsetail fashioned out of strands of silk.

Nikolas let out a low whistle. 'Look at the size of that ruby.' He was looking at the jewel set into the turban beside Tamerlane.

Khan-zada whispered: 'It's from the King of Ceylon, the one his ancestor wouldn't sell to Kublai Khan. The turban is also his shroud. It is sixty feet long and goes everywhere with him in case he dies while travelling.'

One of the grandchildren, a boy of perhaps twelve, had walked to the front of the dais and knelt down on one knee. He opened a scroll and read. 'The ambassadors from the Sultan in Cairo and the King of Castile bring you gifts, lord.'

Temur beckoned the boy to come closer. 'And the Chinese? What does the Ming Emperor bring me?' he asked, peering at his grandson. He was smelling him too, his lips working as his nostrils dilated, an old animal testing his senses. His voice was like raked gravel, deep and dry and cracked with use.

The boy glanced at the older men beside the throne. When he spoke again, his voice was clear. 'They bring you a demand. The Ming Emperor demands that you acknowledge vassalage to him.'

For a time, no one spoke and even the peacocks seemed to wait.

Then Tamerlane laughed, a terrible sound rising from deep inside him. 'Bring all the ambassadors in.'

The gifts arrived first. A jornufa from the Sultan of Cairo, perhaps brother to Bayezid's, and an ostrich from the court of Castile, both led by grooms carrying chests. Behind them came the ambassadors in the finery of their nations, each man carried at his armpits by two guards as was the custom for all foreigners approaching the throne. The watching Mongols laughed.

'Why do they laugh?' whispered Shulen.

'Do you see that man there amongst the Spanish envoys, that one of our race who is dressed in the fashion of Castile?'

Shulen nodded.

'His name is Mohammed al-Cazi and he was sent back to Spain to learn their ways three years past. It seems he has learnt too well. He looks ridiculous.'

The ambassadors were set down in front of the throne and had begun to arrange themselves. The envoy al-Cazi was looking at the ground, his face crimson. Tamerlane was shaking his head. He grunted: 'You are all the wrong way round.' He lifted a hand, its back a mosaic of veins. 'Where are the knights Clavijo and Sotomayor from Castile?'

One of the Spaniards stepped forward and sank to his knees. He was dressed in a pourpoint of black double-cut velvet and around his neck hung a chain of gold with a unicorn at its end.

'Welcome back, Clavijo. How is my brother King Henry?'

Luke saw Tamerlane wince as he levered himself forward from his cushions to look more closely at the ambassador. He was in pain.

The Spaniard lifted his head. 'His Majesty is well and rejoices in the continued health of his brother Temur,' he replied in Turkic.

Tamerlane looked down at his ring. Then he pointed at the Spaniards. 'But you are in the wrong place, Clavijo.' He looked over to where the Chinese ambassadors stood. 'You men from the Ming? You should be behind the Spaniards. Move there.'

Before the Chinese could give each other a glance of surprise, they had been lifted again and taken to the rear of the Spaniards. One of them rose to speak.

'Down!' roared Temur, thumping the side of the dais so hard that the wood shook.

The Chinese sank to their knees and five pig-tailed heads went to the ground. The only sound was the heavy tide of Tamerlane's breathing.

'Tell your master Hongwu this,' he said through clenched teeth. 'Tell him that Temur Gurgan sets the King of little Castile above him in his estimation. Tell your Ming emperor that he is but a pawn to me, a slug. Tell him that China ceased to deserve tribute when the last of Kublai's line left the earth. Tell him that the only reason he has not been crushed yet is because I leave the easiest task to last. Tell him that my only wish is that he should live to see the shame heaped upon him by my army.'

He lowered his voice to one of hissed menace. 'And, last of all, tell your master that the only reason his ambassadors return to him with their heads on their shoulders is because Temur

Gurgan wishes them to give this message to him in person. Have you seen my army?'

A translator was working desperately to keep up with this speech and there was some delay before the Ming ambassadors were able to nod.

'Good. Now go.'

When the Chinese had been lifted from Tamerlane's presence, he turned again to Clavijo. His voice was calm. 'The ostrich pleases me better than the gyrfalcon sent by the King of Portugal. How fast does it run?'

'As fast as a horse, majesty.'

Tamerlane nodded. 'Then it can chase the Chinese army as it flees. How is my sister Catherine?'

Clavijo again lifted his head. 'Both of Their Majesties excel, lord. They wish me to convey a message with these gifts, a message which is personal to you.'

Tamerlane nodded. 'My grandson will read it to me later.'

Clavijo motioned to his colleagues and they began the process of backing away from the imperial presence without looking behind them.

'Where is my daughter Khan-zada?' asked Tamerlane.

The Princess stepped forward. She was royal, unafraid and beautiful. All the heads in the garden turned to look at her – all except one. 'I am here, lord.'

Tamerlane looked up. 'And where is your husband, the Prince Miran Shah?'

'He is in Sultaniya, majesty.'

'Does he know you are here?'

'Yes, lord.'

'And does he approve of it?'

'No, lord.'

'So why are you here?'

There was no reply.

All of this exchange had taken place in the most civil of tones. Now there was menace in the question repeated. 'Why are you here, daughter?'

Khan-zada began to walk forward, stepping past the wives on the carpets and the deer drinking from the pool, until she stood directly in front of her father-in-law, less than three feet from his dais. She spoke quietly. 'What I have to say to you, Father, is for your ears only.' She paused. 'It is not seemly that it be heard by others here.'

Tamerlane looked at her for a long time, his pupils moving around the whites of his eyes, trying to focus on her. 'If you have anything to say against my son, then all should hear it,' he said evenly. 'Let us see how my ring likes your tale.'

The Princess breathed in deeply. She lifted her head and spoke loudly and clearly. 'Your son, the Prince Miran Shah, plots against you, lord.'

Luke glanced at her two sons beside the throne. They were staring at their mother in disbelief. There was complete silence in every part of the garden.

Tamerlane's big head shook slowly from side to side and he leant back against his cushions. His voice was calm. 'My son is wayward, nothing more.' He looked down at his ring. 'It is true that he has ruled sometimes unwisely, that he has not won every battle. But revolt against his father? Against me?' He paused. 'Never.'

Khan-zada glanced at her sons. 'Will you allow me to read something to you, lord?' she asked. 'It is a letter he would have sent you had I not stopped it. May I read it?'

Tamerlane signalled for wine. He gestured to her to begin.

The Princess took a scroll from the sleeve of her tunic. It had a broken seal. She unrolled the paper, glanced once more at her sons and then read:

'"Certainly through your advanced age and weak constitution and infirmity you are now unequal to raising the standards of empire and sustaining the burdens of leadership and government, and above all things it would befit your condition to sit as a devotee in a corner of the mosque and worship your Lord, until death came to you. There are now men among your sons and grandsons who would suffice to you for ruling your subjects and armies and undertake to guard your kingdoms and territory . . ."'

'Enough!' Tamerlane had wrenched himself to his feet, one hand on the rail. He was shaking with rage. 'Give me the letter.' He thrust out his hand for it. 'He has warned me of this.' He turned to a grandson. 'Bring your uncle.'

Pir Mohammed went over to the tent from which Tamerlane had been carried. He pulled back the flap and a man appeared, walking with a stick. As he came closer, Luke could see that he was a younger version of Tamerlane but the face was etched with madness. His long hair and beard were unkempt and still streaked with dust from his ride. He had the blotched cheeks of the drunkard and blooded eyes that roved the room as if seeking a means of escape. They came to rest on Khan-zada and stayed there.

Khan-zada had started to back away. Her face was white. She hadn't imagined that her husband would beat her to Temur. She glanced at Miran Shah, then at Mohammed Sultan.

Tamerlane asked: 'Where are the Greeks?'

Khan-zada's voice was less certain now. 'The Greeks have nothing to do with this, lord.'

By now, Miran Shah was leaning on the dais, pushing hair away from his eyes in frenzied movements and staring at Khan-zada in fascination as if he'd never seen her before.

Luke stepped forward. He felt Shulen's hand on his arm. 'We are here, lord.'

Tamerlane looked up. 'Approach.'

Luke walked forward as Khan-zada had done, followed by Matthew and Nikolas. He walked past the gaze of Tamerlane's eight wives and their children, past the courtiers and grandsons and peacocks. As they approached the dais, the three Varangians stopped and men lifted them the rest of the way.

When they were on their knees, their noses sunk into the soft grass, Tamerlane spoke to them. 'Greeks, you have corrupted the ears of my daughter.'

Khan-zada was standing next to them. She said: 'Lord, look to your ring. Ask them to answer this charge and then look to your ring.'

Tamerlane turned his milky eyes to his daughter-in-law. 'They are Byzantines, daughter,' he said simply. 'I do not have to look at my ring to know that Byzantines lie. They forged this letter and they lie.'

Miran Shah laughed and hit the ground with his stick. 'All Byzantines lie. Ha!' His voice was shrill. 'They must die!'

Now Luke dared to speak. 'We are Varangians, lord,' he said, looking up. 'We've come from Kutahya. I have lived among the gazis of the Germiyan tribe and think as they do, not as a Byzantine.' He could hardly breathe for the beating of his heart. But he had nothing to lose: he was about to die. 'There is someone who can prove it, someone of the Germiyan tribe. May she speak?'

Tamerlane growled, his head sunk deep within his shoulders.

The letter was still in his hand, unread because he couldn't read and was almost blind. Mohammed Sultan approached the dais and whispered in his grandfather's ear. There was silence, another growl, and Tamerlane nodded.

Luke turned to Shulen. She had already begun to walk towards the dais. Her red dress had long flared sleeves that swept the grass as she came. Her hair shone like brushed velvet. She swept through the peacocks and pheasants to stand next to Luke. She looked down at him and then, after arranging her skirts, knelt carefully on the ground.

Tamerlane had seen only in the final stages of Shulen's approach but had heard the whisper around him. Something interesting was happening. 'Who are you?' he asked.

'Can you not see me, lord?'

There were gasps of astonishment from around the throne. No one, ever, had asked that. Tamerlane shook his head in disbelief. 'You dare to question my eyesight, girl?'

Shulen said nothing. She sat back on her haunches and stayed perfectly still.

Tamerlane spoke again. 'The Varangian says you will speak for him.'

Shulen seemed to consider this. Then she said: 'I would rather help you see.'

The silence was deafening. A thousand breaths were suspended. The world paused. Tamerlane frowned and scratched his head. 'Why do you dare to speak thus?' he asked quietly.

Shulen took a deep breath. 'Because if you could see, lord, you would know that the letter you hold was written in the hand of your son.'

Tamerlane was shaking his head in bewilderment. Shulen leant back. 'I have the means to let you see it.'

She had pulled a casket from her sleeve. It was the one found in the Venetians' baggage. She opened it and brought out something that caught the light as it turned. She waited.

'What is it?' asked Tamerlane, his beard jutting forward in the effort to see.

Shulen did not answer but instead rose and walked up to the dais. She held the object out to the man sitting there. 'Put them on, lord.'

Tamerlane leant forward to her and examined the two bits of glass joined by metal that were in his hands. Shulen had rested her knee on the front edge of the dais. 'Here, let me help you.' She took them from him in both hands and, very gently, put them on his nose.

Two enormous eyes blinked from behind the pieces of glass. Tamerlane's hands rose to adjust the metal that bridged them across his nose and fed back to behind his ears. His head was moving from side to side, his mouth agape. He was breathing deeply and quickly.

'What magic is this?' he whispered. 'What have you done?'

Shulen smiled. 'I have made you see, lord.'

Tamerlane looked down at his ring. He spread out his hand and examined his fingers, one by one.

'Are you a witch?'

Miran Shah had sprung forward. 'They send a witch to you, Father!' he cried. 'She is a witch and her potions will kill you if that thing you wear doesn't. Give her to me!'

But Tamerlane was smiling now and the huge eyes were turned to Shulen, seeing her for the first time. 'These are for me?'

She bowed. 'For you, lord.'

Luke had watched this with relief. It had all gone to plan. He saw Mohammed Sultan, Tamerlane's heir, shaking his head in disbelief, a strange smile on his lips. He was staring at Shulen.

In front of them, Miran Shah was now pleading. 'Father, give her to me. I will punish her for her sorcery.'

Tamerlane stayed looking at Shulen for a long time, turning his head from side to side to take in details of her face, her dress and of the garden around. The smile remained on his face throughout. Then he turned back to his son and his voice was low. 'You will do nothing. You will place a rope around your neck and go to my tent to await my pleasure.' He lifted the letter and thrust it towards his son. 'This is your handwriting.'

Luke let out a long sigh. He looked at Mohammed Sultan. Tamerlane's heir had not taken his eyes from Shulen.

PART THREE

PERSUASION

CHAPTER EIGHTEEN

SAMARCAND, SUMMER 1399

Without Shulen, Luke, Matthew and Nikolas were removed from the Garden of Heart's Delight. Lost behind the magnified wonder of Shulen's glasses, the Conqueror of the World had immediately forgotten the Varangians' existence and it was left to his heir, Mohammed Sultan, to slip them discreetly from the tent and take them into Samarcand.

On their way into the city, they passed through the gardens of Paradise and Model of the World, through orchards and vineyards and a suburb called Delhi, until they reached a city under construction. For Luke, it was the opposite of Constantinople. The sun was setting and the workers gone, leaving behind a landscape crenellated with unfinished building, its gleaming stone fresh from the quarry, its mortar still wet to the touch. He thought of the dust that hung over Constantinople's crumbling masonry and of what Ibn Khaldun had said about the rise and fall of empires.

Not yet.

As they came into the centre of the city, riding down a wide boulevard bordered by young plane trees and palms fronting shops selling an empire's produce and pillage, the buildings turned from large to enormous, and stone became majolica. A sea of blue and gold broke over them from every direction, dome climbing on dome, minaret on minaret, and they rode on in silent stupefaction.

They were housed in a building that had been furnished for ambassadors. There were bedrooms and bathrooms and rooms with rich tapestries and pools where red apples bobbed beneath little fountains. They were given food and wine and the stuff to wash themselves and servants to attend them. But when they tried to leave, their Mongol guards shook their heads solemnly.

'We are prisoners,' said Matthew. 'I had hoped for some sightseeing.'

They spent a week seeing Samarcand from a window, watching slaves from a hundred countries toil beneath the whip to create beauty on a scale unimaginable to men born in a small city on the edge of the sea.

With nothing to do but talk, they talked and wondered what had happened to Khan-zada and Shulen. Any question they'd had about Shulen's contribution to their cause had disappeared with her performance in the Garden of Heart's Delight. She'd given Tamerlane the gift of sight and his gratitude had saved them all. But they'd also witnessed the precarious nature of survival in the court of the Celestial Conjunction. Where was Shulen now? Was she safe from those new-seeing eyes?

As to their future, it was as opaque as it had ever been. They were in Samarcand but inside a gilded cage whose doors were locked. Would they still be there when Tamerlane marched north into China? Or would they be dead?

At last, one morning, they received a visit from Mohammed Sultan. The Prince entered smiling. 'You are fortunate,' he said. 'You are to have some entertainment.'

Luke had risen from a couch where he'd been teaching Matthew to play chess. He bowed. 'We can leave?'

'You are invited to join the clans. My grandfather has announced a *qurultay* on the plain of Kani-gil outside the city. Five grandsons are to be married and there will be feasting for sixty days. You will be our guests.'

The Varangians exchanged glances. The Horde was to feast rather than march on China. That was hope.

'Where is our friend, highness?' asked Luke. 'Where is Shulen?'

Mohammed Sultan was already turning. He stopped and looked around, a slight frown above the smile. 'She is safe, Greek. Temur Gurgan has taken a liking to her. She is with him constantly.'

The Prince seemed about to say something more, but instead put a finger to his lips. He nodded. 'We will talk more of this. Now you must come.'

Their horses were saddled and waiting for them outside, as was a guard of Mongols, richly armoured. The square was alive with excited people moving in the same direction. Children sat on shoulders with flowers in their hair and hats on their heads against the sun. The Varangians rode back down the boulevard they'd ridden up a week past. The traders on either side were shutting up shop.

'Temur has ordered all trades within the city to go to the Kani-gil plain,' the Prince explained. 'They will serve the clans. You will see a second city built there within two days and this one emptied.'

They left the city and then the road and climbed to the top of a modest hill from where the plain of Kani-gil stretched out before them. It was an astonishing sight. The clans of the

Chagatai Horde were indeed building a second city of tents, perhaps fifty thousand of them spread over the landscape, each in its own ordered street, with bakers and bath-houses in between. In the centre, in the meadows beside the great Zarafshan River, stood the imperial enclosure, a vast sea of silk and rope with gardens around. Mohammed Sultan pointed with his whip.

'The big tent in the middle is Temur's feasting tent. Around it are the tents of the royal family, the emirs, the sayyids, the shaykhs, the muftis, the kadis, each in their appointed place. There are ambassadors from Castile who will want to meet you. I will take you to them.'

They rode down the hill and entered a street thronged with people of all ages. A man selling meat from a cart was surrounded by Mongol women shouting and laughing. The air smelt of horse and Luke wondered if it ever left these people whose lives were joined to this animal between birth and death. They came to an open space in which a row of gallows had been erected. Mohammed Sultan turned in his saddle.

'The governor of the city is to be executed this afternoon,' he said, 'alongside some architects.'

Luke brought his horse up beside him. 'What is their crime, lord?'

Mohammed Sultan shrugged. 'The governor ruled badly while Temur was away in India. The people were taxed too much.'

'And the architects?'

'The portal for Temur's new mosque was too small.'

Luke heard Nikolas whistle softly behind him. Tamerlane wanted his people to celebrate but only under the familiar shadow of fear. He looked to one side and saw a steaming wooden shed with its door ajar and men queuing for the bath inside. This was a strange world of fear and horse and sudden cleanliness. They came to the imperial enclosure and the Mongol guards at the entrance prostrated themselves as they recognised Mohammed Sultan. The gates were covered with plates of silver gilt ornamented in blue enamel. On one door was the image of St Peter, on the other St Paul.

'The gates of Bursa,' said Mohammed Sultan as they rode through. 'Probably made by you Greeks when you had the city. Now they're ours.'

It was hardly a boast. This was an empire that had sprung from nothing to the greatest in the world in twenty years, an accumulation of riches beyond anything yet seen in history. Luke stared at the helpless saints, strung up on their gilded hinges for heathen scrutiny, and remembered Plethon's loathing for them, alongside relics and all the other paraphernalia of superstition. They arrived at a tent outside which two men were examining coats threaded with gold. When they saw Mohammed Sultan, they swept their hats from their heads and sank to their knees.

'Please, Ruy González, Sotomayor,' murmured the Prince as he dismounted, lifting the men to their feet. 'I bring you friends.'

The Spaniards rose and bowed to Luke, who had also come down from his horse. They were small, dark men whose gathered hair was streaked with grey. They wore Spanish black and their demeanour was grave. The taller of the two turned to Mohammed Sultan. 'Your grandfather has given us these robes. And horses too. We are indebted.'

Mohammed Sultan laughed. 'But you must start drinking, Clavijo!' He patted him on the shoulder. 'Temur has noticed you never touch your wine at banquets. He wonders if Spain is full of monks.'

The man from Castile bowed again. He turned to Luke. 'You will find it difficult', he said, quite serious, 'to keep up with them. They drink until they cannot stand.'

Mohammed Sultan had turned towards his horse. 'Look after the Greeks, Clavijo,' he said over his shoulder. 'Temur has decreed the suspension of every rule and law for sixty days. There will be more abandonment on this plain than you can possibly imagine. I suggest you put on Temur's robes and let your own cloak your statue of the Virgin. Hide her from view. And from seeing.' Then he mounted and rode away.

For sixty days, the Mongol horde feasted and drank and copulated on the plain of Kani-gil. There were no rules so anything was possible. Widows straddled teenagers, men went with men and the bath-houses were busy with the washing of exhausted bodies. It was a time of entire and absolute excess where the Chagatai counted themselves ill used if they were not drunk by noon. By day, there were acrobats and jugglers and tightrope walkers. There were games of daring where men jumped hurdles while others strung bows to fire at them. By night, there was endless feasting and enough wine and koumis to drown Samarcand and all its suburbs. This was the mirror image of conquest: immersion in wine instead of blood.

Luke, Matthew and Nikolas tried to keep up with it all. They spent their evenings eating and drinking their way through horse, mutton and wine, and afterwards did their best to avoid staying the night. Hardest of all was the need to keep sober enough to make their way home to their tent.

By day, and free of any guard, they could wander where they wished. But despite their deels and squirrel hats, they were never invisible. At least a head taller than the biggest Mongol, they attracted attention of the worst kind. Drunken Chagatai tried to provoke them into fights so in the end Luke decided that they should themselves become part of the entertainment.

One morning, they rose, put on their Varangian armour and picked a spot to engage in Varangian weapon practice. They fought with the sword, the axe and the lance and drew crowds of sore-headed Mongols to the spectacle. When they stopped, no one picked a fight with them again.

They saw little of the Spaniards. The envoys from Castile were serious men who wore their religion like armour. They had travelled six thousand miles for fifteen months, been shipwrecked and robbed, arriving at the court of Tamerlane unprepared for its scale and decadence. Clavijo and Sotomayor, the two ambassadors, spent their days trying to find ways to meet Tamerlane again, shocked to realise that their king, Henry III, was counted of lesser importance than the Mamluk Sultan of Egypt or even the King of Badakhshan.

At last the day of Tamerlane's grandsons' weddings arrived and the Varangians and Spaniards were woken early to be told that they would attend the feast to follow the ceremony. It was to be held in Tamerlane's great tent with the Lord of the Celestial Conjunction present. They were given new robes of exquisite design and escorted to the banquet by giggling girls who offered to return to them later.

Inside the tent was more space than Luke had thought possible to embrace within silk. It was filled with long tables on which whole sides of horse and mutton steamed on plates ringed with coloured rice. To either side sat the captains of

Temur's army dressed in their finest deels. Behind them were tapestries, shag velvet screens and furs of ermine. Luke strained his eyes through the smoke to see to the end of the tent where raised daises, each at a different level, had been placed beneath an enormous dome. Upon them were empty thrones with low tables in front of each.

'Where do we sit?'

Nikolas was looking down the long line of Mongols. There seemed to be no empty seats. Sotomayor gestured.

'We sit at the end. In front of the daises. There will be seats for us.'

He began to walk forward. They had reached perhaps halfway down the tent when they heard a blast of horn behind them.

'Kneel!' hissed Clavijo, his hand pressing down on Luke's shoulder. Three Varangians and two Spaniards fell to their knees. Luke glanced towards the end of the tent. Mongols had entered and lined up in front of the tables, their heads bowed, their hands pressed, palm to palm, in front of them. At a command, they fell to the ground. The tent had fallen silent.

There were more blasts and Tamerlane entered. He was dressed in a long robe of red and gold, lined with fox and open to a tunic of simple white cambric beneath. On his head was a crown girded with gems and against the white of his chest rested an enormous ruby. He shuffled past the tables, dragging his lameness behind him. As he approached, Luke dared to glance up. Tamerlane was frowning and his eyes, unencumbered by Shulen's glasses, were bloodshot.

Behind Tamerlane came his eight wives, led by Saray Mulk Khanum, Bibi Khanum, oldest, largest and most senior of them all. It was for her that the biggest mosque in the world was being built, for her that its architects had been hanged on the plain of Kani-gil for not making its portal equal to her magnificence. She made an impressive sight. She was dressed in a tent-robe of blue Zaytuni silk, embroidered with gold circles, whose train was carried by fifteen ladies-in-waiting. By her side walked twenty more ladies supporting a headdress of a size that took Luke's breath away. It was a mountain of pearls and balas rubies and turquoises at whose summit sprang a riot of coloured feathers, some bent to fall to her shoulders. Her face was a mask of white lead through which two tiny eyes blinked to right and left behind a veil of finest gauze.

After the Great Khanum came Tamerlane's other seven wives, who were of varying size and age but all dressed in glittering attire. At their back was Shulen. As she passed Luke, she caught his eye and smiled. It was weak, but it was a smile.

Tamerlane settled himself into his throne on the dais, Bibi Khanum on his right, Shulen on his left. The other wives took their places on lower daises to either side. As Luke hurried to his seat, he saw Mohammed Sultan and Pir Mohammed sit amongst the other grandsons and their new wives further down.

There was another blast of horn and a gorgeously attired man, not of Mongol origin, strode down the length of the tent until he reached Tamerlane. Behind him came a trolley with something tall and cloaked upon it. Luke turned to Sotomayor for explanation.

'The King of Badakhshan, ten days' march from here,' whispered the man from Castile. 'Very rich. They mine precious stones there.'

The King had dropped to his knees and was gesturing to the covered shape behind. He stopped talking, there was a drumbeat, the cloak was removed and Luke's breath left his body.

'My God,' whispered Nikolas.

It was a tree, about the height of a man, made entirely out of gold. Its trunk was as thick as a man's leg and the fruit that hung from its many branches, beneath leaves delicate as paper, was emeralds and rubies and sapphires and every other gem imaginable. Dozens of little birds of gold and painted enamel crowded the tree's branches, some with their wings spread ready for flight, some feeding on the fruit, some with their beaks open for song. It was extraordinary.

Tamerlane thought so. He'd risen to his feet and lifted a chalice in toast to the King of Badakhshan. Luke saw him drain the wine in a single gulp and then watched as Bibi Khanum lifted her veil and did the same. She let out a burp that carried to the other end of the tent. She patted her stomach and Tamerlane roared his approval and sat down.

Then the Conqueror of the World turned to his left and leant towards Shulen. He was whispering something into her ear and Shulen was shaking her head. At last she pointed at Luke and his heart missed a beat. Tamerlane was looking at him.

'Come forward, Greek!' Now he was beckoning him. Luke took a deep breath and got to his feet. The dome above him seemed to rise into eternity, the space around him stretch beyond horizons. He was among ten thousand Mongols and their master had called for him. He walked forward, past the King and his golden tree, past staring generals and emirs and shaykhs, until he stood at the bottom of the dais from which Tamerlane, Bibi Khanum and Shulen looked down. He felt light-headed.

Tamerlane gestured to Shulen. 'I have named her Jawhar-agha,' he said, 'which in your language means "Queen of

Hearts".' He frowned then. 'But you know this, Greek. You already have her heart.'

Luke glanced at Shulen, who was staring straight ahead with no expression on her face. She was simply dressed in purest white silk, high-collared, her jet-black hair falling unadorned to her shoulders. She seemed of a different species to Bibi Khanum.

Tamerlane continued: 'She says she is married to you, which is unfortunate since I wish her to be my wife.'

Luke was too surprised to reply. He glanced at Shulen and then further down to where he saw that Mohammed Sultan had risen from the table.

'You will divorce her,' said the Lord of the Celestial Conjunction. 'And I will take her to my bed. She has given me sight, read to me and salved my joints. Now I would bed her.' He paused and turned his bloodshot eyes to Shulen, who continued to look into the distance, her lips set. Tamerlane's knotted hand covered hers, one animal mounting another. 'She has my favour.'

By now Mohammed Sultan was standing behind Tamerlane's chair, stooping to speak into his ear. He spoke loud enough for Luke to hear. 'Grandfather, the Holy Book forbids taking another man's wife against their wishes. Is it wise to offend God?'

Tamerlane frowned. He drank and wiped the wine from his beard with the hand not covering Shulen's. He wrinkled his nose as if a noxious smell had crept beneath it. He leant forward. 'Do you have any objection, Greek?' he growled. 'I want Jawhar-agha to be my wife. Will you divorce her?'

'No.'

Had he spoken? He had spoken. He had said no. He had denied Tamerlane.

'No, lord,' he amended, his heart pounding. 'She is my wife before God. I will not divorce her.'

Tamerlane's frown deepened. He shook his head suddenly as if trying to escape an unwanted thought. He opened his mouth but his grandson spoke first.

'You will need God's favour to conquer China,' he continued quietly, his ear close to Tamerlane's. 'You will need his blessing to finally unite the kingdoms. Why risk it, Grandfather?'

Tamerlane blinked twice, his head slightly tilted to listen. He drank more wine.

Mohammed Sultan went on, speaking faster. 'Think of it, Grandfather. The Chagatai here feasting with you. Persia. The Golden Horde. You have one more khanate to conquer to create an empire bigger than Genghis's: China, the kingdom of Kublai Khan.' He paused. 'You are so close.'

Tamerlane was fidgeting with the sleeves of his robe. He was breathing hard, his breath escaping in short spasms. His great brow was ever more furrowed, sweat within its folds. He was thinking. At last his hand moved away from Shulen's. He grunted and lifted his chalice only to find it empty. 'Wine!' he roared. A eunuch appeared with a pitcher. He gestured to Bibi Khanum's cup. 'And for her!'

Mohammed Sultan had taken a step backwards. He looked at Shulen who continued to stare ahead. He glanced at Luke and nodded. Then he turned to walk back to his seat.

Tamerlane leant forward again. 'Why are you *here*, Greek?' he growled. 'Why are you at my court?'

Luke straightened. He'd not practised what he would say were Tamerlane to speak to him. His mind raced. He thought of all that Ibn Khaldun had told him. 'Before you go to China,' he said, summoning the words, 'there is the Khanate of Persia's conquest still to complete. Genghis's grandson, Hulagu, went as far as the land of the Turks. You have to reconquer those lands, lord.'

Tamerlane squinted at him. 'You are telling me where I should go, Greek?'

'I say no such thing, majesty. But you should know that the tribes there are weary of Bayezid's rule. You would be welcomed.' He paused and glanced at Shulen, who was now staring at him. 'You would be welcomed as the Sword of Islam.'

Luke's heart was now beating faster than Eskalon's at full stretch. He knew that his life was balanced as precariously as the tightrope walkers he'd watched this past month. He felt giddy with adrenalin, almost drunk.

Tamerlane said: 'Bayezid is a tick that I'll flick from my body when I remember to do so. Until then I will send him letters to anger him. It pleases me.' He turned to Shulen. 'Your husband is brave but foolish. Take him from my presence before I remove him from you.'

Shulen rose and came down from the dais, took Luke's hand as a wife should, and led him through the silent tent, past the ambassadors and shaykhs and generals of Tamerlane's army. And as they walked, the silence was broken as men dared once more to revel. Shulen turned to Luke, speaking from the corner of her mouth.

'That was frightening. From now onwards, I am your wife. If Temur finds out the truth, we're both dead.'

CHAPTER NINETEEN

SAMARCAND, WINTER 1399

As summer turned to autumn and then winter, the leaves on the trees in the Garden of Heart's Delight turned first red, then gold, then as brown as the grass to which they fell. The poles in Tamerlane's tents were seasonally repainted but the roof above stayed blue, for such was the sky outside: day after day of brittle blue dusted with clouds of cotton fleece.

After the qurultay had run its riotous course, Luke and his friends had been given their own tent in the garden with everything they desired and some they didn't. For Luke at least, the slave girls were a temptation but nothing more. His greatest pleasure had been to have Eskalon, then Arcadius, delivered to him repaired and well; his constant pain, to know that day by day the marriage of Anna to Suleyman was drawing closer.

Shulen's tent was placed next to Tamerlane's. She might be married to another man, but the Lord of the Celestial Conjunction wanted her near to him. She spent most days in his tent, often with Mohammed Sultan. Tamerlane was sixty-three and the pain of his knee worsened as the days got colder. While Mohammed Sultan read to them both, Shulen would spend hours at a time mixing lotions and applying them to the tired joints of the man who terrorised the world. And when she wasn't doing this, she was, very secretly, teaching him to read.

The Spaniard Clavijo left Tamerlane's court to go home, leaving Sotomayor behind. He would travel by way of Edirne to deliver another letter to Bayezid and, it was assumed, awe the Sultan with tales of Tamerlane's splendour.

Luke spent much of his time hunting with Mohammed Sultan in the parks around Samarcand, whenever the Prince could be plucked from the company of Shulen. Tamerlane's heir seemed keen to learn as much as Luke could tell him of the West. Matthew and the other Varangians got used to riding by themselves, but while Nikolas and Arcadius joked about Luke's new friendship, Matthew remained silent. He'd grown up with Luke in Monemvasia, spent barely a day apart from him since birth; they were as two brothers. Now there was another.

One morning, Luke found himself riding through the Zarafshan Valley towards the mountains in the south, passing channels that carried snow-melt to the cotton fields. Against Shulen's advice, Tamerlane had decided to hunt and desired her company and that of Mohammed Sultan. The Prince had asked that Luke join them too.

The next day found them high up on a plateau, riding between groves of mulberry trees, the winter sun a liquid mess that spilt across the sky. Luke was riding Eskalon beside Mohammed Sultan. He was wearing a thick deel of padded fur and had Torguk's bow beside him on the saddle. Far behind were guards wrapped in fur, who tickled the hooded necks of eagles and gyrfalcons sitting on their padded arms. Shulen was up ahead with Tamerlane.

Tamerlane's favourite eagle had been released and had already snatched a hare from the snow. Mohammed Sultan had been inspecting the mulberry trees and looked up. 'What must the silkworms think when they see that fly above them?'

'The silkworms, lord? Can they even see?'

The Prince laughed. 'No, I don't believe they can. They only have a month on this earth, all of it spent eating.' He reined in his horse, happy to separate them further from his grandfather and Shulen. He looked up at the eagle again, his hand shielding his eyes. 'They can eat, grow, fornicate, and give us the most precious thing on earth, but they can't fly.' He paused and glanced at Luke. 'Imagine having everything in the world except the one thing you want. Can you imagine that?'

Luke remained silent, guessing the point of it all. Over the weeks, he'd seen how Mohammed Sultan's admiration for Shulen had grown, day by day, into something else. He changed the subject. 'Do you know where Temur plans to go next?'

Mohammed Sultan laughed. 'Probably not where you'd like him to go.'

'The army hasn't moved yet.'

'Which shows Shulen's having some success, perhaps. But I wouldn't count on it. My grandfather does what he wants to do.'

Luke pondered this.

'You think him mad,' Mohammed Sultan continued, 'and you think him cruel. You'll see terrible things next year if you're still with us, but his cruelty has its purpose. Cities open their gates to him.'

'And he slaughters their inhabitants anyway,' said Luke.

'You speak of Delhi. But the inhabitants rose up after the city had fallen. It was the same in Herat and Isfahan. They were lessons.'

'But lessons not heeded by all,' said Luke. 'Tell me of

Toktamish, highness.'

Mohammed Sultan smiled and patted his horse's neck. 'It was eight years past, Pir Mohammed's and my first campaign,' he said. 'It was a glorious thing.'

The Prince kicked his horse into a walk.

'It was winter and Toktamish of the Golden Horde, who'd been given his throne by my grandfather and was treated as a son, chose to invade Mawarannahr from the north. The generals advised waiting until spring to confront him, saying that the snow would be too deep. But Temur Gurgan wouldn't listen. He gathered the tribes and led an army up into the lands of the Rus, snow up to the withers. We moved by forced marches and the army of Toktamish fell back before us, always staying one march ahead. When the food ran out, Temur arranged a great hunt across the steppe, with the whole army sweeping game towards archers waiting in the hills. We marched further north into the wilds of Siberia, the Land of Shadows, and still Toktamish refused battle. We came to the Samara River, a land of mists and marshes, with no food for the army for Toktamish had destroyed everything behind him. The air was so dark and the rain so heavy that we could barely see three paces. Then the sky suddenly cleared and there was the Golden Horde, stretched out on the other bank. Their army was immense, twice the size of ours, and at its centre stood the standard of Toktamish, crowned with a human skull. Temur chose that moment to erect his tent and call for food as if the enemy wasn't there.' The Prince laughed. 'I thought it the most wonderful thing.'

He sat back on his saddle. 'The Kipchaks had guarded the ford and it would be suicide to cross. So for three days we marched along that riverbank, their army shadowing ours. Then one night, when we were in camp, Temur had all the women don the men's helmets and sit around the fires while the army moved silently away, its horses' hoofs muffled by hessian. He force-marched us back to the ford. Then we crossed and came up on the Kipchaks from behind.'

Luke was astonished. The discipline that would have made such a thing possible was beyond belief.

'But it was close. At one stage Temur was dismounted, fighting hand to hand with a half-pike shattered in his hand. Then I rallied the right wing and pushed the Kipchaks back to the river and the day was ours. A hundred thousand dead, mainly theirs.'

Luke suddenly understood why Mohammed Sultan was the favourite grandson of Tamerlane, why his name was read out at Friday prayers and was minted on the coinage. They rode on in silence. Then the Prince spoke. 'My mother is fond of you. Perhaps you understand her better than I do.'

Luke was bewildered. 'Highness?'

'She has told me that you're not married to Shulen yet she forbids me to pay court to her.'

Luke frowned. He'd not realised that Mohammed Sultan knew. 'Perhaps she fears Temur learning the truth.'

'No, she knows me better than that. It's because Shulen is not exalted enough in rank to marry the heir to Temur. But it makes no sense. Few of Temur Gurgan's wives are royal.'

Luke said nothing.

'I don't understand it,' said the Prince. 'Her love for my father Jahangir was beyond passion. Why will she not allow it for her son?'

Luke glanced at him. 'You love Shulen that much, lord?'

Now the Prince was silent and seemed intent on the mane

he was pulling through his fingers. 'Yes, I love her. But you, Luke. Do you love her too?'

Before Luke could answer, there was a shout from behind them and both men turned in their saddles.

'A wolf!' cried the Prince, kicking his horse. 'If they've released the second eagle it must be a wolf!'

Tamerlane and Shulen were too far ahead to be seen. Mohammed Sultan and Luke cantered through the mulberry groves and into the wood at the bottom of the rise, the falconers hard on their heels. Then they were up and out amidst the silver birch and the eagles were circling above them, giant black crosses with their jesses trailing in the air behind. They couldn't see the wolf but the birds could and they began their dives, one behind the other, until they were only feet above the ground.

Then Luke saw it. It was a cub and it was running for its life across the frozen ground, stirring up a blizzard as it went. The first eagle crashed into its neck, rolling the animal head first into the snow. The second sank its talons into the wolf's rear as it landed and a spray of blood arced into the air and pitted the white ground with red. There was a flash of fur and teeth and the wolf lay still.

From below them came a shout. Tamerlane had called for his eagle.

'Allah,' whispered Mohammed Sultan, already turning his horse, kicking hard. 'He promised he wouldn't hunt. His knees are too weak to hold the horse when the eagle lands.'

Already, the piece of meat would be on Tamerlane's arm and he'd be stretching it out for the bird to land on. The Emperor had forgotten his age.

'What will the horse do?' shouted the Prince over his shoulder, lashing the flanks of his own mount.

'God knows! Why don't the falconers recall it?' shouted Luke.

Mohammed Sultan was riding hard. 'It's Temur's eagle!'

They were in the trees now, ducking branches and urging their horses through the snow-covered debris. Above the canopy they could see snatches of the giant wingspan as the bird circled, tighter each time as its eyes fixed on to the man on the horse below. Every second the eagle was nearing the moment when it would begin its fall, when it would land on Tamerlane's arm.

There was a cry. Not of human but of beast. Mohammed Sultan kicked his horse on through the trees. Beyond was the sound of a whip striking again and again and the scream of an animal and then they were out of the trees and before them, at the bottom of the valley, was the Emperor, still on top of his horse, the eagle clutching a gloved arm that was dripping with blood. The bird's wings were spread and it jerked its head left and right with each screech of alarm. The horse was wheeling and at any moment Tamerlane must fall.

Shulen was doing her best. She was trying to catch hold of the reins to stop the horse, but she couldn't get past the flailing hooves and Tamerlane's whip.

Luke pulled Eskalon up and shouted something. Tamerlane's horse looked and saw Luke and came to a standstill, breathing hard and blowing through nostrils wide with fear. Tamerlane jumped from its back but stumbled as he hit the gound. Then he was on one knee and his arm was above his head with the eagle still on it, shrieking with alarm. With every cry, the bird drove its talons further into Temur's arm. Luke turned to Mohammed Sultan.

'Tell the falconers to call back the eagle,' he said. 'Do it now.'

'But . . .'

'*Do* it!'

The order was given and the call made and the eagle released its grip. Tamerlane roared with pain as the bird rose into the air, its jesses trailing. Luke dismounted and ran to Tamerlane, who was kneeling in a pool of blood, one arm cradling the other. He tore off his deel and then the sleeve of the shirt he was wearing. 'Lord, let me bind you.'

But the face that turned to Luke was twisted with rage. Tamerlane lifted his whip with his good sleeve and hurled it at Luke.

'You dared to call my eagle?'

Luke stood. 'Lord, you were about to fall.'

'Temur Gurgan fall from his horse? You dare to say this?'

'Luke . . .' Shulen had dismounted and had taken his hand. He felt something warm and looked down to see her blood seeping through his fingers. 'I tried to calm the horse by taking the reins,' she whispered, squeezing his hand, pulling him down to kneel. 'That was the mistake. Don't make it worse.'

Tamerlane was drawing his sword.

'Wait, Grandfather!' Mohammed Sultan was now in front of Tamerlane. 'What would you do, Grandfather?'

'I would kill him,' the Emperor growled. 'Does he deserve less? He recalled my eagle.'

The Prince lowered his voice. 'You would kill the man who has just saved your life?'

Tamerlane looked at his grandson in astonishment. Some of the colour was beginning to leave his face. 'You take his part against mine? Against your grandfather?' he said more in wonder than anger. 'You would do this? You, my heir?'

Mohammed Sultan remained silent and looked at his

grandfather, his head held high. Tamerlane stared back. Then he laughed.

'I know what it is!' He slapped his thigh. 'You want the girl! Ha! I have seen how you look at her! Well, she is mine.' He paused. 'What do you say to that, heir?'

Still the Prince said nothing. Then he unhooked his sword. 'The girl is married, Grandfather,' he said evenly. 'If you take her to your harem, I cannot be your heir.' He laid his sword on the ground and knelt.

There was no sound except the rasp of Tamerlane's breathing. At long last he let out a long sigh. He said: 'Get up.' There was no trace of anger left. 'You speak well, Grandson, and you're brave. That is why I favour you above all others. That is why you are my heir.'

Mohammed Sultan rose. He gestured to Luke and Shulen, still kneeling. 'And these, lord?'

Tamerlane was trying to take off his glove. The leather was sticking to the holes in his forearm and he winced with the pain. 'The Greeks can go home, all four of them. There is nothing for them here. The girl stays. She can mend my arm.'

Then Luke spoke. 'We are Varangians, lord, not Greeks. I have lived among the gazis of the Germiyan tribe and I am as much a man of the steppe as any who serves you.'

Tamerlane looked puzzled. 'A man of the steppe?' he asked. 'You?' He wiped his beard with his hand. 'I don't think so.'

'Then let me prove it, lord,' Luke said. 'Let me prove that I am as good with a horse and a bow as any you lead. If I am what I say, then perhaps you'll allow me to stay.'

Tamerlane had managed to remove his glove. His arm was a mangled piece of meat, dripping gore. He spat on it and winced again. He looked at Luke, his face expressionless. Then he spoke. 'You are brave but you are a fool.' He turned to his heir. 'Mohammed Sultan, do you take up this challenge?'

Mohammed Sultan had been watching Luke carefully, curiosity in his eyes. 'As you wish, lord. What is it to be?'

Tamerlane thought awhile, his fingers stroking his beard. 'The eagle. No, five eagles. Two on poles, three held by your friends. If you miss, they die. Then you.'

CHAPTER TWENTY

SAMARCAND, WINTER 1399

The eagles were three feet in height and made of wood. Their heads were turned to one side so that their hooked beaks were in profile. On their chests were circled targets of padded straw that would be hard to hit in perfect light. By the time Tamerlane had risen from his bed, it was nearly evening.

Shulen had tried to wake him sooner but he'd given orders that he was not to be disturbed. They'd arrived back from the mountains at midday and Tamerlane, weak with blood-loss and with his arm splinted across his chest, had gone straight to his tent.

So it was in half-light that Luke and Mohammed Sultan rode out on to the ground side by side from a tent where they'd been given their horses. Luke's was a pony of the kind he'd ridden with the Germiyans: swarthy, intelligent and agile. He'd been denied Eskalon but at least had been given Torguk's bow.

Mohammed Sultan turned to him as they rode. 'Can you hit those targets at the gallop?'

Luke looked at the long stretch of beaten earth, planted with two poles with eagles at their tops, perhaps fifty paces apart, and further along Matthew, Nikolas and Arcadius, all with targets strapped to their fronts. On both sides were ropes, which the riders could not cross, at least a hundred paces wide of the targets. The range was more difficult than anything Luke had yet attempted and the light was fading fast.

'If I had my horse, yes. But I've not been allowed my horse.'

Mohammed nodded. They were getting closer to the dais and he spoke out of the corner of his mouth. 'My mother told me this: that you speak with horses and that they do your bidding. How much time do you need with this one?'

Luke looked at the man by his side. He could see Khan-zada in him: the pointed nose, the high cheekbones and sweeping forehead, the head set back upon the shoulders. 'A few minutes, no more.'

'You shall have them. I will ask to ride first.'

'And you will hit them all?'

'Of course, at the first pass. To miss any would raise suspicion. I will miss on the second pass. You will have to hit them all every time. Wait here.'

Luke watched the Prince trot away towards the dais. He looked down at the horse beneath him. He jumped down and walked round to its front and took the head between his hands, allowing his fingers to stroke the loose flesh between the animal's jawbones. He looked into eyes full of bewilderment and suspicion and he began to talk: gently, softly.

We don't have much time. I need you to help me.

The horse was good; they'd given him one with intelligence. It was listening.

This is what I want you to do.

There was a shout from behind him. Luke ignored it and continued to talk. There was another shout, this time from more than one person; what he was doing hadn't happened before.

That's it.

Luke had done all he could. He remounted. Mohammed Sultan was sitting on his horse across from him, no more than ten paces away, his head slightly tilted. Two men with arrows were walking towards them.

'Varangian,' called the Prince, 'I am to ride first. Five arrows, one for each target, and your horse must never slow to a trot. Is that agreed?'

Luke nodded.

Mohammed Sultan took his bow and the quiver of arrows and rode his horse to the end of the course and out beyond the rope. He was in no hurry and Luke spent the time talking to the creature below him: talking with his tongue, his hands, his knees.

Trust me as I trust you. Do not fail me.

A man with a flag had walked into the centre of the course. He turned and looked towards the dais where Tamerlane sat. There was the murmur and shuffle of many people and, looking around him, Luke saw that the ground was now ringed with Tartars in their deels and high hats. Row upon row of Tamerlane's inscrutable army had come to see the foreigner humbled by their prince. Then Tamerlane raised his hand and the flag came down. The contest had begun.

Mohammed Sultan pressed his knees to his pony's flanks and it broke into an easy lope. In one hand he held the bow, an arrow already on its string; in the other his reins. A cheer rose from the men watching and there was the clatter of swords against shields.

The horse accelerated as it approached the first target and

Mohammed Sultan let go of the reins and, in one graceful movement, turned in his saddle and shot. By the time the arrow had embedded itself in the eagle, there was another arrow on the string and seconds later it had hit its target too. Luke glanced at his three friends further down the course. It was too far to see if their eyes were open.

He closed his.

He heard cheers and opened them to see Mohammed wheeling his horse round at the other end of the course. His friends were still standing, arrows in the eagles before them.

It was Luke's turn.

He trotted his horse to the end of the course, talking to it all the way. He had Torguk's bow in one hand and a quiver of arrows slung across his back and he tested the bowstring with his finger and found the tension as it should be. Everything would depend on the animal beneath him.

Have you understood?

At the rope, he turned his horse to face the line of targets and waited for the flag to fall. There was quiet in the ranks of the Mongols and on the dais where Tamerlane sat, a grandchild at each ear to describe the scene. The sun was low in the sky and the colours of the landscape were beginning to merge with the lengthening shadows. Minute by minute, a little more detail disappeared. Luke kissed Plethon's ring.

For luck.

The flag fell and he used first his heels, then his knees, to set the horse in motion and calibrate its speed. He knew that his only chance of hitting every target, and of getting another arrow to the string in between, lay in controlling his horse in its canter. Mohammed had deliberately ridden fast. He would ride as slow as it was possible to do.

The first eagle was approaching. He took aim and released his first arrow and heard the thud of its impact as he reached for his second. That too hit its target and now his friends were in front of him, standing with their eagles strapped to their chests and their heads turned away. Luke used his knees in the way that he'd been taught by Garkil.

That's it. Slow down but not to a trot. And keep it even.

There was a moment of panic as he focused on his target.

It's not Matthew. It's an eagle.

Then he shot and renocked and shot again and again and he heard the cheer around him and looked back and saw three arrows sunk deep inside straw and three faces grinning above them. He felt sick with relief.

His hands went back to his reins and he pulled up his horse, patting its rough neck and talking, talking. He looked at his hands and saw that they were still.

I can do this.

Mohammed Sultan had kicked his horse to begin his second pass. He looked relaxed, as if he did this every morning, as if he'd never missed a target in his life. He glanced at Luke and he nodded.

The Prince rode back down the line of targets as fast as he had before, his horse picking up speed all the time. His arrows thudded into the three eagles held by the Varangians and the fourth found its target.

Then the horse reared.

Afterwards, no one could explain how it had happened. Some had seen a shrew dart out in front of him, others the sun reflected from a shield into the horse's eyes. What all agreed was how remarkably the Prince had controlled his horse, keeping to his saddle despite having no hand on the reins. Of course the last arrow went wide.

Luke sat on his horse and wetted his lips with his tongue. The shadows around him were getting longer by the minute.

One more pass. Five targets.

He kicked his pony and started back down the line of targets.

Arcadius first, then Nikolas, then Matthew, but his horse was going too fast; it wanted to end this game. Luke's hand went to the reins but he was too close to Matthew to pull them. He aimed the bow and fired and knew he'd hit the target and reached for the next arrow. But he was not where he wanted to be. Nikolas was level with him before the next arrow had been fitted. But it was too late and the arrow that should have hit his eagle flew instead into Matthew's.

Then he was at the end of the course. He'd not had time to hit the two last targets and Mohammed had hit four.

He kicked his horse towards the dais, seeing Mohammed do the same from the other end. They arrived together to find Tamerlane with Shulen by his side. She was still wearing the clothes from the hunt, Tamerlane's dried blood on her tunic.

The riders dismounted and prostrated themselves on the ground. Mohammed Sultan lifted his head and spoke. 'He did well, lord. The light was bad. The Varangian did well.'

Tamerlane grunted. 'Well? He lost. Why is that well?'

'He rode well, lord. Like a gazi.'

By now, the three Varangians had been untied and brought over to stand before the dais. Their hair was dishevelled and their tunics filthy from the targets. Arcadius was rubbing his wrists.

Tamerlane grunted again. He pointed to Luke. 'Give him his sword.'

A man came forward with the sword. The dragon head was dull in the narrowing light and Luke took it and looked into the ruby eyes.

Tamerlane gestured towards the Varangians beside him. 'Give one of them a target and send him away twenty paces.'

Arcadius was hauled forward. The target he thought he'd escaped was strapped again to his front and he was led away.

Tamerlane watched it all. 'Put the sword in it,' he said, turning to Luke. 'From here. Put the sword in it and you can stay.'

Luke looked at the target, twenty paces away, already in shadow, his friend behind it. It was impossible and, if he missed, Arcadius would die. But this moment had been long coming and he couldn't fail. It was his only chance and he'd have to take it. He turned to Tamerlane. 'Lord, you know the throw is impossible. It can only succeed by the will of Allah. If I succeed, could it be because Allah has heard what I say and wishes the Sword of Islam to go west and lead the gazi tribes against Bayezid?'

He heard Mohammed Sultan draw breath beside him. He'd gone too far. They were all dead. But Tamerlane merely grunted.

'Perhaps.' He was growing impatient. 'Throw the sword.'

Luke held the sword by its perfect blade, finding its point of balance on the flat of his palm. He positioned himself to throw it, legs apart, head up. He glanced down. The dragon eyes looked up at him, suddenly alive. Then Luke stared at Arcadius; judging, judging.

He threw the sword.

The sound was the right one. Not the hard sound of sword on stone or the softer one of severed flesh; it was the solid thud of blade entering straw and never had a sound been so good. He heard Arcadius whoop with relief.

Tamerlane was staring at the target. Then he nodded slowly. He turned to Luke. 'It is Allah's will that you stay. You will make your Varangian oath to me. You will pledge yourselves to me, all of you.' He rose. 'And I will consider further what is the will of Allah.'

CHAPTER TWENTY-ONE

EDIRNE, WINTER 1399

It was nearly the end of the century and a thin, cold wind blew in from the east to carry it away. Few would regret its passing. It had been a fearful time of plague and war and its survivors awaited the new one with unease. Many said that it would bring not only the end of the Empire but the end of time itself.

The harem in Edirne was preparing itself for hibernation. The east wind patterned its windows with leaves blown in from the gardens, nudging aside the velvets hung to keep it out. Pot-bellied stoves were brought in to heat the rooms and furs spread across their marble floors. Brisk massage replaced caress and the palace cooks turned their attention to making soup.

The harem's hibernation relied on the stored nutrition of story that was released nightly for sharing. Anna, having once told Suleyman that she never wanted to set foot in it again, now spent every night there. Gülçiçek's absence was as a brick taken from a dam. The evenings were flooded with stories told by this slave sisterhood collected from every part of the Sultan's western empire and beyond. Some were noble and educated, others could barely write their names; some as fair as Anna, others darker than Zoe. All had a past and wanted to talk about it.

Theirs was a world cocooned from events outside and the news that made it through the filter of palace servants was not always accurate. They heard that Bayezid's cannon had arrived at last at Constantinople and that dark portents had been seen in the skies above the city. They heard that Bayezid himself had taken a small army up to Wallachia to punish the Voivode for some misdemeanour, leaving Suleyman to run the siege. The Sultan would be away for a month at least and that, to most, was a relief. Although he rarely visited the harem these days, his very presence in the palace spread unease through every room like an invisible gas.

Anna listened to it all and made her own store of fact and fiction, ready to unpack later when she reported to Angelina.

The Princess from Hungary had been ill for some weeks now. To begin with, it was thought to be a summer chill and Anna had felt guilt over the pool games she'd introduced. They'd put her to bed and shut out all draughts and fed her hot soups larded with herbs and Anna had even lent her the *Alexiad*. It was the book that Luke had given her in the cave, her only link to him and the most precious thing she possessed. She missed it nightly but knew that Angelina might miss it more. But the Princess only seemed to get worse.

Then Zoe came to the harem.

On an evening of fog and chill, Anna was shocked to see Zoe present at the evening storytelling. She had news she wanted them all to hear, especially Anna. It came from an Italian girl who'd been asked to help in the interrogation of four merchants from Venice. They'd been brought to Edirne by emissaries from Qara Yusuf of the Black Sheep Turcomans.

The women of the harem were gathered in the audience hall, warmed by wood stoves, and the hum of conversation had turned to silence as the story unfolded. It was a good one. Four tall Varangians, Nordic gods apparently, had arrived in Tabriz disguised as servants to a Lady Fatimah, a rich merchant's daughter. Three of them had been captured and almost died in the arena before their leader arrived with Prince Yakub to save them. Anna hadn't breathed during the telling, her head dizzy with what she was hearing.

Someone asked: 'These Varangians, where had they come from?'

'Kutahya, Prince Yakub's capital.'

'And the Lady Fatimah?' asked another.

'She was in disguise too. She was from Yakub's tribe. No one could work out why she was there until . . .' Zoe looked at Anna and saw that she had her full attention. 'Until . . . well, it doesn't matter why.'

But the harem girls were captivated. They liked this Lady Fatimah. Maria said: 'You cannot stop it there, Zoe. Why was she there?'

'Well,' Zoe said carefully, again glancing at Anna, 'it turned out that she was married to the leader of the Varangians. They had been married in Kutahya. It was he who rescued her from Qara Yusuf's harem.'

'And the hero's name?'

'They called him Luke. He was from Monemvasia.'

Anna grasped the arm of the chair she was sitting in. Beside her, Maria asked: 'Married?'

Zoe turned to her and smiled. 'Yes. Married to this Lady

Fatimah, the merchant's daughter. The Venetians were very certain.'

Anna had looked away, closing her hands to stop them shaking. She rose with all the dignity she could muster and smiled with her lips but not her eyes and left the room. She went to see Angelina, finding her in her room lying against pillows with the *Alexiad* in her hands. Anna sat down the bed and closed her eyes.

'You look tired,' said Angelina, her voice a whisper. 'You should go to bed. Would you like your book back?'

Anna looked at the book. It was no longer a thing of comfort and memory. It was just a book that she'd read too often. 'You can keep it,' she said. She rose and went to her room where a fire was burning. She sat down on her bed.

Luke married. Can it be true?

Of course it could be true. Hadn't she seen Shulen in Kutahya? What possible other reason could there be for her to have been there? What other reason for her to be on so dangerous a mission?

She stayed like that for a while, then rose and went over to a desk in the corner of the room and opened a drawer. In it was a rolled parchment and next to it Suleyman's seal. It was the annulment of her marriage to Damian Mamonas, signed by an anxious Patriarch and brought by her out of Constantinople after her meeting with Luke.

Why did you even send for me?

To say goodbye, of course. He knew that she was to be married to Suleyman and was about to complete the symmetry. He'd just wanted to say goodbye, that's all. She closed her eyes against the pain, screwed them shut to hold out the blast of understanding. Then she opened them, picked up the scroll and read it through. There was nothing more to stop her marrying Suleyman. She looked at the seal.

Suleyman's seal. My seal when I marry him.

Inside Constantinople, the citizens saw portent in every starfall.

Already, strange lights had been seen dancing across the night sky, the moon had somersaulted and an owl flown three times around the dome of the Church of Holy Wisdom. And, most poignantly, a tree in the orchard of the Church of St Saviour in Chora had been split by lightning, only to re-form itself into a crescent.

The most potent relics of the city were once again revealed and the Patriarch mounted the walls to process with his clergy, clamping his battered vestments to his knees with one hand, lifting a splinter with the other and jumping every time the cannon fired.

That was not very often. The cannon needed two hours to cool between firing and the Patriarch, who scorned secular time, found himself unprepared whenever they did so.

The citizens of the city were more often on their knees, either praying or burying their gold, while their anxious wives cut their daughters' hair to the scalp and scoured the Koran for the Prophet's injunction on rape. They knew that it was only a matter of time before their city would fall.

There were no stars in the sky on the night that Benedo Barbi stood at the entrance to a mineshaft next to Marchese Longo. The mineshaft was inside the city's walls and its tunnel went deep beneath them before rising to meet the tunnel dug by the Turks.

Barbi, Longo and Dimitri had arrived from Chios a month earlier, slipping in through the Turkish galleys in submarines of the engineer's own design. The vessels were, in fact, three Greek fire canisters, emptied and kept buoyant by pigs' bladders, with periscopes and tubes for breathing. Launched from boats outside the Turkish blockade, the three men had worked stern paddles with their feet to propel them silently past the galleys. They were blue from cold when they'd been fished from the sea.

Now they were almost as cold for the wind was keen.

'It's from the east,' said Longo. 'It's been blowing for weeks now. Comes straight from the steppe.'

Barbi pulled his fur cloak tighter around him and stamped his feet. He peered into the mine. 'What are they doing in there? Can you hear anything?'

Longo leant forward and listened. 'Nothing,' he said. He straightened up. 'In fact, nothing anywhere. Perhaps they've all frozen to death.'

It was very still. Apart from the rustle of the wind in the trees, tentative as if exploring things unknown to it on the steppe, there was nothing beyond the occasional bark of dog or call of sentry. They were on the very edge of the city among shadowed fields set aside for burial and agriculture, the one perhaps helping the other.

Longo lifted his nose. 'Chestnuts,' he said with certainty. 'One of the sentries is cooking chestnuts on his brazier.' He'd seen the braziers that very morning when he and Barbi had mounted the walls to inspect the damage done by the new cannon. The damage was, so far, slight. This was because the cannon could only shoot ten times in a day and Barbi had persuaded the Emperor to order the construction of vast leather blankets to hang over the walls to absorb their impact. But it was only a matter of time before they would have an effect.

It was three weeks earlier that the engineer had noticed the cannon were aiming their fire at the same part of the wall every time. And he'd noticed something else. It was known that the Turks were digging a mine under the city walls but no one had any idea where. Barbi had guessed that the mine was being dug to that part of the wall being weakened by the cannon. The Turks were going to dig under the wall, prop oak piles beneath the stones and then set fire to them. When the piles collapsed, the walls would come down too. Almost immediately he'd ordered the digging of the counter-mine.

Now it was almost ready. Barbi had ordered thin sheets of bronze to be placed in between the tunnel props that would vibrate to the sound of the Turks' digging. That way they'd gradually learnt the exact path of the enemy mine and, the night before, a man had reported hearing voices. It was time to break through.

'Here they come.' Barbi had knelt and was holding his torch into the opening of the shaft.

A moment later a head appeared, its hair clogged with earth, and one of Longo's men climbed out of the hole. 'They're about to change teams,' he said, turning to help the next man up. 'And we're inches away from them.'

Three more men appeared, the last holding a small brass lamp lit by oil. He said, 'The air's foul down there, lord. The lamp nearly went out.'

Barbi handed him a cloak. 'Here, wrap yourself in this.' He turned and patted a brass siphon lying on the ground beside him. 'There's no danger of this going out, I assure you.'

The plan was a simple one. The entrance to the Turks' mine was situated between the two cannon lying in their cradles, perhaps twenty paces from each. Barbi intended to wait until the Turkish digging teams changed, when the men were most tired, and then break through. He'd taken a giant bellows from the city's blast furnace and connected it by tube to an incinerator that would produce thick smoke. He meant to blow smoke into the Turkish tunnel to clear it before sending in a party with Greek fire. They would emerge from the mine, using the flame-throwers to scatter the guards while others spiked the cannon. Then, coming back through the tunnel, they'd set fire to the Turkish props and collapse their mine.

It was a simple but dangerous plan and Marchese Longo had volunteered to lead the party that was now standing around him. He was a father now and had a wife nursing a two-year-old son called Giovanni and he knew it was reckless. But he was also a Genoese lord from one of the oldest families of the republic. He turned to his friend. 'Are you ready?'

Barbi was helping a man to strap on his canister. It was big and bulbous and shone dull gold in the light of the torch. It looked as if the man was carrying a knight piggyback. Another was donning the second siphon. 'I think so. Here are the flints.' He gave Longo a tinderbox.

Marchese Longo led the way into the shaft, lighting their way with the oil lamp as they climbed down. The tunnel at the bottom was the height of a tall dwarf and they had to stoop to walk. It was cold and damp and the air was thin and gaseous. Behind him came the man with the bellows, its tube snaking after him, followed by the first of the siphons.

They made slow, shuffling progress but eventually they reached the Turks' tunnel. Longo lifted the spluttering lamp so that its light fell on a wall of earth in front of him. He turned and the light played across the brass plates to one side. He put his finger to his lips. Voices could be heard on the other side of the wall, and the sound of scraping. He signalled for the man with the bellows to come forward.

With some difficulty, they changed places and the bellows-carrier began slowly making a hole for the snout of the bellows to fit through. Then he stopped, turned and nodded. One push and the snout would break through to the Turkish tunnel. The moment had come.

Longo waited for the signal to be passed up from the rear that the smoke was ready.

He gave the signal.

The bellows snout was pushed through and the man behind it began to pump. Almost immediately there were cries from the other side as the smoke filled the Turkish tunnel. Longo and his men put wettened cloths to their faces.

The man with the bellows had stopped pumping and was now digging through the rest of the wall-face. The shouts from the other side were getting fainter. Longo came alongside him to help. Soon the hole was big enough to crawl through and one by one the raiding party pushed themselves into the tunnel.

Longo knelt next to the man with the siphon once he was through. Then Marchese took the tinderbox from his belt, opened it and took out the flint, fire steel and tinder. He nodded to the man and they rose and began to move down the tunnel as fast as they were able. It was taller than their own and the wooden props more frequent. Through the smoke, they could hear panic.

Then there was light before them. They were nearing the shaft of the Turkish mine. They could see a torch and the flash of steel ahead through the smoke. Armed men had entered the tunnel to stop them. Longo knelt and gestured for the siphon.

When it was level, he struck the flint against the fire steel and lit the tinder.

A moment later, there was an almighty roar and flames spat out of the siphon's nozzle, shooting the length of the tunnel. For a second, they lit the terrified face of a man aiming a crossbow. Longo raised his hand and the nozzle was closed. The flames subsided, leaving an avenue of burning props on either side of the mine. 'Quick!' he yelled.

Barbi had calculated that they'd have about five minutes before the wood burnt through and the mine collapsed. Five minutes to scatter the guards, spike the cannon and get back through the tunnel. It wasn't long.

They hurried forward with the cloths still pressed to their faces, their lungs bursting and their eyes streaming with tears. They found the steps and fired a tongue of flame up them to clear any ambush at the top. Then Longo climbed outside and began to pull the first siphon-carrier up behind him. An arrow whistled above his head.

'Quick!' he shouted again and scanned the ground for the cannon.

There they were, one on each side of the mineshaft, armed men in front of them. He ducked as another arrow embedded itself in the wattle fence. By now, the second siphon was out and its carrier already opening his tinderbox.

'When you're ready . . .' shouted Longo, his sword raised. '*Now!*'

The two siphons spewed fire and, free from the tunnel, their flames arced high and wide through the darkness, turning men into fireballs on either side. There were more screams. The wicker palisade was alight and a janissary was scrambling towards a water butt when a flaming swing door fell on top of him.

Arrows hissed through the air and one of the siphon-carriers grunted and fell forward. Longo ran to him and pulled the contraption from his back. The siphons still had work to do. It was time to spike the cannon. He turned to the man beside him. He was a young officer of the guard and his eyes shone with the excitement of at last striking back at the enemy. 'You have the nail?'

'And the hammer,' yelled the young man. He turned and beckoned to another, who had struggled into the siphon harness. They rose and ran towards one of the cannon. A moment later, Longo ran to the other. It was dug deep into its pit and resting on a thick cradle of oak. In front of it the swing door and wicker fence lay on their sides, both alight.

The siphon-carrier got down on one knee at the rim of the pit and sprayed flames in a circle to keep any help from coming. Longo jumped into the hole and began hammering his nail into the firing hole of the cannon. It was hard work for the bronze was thick. Then, after several strikes, it split. The cannon was broken.

But it had taken time.

Longo and the soldier pulled themselves out of the hole. Longo shouted, 'Fire the cradle!' The man turned, opened his nozzle, and soon the cannon was surrounded by flame. Longo looked across at the other cannon. Its cradle was already alight. Good.

But it has taken too long.

He glanced over towards the mineshaft. Would they really be able to make it back through the tunnel? It seemed unlikely. He turned to the siphon-carrier. 'Give it to me.'

The man struggled out of the harness. The canister was hot. Longo took hold of one of the straps and began dragging it towards the mineshaft. 'Follow me!'

As he approached the shaft, he saw that the young officer and the other siphon-carrier were already there. They were crouched behind piles of bodies, pinned down by arrows.

'They're getting closer,' said the officer as Longo crawled up beside him. A crossbow bolt thudded into the body to his front. 'We won't make it back through the tunnel. It's aflame.'

Longo looked behind him. The shaft's opening was crimson with fire. He turned back. 'Get your siphon.'

The young officer rolled his way over to the man with the canister. He cut the straps with his dagger. Moments later he was back with Longo, the siphon beside him. 'What do we do now?' he asked. 'We're trapped.'

Longo looked above the bodies to his front and saw Turks readying themselves for an assault. 'They mustn't get the canisters,' he said. He was opening his tinderbox. 'We can use them to hold the bastards off a bit longer then we'll have to throw them into the mineshaft. And we must do it before the tunnel collapses. Understand?'

The officer nodded. Longo looked at him and smiled. He reminded him of Luke. He turned to his front. 'Now let's take some with us.'

Longo lit the nozzle. The young officer did the same. They rose and stood shoulder to shoulder, screaming defiance at the enemy as they hosed it with fire. Their two flames soared into the night and the men before them ran. There were shouts and the clash of metal and a riderless horse suddenly emerged to one side, reared, and galloped away. They sprayed fire until there was no more left to spray. Then Longo turned. There were flames leaping up from the shaft and the heat was intense. It was the mouth of hell.

'Now!'

The young officer threw his canister into it and Longo followed suit. There was the sound of hoofbeats behind them and they turned once more. A hundred paces to their front, a troop of sipahi cavalry was lining up for the charge, their swords drawn. Longo looked around for a weapon. There was a pike and a crossbow lying on the ground. He chose the pike. 'Start running for the walls,' he yelled to the other men. 'We'll hold them off for as long as we can.'

He heard hoofbeats and looked at the sipahis, but they hadn't moved. There were more riders behind them.

We're surrounded.

He lifted his pike and spun round, ready for the first lance. The soldiers gathered around him, forming a little ring. The flames from the mineshaft were higher now, and they could see nothing beyond them. They could only hear.

The hoofbeats were getting closer. They might take one or two with them if they were lucky. Longo looked up at the sky.

Fiorenza. Giovanni.

Now there were shouts. One shout. In Greek.

Horsemen emerged from the night: Dimitri followed by several others. They had bows and big quivers by their sides. Some led horses without riders. Dimitri reined his horse in. 'Get on the horses and ride!'

His men were already forming a line beyond the mineshaft. They unleashed a volley of arrows at the sipahis. Then another. Longo turned to the wounded man who was sitting by his side. He put his arm around his neck and lifted him. Dimitri was holding a horse. They managed to get him into the saddle but it took time.

'Quick!' Dimitri cried. He'd grabbed the reins of another horse and was holding them out to Longo. 'Get on and ride!'

Longo mounted. He felt the ground shake and heard a low rumble beneath him as if some giant was turning in his sleep. He looked over to the mineshaft and saw a smoke cloud rising into the night sky.

The Turks' tunnel has collapsed.

He dug his heels into the sides of his horse and it sprang forward towards the city walls. Dimitri was behind him shouting at the horse archers. He looked up. The city walls were closer than he'd thought they'd be. He could see men lining their ramparts, shouting and waving.

Then Dimitri was by his side. 'This way!'

Longo turned his horse and saw before him the Romanus Gate, open with archers on its battlements. They unleashed a hail of arrows high into the sky over his head.

'Come on! We can make it!' Dimitri was ahead of him, riding low in the saddle. Behind were the horse archers and behind them the sipahis. Arrows were thudding into the ground around him.

He heard a cry to his side and looked over to see the young officer slump forward in his saddle, an arrow in his back. The horse behind him had an empty saddle.

'Don't look back!' yelled Dimitri. 'You can't help them!'

The gate was much nearer now. If no arrow hit his horse, or him, he might just make it. He kicked harder.

He looked up at the open gate again. Closer. There was a man in white standing there waving, urging them on.

Plethon.

More arrows were being fired from the walls now. He heard screams behind him.

I'm going to make it.

One last kick, one more shouted encouragement into the ear

to his front and he was passing Plethon and galloping through the gate. Men were already pushing it closed behind him. He heard the clatter of hoofs on stone as the horse archers came through. He turned and saw the garrison's archers run in and the gates close behind them.

I made it.

CHAPTER TWENTY-TWO

FLORENCE, SPRING 1400

It was spring in the Tuscan countryside, yet the couple that rode up to the walls of Florence were dressed as winter and summer.

Plethon and Fiorenza looked like allegories. The philosopher was robed in his usual toga while Fiorenza was dressed in dragon-green damask, every inch the Byzantine princess that she was. He was Father Frost, Old Man Winter: white of hair, beard, toga and horse. She was the early blush of summer, buttercups and ripened corn. People had stood by the side of the road to stare at the strange pair since they'd landed in Italy. They'd stared at them in Naples, in Rome, and all spaces between. Now they were staring at them from the walls of Florence.

Plethon had spent Christmas at Constantinople, thinking it less merry than the one he'd spent in Mistra. The Emperor Manuel had been moody and his court's new ceremonial hadn't lent itself to the festive season. And then there'd been Armageddon to think of. The end of the world was apparently nigh.

So it was with some relief that he'd taken ship for Chios in early April in a world that was still intact. With him had gone Marchese Longo, Dimitri and the engineer Benedo Barbi, who'd done what they'd come to do to the Turkish cannon and whom no amount of Manuel's flattery would compel to stay in Constantinople. The city was safe until new guns arrived from Venice and who knew when that might be? After all, Chios was still Genoese.

The Turkish galleys in the Propontis had hardly given the Genoese round ship that slipped out of Pera a second glance, minding more about things going in than out. Plethon was surprised to note that there were only half the galleys that there'd been the week before.

It had taken two days for them to get to Chios and two more to decant Dimitri and Barbi and swap Longo for his wife, a good deal of gold and a small army for an escort. They'd then sailed to Methoni and, from there, ridden straight to Mistra.

They'd stayed in Mistra for only a day, Fiorenza befriending the Despoena while Plethon spoke to the Despot. When he'd finished doing that, he'd ridden out of the city with a guard of three Varangians and some spades.

From Mistra, they'd gone back to Methoni, reboarded their ship and crossed the straits to the Italian mainland, landing at the port of Otranto on its southernmost tip.

For Fiorenza, the ride up through the Kingdom of Naples had been a depressing one. Ever since the murder of the childless Queen Joan eighteen years earlier, the country had quivered to the tread of Angevin armies and the once-fertile region of Apulia was a place of derelict fields and beggars. Their Genoese escort had ridden up beside them to shield them from outstretched hands, shaken fists and the curses of people with little left to lose. In Naples they'd met one of the Angevins.

King Ladislaus was of the senior branch and had finally

dislodged Louis of Anjou from his capital the year before. Plethon and Fiorenza had made their reverences and tried not to notice the royal stutter, an inconvenience that had dogged Ladislaus ever since the Archbishop of Arles had tried to poison him ten years before. Life seemed precarious in Naples.

Plethon had explained as they'd ridden out of the city. 'Ladislaus and Louis are both of the Angevin line,' he'd said. 'They both lay claim to the Kingdom of Naples and each is supported by a different Pope: Ladislaus by Rome and Louis by the Antipope in Avignon. This poor kingdom is where the two Popes fight each other by proxy.'

From Naples they'd ridden north to Rome to meet with Pope Boniface and King Sigismund of Hungary, the man who'd commanded half the Christian army at Nicopolis and so nearly turned defeat into victory.

Rome had once been a city of a million souls, the marble centre of the Roman world. Now its inhabitants numbered fewer than twenty thousand and it was a place where wild animals scavenged among the grass that grew beside its ancient ruins. It was a place of riots and anarchy and they'd been obliged to meet in the fortress of Sant' Angelo where the ashes of Roman emperors lay.

While Fiorenza had tactfully gone to Roman mass, Plethon had met Pope and King in a room without windows. The meeting had been one of reference: oblique, opaque; the vaguest of threat cloaked in mantles of velvet courtesy, the mantles changing colour at a speed that made the change unseen. It had been a dialogue of shadows in which the treasure had been mentioned only once.

The day of their departure was bright and clear and Fiorenza filled her lungs after the fug of Rome. The fields around were full of men sowing seed, of donkeys and windmills and apple orchards with nets beneath the trees. There were meadows and breezes and the murmur of brooks. She wanted to know about the schism in the Western Church.

'It began just after the turn of the last century,' Plethon explained. 'Pope Clement refused to go to Rome and be the victim of robber bands. So the whole papal nonsense moved to Avignon in France.'

'Where it prospered?'

'Where it certainly prospered. The new air of France inspired new ways of fleecing their flock. They came up with a "Treasury of Merit", funded in heaven by Christ and the saints, from which the Pope could draw to issue indulgences.'

'Indulgences?'

'I don't think we have them yet in the Eastern Church. They shorten your time in purgatory. Ha!' Plethon sat back and snorted at the miracle of purgatory and the monumental deceit of the Catholic Church. It was so loud that his horse started, thinking, perhaps, that it was carrying another.

'So why are there two Popes now?'

'Now that's a good question,' Plethon continued. 'Twenty years ago, an unusually virtuous Pope decided that the swill of Avignon was too much even for the papal nose and moved back to Rome. But his successor was so bad that the Cardinals made another Pope and put him back in Avignon. Now the whole of Europe is split in its allegiance and, of course, the Pope in France has become an instrument of French policy and the Italian one the pawn of the City States.'

'Which is where Ladislaus and Louis come in?'

Plethon nodded. 'Indeed. It's as I said. Ladislaus is backed by Boniface and Louis by Benedict in Avignon. A quartet of Christian fools.'

Fiorenza, smiling, said to him: 'Plethon, you don't believe in anything, do you?'

The philosopher turned, the image of outrage imprinted on his face like a Greek mask. 'Lady, to say such a thing! I am a man of unwavering Hellenic principle!'

'Ah, "Hellenic",' she laughed. 'Now, there's a word.'

'Which has meaning,' continued Plethon, now speaking with his arms. 'It means that we stop all this Christian nonsense and go back to our roots: Athens and Sparta and a people in control of its own destiny!'

'Like Luke?'

Plethon chose to ignore the question. 'We need to reimagine the same culture, the same society that bred men like Leonidas to defend the pass at Thermopylae. Three hundred stopped a million. It can happen again.'

'But the Persians won at Thermopylae.'

'They won the battle but lost the war. Greece remained free and became Rome. Now we must do it again.'

'Which is why we're here.'

'Which is why we're here. Greece and Rome have always been one. There's something interesting happening in this country which we can help with. Perhaps it's time for a reunion.'

'As a last resort?'

Plethon looked across at her. She was beautiful and clever beyond measure. She knew exactly what the plan was. Ultimately. 'If all else fails, yes,' he said quietly. 'A reunion.'

Fiorenza was silent for a long time, deep in thought and oblivious to the flies that made her horse nod. At last she asked: 'So why do you hold out any hope of this schism ending?'

'Because the French want it to. Theologians at the University of Paris have persuaded their mad king to rise above national concerns for once. He must be very mad.'

Fiorenza knew about the French King. All the world knew that Charles *le Fou* of France thought he was made of glass, refused to wash and ran naked through the corridors of his palace. It was said that they'd had to wall up the doors of the Hôtel Saint-Pol to stop him getting out. 'Would that be enough to end it?' she asked.

'Probably not,' Plethon replied. 'But then I have something else. Something better.'

It took a week to ride to Florence and the days remained fair throughout. Fiorenza had been looking forward to entering its walls and seeing this new rival to Venice in power and beauty. But she was to do so alone.

Plethon stopped his horse at the city gates. 'I am to meet someone outside the walls,' he said. 'You go in with the escort. Remember we are to present ourselves to the Signoria tonight.' Fiorenza frowned. Plethon hadn't mentioned his meeting.

At leisurely pace and enjoying the sunshine upon his scalp, the philosopher rode alone up one of the hills that surrounded the city until he reached a long flight of steps where he dismounted. Leaving his horse, he climbed slowly up, passing the Stations of the Cross, until he reached the Church of San Miniato, which sat amidst belvedered gardens at the top.

He was greeted by buzzing and the pleasant smell of honey. There were monks everywhere, men of the Olivetan Order who wore gloves and veils beneath broad-brimmed hats and who tended a row of beehives. Others were working on a garden where sleepy cats stretched out like courtesans between the undulation of ridge and furrow until nudged aside by hoes.

Plethon was investigating gooseberries beneath a net designed to foil starlings when a man beside him spoke. 'The bees do their work twice. They make the honey and they pollinate. What could be a better example of godly industry?'

The philosopher turned and found himself looking at a man of startling ugliness. Giovanni de' Medici was around forty years of age but looked much older. He had a large nose set within a warted face and his hair was thin and began somewhere far above his temples. He had bulging eyes and thin lips that were, so it was said, designed never to smile. But he was smiling now.

'You are Georgius Gemistus Plethon,' he said. 'News of your toga travels ahead of you.'

Plethon bowed, just missing the head of the other who'd chosen to do the same. 'And you are the banker whom my friends on Chios have much to thank for. It seems your investment was a sound one.'

De' Medici nodded. 'I hear that one of these friends is with you. My agent on the island is much taken with her.' There was a loud curse behind him and the banker turned. 'Careful with that eagle!' he shouted. 'One feather lost and you'll never hoist again!'

Workmen, stripped to the waist, stood upon scaffolding set against the front of the church. Two of them were at the top, pulling on a rope to which was tied a large stone eagle clutching a bale of wool cloth. Two more straddled the top of the church, waiting to guide the bird to its nest.

Giovanni de' Medici turned back to Plethon. 'The eagle is the sign of the Arte di Calimala, who maintain this church. They are the guild of cloth-finishers, hence the bale of wool. We take pride in the church.'

The explanation was brief and without waste and Plethon hoped that the discussion to come would be equally succinct. But where were they to have it? The banker's message had promised somewhere discreet.

De' Medici took his arm. 'Let me show you something.'

The two men walked over to the belvedere. Before them stretched a city cradled between hills, a pearl set within a band of emeralds. It was a walled sea of red and orange tiles that washed up against a lighthouse at its centre, striped black and white.

Giovanni was pointing at it. 'Giotto's *campanile*.' He turned. 'Why so tall? Because we are a city fond of masses, public meetings and curfews, all of which require bells. And when they clamour, we are at war.' He paused. 'I mean to tell you that you have arrived at a place which takes its civic responsibilities very seriously.'

Plethon looked down at the campanile and the great church beside it, equally striped. He thought of a new animal he'd heard about from the land of the jornufa, a horse that looked like this. There was something missing.

'Yes, it needs a dome,' said Giovanni. 'But such a dome! No one has yet come up with a design that will carry the weight.' He turned. 'Shall we go and talk?'

The man was already on his way and Plethon hoped that it was to a place where they could sit. His legs ached after the long climb. They walked through the gardens and into the darkness of a big church where heaven flung its promise through windows high in the walls. There were eagles everywhere.

At the back of the church were steps leading down to a crypt, and Plethon found himself being led into a low forest of pillars and vaults with tiered candles playing their light against saints and sinners that covered every inch of the walls. The place was discreet but eternity would watch over them.

They sat on a bench in front of the altar and Plethon looked around him. The crypt was empty and the columns too slender to hide anyone. The air was cold and he pulled the folds of his toga over his arms.

Giovanni de' Medici was watching him carefully, one eye closed as if taking aim. He said: 'I have been asking myself why the great Plethon should wish to meet a humble merchant from Florence. I would ask you to tell me.'

Plethon was pleased to note that the crypt did not carry sound. Eternity held no echo. 'It is', he said, 'to do with what you are, de' Medici. And that is not a merchant.'

The Italian opened the eye that had been closed. 'Not so? My family imports wool from Flanders. We dye, stretch, full and calendar it. Then we sell it. Is that not the work of a merchant?'

Plethon nodded. 'It is. But you have not done that for many years. Do I need to describe your life?' He paused and then, getting no answer, continued. 'Fifteen years ago, you were working for your cousin Vieri di Cambio in his bank in Rome where you learnt the business of the papacy. Now you have your own bank in partnership with Benedetto di Bardi who runs the branch in Rome. Your bank is small and therefore has the benefit that kings do not ask it for loans and then default on them, as King Edward of England did fifty years past. This happened to the Alberti family who've lost the Pope's business, so there's a vacancy. You are small, you need to get bigger and you want the Curia's money. Which makes you invaluable to my plan.'

The man next to him leant back in the pew. He ran his hand through his wisps of hair. 'Ah, your plan. I was hoping we'd come to that.'

Plethon glanced around once more. The only movement in the crypt came from the candlelit martyrs; the only sound was the murmur of monks chanting somewhere outside. He leant forward and his voice was little above a whisper. 'I am told that you are a man of discretion, de' Medici. I will have to believe it so.' He paused and brought his hands together as if they held the plan. 'My wish is to reunite the Christian Churches. First to heal the schism in the West and then to bring together the Churches of Rome and Byzantium.'

De' Medici whistled softly. 'You wish for a lot, Plethon. Why? Is it for the good of your eternal soul?'

Plethon sat back. Then he gestured slowly to the crypt around them. 'What will happen to this great Church of San Miniato when the Turks come?' he asked quietly. 'How will Giotto's campanile suit as a minaret, do you think, its bells replaced by a muezzin?' He leant forward. 'What will happen to the profitable profession of banking in a Muslim world? Do you know how quick it is to cross the sea from Methoni to Taranto as I have just done? Do you know how close the Turk is to taking Mistra?'

Giovanni de' Medici was no longer smiling. Plethon went on, 'I know that you prefer trade to politics, that you've paid fines rather than perform the duties of *gonfaloniere* for your city, but self-interest should inspire you in this matter, de' Medici. My plan can make you very rich.'

Both men were silent after that, each contemplating treasure of a different kind. Then the banker said: 'So what is your plan?'

Plethon looked down at his hands. Their fingers were interlinked but the palms were open. The plan was to be revealed. 'Both Popes are old and cannot be expected to live long. My plan is to persuade each to ask their cardinals to swear that, when they die, whichever of them is elected Pope will resign his office immediately. Then the combined cardinals will meet in council to elect a single Pontiff who will rule from Rome.'

Giovanni de' Medici was already shaking his head. 'But what would it take to achieve such a thing? Why would the Pope agree?'

'One already has. I come from Boniface in Rome.' Plethon moved along the bench to his companion so that he was closer than he might wish to the other's warts. 'As for the cardinals, it would take what it always takes. Money and force. Money to bribe, force where the bribes fail.'

'And I supply the money? Why would I do that?'

Plethon smiled. 'Because, my dear Giovanni, you wish to be the richest banker in Florence. You want Brunelleschi to build your new palace. You want the Peruzzi to stop talking behind their hands about upstarts from the Mugello. And the only way to do all this is by becoming God's banker.' He paused, letting the words settle. He said softly, 'The Pope that returns to Rome as the only Pope will be a grateful man. And, with the entire papal revenues once more intact, a rich one.'

But de' Medici looked far from persuaded. He pursed his lips thinned in concentration and looked over to the altar, perhaps hoping for some sign of divine will. 'What about the force? Who provides that? Ladislaus?'

Plethon said, 'Possibly Ladislaus. And he might soon have some money since he told me he's to marry Mary of Lusignan who'll bring Cypriot sugar to the match. But Ladislaus might not be acceptable to the French. Remember, Pope Boniface crowned him King of Naples when Clement in Avignon had already crowned his cousin, Louis of Anjou. Anyway, he probably doesn't want to get poisoned again.'

'Who then? Visconti of Milan? Niccolò d'Este of Ferrara? He's merely a boy.'

Plethon continued to shake his head. 'No, I had in mind someone else.'

'Ah, then Carlo Malatesta, Lord of Rimini? He is friend to Florence, Venice and the Papal States. He would bring in Mantua through his Gonzaga wife and the French like him for his opposition to Visconti.'

Plethon said, 'He is Italian and Italian will not serve.' He paused. 'What do you know of Sigismund of Hungary?'

The banker looked surprised, then less so. He nodded. 'I know him well. I lend him money. He was at Nicopolis where he got away but his daughter was taken by the Turk: the beautiful Angelina.'

'Yes, and he vowed he would avenge Nicopolis. Without Burgundy next time.' Plethon looked at his companion closely. 'Is he a good Christian, do you know?'

De' Medici thought before he spoke. 'He is a practical man. And he'd like to be Holy Roman Emperor one day.' He paused and narrowed his eyes. 'You know, of course, that he and Ladislaus are mortal enemies, both claiming the crown of Hungary?'

Plethon nodded. 'I had heard.' He scratched his beard. 'This daughter . . . Angelina. She is illegitimate. Is he fond?'

'No father is fonder. She is his only child.'

Plethon nodded. 'Well, I saw him as well in Rome. He agrees to the plan.'

There was silence in the church. De' Medici was looking at the man next to him in admiration. Then he said, 'Your grasp of Italian politics is impressive, Plethon. Do you even have a candidate for Pope?'

Plethon smoothed his toga over his knees. He lowered his voice to just above a whisper. 'No, but you do. Tell me about Baldassare Cossa, Giovanni. He sounds interesting.'

De' Medici let out a long breath. 'Now that *is* impressive. What do you know?'

'That you've just bought him his cardinal's hat. Ten thousand florins, I believe: a fabulous sum. There must be some purpose to such magnanimity.'

The Florentine laughed. 'There's competition. Venice wants Angelo Correr, cousin to the Doge. And he should be persuadable on union. After all, he was titular Patriarch of Constantinople and has been discussing *Filioque* issues with your own Patriarch Matthew.'

Plethon shook his head. 'Too old, too godly. The battle will be fierce. Baldassare Cossa is well chosen: he is greedy, ruthless and intelligent, a winning combination for Pope.'

De' Medici was silent for a long time. The only indication that he'd found interesting matter in what Plethon had said was in his breathing, which had quickened. His goggle eyes were a little wider, his cheeks pinker, and his templed hands were raised to his lips in thought.

Eventually he turned and asked, 'But how will you persuade the two Popes to do this when they have excommunicated each other? How will you get them to persuade their cardinals?'

Plethon looked into the banker's eyes. 'You will just have to trust me on that. I have the means to do it and, to judge from my meeting with Boniface in Rome, it will work.'

The Italian nodded slowly. 'And you go on from here to Avignon?'

'Yes.'

De' Medici was still nodding, this time with his fist beneath his chin. 'It might just work,' he said. Then: 'Where does the Princess come in?'

For a moment, Plethon didn't know who he was talking about. Then he realised.

Fiorenza.

'She is here to give you gold.'

De' Medici smiled. 'Ah, the final carrot. Would this be the repayment of the loan to Chios?'

'The final part, I believe. Delivered to you with interest, although I gather you don't call it that.'

The banker laughed, a thin sound from an unused organ. 'My agent there will be disappointed. He's in love with her and needs a reason to stay.'

Plethon shook his head. 'They think he's a spy. For Venice.'

Laughter again, this time louder. 'Tommaso Bardolli a spy? Don't be ridiculous! He's too busy being in love. She encourages it.'

Plethon frowned. 'The Princess Fiorenza encourages it?'

'She flirts with him. It was she who told him to stay on the island.'

In fact Tommaso Bardolli had little choice but to stay on the island. Not long after Fiorenza and Plethon had set sail from Chios, the galleys that the philosopher had noticed weren't at Constantinople turned up in the bay of Chora.

Their admiral was a nervous man. He had been given strict and challenging instructions. He was to take ten ships, fill them with two thousand janissaries, sail to Chios and take it. And he was to do it in two weeks. Now the two weeks were up and the island still hadn't been taken.

Prince Suleyman, still smarting over the loss of the cannon, had been the one who ordered them there. He'd not take Constantinople until he had more cannon, and the Serenissima had made it clear that they wouldn't even start making them until Chios had been delivered to them.

Now, standing on the battlements of the castle at Chora, Marchese Longo was thinking about snakes. Since antiquity, Chios had been famous for snakes, its Greek name Ofioussa meaning 'having snakes'. Some said that the gods had given the island mastic as the means to live with them. At that moment, it seemed to Longo that the bay was full of them, its surface a churn of writhing bodies that rose and turned and spat, their darting tongues breaking out to lick the air.

The meltemi.

Thank God for the meltemi. The wind was early this year, early and strong. It had started almost the moment that the Turkish galleys had broken the horizon two weeks ago and had yet to stop. The Chians saw it as proof that God was with them and put their swords to the grindstone with new fire in their bellies.

Around Longo stood the men from the campagna, all armed and grave. Zacco Banca turned to him.

'Marchese, we thought that our mastic would protect us. Has the Sultan changed his mind?'

Longo shrugged, pulling his cloak tighter to his shoulders. 'Perhaps it is not Bayezid we are facing. They say that he's gone to Wallachia.'

Gabriele Adorno nodded. 'In which case this has been ordered by Suleyman. He means to take our island and hand it to Venice. What do we do?'

Longo looked at the galleys lined up at the mouth of the bay. They were rocking like cradles and presumably the poor wretches within were mewling and puking as the contents of cradles do. The ships were crammed with men desperate for dry land, yet every attempt to disembark them had, so far, ended in disaster. The landing craft were flat-bottomed and didn't stand a chance in such a sea.

'Perhaps nothing. The wind does our work for us.' It was Benedo Barbi who'd spoken. He was standing between Longo and Dimitri and had had to raise his voice to be heard. The wind made noise of everything it met: ropes, flags, cloaks; each snapped its own particular protest.

'How much longer will they bear it?' asked Dimitri. 'The decks must be awash with vomit.'

Longo nodded. He looked up into the sky. It was blue and without cloud and the sun was at its zenith which meant that the wind was about to blow more strongly. It always did in the afternoons. 'If it will just continue for a few more days,' he said. He turned to a man behind him whose vestments were billowing like sails. 'Monseigneur, keep those masses going. I want one an hour.'

The priest bowed, his hands clamped to his knees. 'It is to be wished that the Princess Fiorenza's passage was safe in such seas. We will pray for that too.'

Longo frowned. He'd hoped she would be in Florence by now, delivering gold to Giovanni de' Medici and telling him that they had no more use for Tommaso Bardolli on the island. It seemed an unlikely coincidence that the Turks had appeared two days after a large part of the garrison had left. Where was the agent now? He'd have to have him followed.

In Edirne, it was evening and the daughter of the King of Hungary had just been visited by a priest found somewhere within the small Christian community that resided in that city. He was a small man, tonsured and smelling of cheese, whose gloom had preceded him into the room and stayed long after he'd left.

The Princess's condition was deteriorating by the day. She was whiter than the sheet beneath her and her eyes were sunk deep into a face washed with perspiration. She drifted in and out of fever and could hold nothing down. The only thing she could do was read and she did this continuously, finding it easier than talking.

It was now five months since she'd taken to her bed and the palace doctors had tried everything they knew to try. She'd been starved, bled, wrapped in wool, fed every disgusting herb under heaven and, moment by moment, the life had drifted away from her like pollen from a flower. Anna and Maria had sat by her bed day and night, rigid with cheer, and only once had they broken down. It was the day her hair had been taken from her.

Now, shaved and shivering, Angelina lay asleep in sheets drenched with sweat and the first traces of blood. They'd given her a sleeping draught an hour past and she would not wake. Maria had pulled back the sheet to change it and was the first to notice the stain.

'It must be in her urine,' she whispered. She'd gone as white as the patient, her eyes wide with horror. 'Look, it's between her legs, from where she's wet the bed.'

'What *does* that?' asked Anna.

Maria was shaking her head. 'There is something in India they call *cholera* which comes from bad water. Otherwise . . .'

'Otherwise?'

Maria looked at her and there was dread in her eyes. 'Otherwise, it could be arsenic or certain snakes' poison.'

They stared at each other without speaking, both thinking the same thing. Only one person in the harem would have access to such poison.

Gülçiçek.

'We need to find the doctors,' said Anna, rising. She bent over Angelina to kiss her forehead, prising the book from her sleeping fingers. She held Angelina's hand in hers, staring at it.

The fingers.

Something about Angelina's fingers was wrong. She looked closely at them, at their flaked tips; then she raised them to her nose. She looked at the book.

Of course.

In the corridor were the palace doctors. Their heads were joined and they were speaking in whispers. Beside them stood the Chief Black Eunuch. Anna motioned him to join her.

'It's poison,' she said, 'I've seen it on her fingers. Someone coated the corners of the pages in the book that I lent her.'

The Kislar Ağasi was a giant from Mali and famous for his calm. Early in his Timbuktu upbringing, his calm had been mistaken for stupidity and he'd been sold as a slave. He'd secured his role as ruler of the Sultan's harem through deploying that composure to best effect. Now he said nothing.

'You know who's done this,' Anna said, looking up at him.

The eunuch remained silent. He was dressed in a thoub of flawless white and not one muscle in his giant, impassive face moved.

'Angelina is near death. The priest has been. Our only chance of an antidote is in knowing the poison.'

The eunuch wasn't looking at her. His half-closed eyes were fixed on something beyond and above her.

'In the not very distant future,' Anna continued, her voice

even, 'I shall be married to the next sultan and you will either be free and rich or have died in as agonising a way as someone crueller than I will have devised.' She paused. One tiny bead of sweat had appeared on the man's temple. She rose on tiptoe to it and whispered: 'I want to know the poison, Kislar Ağasi.

CHAPTER TWENTY-THREE

EDIRNE, SPRING 1400

Three days later, Bayezid's mother was dead. No one had known the Valide Sultan's age, only that she was infinitely old and infinitely powerful. Some said that she'd exercised her power well, others that she'd been a scheming witch. Anna felt that her only good act had been the one she'd performed on her deathbed. As to how she'd been persuaded of it, Anna preferred not to know.

The man had set off for Venice as soon as they knew where the poison had come from. Now he'd returned with bad news. The Kislar Ağasi was passing it on to Anna and Maria. 'The Jew had no antidote.'

'Did he even say what poison it was?' asked Maria.

The giant shook his head. 'He said that it was poison from many different snakes. Snakes from the island of Chios.'

Anna put her hand on his arm. 'Chios is close. We can send for someone.'

The eunuch frowned. 'I fear not, lady. Chios is under attack.'

On Chios, the meltemi was over. Despite the Monseigneur's many masses, the wind had blown itself out. Or almost.

From Marchese Longo's vantage point on the castle walls, he could see smoke from the burning fields drifting north into the foothills of Mount Aipos and, closer, the dust of pounded masonry following it. The Turkish galleys had hove to beneath the walls and were firing their cannon. The guns were small and the firing infrequent but dust had obliterated the sun. The sound was deafening.

'There they are.' Dimitri was pointing south across the plain towards the Kambos where the fields had been set alight. Emerging from the smokescreen were the janissary ortas and they were advancing in good order. They had been dropped further up the coast an hour before.

First came groups of infantry behind large wicker screens, then archers who stopped behind them to loose volley after volley of arrows. Next came the water-carriers who would also tend to the wounded. It was an impressive and entirely silent manoeuvre and Longo found himself nodding in approval.

'No wonder they win,' he murmured, turning to Benedo Barbi, who was on his other side. 'Look at them.'

'Look at their clothes,' said Lara, who'd arrived later. She and the monks of the Nea Moni monastery had set up a hospital inside the castle. The meltemi had at least given them time to prepare.

The janissaries were certainly fine. Each wore a tall white *börk*, and beneath they wore mail hauberks over long tunics and boots of red leather. Some carried banners with crescents and the hand of Fatima on them. In front of them, soldiers of the campagna were streaming back through the suburbs of the town, some carrying wounded. The town's population had taken shelter inside the castle.

'I'd better go back to the monks. I wish the Princess was here.'

Longo wished it too, and not just for her healing. He missed every part of his wife.

Barbi said: 'If only we had some cannon. We'd make better use of them than these clowns.'

The Turks' first rounds had been aimed at the row of windmills on the harbour front. Every one had missed and one of the cannon had exploded, setting fire to the sail above. Now they had chosen the easier target of the walls.

'They are keeping our heads down in the castle while they burn down the town around us,' said Dimitri. 'We don't have long.'

Longo nodded. With half of the garrison in Italy, they were outnumbered twenty to one. They had no cannon beyond the little ribaudekin given by the Duke of Milan and all the Greek fire had been used up in Constantinople. It would be over quickly.

Longo looked up to the sky. His fingers eased the top of his cuirass, which was digging into his neck. The sun was hidden by the smoke and the air smelt of burning. From the town he could hear the shouts of panicked men and animals. Somewhere a donkey was braying without cease.

He thought of Giovanni. Would he become part of the *Devshirme?* Would he be sent away to become a janissary as they'd meant to do to Luke? He'd heard that Greek families on the mainland were now offering their children for the levy with bribes.

Not Giovanni. Not while I am alive to prevent it.

His son was in the new port of Limenas. He was in the care of a fisherman and his wife who'd been given money to take him to Mistra where he would be reunited with his mother. He'd agreed the plan with Fiorenza before she'd left. They would leave as soon as the messenger told them that Chora had fallen.

Longo looked back at the janissaries. They were almost at the castle walls now and scaling ladders were being brought forward. The huge gates of the castle had shut behind the last of the fleeing men. Everything in the town was being set alight and plumes of black, acrid smoke rose from the houses.

It won't be long now.

A horn sounded. It did not come from the town but from the ships. Longo walked to the walls overlooking the harbour. The Turkish cannon had fallen silent and the flagship had hoisted a new pennant. The galleys were turning, their oars digging deep to bring them around.

The engineer arrived beside him. 'What are they doing?'

Longo shrugged. 'Perhaps they don't want to hit their own men now that they're at our walls.'

Barbi shook his head. 'Their aim is certainly wanting, but you'd think that this would be the time to increase their firing. Look.' He was pointing back down the coastline to the place where the Turks had first landed. The boats that had brought them from the ships were working their way along the shoreline towards the town.

Dimitri had joined them. 'Do they mean to come off and attack from some other direction, do you think?'

The others remained silent. It seemed inexplicable. Longo led them back across to the walls above the town. The Genoese archers on the ramparts were shouting into the smoke below.

'They're calling them cowards,' said Barbi as they approached. 'Is that wise?'

They came up to the archers and saw what they saw. Through

the smoke billowing up from the houses were janissaries in retreat. Maintaining their impeccable discipline, the men were marching back through the streets of Chora in the direction of the boats that were coming to get them.

Longo heard footsteps behind him. Members of the signore were approaching, Gabriele Adorno at their head, Zacco Banca beside him.

'What is this, Longo? Do they come at us another way now?' Adorno's white beard brushed his black armour as he spoke. 'Where are they going?'

'I couldn't say,' replied Longo. He glanced up at the sun, fierce now without the dust. He put his hand to his brow and looked out to sea. 'There's a boat coming towards us.'

A pinnace had detached itself from the flagship. It was more a *barche* with a tassled awning at the stern. It had an ornate ribaudekin set into its prow and a turbaned man stood astride the muzzle. The sea was still choppy and its scalloped waves rocked the boat from side to side and Longo wondered whether the man would make it to the shore.

He did. Ten minutes later the men of the campagna and Benedo Barbi were assembled at the top of the harbour steps watching the man straighten his turban as he stepped from the boat. On dry land, he was impressive. Everything about him was large, from his turban to the curl of his moustache; from his sash to the sword it held to his waist. In one hand was an enamelled mace, in the other a scroll.

He reached the top of the steps and bowed. 'I am the Yeniçeri Ağasi. I command the janissaries. Which of you is the Lord Longo?' The man spoke Greek as if he was native to the tongue.

Marchese Longo exchanged glances with Gabriele Adorno. 'I am Longo.'

'I have a message from the Prince Suleyman,' said the Aga, lifting the scroll. 'There is to be a truce for a week. We need someone with the skill to heal snake poison, snake poison from this island. Do you know of such?'

Zacco Banco stepped forward. He was shaking his head. 'Are we to understand that you intend delaying your attack so that we can *help* you?' He sounded incredulous. 'What will you do at the end of the week?'

The janissary turned to him. 'We will return the person and renew the attack.'

Banco snorted. 'Why would we help our enemy?' he asked. 'It is unnatural.'

The Aga turned back to Longo and held out the scroll. 'It is to be read by you, Lord Longo. It has the seal of my master and has not been opened.'

Longo took the scroll, broke the seal and opened the parchment. He read the contents twice, then rolled it up and tucked it into his belt. He turned to Benedo Barbi. 'Go and find Dimitri. And tell him to bring Lara.'

Two days later, Bayezid was in the throne room at Edirne, with his son Mehmed, and was in a dark mood. One of his fillings had fallen out. The doctors had prescribed the same opiates given to Angelina but they'd only delivered nightmares. To make it worse, he'd just had to endure a dirge from the janissary *mehter* band for two hours and the beat of the *davul* was still thumping in his temples.

'Thank Allah we're not widows,' he said to his second son, his eyes closed and a finger to each temple. 'The Koran dictates four months and ten days for them. We'll only have to mourn her for three days.'

Bayezid had returned from Wallachia immediately on hearing of the death of his mother. He'd left his army there to persuade the Voivode Mircea not to repeat the mistake of Nicopolis. Now he was pacing up and down, speaking through lips that hardly moved, his hand nursing his jaw. In middle age, the Sultan had lost all the dash of his youth. He was bloated, puffy of face, and his breath was a mix of new wine and old food. Yildirim was long dead.

Mehmed was wearing a simple tunic without adornment or jewellery of any kind, the Koran being specific on the matter of what to wear in mourning. At sixteen, he was well made and had the darkness of his mother Devlet Hatun, wife to Bayezid and sister to Yakub Bey. He was a gazi to his fingertips. 'Are my brothers here yet?' he asked.

Bayezid shook his head, fingers still attached. 'Musa is here somewhere with that Bedreddin creature, the one who talks in riddles. Suleyman? He's here somewhere but I suspect avoiding me.' He came over to Mehmed, sat and looked at his son. 'What was she like?'

Bayezid was speaking of Mehmed's future bride, Emine, daughter to Nasireddin Bey who ruled the beylik of Dulkadir, from where he'd come.

'She's twelve, Father. We didn't talk.'

Bayezid opened his eyes, laughed, then winced. 'You are fortunate.'

They were sitting on a wide divan covered by thick carpet. Mehmed ran his palm over its surface. 'There was news of Tamerlane,' he said quietly. 'I got it from the Portuguese ambassador. He was visiting Nasireddin Bey on his way back from Samarcand where he'd seen the Chinese envoys treated with contempt at Temur's court. He believes Temur will invade China.'

Bayezid nodded. More pain. 'We know that he hasn't left Samarcand yet.' He paused, putting his hand on his son's. 'You think we should go east?'

Mehmed nodded. 'As do you, really. Why else am I marrying the Dulkadir Princess?'

Mehmed led the court faction that wanted to strengthen the eastern borders of the Empire. Dulkadir was on the frontier with Qara Yusuf's Black Sheep Ilkhanate, was still independent and a more reliable ally than the Karamanids.

In fact, Bayezid had thought that if Tamerlane was on his way to certain defeat in China, he might look at alternatives for his son. But he was still smarting from the snub delivered from Cyprus: Mary of Lusignan was to be wed elsewhere. After that, he'd resolved to avoid further humiliation in the west. 'Yes,' he said. 'The marriage is important.'

They heard the sound of steps in the hall beyond the throne room. They looked up to see the curtain part and Suleyman enter. He was dressed in armour spattered with dust, suggesting a hard ride from the siege. He looked at his father and brother in turn, then at their joined hands. Bayezid rose. He stared at his heir but said nothing.

Suleyman broke the silence. 'It was to get the cannon, Father. Venice would not have provided them otherwise.'

Bayezid walked slowly over to a table on which stood a cup and a bowl of sugar. He drained one and set his eye on the other. His tongue sought out the hole in his tooth. 'You disobeyed me.'

Suleyman shook his head. 'Father, what is more important, Constantinople or Chios?'

'That's not the point.' Bayezid was shouting now. 'You disobeyed me. I told you not to touch Chios and you invaded it.'

'For the cannon . . .'

'Which you've already managed to see destroyed.' Bayezid looked at his eldest son with contempt. 'And there's worse, isn't there? Your red-haired concubine used your seal without you knowing. She has humiliated you.'

This was the awful truth that Suleyman had heard on his arrival. Anna had used his seal to bring Lara from Chios. She'd committed something close to treason. 'Father . . .'

'This is the girl you were proposing to marry,' Bayezid continued, walking over to a window and looking out. 'Well, you must sweep from your mind any notion of that now. She must be punished. How will you punish her for what she has done to you?'

Suleyman thought quickly. Was his father finding reason to kill Anna? He said: 'She is the daughter of the Protostrator of Mistra. If we kill her, she will be another martyr to their cause. Another relic. If we banish her, it will be what she wants. I will imprison her.'

Bayezid considered this. Gülçiçek had wanted Anna dead but he saw no merit in creating martyrs. He nodded. 'Temur will winter in the Qarabagh where he always does. You will take half the army and march east to keep watch on him.'

Suleyman recoiled. 'But, Father, you have tasked me to take Constantinople.'

'And you have failed.' Bayezid glanced behind him. 'We will see if your brother Mehmed fares better.'

Suleyman closed his eyes. A memory: he was in a tent and speaking to Zoe.

If we go east, it will be because Constantinople hasn't fallen. Mehmed will inherit this empire and I will go to the bowstring.

Much later, Anna went to sit alone in the place where she knew Suleyman would find her. It was the place where she'd watched the jornufa and heard of Luke's execution. It was the place where Suleyman had kissed her. It was a place of memories, sweet and less so.

The evening was heavy with the scent of flowers newly arrived to the world, breathing deep after the daily exertion of growth. The air was as still as death but Anna felt alive, giddy with the success of her plan. Lara had been brought from Chios, bringing with her the pharmacy she'd created with Fiorenza. Within it had been found the antidotes for Angelina's poison, the fine balance of kill and cure that would fight the toxin on equal terms. The effect had been immediately encouraging. Angelina would live.

Now she had to face Suleyman, the man she'd betrayed completely. She saw a shadow approach amongst the geometry of lawn and hedge and knew that it was he.

Then he was there, mounting the steps of the chiosk as if each was a mountain. He fell on to a bench. Anna looked at him and was shocked. His face had lost its structure, the fine cheekbones collapsed, the chin sunk deep into his chest as if attached by the thin chain of his beard. He looked angry and broken.

She felt a surge of pity. She came and sat beside him. The cicadas chattered of the cycle of day and night and the space in between that belonged to them, unchallenged in their chorus since the caged birds had been set free.

'I'm sorry.' It was all she could think of to say.

There was no movement beside her. The man was either deep in thought or too angry to speak. She hoped for the latter: a sentence of sorts. She wondered, without urgency, if her life was now forfeit.

'Am I to die?'

Suleyman stirred. He lifted his chin and exhaled through pursed lips. He rubbed his eyelids between thumb and forefinger, bringing them together at the bridge of his nose. He spoke, his eyes closed. 'Why did you do it?'

'To save a life.'

'And lose another.'

'Yours or mine?'

He nodded slowly. 'Mine, of course.' He turned to her. 'I'm to leave the siege and go east to watch Tamerlane. When I return, there'll be a new heir.'

'Am I to go with you?'

Suleyman shook his head. 'You are to be imprisoned but released from marriage to me.'

Anna frowned. 'And if I don't want to be released?'

Suleyman glanced at her. 'What you want is immaterial. My father forbids the marriage.' He looked at his hands. 'And you still love another.'

'He is married. I am annulled.'

'Yes, he is married. A Spaniard arrived from Tamerlane. He told us that Tamerlane's mood had not been improved by the refusal of a woman to marry him because she was already married to another: a Varangian. It seems he is still alive but has chosen someone other than you.'

Suleyman looked away. The garden was losing substance, its content merging into different shades of black. Anna rose and walked to the balcony on which she had draped her shawl. She put it over her shoulders and held it to her front with one hand, the other resting on the stone. She'd been shocked by this latest proof of Luke's desertion and needed time to compose herself. She studied the bowed head of the man before her, broken by his love for her. She had dared to hope that news of Luke's marriage was false. Now she knew it to be true.

She said: 'You'll take an army with you?'

'Half the army.'

'And Constantinople?'

'The siege will go on. But without cannon, it can't be taken. So only half the army need remain.'

Anna nodded slowly, considering this. 'Half the army is a lot of soldiers. What would your father have you do in the east?'

'Stay within our borders. Watch Tamerlane's every move and not let him get between us and our new allies.'

'And what if you strayed beyond your borders? What if you brought new territory into the Empire?'

Suleyman glanced up at her. Was this Zoe or Anna speaking? 'Then I would be disobeying orders,' he said carefully.

'Which your father must be getting used to.' She paused. 'It would strengthen your position. No one puts a hero to the bowstring.'

Suleyman straightened. He looked at her for a long while and then, for the first time, smiled. He rose to leave. 'What a Valide Sultan you'd have made.'

CHAPTER TWENTY-FOUR

QARABAGH, OCTOBER 1400

As Bayezid had predicted, that autumn Tamerlane moved his army into its winter camp in the high valleys of the Qarabagh, west of the great Hazar denizi Sea, and not a man within it knew where he planned to go next.

The land was shaped as a kidney bean and bordered on three sides by the mountains of the Great Kirs, where dense forests of oak, hornbeam and beech rose up to white-barked birch and meadows of startling green. It was a place of streams and lakes and rolling pasture. It provided good hunting and clear air where an eagle might spot its prey a mile distant. It was a place, so the army hoped, of rest before the onslaught began.

But the signs were not good. A large Ottoman army under Prince Suleyman had moved east and taken Armenia, which bordered Georgia, a vassal state to Tamerlane. Moreover, a year past, the Georgian King Giorgi had revolted and his punishment could not be delayed to the spring. So the army sharpened its swords, looked to the battered fur of its deels and wondered if Temur himself would lead them into Georgia that winter.

However, it wasn't Tamerlane but Mohammed Sultan who led fifty thousand men into the Land of the Golden Fleece. It was the Prince's first command, a gift from his grandfather to reward and test him. It was the fourth time that a Mongol army had had to invade the troublesome country and Mohammed Sultan was told to make it the last.

King Giorgi was little older than Mohammed Sultan and had already garnered a reputation for daring. He'd led an army to the rescue of his ally Emir Ahmed of Azerbaijan, besieged in the city of Alanjiq, and put Miran Shah to flight. Now he was harbouring Ahmed's son Prince Tahir at his court in Tiflis and, despite Tamerlane's repeated demands, had refused to give him up.

Instead he sent gifts. Envoys had arrived in the meadows of the Qarabagh carrying gold coins struck in the Emperor's name, a thousand horses, vessels of gold, silver and crystal, crates of silk and a balas ruby the size of a walnut.

But Tamerlane remembered similar gifts from the King's father, Bagrat, after the last invasion, including a coat of mail said to have been forged by the Prophet David. The King had converted to Islam, declaring, as was required: '*La ilaha illa'llah Mohammedan rasul' Allah*,' and all his court had knelt and done the same. But once the Lord of the Seven Climes had left, Bagrat had recanted. Now Mohammed Sultan was to wipe away this unsightly stain of Christianity from the cloak of Islam once and for all.

Tamerlane's heir led the army into a country of peaks, gorges, valleys and torrents where spies reported his progress from every hilltop and villages emptied before them, their inhabitants taking their last ear of corn into the mountains behind. But he didn't burn everything to the ground as his grandfather had done. He didn't fire the Georgians' homes and desecrate their churches. He didn't send spies ahead to spread terror. Instead, he invited the villagers to return to their homes and live in peace under Mongol rule.

Luke was responsible for this, helped in large part by Shulen. He showed to her the stream of logic and she led Mohammed Sultan to drink from it. It helped, of course, that the Prince was in love with her. Every day, she rode beside him at the head of the army, deep in conversation, and when the army retired at night, their murmurs could be heard above the mournful *qavvali* of the Sufi *pirs* who never slept.

The soldiers didn't like it and there was soon grumbling about the lack of pillage. But Mohammed promised them greater booty when they reached the capital Tiflis. And so it happened: they took the city and found living inhabitants better able to say where they'd hidden their treasure than dead ones.

The terrain of Georgia suited Luke and the Varangians' kind of soldiering. They'd been trained by their fathers in the mountains of Mistra and knew how to make the terrain their friend. Each was given a *qoshun* of fifty men to command and they soon made names for themselves for the daring of their night raids. Luke began to be included in the evening briefings when the Mongol generals would gather round the map with Mohammed Sultan, and his advice was sought more and more.

One night when he returned late to the Varangians' tent from a briefing, Matthew was still awake. 'Is there any limit to your talent, old friend?' he asked through a yawn.

Luke was removing his armour. He was very tired. He wanted to sleep as deeply as Nikolas and Arcadius were sleeping.

But Matthew had propped himself up on an elbow. 'You seem to be able to do anything you set your mind to. You'll leave us behind.'

It had been coming. Luke rubbed his eyes. 'How so?'

'Well, you're best friends with Temur's heir. You'll be given a command soon – more than a qoshun. He has you at every briefing.'

It was true that he was the only Varangian invited to the briefings. He laughed. 'Are you jealous, Matthew?'

His friend lay back on the rolled tunic that served for a pillow. He'd not laughed. 'Of course not.' He was silent for a while. Then he asked: 'When you ride together, what do you talk about?'

Luke shrugged. 'Everything. He's interested in everything.' He turned to his oldest friend. He'd never seen him jealous. 'Matthew, I have to befriend him,' he said quietly.

Matthew asked: 'Has he told you where the army's going? I mean after this?'

Luke shook his head. 'Only Tamerlane knows that.'

Matthew grunted. He rolled over and pulled the blanket up over his shoulders. Very soon he was either asleep or pretending to be. But Luke lay awake, deep in thought.

It soon became apparent that Mohammed Sultan had a problem. He hadn't brought the Georgian army to battle. Mongol patrols fanned out across the frozen country and soon word came back that King Giorgi had taken refuge with his army in the cave city of Vardzia, a hundred miles north-west of Tiflis.

Vardzia was a warren of houses, palaces and churches built into the side of a mountain. The only way into it was through a tunnel that led up from the River Mtkvari below. It was said to be impregnable.

They reached Vardzia in a blizzard. Through the driving snow, it was difficult to see the thirteen storeys of cave dwellings that pitted the side of Mount Erusheli, and impossible to see the row upon row of terraced farmland built into the slopes below that sustained it. The army set up camp and wondered what to do.

That evening, the briefing was subdued. 'Queen Tamar designed it well,' said the Prince, looking up at the faces gathered round the map. 'It's too high for scaling ladders and too deep for siege engines. There's an underground spring and the army has food for a year. We can't get at them.' He turned to Luke. 'My generals suggest the usual assault which, if it even succeeds, will kill most of the army. Have you any ideas?'

Luke studied the plan of the cave city drawn up by the army's engineers. In many ways it resembled the villages he'd designed and built in Chios and the problem was similar: how to dislodge an enemy holding the advantages of height and limitless cover. He thought hard. Then it came to him. The difference here was that there was something above. There was high ground above the caves. 'Baskets,' he said.

Mohammed Sultan frowned. 'Baskets, Luke? Is the campaigning too much for you?'

'No, I'm serious, lord. We make baskets and put archers into each. We lower the baskets down from the top of the mountain and the archers shoot flaming arrows into the caves.' He paused and looked at the Prince. 'We smoke them out, highness.'

And so it happened.

Luke led a *hazara* of a thousand archers a mile downstream of the Mtkvari River to a ford where they crossed and then began the ascent around the back of Mount Erusheli. They climbed through thick pine forest, then scree, carrying baskets of saplings bound by leather, and the pulleys to lower them.

At the top, they found the plateau empty of sentries and the archers rested while the engineers erected the pulleys. Then, three to a basket, they began to lower them.

Luke was in the first basket with two archers and a bucket of burning pitch. The archers' arrowheads were wrapped in pitch-soaked hessian. The pulleys had been coated in grease but still squeaked with each lurching drop. Luke held his breath, eyeing the flames beside him and praying that no sudden gust of wind would upset the container. Below them, the sheer side of the mountain fell into an abyss with rocks below. The hand that held his dragon sword was wet with tension.

Silently, silently they came level with the highest caves and saw that the Georgians had barricaded their mouths with defences of wood, straw and mud packed tightly together. There was no sign of any soldiers. Luke looked out to see that the other baskets had reached the caves. He saw Nikolas in one, peering nervously over the side. Matthew and Arcadius were above, waiting to come down next. He raised his sword and turned to the men beside him. 'Light your arrows,' he whispered.

The arrowheads were lowered into the flames.

His sword dropped and he yelled: 'Fire!'

A hundred flaming arrows flew through the air and struck the barricades. Within moments, the fires had spread inside the caves and smoke was billowing out. The Mongol archers had covered their noses and mouths with masks and were able to keep firing. Soon, flaming Georgians were jumping to their deaths.

But the Georgians in the caves below had seen what was happening. They threw aside the barricades and fired up into the baskets. Luke had thought of this. He'd had each basket padded with thick mattresses and the Georgian arrows thudded into straw. He looked up to see more more baskets coming down the mountainside with Matthew in the first. 'Hurry!' he yelled.

The Georgians below had recovered and the arrows now coming at them were aflame. The basket next to Luke's was set ablaze and three Mongols, fire covering every part of them, fell through the air.

Luke looked up. 'Faster, Matthew!' he shouted. 'And swing into the cave-mouths when you get level!'

Already Luke and his companions were pushing and pulling the sides of their basket, trying to get near enough to jump into the caves. Others were doing the same. Then they were close enough.

'Jump!' yelled Luke and he launched himself into the air, his arms flailing, landing inches from where the cave fell into nothing. He threw himself forward, his hands clawing the sand. An archer landed beside him and grabbed his tunic, pulling him in. Then he drew his bow and fired and Luke heard a scream from inside the cave. The other archer landed.

There were a dozen Georgian soldiers in front of them, their shields locked, burning debris all around.

Luke leapt to his feet. 'Charge!' He raised his sword and ran forward, the two archers behind him. The dragon head flashed and came down on a shield, breaking it in two. He raised it again and smashed open a helmet. He swung it to left and right and men fell before it. The sword was possessed by demons; it had a will of its own.

By now, there were others behind him and the shield-wall was backing away, slowly at first and then in panic. A hole opened behind them and the Georgians were jumping through it to the next level down. Luke followed them.

Below were more soldiers, most trying to escape through a tunnel at the back. They turned but it was too late. Luke was on top of them, hacking and stabbing and pushing the dying out of his way. He looked round to see Arcadius at the mouth of the cave. He was grinning. 'It's working!'

It was. The Georgians were in full retreat, running into the tunnels that would join with the main one down to the Mtkvari River. The Varangians followed them as far as the junction, then went back up to the mouth of the cave. They looked out to see hundreds of baskets coming down to pour more Mongols into the battle. Smoke was billowing into the air at every level. The cries of pain echoed from deep inside the mountain behind them. Luke felt a hand on his arm. 'Matthew! Not hurt?'

His oldest friend shook his head. 'No more than anyone else. We've lost hardly a man.'

In an hour, it was over and the Georgians had sued for peace. Luke and his friends emerged from the tunnel at the bottom to find Mohammed Sultan and Shulen watching lines of Georgian prisoners being led away. The Prince put his arm around Luke's shoulder, drawing him to one side.

'Your victory, my friend,' he said, smiling. 'And we'll not slaughter the prisoners as we usually do. It seems that word had reached them of our clemency so they were happy to surrender.'

Luke glanced back at his friends. 'All four of us took part, lord,' he said quietly. 'You should congratulate Matthew especially. He led the second wave.'

The Prince nodded. 'I will. And then we march back to the Qarabagh without delay. The men need rest.'

'And Prince Giorgi?'

'He escaped with Prince Tahir. I've not ordered a pursuit. He'll know these mountains better than we.' Mohammed Sultan called for his horse. He turned with his foot in the stirrup. 'You'll return to a hero's welcome, Luke. My grandfather will be pleased.'

But the welcome they received was not what they'd expected.

News of the baskets had preceded the army and by the time Mohammed Sultan, the four Varangians and Shulen presented themselves to Tamerlane, he knew the story well. To begin with, the Lord of the Celestial Conjunction was jovial. 'Baskets!' he chuckled, his glasses bobbing up and down on his nose. 'You had my army weaving baskets?'

It was a stratagem even Tamerlane would have been proud of but Mohammed Sultan would take none of the credit. He was on his knees in his grandfather's castle-tent and beside him knelt Luke. He gestured to him. 'It was Luke's idea, Grandfather. We do not have King Giorgi but his country has sworn vassalage.'

Tamerlane's face darkened. 'No Giorgi? What about Prince Tahir? Did you capture him?'

Mohammed Sultan shook his head. 'Lord, he fled to Suleyman who was still in Armenia.'

'But who has now returned to Bayezid, who already gives refuge to his father Ahmed.'

Miran Shah, whose advisers had shouldered the blame for the plot against Tamerlane and unshouldered their heads in consequence, now said: 'Bayezid has allied himself with the Mamluks and Qara Yusuf of the Black Sheep. Your spies have said it, Father. He gets stronger.'

Tamerlane's spies were numberless, nameless and ruthless. He had informers in every court – itinerant monks, strolling vagabonds, physicians, procuresses – all of whom used the empire's courier to send news to their emperor every day.

'Perhaps', said Mohammed Sultan tentatively, 'it is therefore time to strike Bayezid before he can link up with the Mamluks? Their combined army would be very great.'

Tamerlane grunted. Then a smile spread across his lips. 'Would you like me to read you the letter I'm sending Bayezid?' he asked.

Mohammed Sultan exchanged a glance with Shulen. Had Tamerlane taken his lessons further in their absence?

The Emperor adjusted his spectacles and, very slowly, read the letter:

> 'Since the ship of your unfathomable ambition has been shipwrecked in the abyss of self-love, it would be wise for you to lower the sails of your rashness and cast the anchor of repentance in the port of sincerity, which is also the port of safety, lest by the tempest of our vengeance you should perish in the sea of punishment which you deserve.'

Tamerlane looked at Shulen, his two eyes huge behind the spectacles. 'Well, is it good, teacher? Or is there too much water?'

Shulen spread her hands before her. 'Lord, you are magnificent.'

Miran Shah was now looking at Mohammed Sultan, mischief in his eyes. 'We will have, of course, the news of what you did in Georgia to spread terror west. How many Georgians did you kill, do you think, nephew?'

Mohammed Sultan shook his head. 'We did it another way.

Georgia is not like the plains of Persia. Their army could hide in the mountains. We were merciful and the people helped us.'

Tamerlane was frowning. 'So how many did you kill?'

For the first time, Luke felt a knot of fear inside him. The conversation was taking a dangerous course. He decided to speak. 'Lord, I advised the Prince to be merciful. The booty we bring back is very great and the Georgian people might be persuaded to stay vassals this time.'

It was a mistake and Miran Shah pounced on it. 'So are you suggesting, Greek, that my father's tactics have been wrong these last years?' he asked quietly. 'Has the Sword of Islam been fighting the wrong wars all this time?'

Luke had seen the trap too late. He was in it and its walls were very steep. He decided to say nothing.

Tamerlane's eyes were fixed on his heir. 'How many did you kill?' he asked again.

'Few, lord,' answered the Prince. 'Their army surrendered soon after the baskets had done their work. I let them live.'

For a long time, Tamerlane sat there, staring at his heir in silence. Then he said: 'That was very wrong. We will have to make up for it.'

A month later, Bayezid was in his harem in Edirne, leaning naked against the sides of a shallow bath in which, amidst rose petals, floated a smaller version of his navy. All of the galleys had masts except one that carried a beaker of wine. Two page boys swam around him in the water, one on his back, while a third rubbed ointments into his shoulders. The smell in the room was a mixture of herbs, wine and something else that made the man who'd entered feel nauseous.

'Father, you wished to see me,' said Suleyman.

The Sultan raised his eyes from the boy floating on his back. 'Yes,' he said. 'We have news of Tamerlane. He's taken Sivas.'

Suleyman rocked backwards on his heels. Sivas was only four hundred miles east of Bursa and Tamerlane was in the Qarabagh. Or was. 'But I regarrisoned it. I put in four thousand Armenian sipahis.'

The Sultan's voice was low. 'Shall I tell you what happened to those sipahis?'

Suleyman didn't answer.

'After a week of siege, the Mongols breached the walls and the sipahi commander offered to surrender to avoid a massacre. Temur agreed and promised that no drop of Armenian blood would be spilt.'

Bayezid laughed then, a dry sound.

'Well, he kept his promise. He had a pit dug and he buried them alive, every one of them. Then he turned on the city's Christians. Five thousand had their heads tied between their thighs – men, women and children – and were thrown from the walls.' He paused and looked at his son with disgust. 'I told you to keep an eye on him and instead you invaded a country we didn't need.'

For some moments, Suleyman was struck dumb with the shock. Then he said, 'I thought he would stay in the Qarabagh.'

'Well, you were wrong. His army's now taken Malatiyah, so it lies between us and the the Mamluks.' Bayezid's face was expressionless. 'He's coming to fight us,' he said quietly. 'And, because of you, we do not have our allies with us.'

CHAPTER TWENTY-FIVE

ALEPPO, WINTER 1400

Luke stared at the child. His throat was open and in his hand he held a wooden sword. He was little older than Giovanni must be now. Three? Four? The eyes that stared back had a strange, faraway look as if they'd ranged over the furthest boundaries of human evil. Luke looked down at his sword. Had those dragon eyes seen anything to match this?

Matthew said: 'Why look at him?'

It was a good question. Why look at him? The square was full of dead children and the birds that gorged on them. A mosque stood to one side, little more than smoking rubble after four days of desecration. Adjacent was another ruin with charred benches propped into a pyre. Next to it, a Mongol lay on his front. He was wearing a woman's dress and in his hand was a flask from which wine had run into blood.

'It must have been a school,' said Nikolas.

Beyond the boy lay a girl of the same age who'd lost her eyes to the birds. She was rolled into a ball, naked, blood all around her. Arcadius was kneeling beside the little body. 'He was trying to defend her,' he said. 'With his sword.'

Tamerlane had come to Aleppo. Leaving Malatiyah, he'd

struck south into Syria, part of the Mamluk Empire, and Luke and his friends had seen all that had ensued. Every town, every village, every living thing in this army's path had been destroyed and the towers of skulls left behind were the tallest yet of Tamerlane's hideous career.

Luke had been numbed by it all. To find some path back to humanity, he'd tried to imagine the last bit of life before the death that he saw all around him. Had it been the shake of the ground to the sound of a million hoofs, or the black cloud on the horizon that had first warned of the apocalypse to come? Had the people prayed to a God that seemed no longer there? Had they hugged children to their breasts, shielding eyes from the horrid face of Armageddon?

Luke had begged God for forgiveness for his pride, his stupidity, for surely these new heights of savagery had everything to do with the restraint he'd urged on Mohammed Sultan in Georgia? His friends tried to persuade him otherwise.

'It's because he has no cannon,' Matthew had explained. 'He can't open gates with cannon, so he has to do it with terror.'

Certainly the terror had worked. As usual, Tamerlane's agents had fanned out ahead of the army; the beggars, mercenaries and wandering *ozanlar* that crept into cities after dark and sat in public places murmuring of the terrible things they'd seen; telling of small men with flat faces, drunk on the mare's milk they called koumis, eating half-raw meat taken from beneath their saddles, washing it down with the blood of their horses. These were the creatures the Greeks had named from the blackest part of their hell: *Tartarus*. And they were on their way.

Aleppo was 160 miles south of Malatiyah and Tamerlane's army had covered the distance in three weeks, stopping only to slaughter. The city was an ancient place where Ibrahim had performed his devotions. It was a place of commerce and culture at the crossroads of trade routes and its markets were crammed with the produce of continents. Its governor, Damurdash, knew that there'd be no time for the Sultan to send an army from Cairo, so he'd gathered what troops he could from Antioch, Acre, Homs, Ramallah and Jerusalem.

Within the city were two factions: those who wished to fight and those who didn't. The fighters won; their army was large and their walls strong. So Tamerlane set out to tempt them out with skirmishing parties that rode up the walls and hurled abuse at those above. It worked. The gates opened and the Syrian army drew up in battle formation outside. But Tamerlane's war elephants filled them with terror and, when they charged, the Syrians fled back towards their city. In the mayhem, thousands were trampled to death and soon the city's moat was piled high with corpses.

Damurdash had little option but to surrender and a long line of priests, doctors and sharifs, loaded with priceless gifts, left the city to sue for peace. Tamerlane agreed to spare the city, then entered it, slaughtered the envoys, and began four days of general massacre. The women and children fled to the city's mosques but the Mongols followed them there. They took the children from their mothers and killed them, then raped the mothers before killing them too. Finally they killed the fathers and brothers who'd been forced to watch it all.

And Luke, Matthew, Arcadius and Nikolas, bound by oath to Shatan, were forced to watch it all as well. Now, with no one left to kill, the Mongols had left and Luke was in a square staring at a boy with his throat open.

He turned to Matthew. 'No, this is the result of the mercy

shown in Georgia,' he said quietly. 'The world has only so much blood and Tamerlane must have his fill.'

Nikolas then said what they'd all been thinking: 'Why will he stop at Constantinople?'

It was what Luke had been asking himself since leaving Malatiyah when he'd last seen the grim set of Tamerlane's face beneath his tasselled helmet. The question had tormented him every mile of the way. Why would Tamerlane stop at Constantinople? Or Mistra for that matter?

Or Chios?

Had he brought an unstoppable Shatan west to do worse than Bayezid could ever dream of? He'd hardly slept on the march so far. He'd certainly not sleep tonight. Not after this. Luke shook his head slowly and said what he didn't believe: 'No. His army is tired. His generals urge him to turn back. He'll go on to Damascus and then take his booty home.'

But will he?

In the Ottoman camp outside Constantinople, that very question was being debated between Bayezid and his sons. With them were the Grand Vizier and Yakub Bey. They were standing, or sitting, in a tent behind the Turkish lines and from outside came the sound of an army engaged in the business of siege: the thump of trebuchet released, the crash of stone on wall, the desultory cheer of men pausing in their work to watch. It was midday and the sky was overcast, promising rain. Soon the cheers would turn to grumbles – though not loud, for this was the Ottoman army.

Prince Mehmed was reading a letter to his father. It was from the Kadi Ibn Khaldun and it told of terrible things.

'They fell on Aleppo as ravening wolves, as jackals of the steppe. Children were slaughtered before their mothers, mothers violated before their husbands. The very streets ran with blood. Oh my Lord! It is only the owl and vulture that now take refuge in the city of Ibrahim and there is no birdsong there. It is a place of skulls built into towers taller than minarets. It is a place of death.'

He paused. 'Shall I go on?'

Bayezid shook his head. 'No, I think we understand the calamity. I suppose he wants us to send an army?'

Mehmed laid the letter down on the table next to a bowl of sugar. 'Of course, Father. As we are obliged to do by the alliance brokered by Prince Yakub. We are each to come to the other's aid if attacked.'

'But we'll be too late.' This was Suleyman. 'He'll have taken Damascus by the time we get there.'

Mehmed shook his head. 'Not if they defend it, which they will if they know we're coming.'

Bayezid leant forward to the sugar bowl. 'Remember we have a counter-offer.'

The offer had just been put to them by Tamerlane's envoy, who was waiting outside. He'd brought with him a different sort of letter from the Lord of the Celestial Conjunction. It was a promise not to attack Bayezid if he sent no army to help the Mamluks and delivered to him the Princes Ahmed, Tahir and Qara Yusuf, all vassals of his who'd taken refuge in Bayezid's court.

Mehmed snorted. 'What worth has any promise from a madman?' He paused and lowered his voice. 'Father, you are Yildirim and you've never lost a battle. Our combined armies will be twice his number. This is our chance to rid the world of this scourge.' He glanced at Yakub, then back at his father. 'Remember Ain Jalut.'

Ain Jalut was the only time the Mongols had been stopped before. The battle had been fought not far from Aleppo a century and a half before. The Mamluk Sultan Baybars had defeated the Mongol horde and sent it home. The world had been delivered. Could it happen again? Bayezid looked at his second son and nodded slowly.

Ain Jalut.

He said: 'You will take half the army and march to our borders and wait. We'll see if this young Sultan will choose to defend Syria or remain in Cairo.'

'And what do we tell Temur's envoy?'

'We tell him that Temur will get Ahmed and the others when we've seen him return to Samarcand. Not a moment before.'

Zoe was standing at the entrance of Suleyman's tent, her fingers pulling aside the tent-flap enough to see the Mongol envoy emerge from his audience with Bayezid and walk towards his horse. She was frowning.

It was evening by now and the shadows were lengthening. The rain had come and gone and the work of the siege was dying with the day. From every direction came the pinpricks of twenty thousand fires being lit and the murmur of an army sitting down to eat. The air smelt of wet earth and leather and canvas and soon it would smell of food.

Zoe narrowed her eyes. The horse was familiar. It was large and richly caparisoned and, without any doubt, was Eskalon. It made sense. The Mongol horses were small, shaggy creatures, ill fitted to diplomacy. Eskalon would impress. But why was the envoy here at all? Was it to make peace with Bayezid so that

Tamerlane could plunder the riches of Egypt unhindered? And if so, where did that leave Suleyman?

Zoe had not enjoyed her time at the siege. First had come the news of Damian's death. It seemed her twin brother fallen from the Goulas after some fight with her father. He'd been drunk. She remembered a man standing before her in this very tent telling her how it had happened: a smaller, older, frailer man than her father, yet her father nonetheless. He'd not looked at her when he'd spoken.

'It was an accident. He was drunk and he slipped.'

It was a lie but what was the truth? Had her father killed him? Had that been the only way for Zoe to inherit? She'd felt sick every time she'd considered the question since.

She'd not seen her father from that day. They said he never left his palace in Venice these days, had handed all business over to his lieutenants. Zoe wondered sometimes what sort of business she would inherit at the end of it all.

Worst of all, Suleyman had not yet proposed marriage to her and seemed to spend more and more time at Edirne. There, Zoe had heard, he rode out with Anna, even though she was supposed to be imprisoned.

Then there was the problem of Suleyman. His absences from the siege had been noticed by Bayezid. If Tamerlane wasn't coming, then Constantinople would surely be taken by Mehmed who would reap all the glory.

And what would Suleyman reap?

Now she watched the envoy approach Eskalon and pat his neck. The horse dipped his head twice and snorted through the silk. Zoe thought of Luke. How could she persuade him to come and take Anna away from Suleyman?

He won't know that Anna thinks him married. What if he did?

She wasn't sure herself. She'd doubted the Venetians' story even as she'd enjoyed telling it to Anna. But then the man from Castile had arrived to confirm it. It hardly mattered.

If he learns that Anna thinks him married, he might come and get her. Especially if he also knows she's free of Suleyman.

Would he? Yes. Zoe stepped from the tent and, as she did so, Eskalon's head turned. The envoy watched her approach, bowing and then straightening up. He was a man of middle years with a small, intelligent mouth beneath a beard streaked with grey. Zoe arrived beside the horse. She ran her fingers through his mane.

'Eskalon.'

The envoy nodded. 'You know the horse?'

'I know his master.' She looked at the Mongol. 'Not you.'

The envoy smiled. 'No, not I. One who has found favour with my master.'

'One who is a Varangian.' She paused. 'I hear he is married. To the woman called Shulen.'

The man remained silent.

'Will you give him a message?'

The envoy frowned. Then he nodded.

'Please tell him that Anna has heard of his marriage to the girl Shulen and is greatly distressed. Tell him that she was engaged to be married to the Prince Suleyman but is now released. But she is his prisoner.' She paused and put her hand on the envoy's arm. 'He will want to know this.'

The envoy had gathered his reins, perhaps thinking that he had more important business to attend to. He put his foot into the stirrup and pulled himself high into the saddle. He took the reins. 'And who should I say has sent this message?'

'A friend.'

CHAPTER TWENTY-SIX

DAMASCUS, JANUARY 1401

Luke looked across the orchards and gardens that led up to the walls of Damascus and saw the shadow of death stretched over them. It was early evening and the winter sun was an orange ball poised above the mountains to the west that rose ten thousand feet before sweeping down into the Middle Sea beyond. To the east, the wastes of the Badiyat ash Sham desert spread out to a desolate horizon. The air was still and held the promise of cold to come.

The walls of Damascus looked red and strong in the evening light; not as impregnable as Constantinople's perhaps, but robust enough to withstand the Mongol army's siege engines. From their battlements shone the busy glint of shield and spear, and above, rising into clouds of birds, rose the three minarets of the Umayyad Mosque, noblest building in the province of Islam, matchless in grace and beauty. There flew the green flag of the Prophet.

Luke pulled his cloak tight around his shoulders and wondered if the long line of refugees waiting to enter the city would manage to do so before the gates shut for the night. There were thousands of them, mainly women and children who'd somehow escaped the inferno of Aleppo. They'd tell the story of Tamerlane's terror far better than any of Tamerlane's agents could.

He looked behind at his three friends. Matthew was in the centre, carrying the white flag of parley; Arcadius and Nikolas were on either side: three Varangians sworn to a monster that wanted to wash this desert with blood. Beyond them, five miles distant, was the Mongol army, stretched out between mountain and desert in a vast, hundred-mile scythe of destruction. Behind it were ruins and towers of skulls.

Luke leant forward to pat Eskalon. He placed his hand on the dragon head of his sword, enjoying the cool, scaled silver against his palm. He said his first words of the ride: 'I can't see it.'

There was no reply from behind, only the shuffle of harness and the snort of horses ridden hard. His friends exchanged glances and Matthew stood in his stirrups and shielded his eyes.

'It's out there somewhere, Luke. The patrols said at least fifty thousand.'

Nikolas rode up to Luke's side. 'We need to give the city a wide berth. Let's head out into the desert.'

Luke nodded. He was in no mood to meet a sortie from the city. In fact he was in no mood to meet anyone. The numbness that he'd felt in the ruins of Aleppo had stayed with him every mile of the two hundred they'd ridden to Damascus. On the way, he'd witnessed the obliteration of Hama, Homs, Baalbek, Sidon and Beirut with a sort of dread detachment, as if the horror belonged to a world he didn't inhabit. His eyes had seen deeds of savagery that his brain would not admit, had witnessed evil that could find no place in his matrix of experience. He'd learnt to withdraw, putting on armour, better than any Varangian mail, to survive this apocalypse. He'd taken refuge in silence.

And throughout it all, he'd clung to one truth that no amount of blood could wash away: Anna was not to marry Suleyman.

But the envoy had told him something else: that Anna believed *him* married to Shulen. If she thought him married, she would think him lost to her. His first impulse had been to ride west to Edirne as fast as Eskalon would take him. But he was oath-sworn to Tamerlane, as were his friends. And something deep, deep within him knew that he couldn't ride to her until he'd done what he had to do.

Luke turned Eskalon's head towards the desert. 'Follow me.'

Half an hour later the four Varangians had arrived at the Mamluk army and were shown into the presence of Ibn Khaldun. As soon as Luke had heard that the Kadi was with the army, he'd volunteered himself for the task of parleying with a man he knew he could trust. He'd gone to Tamerlane and offered himself, not expecting to be accepted. He was.

Now the old historian was before him in a tent full of sculpted armour, sherbet and exquisite creatures who tiptoed around on bare feet. Ibn Khaldun explained: 'They're my bodyguard, believe it or not, and it's their armour around the walls. I've never seen them in battle so I don't know how safe I should feel.' The old man had risen from a furred divan and placed his hand on his heart. He bowed. 'May the peace of Allah be upon you, Luke.' He looked around. 'And no less upon the rest of you.' He gestured to one of the creatures. 'I never got the chance to see you fight in Tabriz. Would one of you like to wrestle now and we can finish this business without further bloodshed?'

Luke produced a smile, his first in a month. 'Ibn Khaldun, we're here to parley, not wrestle your bodyguard.' He heard a sigh of disappointment from behind him: Nikolas. 'How big is your army?'

'As the sands of the desert. Numberless.' The old man paused while he sat again. 'Shall we say sixty thousand? With cannon.'

'So less than half Temur's.'

The historian arranged the folds of his tunic that swept to the floor in patterned silk. 'If you say so. But you're forgetting Bayezid.'

Luke shook his head. 'Not Bayezid but Mehmed. And he's stopped at the border.'

The Kadi's face remained composed. 'So why are you here? Temur seems to have the advantage. Please sit.'

Four of the bodyguard had appeared with folding chairs. Luke was the first to sit. He leant forward. 'Ibn Khaldun, I am here to prevent further massacre, if I can. I've seen too much these past weeks. I'm tired of blood.'

'But your master never tires of it,' said the Kadi. 'It's his elixir. It keeps him strong, so they say.'

'His army is tired. His generals tell him to rest in the mountains of Lebanon. He has no cannon and you have strong walls. He is persuadable.'

'Because he can see that even if he wins this battle, he'll be too weak to beat Bayezid as well.' Ibn Khaldun drank some sherbet and patted the neat beard beneath his smile with a napkin. 'And, of course, that's what you want: Tamerlane strong enough to beat Bayezid.' He put down the cup. 'But what makes you so sure he'll go back to Samarcand afterwards?'

'I'm not,' admitted Luke. 'Sometimes I wonder whether Constantinople wouldn't be better off with Bayezid's army on its walls.'

'Ah, but that wouldn't fit with the plan,' said Ibn Khaldun. 'Plethon wants the Roman Empire to recapture its birthright, a re-merger of Greek and Roman culture, as it always was. But at the right time, which isn't yet.' The historian joined his hands beneath his chin and looked at Luke, then his friends. 'But what do *you* want, all of you?'

Matthew spoke. 'We want what Luke wants,' he said. 'To save our empire from Bayezid. And we want to stop this bloodshed and go home; Luke to Chios, us to Monemvasia. We're all tired.'

Ibn Khaldun nodded. 'Very sensible. So how do we achieve this? We have two armies either side of Damascus and some excitable generals. How do we stop them fighting?'

Luke said: 'With money. One million dinars and he'll turn round and go away.'

Ibn Khaldun looked surprised. 'Really? And why would we believe him?'

'Because Temur may be unpredictable but he's not stupid. You've said it yourself: he doesn't want to be weakened with an Ottoman army behind him. ' He paused. 'And perhaps he thinks Egypt too big a prize just now.'

'Where will he go to rest?'

'To Lebanon.'

'And then?'

'To Bayezid. He'll have been persuaded by then.'

Ibn Khaldun was silent for a long time then, seemingly absorbed by the patterns on the sleeves joined in his lap. 'One million dinars is a lot of money.'

'Not for Damascus. It's one of the richest cities on earth. You can find it.'

The old man nodded. Then he rose and clapped his hands. Two of the bodyguard appeared, this time in armour. 'These ladies will escort you out of our camp. Tell Tamerlane that he will have his money by sundown tomorrow.'

'And how will it be brought to him?'

'I will bring it myself. I will go into the city.'

The Varangians' ride back was shorter than the ride out because Tamerlane had moved his army forward into the orchards around the city walls, well out of arrow-range. It had been done, Luke supposed, to concentrate the minds of those collecting the ransom.

The army was a fearsome sight. In the fading light, it seemed that the entire landscape was made up of Mongol horsemen standing stirrup to stirrup. At their centre were the huge hulks of the elephants with towers on their backs and giant scimitars on every tusk. As Luke rode closer, he could see that every Mongol had his four spare mounts tied by his side so that the army seemed, in this light, even bigger than it was. This was a familiar Tamerlane ruse. On the approach to Aleppo, Tamerlane had ordered brooms tied to the horses' tails so that the dust cloud seen from the city would stretch across every part of the horizon.

In front of the army sat Tamerlane with his sons and grandsons beneath the various flags and skulls that told of God and superstition. A shaman was mounted to the rear. Luke and his companions rode over to Tamerlane, dismounted and prostrated themselves in the sand.

'What did they say?'

Luke looked up. Tamerlane was mounted next to Mohammed

Sultan with Shulen on his other side patting a pretty palfrey that looked out of place in this army. She smiled at him.

'They will pay you one million dinars by this time tomorrow,' said Luke. 'It will be brought out to you by the Kadi himself. He has gone into the city to collect it.'

Tamerlane grunted. He had his eagle on the arm that still bore the scars from its talons. He tickled the top of its head with his gloved finger.

'That is a pity. They are cowards.'

Mohammed Sultan coughed. 'Father, it is a fabulous sum. Enough to clad the Bibi Khanum's dome in gold. We can rest for the winter, then come back later in the year.'

Tamerlane nodded slowly. He took a lump of offal from the pocket of his deel and fed it to the bird. He grunted again. 'Very well. Turn the army around.'

Tamerlane had retired his army partly because he'd apparently accepted the Mamluk agreement and partly because he didn't want the ruse of the riderless horses to be seen by the light of day. The citizens of Damascus saw the manoeuvre very differently.

Ibn Khaldun had entered Damascus to find its people more belligerent than he'd hoped. He'd ridden straight to the citadel to meet the governor, a man of ninety who had none of the wisdom of age. With him were the leaders of the city's garrison, merchants and clergy. The imams had just arrived from the Umayyad Mosque where they'd been seeking the guidance of Allah. The words 'Ain Jalut' were, in Ibn Khaldun's opinion, on too many lips.

'One million dinars!' said a fat merchant, trembling with outrage. 'It's an extortionate sum.'

'Extortion is what Temur does,' said the historian calmly. 'The alternative is worse.'

'But we have the sultan's army behind us,' said the governor, 'and Bayezid's coming. We just have to wait.'

Ibn Khaldun shook his head. 'Bayezid has sent only half his army with his second son who is currently sitting on the border and doesn't seem to be in any hurry to cross it. I expect Tamerlane has made a separate agreement.'

It was late evening and they were standing in a room high in the citadel tower. Through opposite windows they could see the shapes of two armies, one much larger than the other. The sun had set and soon it would be dark. A slave had just entered with a taper to light the torches on the walls.

'Don't light them,' said Ibn Khaldun to the man. 'These gentlemen need to see the armies outside.'

'We have our own garrison as well,' said a general. 'Twenty thousand at least.' He turned to the governor. 'We should strike now while they're tired. They've had nothing but forced marches since leaving Sivas.'

Someone else agreed. 'If we let them rest the winter in Lebanon, they'll just return stronger in the spring.'

'But you might have a proper army sent from Cairo by then,' said Ibn Khaldun.

'They have no cannon and our walls are strong.' The governor turned to the imams. 'What does Allah tell us to do?'

A man with a voluminous beard, eyebrows and a look of religious ferocity spoke. 'He tells us to wait. Not pay this ransom and wait.'

This was what might have happened if, at that moment, a merchant standing by one of the windows hadn't seen something extraordinary. His back was to the meeting and he was looking out to the north.

'The Mongol army is marching away,' he said.

It was nearly dawn and Luke was walking with Shulen among the elephants, all of which were standing, for elephants sleep standing up. Their mahouts slept beside them, well within trampling distance of their chained feet. It was this mutual trust that had brought Luke here every night when he couldn't sleep. In a world that had been lost to evil, it reminded him that humanity still existed somewhere, even if not within humans.

The mahouts, one to each elephant, had come with them from Delhi and were suffering from the winter cold of the desert. Shulen had found furred deels to give them.

'Are they all boys?' she whispered as she laid a deel over a sleeping mahout. 'Why not girls?'

Luke shrugged. 'The elephants are all male so I suppose their keepers have to be male.'

'But why must the elephants be male? Are men so much fiercer?'

Luke knew the answer to this. 'In battle, the she-elephant will run from the male. A mahout told me this.'

Shulen thought about this. It seemed strange. She looked down at the sleeping boy lying in the night-shadow of his colossal friend. 'It's a curious friendship,' she murmured. 'What's that by his side?'

'The bag? Inside is a chisel-blade and hammer. If the mahout gets hurt in battle, the elephant will run amok. Those will cut through its spinal cord and kill it instantly.'

Shulen shivered. She straightened up and the two of them walked beyond the elephants to look south towards the city.

They could hear the sounds of the camp followers and baggage train still coming in. It took a long time for this army to turn around. She looked across at Luke and saw the strain on his face. He'll come tomorrow.'

Luke shook his head. 'He said tonight. There's been a problem.'

Shulen put her hand on his arm. 'A million dinars is a big sum to raise,' she said. 'Imagine all the camels needed to carry that amount of gold.'

'If it was taking time, he'd have sent word.'

Shulen regarded him in silence. Luke had changed so much over the past months. Ever since the Georgia campaign, he'd been subdued, lost in his thoughts. Shulen had learnt one reason for it from Matthew.

'She can't leave Edirne, Luke,' she said softly. 'She's a prisoner.' She looked away. 'She'll still be there when you arrive.'

'She thinks we're married.'

'Well, she'll learn differently. When you arrive.'

Luke turned to her. 'And when might that be, Shulen?' he asked, the bitterness giving edge to his voice. 'We thought he'd go to Bayezid but he came south instead. Who's to say he won't come back here in the spring when he's rested the army? He never does what we expect.'

Shulen had probably spent more time with Tamerlane than anyone else in the army. Her salves for his joints were becoming indispensable and were required daily. When she wasn't talking to him, she was listening to Mohammed Sultan talking to him. She was as mystified by Tamerlane as she was scared of him. 'I think he's had his fill of blood,' she said quietly. 'After the winter, he'll fight Bayezid and then go home. It's what Mohammed Sultan is telling him to do.'

Luke looked away. There were noises in the distance: shouts and screams. They were coming from the baggage train. Then there was an explosion. 'Oh my God,' he whispered.

'What's happening?'

Luke was shaking his head in disbelief. 'They're attacking us. The fools are committing suicide.' Then he was running in the direction of his tent.

When he got there, he found his friends awake and putting on their armour. The Varangians' tent was among those of the *gautchin*, Tamerlane's bodyguard, who were already armed and ready to ride, each man standing next to his horse. A general, known to Luke, was preparing to mount, his foot in the stirrup. Luke ran up to him and put his hand on his shoulder. 'Do you remember what I showed you in Georgia, Torchin? The arrowhead?'

The man nodded. He had a hideous silver face-mask angled to his helmet whose vacant eyes stared up at the sky.

'We Varangians will be the point. You gautchin must follow us as fast as you can. Can you do that?'

The man nodded again and pulled himself into the saddle. He shouted commands to his men and lowered his mask.

Luke heard more explosions from the baggage train. He turned to Matthew. 'We're going to need lances.'

'We've got them. They're coming up with the horses.' Matthew helped Luke to tighten his cuirass straps. 'Here's your sword.'

Then the neck of the dragon was in Luke's hand and he felt a charge of excitement flash through him. He looked down at those ruby eyes and at Plethon's ring on his finger. He kissed it. He heard a neigh behind him and turned to see Eskalon with a groom. He went up and took the horse's head in his hands. 'Today you'll be a destrier, old friend,' he whispered. 'As you were born to be.'

Luke put on his helmet, mounted and took the lance. He turned to the other three, who were already on their horses. 'Let's go.'

There was confusion in the direction they were riding and it became worse the closer they got to the enemy. First it was men scrambling to find their horses and weapons, then it was camp followers: old men, women and children, running to escape whatever was behind them, some hideously burnt. There were more explosions and flashes from in front. Luke kicked Eskalon, shouting at those in their way. They rode on until they could see the attackers.

The first Mamluks were mounted on small, quick ponies and carried *naft* grenades of baked clay, which they were hurling into the wagons of the baggage train. There were flames everywhere. These *jandar*s were dressed in tunics lined with fire-proof talc and had hoods to protect their heads. Some were swinging the grenades in slings above their heads.

'Greek fire!' yelled Luke over his shoulder. 'Close up!'

Behind the grenade-throwers were thousands of Bedouin *ashir* auxiliaries who were firing arrows over the heads of the jandars. The ground was strewn with Mongol dead and dying: men, women, mules, dogs; it was a scene from hell.

'Close up!' Luke shouted again and he slowed Eskalon to allow his three friends to form up on either side of him. Arrows were landing on his helmet and shoulders. 'Lances down!'

They hit the jandars at terrifying speed. Eskalon was twice the size of the Mamluk ponies and tore into them, butting and biting like a huge, rabid dog. The jandar soldiers had small shields strapped to their upper arms, expecting arrows. Instead they got armoured knights at full charge. They were lifted from their saddles by the impact, grenades flying from their hands to explode amongst the ashirs behind them. Now the sounds were of the screams of men.

The Varangian arrowhead drove deep into the Mamluk ranks, cutting a swathe of destruction as it went. The four were too close for the Mamluk arrows to harm them and the lances kept their swords at bay. Jandars and ashirs fell before them by the score and the momentum of the Mamluk attack was stopped, then turned. But the Varangians couldn't keep up their charge forever. They began to slow. They threw down their lances, lifting swords and axes instead. Now they were fighting hand to hand and the Bedouin auxiliaries were all around them, closing in. Luke glanced behind him.

Where are the gautchin?

He swung the dragon sword again and again, slashing with its blade and smashing with its pommel. He had the advantage of height and he used it to cut down on his enemy from above, fighting on one side because Matthew was protecting his other. Meanwhile, Eskalon tore chunks of flesh from the Bedouin ponies on every side.

'Where are the gautchin?' Matthew's voice echoed from inside his helmet. 'Nikolas has been hurt.'

Luke glanced to where Nikolas was fighting. He had decapitated a grenade-thrower but there was blood running down his arm. It was coming from his neck. 'We'll have to break out!' shouted Luke. 'Follow me.'

He turned Eskalon back towards the Mongol camp, dropping an enemy as he did so. From in front he heard shouts and the clash of steel. The men before him were looking over their shoulders.

The gautchin.

'They're here!' he yelled and thrust Eskalon into the confusion. Suddenly he felt exhilaration where there'd been exhaustion. They were winning and they would survive. He lifted his dragon sword and took the bow-arm from a man with a giant swing.

He heard a cry to his left. Nikolas was on the ground and a Mamluk was lifting his sword to strike him. Luke heaved at his rein and Eskalon turned. The man was too far away. He lifted the dragon sword and threw it. It turned once in the air before embedding itself in the man's back. Luke kicked Eskalon's flanks and held out his arm to his friend. 'Get on!'

Nikolas had removed his helmet. He was grey with loss of blood. He took Luke's hand and was pulled on to the back of the horse. Luke bent low to recover his sword. He yelled: 'Hold on!'

Matthew and Arcadius had seen what had happened and had fallen back to protect their friends. But the Mamluks were already in retreat. The shouts of the gautchin were louder now and getting nearer and behind them would come the whole army. Then the Varangians were through the last of the fleeing Mamluks and the gautchin were charging past them with their terrifying masks and howls of the hunt. The Varangians reined in their horses. Men appeared and Nikolas was taken from Eskalon's back and Luke watched him carried away in a cloak.

Matthew said: 'He'll live. It wasn't so bad.'

Arcadius had come up beside them. 'Shall we go back to the battle?'

Luke felt his horse move beneath him. Eskalon wanted to

go back, but the battle seemed to be moving away fast, the Mamluk force in full retreat. They'd have to ride hard to catch it up. He kicked Eskalon.

The three rode towards Damascus, trampling the Mamluk dead and wounded as they went. The Mongol army was now all around them, some only half dressed, some women, all chasing the enemy in every way they could. By now, the day was almost with them and, as the walls of the city drew closer, Luke could see that its giant gates were being slowly closed. Thousands of the city's garrison were still outside but the gates were closing.

The Mongols riding beside them could see it too and roars of anger turned to roars of joy as the prospect of new slaughter presented itself. Luke could see that some of the Mamluks had turned to fight, fitting arrows to bowstrings. Some had fallen to their knees and were tearing their hair. Others ran on.

The Varangians pulled up their horses. They'd seen the way this army did its slaughter and had no desire to get closer. They saw the Mongols fall upon the thousands stranded outside the gates and butcher them with a speed and efficiency that meant that, in less than an hour, it was all over and the vultures could begin their work. Then the Mongols swept back to their broken camp, past the three Varangians who sat in silence on their horses, looking at a field of ten thousand dead. Luke was the first to speak.

'The fools,' he whispered. 'The utter, utter fools. They've given Tamerlane the excuse he was looking for.'

Matthew asked: 'Is that why he pulled back, do you think?'

Luke nodded. 'He must have known what might happen.' He looked at his best friend. 'After all, the gautchin were waiting.'

*

The following night, Tamerlane moved his siege engines within range of the walls of Damascus. They were huge machines, captured from a dozen armies, capable of hurling fireballs into the city at a terrible rate. Meanwhile the elephants dragged battering rams forward to the beat of a drum, the mahouts, deel-clad, on their heads. The army settled down in an arc that covered the landscape and its fires reflected the stars in the sky.

The next morning, Luke, Matthew and Arcadius were summoned to Tamerlane's tent. Nikolas was still in theirs, bandaged and sleeping. They found the Emir seated on a plain chair with his foot raised on a footstool. With him were his two grandsons, Khan-zada and Shulen. The air smelt of herbs and Shulen had oil on her hands. The Varangians prostrated themselves on the carpet. Tamerlane was smiling.

'You Greeks were brave last night,' he said. 'I'm told you led the army.'

Luke spoke from the carpet, 'I was awake when the Mamluks came, lord.' He paused. 'As were the gautchin.'

Tamerlane grunted. 'They're always awake. They guard me. They caught the dervish.'

Three nights past, a Mamluk assassin had stolen into the camp disguised as a dervish dancer. The gautchin had found knives on him and sent him back with no ears or nose.

Tamerlane continued: 'They've sent someone over to parley. The one you talked to. He's waiting outside.' He leant forward. 'You told me to trust him and they attacked us. And where are my million dinars? Why don't I cut off this one's head and send it back?'

Inspiration came to Luke. He said: 'The man who waits outside is a great historian, lord. His writings will be read for centuries. Surely such a man should write of you?'

Tamerlane considered this. His eyes gleamed from behind his glasses. He nodded. 'Show him in.'

Two guards opened the tent doors and Ibn Khaldun walked through them, his hands tied together, He looked tired and dishevelled. He dropped to his knees.

'How did you get here?' Tamerlane blew his nose into his hand and shook it away.

'I was lowered down the walls in a basket, lord,' replied Ibn Khaldun. 'The city is in turmoil. It was not safe to leave by the gate.'

Tamerlane laughed and gestured to Luke. 'That's what he does with my army,' he said, slapping the arm of his chair. 'He lowers them in baskets. In Georgia. You should put it in your histories.'

Ibn Khaldun bowed from the waist, his head to the carpet. He murmured: 'As you desire, lord.'

Tamerlane leant forward and peered at him. 'I've long wanted to meet you,' he said. 'I've had your histories read to me.'

This was a surprise to everyone but Shulen. Ibn Khaldun looked up. 'I am gratified, lord.'

'They're good but they don't include me. You write of empires' rise and fall. Will mine fall?'

Ibn Khaldun paused for only a heartbeat. 'Inevitably, lord.'

There was silence for a time while Tamerlane inspected his fingernails. Then he chuckled. 'You're brave,' he said. 'What of the Mamluks? Will the Mamluk dogs rule longer than the Mongols?'

'Not unless they relearn how to fight. They have abandoned us.'

Tamerlane knew this. His spies had come in just after dawn

to report that the Mamluk army had melted away into the desert.

'They have abandoned you,' said Tamerlane. 'They sent you into the city to get the money, then fled back to Cairo. What is the mood inside the city now, historian?'

Ibn Khaldun said: 'Realistic, lord. They've lost an army and half their garrison. They are assembling gold.'

'Ah, but how much? One million dinars is no longer enough. I've lost men.'

The old man chose not to answer. Instead, he kept his brow to the carpet.

Tamerlane asked: 'Did you come alone?'

'I brought a servant, lord.' He paused. 'Let down in a smaller basket.'

Tamerlane threw back his head and roared, keeping the glasses to his nose with a finger. His vast ring flashed in the light that fell through the toghona. 'I like you, historian. Your servant can return to the city to tell them that the price for their lives has gone up to ten million dinars.' He leant forward to scratch his bandaged foot. 'As for you, I desire that you stay here and write for me a description of the whole country of the Maghreb, detailing its distant and nearby parts, its mountains and its rivers, its villages and cities – in such a manner that I might seem actually to see it.'

Ibn Khaldun stayed in the Mongol camp for a month, first writing of the Maghreb with questionable accuracy, then discussing it with Tamerlane. The Lord of the Celestial Conjunction was obsessed by the rhythm of empires: how they rise and fall, and why. His empire would last, he declared, because Allah was with him. Ibn Khaldun was wise and gracious and often silent and Tamerlane liked him more and more.

Luke watched all this with mounting horror. If Tamerlane was asking for a map of the Maghreb, it was because he was planning to go there next, not to Bayezid. He raised the question with Mohammed Sultan one evening when they were walking with Shulen.

'He doesn't tell me anything,' said the Prince. 'Since Georgia, he's kept his plans to himself even more than usual. I don't know where he'll go next, truly.'

Shulen said: 'And he changes the subject when I give him his oils. His spies come in and I am dismissed.'

Meanwhile, the terrified citizens of Damascus sat within their walls with Tamerlane's horde camped in a menacing circle around them and no Egyptian – or Ottoman – army in prospect. Every now and then, the Mongol siege engines hurled balls of fire among them to hurry the process of surrender and eventually it came. The gates opened and a long line of soldiers, priests and merchants filed out ahead of mules bearing gold. It wasn't ten million dinars but it was as much as they could find. Or so they said.

Tamerlane received the men and the gold and the city's surrender and promised to keep his army outside the walls if the remainder of the garrison were delivered to him. The men duly marched out to the sound of the drum and formed up in front of the victor, laying their weapons on the ground before prostrating themselves.

Their commander begged for the lives of his men but Tamerlane was deaf to mercy. He impaled them, all eight thousand, one by one. It happened through the night, and the screams of agony rose over the city and into the houses and through the trembling flesh of a million hands pressed to ears. The next morning, those few citizens who'd managed to sleep awoke to an army of bloody scarecrows staring sightlessly up at the walls. Only these ones didn't scare away the birds.

By midday, the city had opened its gates and Tamerlane, his usual retinue and a bodyguard of gautchin had ridden through. Accompanying him were the Varangians, Shulen and Ibn Khaldun. The city within made a curious sight. The streets were empty of people and six weeks of siege had transferred most animals from street to cooking-pot. Everywhere were broken doors and the contents of houses thrown outside. It was as if the city had already been sacked.

Mohammed Sultan was riding next to Luke. 'It seems they've tried hard to find the ten million dinars,' he said.

They rode through the streets to the Umayyad Mosque where Tamerlane dismounted and went in to pray. Luke stayed outside in the courtyard, looking up at the fabulous vision of heaven that crowded its walls. His eyes swept up minarets that seemed to pierce the very belly of paradise, pouring green, blue and gold mosaic over a desert city rich enough to have raised them. He was overwhelmed by its beauty.

After the mosque, they rode up to the citadel where the city's leaders awaited their fate. Tamerlane quickly made it plain. 'I want all of your wealth,' he said. 'Since you have chosen not to give me what I've asked for, now it will be everything. Every dress, every jewel, every plate, every cup. Everything.'

The word went round the city as word does and they rode back through streets now filled with people. They'd come to the doors and roofs of their buildings in their thousands and they were silent and sullen. They were people with nothing more to lose.

When they got back to the Mongol camp, Ibn Khaldun came to Tamerlane. He'd seen the way things were going. He wanted to go home but had one last request. 'The officials who came with me into Damascus, also abandoned by the Sultan of Egypt, are capable administrators who can do you good service in your vast empire.'

'What do you wish for them?' asked Tamerlane.

'A letter of security, signed by yourself, lord, which will allow them to leave the city and join your army.'

Not only did Tamerlane agree to this, but he allowed Ibn Khaldun to take his mule and leave the camp as soon as he might wish. There were things to come, perhaps, that Tamerlane did not wish the historian to see.

Tamerlane had posted guards at the city gates with instructions not to allow any part of the army to enter. But the Mongols were tired and bored and some of them found a way inside the walls. They began to plunder and were set upon by the citizens. A thousand Mongols died. Luke was outside Tamerlane's tent when the news arrived. He was with Mohammed Sultan. The Prince was shaking his head.

Luke looked at the Prince, dread in his heart. 'Was this meant to happen?' he asked quietly. 'Did Temur ever intend to spare this city?'

Mohammed Sultan didn't answer. Instead he looked towards Tamerlane's tent where the black flag was already being raised. The storm was about to be unleashed. They heard the cheers of men who saw the flag. They saw the koumis passed from mouth to mouth by men gathering the will to do things that no human should do to another.

And so it began. The Mongol army poured into the city and began to slaughter every living thing within its walls. Fired with koumis, they outdid each other in the ingenuity of their torture so that people begged not to live but to die quickly. To start with, the tide of death was slow, the Mongols wanting plunder more than blood. But once the wagons had been piled with treasure, the mules weighed down with booty and every camel within fifty miles of the city gathered to carry what it could, then the killing began in earnest.

Luke, the other Varangians and Shulen stayed in the camp and wished themselves deaf. From across the gardens and orchards came the dark music of pain. For three days and nights, the screams continued until the sound of fire took over. Having taken everything they could, the Mongols set light to the city. A wind rose up from far into the desert and blew west towards the mountains, bringing the apocalypse on its back. The wind swept over the city walls and fanned the flames so that they leapt from house to house, garden to garden, mosque to mosque, faster and faster until they reached the heart of the city. The Umayyad Mosque sat on a hill and by the time that the fire reached it, the heat was so great that the lead on its dome began to melt. Soon the roof fell in and the fire rose up to devour the beauty it found within. By morning, the greatest building in Islam was no more.

Throughout it all, Tamerlane was deaf to entreaty. Mohammed Sultan, Pir Mohammed, even Shulen tried in vain to reason with him, reminding him that he was the Sword of Islam, but the madness of destruction was upon him and he was consumed by it. He sat outside his tent and drank wine as wagons filed past, some filled with the riches of Damascus piled high, some with heads to build the biggest towers yet.

When it was over, when the city had been levelled and its walls pulled down, Tamerlane ordered the black flag lowered and the army made ready to march away. A quarter of it was sent back to Samarcand with the plunder, and the caravan that carried it was the longest the world had ever seen. The entire contents of Syria were on the move, displaced from a smoking, ruined landscape, to embellish the new centre of the world. Luke and his friends watched it go in silence and thought of Constantinople.

'He can't stop himself,' said Matthew eventually.

'No,' agreed Luke.

'Should we go back to Plethon? He should know of this.'

Luke shook his head. 'We go to Lebanon with the army for the rest of the winter and then see where he takes us next. We have no choice. We are oath-bound.' He paused. 'And we have our empire to save.'

CHAPTER TWENTY-SEVEN

SIEGE OF CONSTANTINOPLE, SUMMER 1401

Zoe Mamonas was lying in her tent reading a letter. She was naked.

Partly this was to do with the heat. It was evening but the summer sun was still strong and the inside of the tent, where no Bosporus breeze could enter, was an oven. Partly, also, it was to do with the man now tending her garden: Yusuf, a janissary of extraordinary size and ugliness. He had come with her from Monemvasia and, when not tending to her garden, applied himself to her carnal needs. With Suleyman so often in Edirne, these were many and frequent.

Suleyman's absences were beginning to concern her. Her plans required him to marry her as Gülçiçek had suggested and, since Luke had not come, Zoe had to think of another way for Anna to disappear. The letter might provide the answer. It had come from inside Constantinople.

The garden Yusuf tended was neat and long and full of tulips. There was a formal hedge around it broken by a gate with little bells on it that opened on to a gravel path. The bells and gravel were Zoe's warning device should Suleyman return without notice. It was an oasis of calm and order in the dirty landscape that surrounded it. Now in its seventh year, the siege had turned the orchards and fields outside Constantinople into desert or quagmire, depending on the season.

Inside, the tent was large and divided into three rooms: one for sleeping, one for washing and one for receiving guests. Zoe was in the first of these because Yusuf had just left it and because she wanted privacy to read the letter. The bells sounded and she looked up, folded the letter and put it beneath the mattress. Footsteps were moving the gravel outside and getting closer. There were voices.

Suleyman.

Zoe rose and put on a dressing gown. There were two to choose from: red and white. She chose the white. It was of weightless silk and it hung from her like rain. She parted the curtains and walked into the audience room of the tent. Suleyman was standing there, dressed for the ride, with dust rising to the top of his boots. He looked exhausted.

'Baghdad is destroyed,' he said. He sat in a chair and put his head into his hands, the long hair parted by ringed fingers. 'Tamerlane has turned it into dust.' He began to remove his boots, shaking dirt on to the carpet as he did so. He looked up. 'You've been asleep?'

Zoe sat down. She crossed her legs, hoping that Yusuf's smell was not on her still. 'There's not a lot else to do. The siege is not entertaining. What happened at Baghdad?'

'He attacked at the hottest time of day, when the soldiers were asleep. The idiots had left their helmets on the battlements and gone to find shade. Tamerlane saw it and attacked.'

'And the citizens?'

'All slaughtered. The Tigris is crimson to the sea.'

'Is this bad news? He's not come here.'

Suleyman shook his head. 'We're next. Bayezid made a mistake; we should have fought him at Damascus.'

'But the Mamluks marched away.'

'Because they knew we weren't coming. Together, we might have beaten him. Now, Tamerlane is rested and his army bigger than ever.' Suleyman had removed his other boot. He sat back and looked around the tent. He rose and poured himself wine. 'Bayezid doesn't know what to do. He's paralysed by fear.'

'Which is why you must act.'

Suleyman drank, sitting back down. 'Act? Mehmed has the army now. It's he you should persuade to act.'

Zoe rose from her chair and came over to him. She knelt and took his hands in hers, kissing each finger in turn. She looked up at him. 'No, *you* need to act. Mehmed has failed to take Constantinople. I have an idea for how you might succeed. You need the walls of Constantinople to beat Tamerlane.'

The following day, Prince Suleyman was riding at the head of a retinue towards the walls of Constantinople. It was early morning and the party raised its closed eyes to the new sun like worshippers. On their left was the Golden Horn, its waters dazzling points of light; on their right, the serpentine siege works running far into the distance.

Watching them from a window high in the Blachernae Palace was Plethon the philosopher, in his hand the most recent letter he had received from Zoe. The correspondence had begun three weeks ago: a letter smuggled into the city suggesting a way for Anna to be set free, to which he had replied. After what had happened in Mistra, when Zoe had nearly murdered Anna, he knew he should never trust her again. But, then again, this plan was better than others she might consider for removing

Anna from Suleyman's presence. He'd heard about Angelina's poisoning.

The Blachernae Palace was one of the cooler places to be in Constantinople during the heat of the summer months. Built on the sixth hill of the city overlooking the waters of the Golden Horn, it was a place of cool halls, terraced gardens and fruit trees with enough unpopulated land between it and the rest of the city for the imperial noses to appreciate their scent.

Plethon watched the party approach the gate of the Blachernae and heard the squeak of chains beneath as the giant doors were pushed open. He moved to another window to watch the party emerge from shadow into a bright landscape of terraced gardens with buildings above. He saw Suleyman dismount and begin to climb the steps. There were lines of Varangian Guards on either side, standing behind axes whose blades reached up to their breasts. They were dressed in coats of silver armour and had long *chlamydes* clasped at their throats.

Plethon drew back from the window. It was time to join his emperor.

He joined Manuel just as Suleyman entered the Hall of Audience, his guard taking up position on either side of its doors. It was a long room at the end of which had been placed a dais with a wide throne on it. On the throne sat the Emperor and Empress, both dressed in purple togas. The room was filled with bearded men who stood between colonnades of porphyry and in front of tall plinths from which gazed the busts of former emperors. Behind them were windows. On the left, the windows were half filled with roof tiles and half with the glittering waters of the Golden Horn.

Plethon watched Suleyman walk slowly between the lines of

functionaries. As he approached the dais, the Emperor rose and came down the steps to greet him. 'Prince Suleyman, welcome to Constantinople. My wife.'

He'd turned and was gesturing to the Empress who'd risen from her throne and was smiling as if Suleyman had come for Christmas. Centuries of breeding were being put to work. She said: 'Your father does well?'

In spite of himself, Suleyman performed the slightest of bows. 'My father does well, highness.' He looked around him. 'Do you have the philosopher who calls himself Plethon among this gathering?'

Plethon stepped out from behind the Varangians who bracketed the throne. 'I am here,' he said, bowing.

Suleyman nodded. Then, to the astonishment of all in the hall, he turned round and addressed them, his back to their emperor.

'Byzantines, it's been seven long years of siege and the time has come for reason to prevail. We have an army you cannot count at your walls with *bashibozouks* in it with no concept of fear or, I'm afraid, chivalry. But they are not your greatest cause for concern.'

Plethon looked down the line of beards, the eyes above them sunk beneath frowns.

Suleyman continued: 'You Greeks have your word for them: Tartars. You have heard what they did to Aleppo, to Damascus; what they did to the Umayyad Mosque, the most glorious place of worship in our world. I'm here to tell you that they've done the same to Baghdad, home of our caliphate for centuries, a city steeped in holiness. If Temur can do this to cities of the Prophet, what will he do to a Christian one?' Suleyman turned, searching the faces before him. 'Temur is God's scourge, sent to punish us for our failure to worship Him as one, for our endless enmity.'

There was an unfathomed silence in the hall. Baghdad had fallen. Was this the end of the world?

Suleyman lowered his voice but still spoke to them all. 'Constantinople has the strongest walls on earth. Only they can stop this thing from hell destroying the world: your world, my world, God's world. You have five thousand on your walls; we have two hundred thousand outside them. Let us defend your city together.'

It had been said and no beard had fallen to the floor. It had been said and it had been heard. Suleyman continued: 'Your great city has stood for a thousand years. Damascus and Aleppo have stood for longer. Do not, for the sake of your wives and children, make your end like theirs. And do not take the whole world with you.'

The silence stretched out. Only the Emperor would break it.

'What are your terms?' he asked quietly.

Suleyman turned and made a bow. 'Surrender Constantinople and receive complete freedom of worship: you in your churches, we in our mosques. Once we have defeated Shatan.' His voice was still loud enough for all to hear. 'Turk and Greek living side by side in peace. As they do in Anatolia and Rumelia.'

'And the rest of the Empire?'

Suleyman glanced at Plethon. Was Zoe right about this? She'd been right so far. 'Mistra you keep. It was, after all, where you Greeks began. You return to your roots.'

For a long time no one spoke, no one shouted out, no one wept. Only fear rose like a formless steam from the men gathered in the hall. Plethon cleared his throat. He walked over to Manuel and whispered something into his ear. The

Emperor was studying the ground, a finger to his lips. Then he nodded.

Manuel looked up at Suleyman. 'Come, we will talk further.'

Not much later, Manuel, Plethon and Suleyman were standing in an antechamber. It was small and had thick tapestries on its walls. There wasn't much light in the room. Manuel removed the *camelaucum* from his head and set it down on a table. He turned to Suleyman. 'We give you Constantinople and we keep Mistra. This is your proposal?'

Suleyman did his best to arrange his features to match those of the Emperor. He said: 'It is as I said, we live side by side in peace.'

Manuel shook his head. 'I'm afraid that won't reassure the very nervous citizens of Constantinople,' he said. 'You'll have to be more specific, Prince Suleyman.'

Suleyman inclined his head. 'No deaths, no slavery, complete freedom to worship how you please.' He paused. 'I have heard it said that this last is of particular importance to your citizens. I have heard that they would rather this than enslavement to the Pope.'

Manuel didn't say anything. He appeared to be thinking very deeply, his hand stroking the full length of his beard. He was staring at his crown. Eventually, he said: 'There is some truth in that, yes.' He turned to the man next to him. 'Lord Plethon, what is your view?'

Plethon walked to a window and looked through it for a while. 'My view, majesty, is that we are not going to decide the fate of a city that has stood for a thousand years in a meeting between three men in a small room with imperfect views. We shall need time to discuss such an idea.'

Manuel nodded. He turned to Suleyman. 'We will need a truce to think about it. But how do we trust you? You are not Bayezid.'

'No, but I am a man of honour.'

Plethon was shaking his head. 'You are, at present, our enemy. We will need a mark of your goodwill if we are to convince the people of such an idea. I propose that you hand over to us certain hostages, men of note, who will be released when you have our answer. Among them should be Anna Laskaris, daughter of the late Protostrator of Mistra. It is understood that you are no longer to marry her so she should be free to leave. Such an act would be popular with the people.'

Suleyman blinked, then blinked again. He opened his mouth to speak but Plethon hadn't finished. 'And the daughter of the King of Hungary as well. That would convince the Kings of Christendom that you are in earnest. She should be handed over too. We hear that she nearly died in your care.'

Suleyman stared at the two men, first one and then the other. He'd prepared his speech to the court but hadn't prepared for this. He thought quickly for alternatives. There were none that wouldn't undermine his case. He was trapped – but the prize was so near. He thought of Anna and he thought of consequences.

Take Constantinople and I can have it all. Including Anna.

'Very well,' he said.

It was only two days later that Anna found herself on a Venetian round ship being pulled up the Bosporus by two skiffs on its way to Trebizond. She herself would not be going so far. She was to be landed at the Black Sea port of Constanza and from there taken to Buda in the Kingdom of Hungary.

Anna was dressed as a cabin boy. She wore a brown leather jerkin over a hose of patched white. On her head was a hat big enough to collect her hair and on her face as much dirt as would hide her beauty. Venetian vessels were the only ones allowed to leave the city and even they were subject to search under the guns of the Castle of Güzelce Hisar further up the Bosporus.

They had set sail the night before from the harbour of Hormisdas where Luke's ancestor Siward had left from. Anna and Angelina had been brought from Edirne and, leaving their Ottoman guard at the gate, had been met by a man with a message from Plethon. Anna had gone straight to the harbour to catch the tide, Angelina to the palace. Siward had taken a casket that long-ago night, a casket they said one day might save the Empire. Anna had opened that casket and knew now that they'd been right. The four letters she was carrying were proof of it.

Three of the letters were from Plethon. The first would be delivered by her to King Sigismund of Hungary at Buda. The other two would be taken by courier to Rome and Avignon. The fourth was from Angelina and Anna was to give it to Sigismund once the King had read Plethon's.

Anna looked out across the water to the banks of the Bosporus, little more than a green haze in this early hour. They were narrowing now and she could see the walls of the Güzelce Hisar coming up to her right. A small galley had put out with bombards on its foredeck. There was no wind and the only sound was the dip of their oars and the bark of seagulls.

Anna put the letters into a pocket sewn inside her jerkin. Then she turned to go below.

CHAPTER TWENTY-EIGHT

QARABAGH, WINTER 1401

King Giorgi's balas ruby was of a size that fitted neatly between the talons of Tamerlane's eagle.

Riding the mountain currents, the bird could see, refracted through the stone, a world in hibernation below, a world measuring out the slow heartbeat of its winter months under a carapace of infinite pink.

Around it was hard blue sky, empty of anything except a smudge that hovered over the horizon. The eagle flew towards it and, swooping down close, found it to be the mixture of smoke and scavenger birds that stood guard above the snow-bound Mongol camp. Tamerlane had decided to rest his army in the Qarabagh rather than Lebanon and no one but he knew the reason why.

The sound from the camp was more animal than human: the scrape of horses digging deep for grass within huge pens that bordered the camp. It was mid-morning and most of the men were still abed, sleeping off the rigours of last night's feast while their women were outside, silently airing bedding, scouring cauldrons and hanging washing up to dry. One or two, summoned from within, might be stirring the concoction of mare's blood and egg-yolk that was said to cure even the worst airag hangover. None would dare to disturb the sleep of this Mongol army. For rest and feasting was what it had been promised.

The feasting had been prodigious. Enriched with booty, the army had summoned more wine from the Lebanon than its vineyards could offer and drunk it night after night until the airag took over. And afterwards, Syrian slaves had warmed their beds through the long winter nights. There was, of course, much to celebrate. Never had the army taken so much from so many cities and the new year would bring more plunder.

The eagle swooped lower, swinging around the pall of smoke, scattering other birds of prey. It glided over the pony pens, diving down to race above the upturned heads of camels and pack-mules. Ahead of it were a wall and a garden with pools and waterfalls and pavilions and a solid perch standing next to an old man who would give it meat. Now the bird was above the wall and its angry eyes blinked twice at the glitter of all that was within.

'Ah,' said the old man, looking up and squinting, 'he returns. And with him the jewel.' He spoke to the girl who was kneeling before him, massaging his knee. The eagle landed on its perch and Tamerlane took the ruby from its talons. He held it up to the sun, turning it between his fingers. 'I win the bet and you do your massage higher.'

The girl laughed. 'You know very well that that was not the bet, lord.'

Shulen waved away a fly that was trying to settle on the leg. Tamerlane lifted her chin with a finger. 'Your glasses help me to read, Shulen,' he whispered, leaning forward so that his rancid breath was all about her, 'but I cannot see what is brought before me. Describe it to me.'

All around him were piled the treasures that had been pillaged from Aleppo, Homs, Hama, Beirut, Damascus and Baghdad. It was a selection of what his generals thought would most amuse their leader. There were bowls of gold dust, helmets full of precious stones, bolts of raw silk, an ingenious clock that also made music and an incense burner, shaped as an elephant, to remind him of his adored beasts sent to winter in warmer climes. And beside his chair reclined a snow leopard with a necklace of pearls around its neck.

Shulen began to list them, occasionally rising to bring something of interest for him to inspect. After a while she brought him a book, its leather covers finely wrought in gold and tiny jewels.

'What's this?' he asked, adjusting his glasses.

'I don't know, highness,' she answered, looking down at it from his shoulder. 'It says it's the work of the Indian sage Vatsya. It seems very old.'

Tamerlane was leafing through the pages, humming to himself. Then he stopped at an illustration and looked at it for a long time, bringing his head so close to the page that only he could see it. He'd stopped humming. Eventually he looked back up at Shulen. 'Can I read to you from it?'

Shulen nodded, smiling. Her student wanted to impress her.

'Well,' said Tamerlane, 'Vasya writes as follows:

> 'Just as a horse in full gallop, blinded by the energy of his own speed, pays no attention to any post or hole or ditch in the path, so two lovers blinded by passion are caught up by their fierce energy and pay no attention to danger.'

He looked up at Shulen, who had gone the colour of the ruby. 'Is that not true, teacher? Here, look at this illustration!'

Tamerlane was so bent with laughter that he didn't witness the arrival of his heir amongst the throng of courtiers who parted to let him pass. Mohammed Sultan, with Luke next to him and the other Varangians behind, was approaching. They all knelt and Mohammed Sultan spoke: 'Grandfather, I bring you news.'

Temur looked down at him, pushing the glasses to the top of his nose. 'The pig-Khan? I know it. For weeks I have known. For what do you think I keep the yams stocked with horses? They bring fresh fruit up from Hormuz and fresher news down from my spies in Chang'an.'

The Emperor of China was dead. Aged sixty-nine, the peasant that had founded the Ming Dynasty was at last floating his way down the sacred river to meet his ancestors and all was chaos in his wake. Mohammed Sultan had been in Sultaniya when the news had come in with a caravan. He had immediately taken horse for the Qarabagh.

'What will you do, Grandfather?' he asked now.

'What will I do?' Temur looked up, surprised. 'Attack them, of course. What would you do?'

Mohammed Sultan glanced at Shulen. 'Is it wise to turn our backs on Bayezid? They say that he's on the point of taking Constantinople. Why not strike while Constantinople is still in friendly hands? And what of the Mamluks? Will they not join with Bayezid if we go north?'

'I have never lost a battle, Grandson. You would do well to remember that.'

'No, lord. But the Ming army is over a million strong. It is a formidable force.'

Tamerlane's frown deepened. He drank wine from a goblet and wiped his beard with his sleeve. 'China will be my jihad,' he said quietly. 'I am old and not long for this world. I need to think of my soul.'

'Jihad, lord? There are better jihads than China.'

Temur looked at him darkly. 'She has told you to say this?' He nodded towards Shulen.

Mohammed Sultan shook his head, his eyes on the carpet beneath him. It was patterned as a garden with intertwining trees' branches. A solitary pear adjoined his toe.

'Anyway, it's too late,' said Tamerlane, putting the empty goblet back on to a tray. 'I've been planning it for years. The spies have done their work. Barley has been sown on the route of march and castles built on the border.' He smiled and looked straight at his grandson. 'And the elephants have been trained.'

Mohammed Sultan was amazed. 'All this has happened?'

Tamerlane nodded, stretching out his oiled leg. 'General Allahdad was sent north two years ago to make maps and develop the land.'

Mohammed Sultan sat back on his heels, his head very still. 'So you never intended to attack Bayezid?' He paused. 'What if Bayezid now comes for you?'

'I don't think he'll do that. I've scared him enough with Sivas.' Tamerlane scratched his knee and examined the oil beneath his fingernails. 'And the letters have stopped.'

'But, Grandfather, he is on the point of taking Constantinople, and when it falls . . .'

' . . . he will go further into Europe,' finished Tamerlane testily. 'Why do you think I have my Jerusalem oil from Pope Boniface and those pretty stallions from King Charles of France? They know where he'll go next.' Tamerlane sank back into his cushions. 'Don't be angry with me, Grandson. We cannot have the Greeks deciding what we do.'

Mohammed Sultan stared at his grandfather. That he, Temur's heir, should be so publicly humiliated. He got to his feet and bowed stiffly. 'Lord, if you will excuse me.'

'No,' said Tamerlane, 'not yet, at least.' He signalled for more wine and leant forward from his cushions. 'I want you to go to Samarcand.'

Mohammed Sultan stared at his grandfather.

'I want you to go and see how Allahdad fares. He's there now. I want you to tell him that we will march in forty days' time. Can you leave now?'

Mohammed said nothing for a while. Then he nodded. 'Of course, Grandfather.'

Tamerlane's heir bowed, turned and walked back through the treasure, looking at the ground. Three of the Varangians had got to their feet, ready to follow him. Luke stayed on his knees.

'You wish to stay?' Tamerlane was peering at him. 'Very well.' He waved his hand. 'The rest of you go.'

When his friends had left, Luke found himself the focus of Tamerlane's full attention. He forced himself to stay calm, to smother the fury he felt that it had all been in vain, that this old man would fight his last battle in China rather than Anatolia. The horror of the past year, denied for so long, engulfed him, revulsion filling every part of his being. He clenched his fists.

It's all been pointless. All the slaughter, everything.

Tamerlane was smiling, his leather cheeks pushing up his glasses. Whatever he could see in Luke seemed to be pleasing him. 'I wish you to go with my grandson to Samarcand,' he said. 'You are good for him.'

Luke didn't reply. He felt numb.

Tamerlane was looking at him with curiosity. 'You have done him service. Me as well.' He paused. 'Perhaps he'll need your baskets again.'

Luke steadied himself, his fingernails dug deep into his palms. Suddenly, waves of fatigue rolled over him and he could think of only one thing he must do: leave this madness and go to Anna.

Keeping his voice steady, he said: 'If I and the other Varangians have done you service, lord, then we ask to be released from our oaths. We ask to go home.'

Tamerlane's smile wavered, then turned to a frown. He shook his head. 'By no means can you be released, Greek. I want you on the campaign. I still favour you.'

'Then let me go home,' said Luke quietly. 'I have nothing more to give you.'

Tamerlane's voice sank to a growl. 'Nothing more to give, Greek? You've just begun. You'll go where I tell you to go: with my grandson to Samarcand.'

Luke opened his mouth to speak. He didn't care any more; he was so tired. He glanced at Shulen. She was staring at him, minutely shaking her head. It was a message, but what? She rose and, placing her hand on Temur's forearm, bent to whisper in his ear. 'Lord, my friend is tired. Let me speak to him.'

The old man turned and blinked at her. Then he grunted, nodding. 'Speak sense to him. Go.'

Shulen swept from the dais and took Luke's arm and half pulled him from the tent. She walked him to where they could be alone. She let go of his arm. 'That was foolish. You nearly lost your head.'

Luke was standing with his eyes closed. He said: 'Shulen, it's over.'

'No, Luke. It's not over. We can still do this.' She paused and took his shoulders in her hands, forcing him to look at her. '*You* must do it – for Byzantium.'

'But do what? You heard him: he's going to China.'

'Not yet,' she replied softly. 'Go with Mohammed Sultan and I will join you later. This is far from over.'

Important news travelled fast, not just for Tamerlane. The Ottoman Empire, only a century old, was as alert to Tamerlane's every movement as a lion guarding its prey. Its spies watched the flurry of activity in the Mongol camp, and its direction east, and carried their interpretation back to Bayezid. Only a month later, the Sultan had had it confirmed.

'The Mongol goes to China.' He was sitting in the throne room at Edirne and before him stood his three sons: Suleyman, Mehmed and Musa. He could barely conceal his glee. 'A million Chinese will destroy his army and he will die of rage and shame.'

Suleyman nodded. It was six months since Anna had left Edirne and gone into Constantinople. She hadn't come out with the other hostages who'd been released at the end of the truce with Manuel's answer that Constantinople would not surrender. After his fury and grief had subsided, Suleyman had set his mind on being the one to take the city. After all, Mehmed's attempts had all failed and his brother's fears about a Mongol attack seemed now to be unfounded.

He said: 'And the news has gone further. Venice wants to give us cannon again.'

Bayezid wrinkled his nose. 'Those dogs point with the wind but this one will blow them away. You talk to them?'

The news of Tamerlane's move on China had reached not only the Doge in Venice but also Pavlos Mamonas, as had Suleyman's visit to Constantinople. The plan had all the hallmarks of his daughter's genius. He'd deduced that Suleyman was on his way back into favour and had immediately reopened negotiations with Venice. The cannon would arrive at the siege by the summer. Suleyman glanced at his brothers and said: 'Yes, I talk to them as I talked to Manuel in Constantinople.'

Suleyman smiled at his father. 'Give me back the siege, Father, and I will take this city one month from the cannons' arrival.'

Bayezid frowned. 'What of Sigismund? He's raising another crusade.'

Suleyman had heard this. The news had reached them a month after Anna had entered Constantinople. 'But how long will it take to come, if at all? What appetite will the Christian Kings have to fight us after Nicopolis? All it will do is give the Byzantines new heart. But it's too late.'

Bayezid looked hard at the man who was still his heir. Then he nodded. 'It is your last chance, Prince Suleyman.'

CHAPTER TWENTY-NINE

THE ROAD TO SAMARCAND, SPRING 1402

The ride to Samarcand took three weeks and would have been shorter if Luke hadn't insisted on keeping Eskalon. To begin with, they'd ridden with an escort of gautchin but Mohammed Sultan had dismissed them on the Persian border and they'd ridden on alone. For the first time in his life, Luke was glad not to be with his friends.

The two men rode south down the shoreline of the Khazar Sea until they came to the trade road and then turned towards Tabriz. The way was busy with wagons of plunder going east and soldiers west to join the Conqueror of the World. But for Luke, no distance was great enough to separate him from Tamerlane. The bustle around him belonged to another world; his was scorched by fire and drowned in blood: red road, red dust, red sun spilling blood across the evening sky because the earth had soaked up all it could manage. In his dreams, the sun was masked by the endless smoke of burning and the only sound was one long scream of agony. He dreamt of destruction and awoke with its smell still with him: the smell of fire, of horse, of fear, of blood. The smell of Tamerlane.

Luke hardly spoke throughout the ride, finding no words

to describe the scale of his torment. He wanted to shout out to those they passed that their world was inverting, that the creatures of hell were coming up to the surface while all that was good was being buried for ever. He wanted to tell them to tear down their churches because neither their God nor the angels could see them through their tears. Perhaps he did shout out, for the people backed away as they passed. They were used to armies and wagons of plunder but not a fair-haired giant with madness in his eyes.

For the most part, Mohammed Sultan let him be. He saw the endless washing of the hands when they stopped to rest and understood. He knew that only time would wash away the blood. Only time or something else.

They reached Samarcand and rode through a city embraced by scaffolding. Blocks of stone and marble, sheets of copper and brass were piled everywhere and between them were vast pits dense with workers of every nation. The streets were full of masons dressing stone and the air was choked with the smoke of furnaces working at full blast. Even from afar, Tamerlane's all-seeing eye watched everything and the fear that hung over his enemies was above Samarcand too.

They spent a week in Samarcand and, while Mohammed Sultan talked with Allahdad, Luke slept. Then the three of them rode east towards China, through the rich Fergana Valley where the water of the Syr Darya sparkled in the sunlight and the fields were full of women sowing wheat and barley for the army to come. The road was the main trade route into China and Allahdad had filled in its holes, built new yams and created whole villages full of warehouses, barracks, bakeries and pens for thousands of horses. They spent two weeks riding east and during that time Luke remained silent. It was only when they'd arrived back in Samarcand that Mohammed Sultan finally confronted him.

'Get up,' he said. He'd entered Luke's bedroom in Tamerlane's palace to find his friend awake, staring at the ceiling. 'We are going somewhere where we can talk and you can mend.'

The forty days were up and the Mongol army still had not marched. The first flowers were knotting themselves into a carpet that would unroll across the valleys to welcome the coming of spring, and still Tamerlane's gers remained in the fields of the Qarabagh.

Tamerlane was ill.

It was night and inside the imperial ger it was stifling. Four Damascene braziers stood at each corner of an enormous bed raised high on a dais, throwing up snakes of flame to add to the heat cast out by the iron stove. On the bed, naked save for a loincloth sodden with sweat, lay Tamerlane, his eyes closed and his grey hair matted to his skull. His body was criss-crossed with scars, some old and puckered, others still livid. Every battlefield was there, every sword stroke of an enemy that had got too close. His bed resembled a pyre.

The ger was simple considering its occupant's wealth and power. On its walls were hung the pelts of different animals, all claws and teeth. On the floor were plain carpets of coarse weave, piled one on top of the other. The furniture was sparse: a table of mother-of-pearl that was also a chessboard, the pair of elephant incense burners, two sitting lecterns, one holding the *Kama Sutra* that had made Shulen blush so, and a tall perch on which stood Temur's eagle, its head sunk deep into its neck and its eye fixed malevolently upon the snow leopard lying at the foot of the bed. Next to the animal knelt Khan-zada and in her hand was a bowl and sponge.

The light played its uncertain fingers over this scene, summoning from the dark one tableau after another to tell the story of this sickness. The man on the bed was covered in boils, seeping yellow fluid that gave off a putrid stench until wiped clean by the hand of the Princess. There was the sound of the ger door opening and Khan-zada turned. 'Close it quick!' she whispered. 'We must keep the heat in.'

Her second son had entered and with him was Tamerlane's greatest general, Burunduk. They stood for a while looking at the emir and then began to untie their deels. Pir Mohammed spoke: 'Is this heat right, Mother?'

She put down the bowl and soaked the sponge in the water, wringing it between her hands. 'I don't know what is right,' she said. 'I don't know what afflicts him. That's why we need her.' She pressed the sponge to Temur's forehead. 'Are they here?'

The general nodded and stepped forward to the other side of the bed so that he was facing the Princess. 'They are waiting outside with the horses, highness.'

'And no one knows how Temur is?'

'No one except those in this room.'

Khan-zada looked over to her second son. He was quieter than his brother and inclined to melancholy but he was good and strong and would do what was right. He had Jahangir's kind eyes, eyes that had always been wise beyond their years. He was Temur's second heir and she prayed every day that he would never have to become his first.

'And Miran Shah? How long can we keep him from this tent, do you think?'

Pir Mohammed knelt down by the side of his mother. He

took her hand in his. 'We'll find a way, Mother,' he said gently, 'until she returns. Now we must go to the Varangians. There's not much time.'

They rose and walked outside the tent, Burunduk behind them. In the darkness were Matthew, Nikolas and Arcadius, each holding a horse, each dressed for riding. Khan-zada went up and kissed them in turn. She looked from one to the other, seeing how young they were, younger than her sons. 'Go, and ride harder than you have ever ridden. Use your paizis to change horses wherever you can. Go like the wind.' She turned to Matthew, taking his hand. 'And bring her back to us,' she whispered. 'Only she can save him now.'

It was evening when Luke and Mohammed Sultan reached the church of the rock. They had followed the road west from Samarcand, then turned south into the hills. As the sun was setting, they came to a giant fist of sandstone on top of a hill into which hundreds of caves had been dug. A rough path led up to it.

'Tombs,' said Mohammed Sultan. It was the first time he'd spoken since waking Luke. 'Thousands of years old. And a Christian church on top of them.' The Prince had turned his horse on to the path and spoke over his shoulder. 'My mother used to bring us here when we were young. To worship.'

With the sun gone, it was suddenly dark and cold. Luke unstrapped his deel from the back of his saddle and put it on. He saw his breath rise before him. 'To worship?' he asked.

'My mother is a Nestorian. It was a sect of your church that came east many centuries ago. Many Mongols are Nestorian.'

'You?'

'No longer. I'm to be the Sword of Islam, after all.'

Luke fell silent. In another mood, he'd have been more surprised at this revelation. Now he merely nodded and looked above him at the beehive necropolis – honeycomb and catacomb – and the cave at its top, which had pillars and steps framing its mouth. When they reached the church, they dismounted and lit torches that they'd brought with them. Luke entered first and raised the flame to see pictures of saints on the rock walls, their colours faded with age. He swung the torch around. The church was empty and had an earthen floor, raised at one end with a niche in the wall behind. Luke walked over to it.

'What was here?'

Mohammed Sultan joined him. 'When I used to come here, a statue of your Virgin Mary. Before that? Who knows? Cybele, Matar – they're all the same.'

Luke turned. 'This was a place of pagan worship?'

'Of course.' Mohammed Sultan gestured towards the niche. 'Before your Virgin was installed, Cybele would've sat there on a throne with two lions at her feet. She would've been fat and many-breasted, giving eternal birth while her worshippers danced to two-piped *aulos*.'

Luke looked around the church again, half-rock, half-building. It was a place of whispers and the tremulous echo of ancient prayer. He suddenly felt very cold. He said: 'We should build a fire.'

Mohammed Sultan rose and led them out of the church and along a path that followed the contour of the hill. The evening was cold but clear, with a million stars emerging in patterns of winking light. Luke turned to look out over the landscape below. He could see a patchwork of grey sewn together with black: the tapestry of old, old fields and broken walls. In between, the road wound its way down the valley, silver and sinuous. They walked to the bottom of the hill where there were trees and gathered wood.

An hour later they were sitting on the floor of the church, a fire between them, their rolled bedding and saddlebags set behind them as cushions. In silence they ate food they'd brought with them, each finding some comfort in the fire. Eventually Mohammed Sultan looked up at Luke, seeing only his face through the flames. He said: 'Luke, the slaughter had nothing to do with what happened in Georgia. What we did there was right and will be remembered.'

Luke made no reply. His eyes were alight, but dull.

'And you did what you could at Damascus with Ibn Khaldun. If the fools hadn't attacked us, they'd still be alive.'

Still no answer. Mohammed Sultan leant forward and picked up Luke's sword, which was lying between them. He raised it into the firelight, turning it, examining the blade, then the hilt. The dragon scales were rapids of silver in the flickering firelight. 'You told me that something was written on the blade. What is it?'

Luke turned to him, as if seeing him for the first time. 'Mistra,' he replied.

'Tell me about Mistra and then tell me about Anna. They are joined, I think.' He paused. 'But first tell me about this sword. It is different.'

Luke looked back into the fire, frowning. He allowed the images to form slowly in his mind, side by side.

Mistra, Anna, the sword. They are joined.

'The sword was made for a Varangian prince called Siward, my ancestor. His descendant brought a treasure out of Constantinople two hundred years ago when it fell to the Franks. Mistra is where it was buried. Now the treasure's been found, by Anna. It is said it will save Byzantium.' Luke lifted his hand and raised his finger. 'This ring', he said, 'is part of it. It's old and it's Hebrew. That's all I know.'

Mohammed Sultan looked up at the ring and whistled softly. He laid the sword down in his lap. The firelight had risen with new wood and the walls around them seemed to close in, the worn saints looming over them, listening. Luke felt something rising within him, an urge to fill the space with words.

'Anna was born in Mistra, I in Monemvasia. She was married to the son of the Archon who employed me to care for his horses. That's how I found Eskalon. Anna's husband was cruel and I tried to take her away from Monemvasia but we were betrayed and my father died as I got away, without Anna. I went to Chios where I fathered a son who doesn't know that I'm his father. Bayezid's heir, Suleyman, fell in love with Anna and took her to his harem. She is there now and I must get to her once I have done what I must do.'

Mohammed Sultan sat very still, absorbing this procession of facts. He said: 'Tell me about you Varangians.'

Luke pushed his fingers through his hair and leant forward towards the fire, one arm hugging his knees. 'We came from an island far to the west called England. They say that it's a place of woods and mists and people who love to fight. Siward left when the Franks invaded and put an arrow in his king's eye. He sailed to Byzantium with five thousand followers to offer their service to the Emperor. A hundred and fifty years later, the Franks took Constantinople and Siward's descendant came to Mistra with the treasure. That's why I was born there.'

'So you're the descendant of a prince, Luke. And this sword' – he picked it up – 'was made for a prince. I begin to understand.'

Luke looked at him. 'Understand?'

'Why you were sent to us,' Mohammed Sultan said quietly. 'It was your destiny.' He picked up a branch and fed it to the fire. The flames rose up and the saints rose with them. A light wind entered the church and Luke pulled his deel tighter to his body. It was the first time they'd talked of destiny. He closed his eyes.

My destiny is to save an empire. And I have failed.

Mohammed Sultan continued, as if reading his thoughts: 'You have not failed in your destiny yet, Luke. That is why we must persuade my grandfather to turn west again. We want the same thing: Tamerlane to fight Bayezid. I want it because I don't want to see my nation perish in the snows of China; you, because you want to save your empire.'

Luke shook his head. 'It's too late. And who's to say that he'll stop with Bayezid? What if he takes Constantinople? Or Mistra? What then?'

Mohammed Sultan stared deep into the fire. He didn't speak for a while and Luke wondered if he'd even heard him. Then he picked up a stick and examined it. 'You've told me some of what's happening in the west,' he said. 'When we rode together in Samarcand, you told me that there's a rebirth of ancient wisdom happening in Italy, that this rebirth is important for the future of the world, of mankind. I believe you.' He turned the stick over in his hand. 'The last time that our armies came into Europe, they were stopped by the death of the Khan. Everyone went home to find a new one. It might happen again. Tamerlane is old.'

They sat there, very still, each considering what had been said and what hadn't. Luke felt the presence of countless worshippers all around him in the dark: pagan and Christian, formless yet watching. They were two young men from different ends of the world united by warmth and an understanding that could not speak its name. For the first time in months, Luke felt the warm flow of blood inside his body rather than without.

Mohammed Sultan changed the subject. 'Tell me more about Anna.'

Anna.

What could he say about Anna? That she had beauty and courage and understanding that meant that he could have no life without her? That his yearning for her was such that he'd almost broken oath to go to her? That he loved her beyond any measurement the world had yet devised? Instead, he said: 'She was the daughter of the Protostrator of Mistra. She found the treasure.'

'So she is part of the plan. And Shulen?' Mohammed Sultan had leant forward. 'Is Shulen part of the plan, Luke?'

There was something new in his voice, as if his words were the reconnaissance for more later, as if they were scouting new ground.

'Shulen is part of the plan to bring Temur to fight Bayezid. Anna will be part of what happens next.'

'And which plan is more important to you?'

Luke sighed. 'Now? I've not liked what I've seen of the Tamerlane plan but if it will save my empire then there may be no need of the other.'

'And which woman is more important to you, Shulen or Anna?'

Luke said simply: 'I love Anna.'

Mohammed Sultan leant back against the roll of his bedding. He was nodding very slowly as if this simple statement had revealed much more. 'And Shulen? You have loved her as well, perhaps?'

Luke considered this. Had he? Had he been more than tempted by her feral beauty? Could fascination ever be mistaken for love?

'No,' he said. 'I have not loved Shulen.'

The Prince turned and brought his saddlebag on to his lap. He opened it and brought out a small phial, which he opened. He proffered it to Luke. 'Drink this.'

Luke took the phial and studied it. It was made of glass, but opaque. 'What is it?'

'Medicine,' said Mohammed Sultan. 'From Shulen. It will cure you.'

Somehow Luke knew it was blood.

Blood to wash away blood.

He sat there looking at the phial for a long time. Then he brought it to his lips and drank. It was warm and thick and Luke didn't care who or what it had come from. He heard a sound from the raised part of the church. He looked towards it and the fire played tricks for there was Cybele, dressed in white, standing in her niche. But she had no lions, or naked breasts. And she wasn't giving birth. She was Shulen.

Luke shook his head, trying to clear it. He closed his eyes.

Shulen. Here.

He heard a voice far away that he knew. Shulen's. She said: 'You will dream of blood and you will be cured.'

He forced his eyes open and looked at the place from where the voice had come, trying to focus. She was with someone else now, holding their hand. It was Mohammed Sultan. He fell back against his bedding and closed his eyes and sleep broke over him like a warm surf and he dreamt.

He was in a pit with bars above. He saw a bull pulled by men with a rope and its throat cut. He felt the rich blood cascade over him, filling the space around, rising, rising, until just his nose and mouth could breathe above it. He was drowning because he couldn't move to keep above the blood. Then he was rising out of it and was standing on a rock in the middle of a river with fish in it and he was spearing them. One flashed past, then another: fat silver-grey trout darting among the rocks and tumbling down the eddies between. He raised his spear slowly while fixing his eye on the little defile through which they'd come. Then he struck and felt the joy of skin pierced. The water turned red.

He awoke to the smell of cooking fish. It was daylight and Mohammed Sultan and Shulen were side by side by the fire, turning fish on a spit and watching bubbling fat break through their curling scales. The fish hissed and spat and Luke felt his mouth fill with the juice of hunger. Mohammed Sultan lifted a fish off its spit by both ends, blowing on its surface and resting it on a stone to cool. He turned.

'You've slept for two days. How do you feel?'

Luke felt unlike he'd ever felt before. He felt lighter than goose-down and his body tingled with sensation. He felt joy and hunger in equal measure. He felt alive. He propped himself up on his arm. 'I feel different.' He turned to Shulen. 'You came.'

'As I said I would.' She laughed. 'You've done more talking in the past two days than you have for a month. It was a torrent.'

'What did I talk about?'

Shulen and Mohammed Sultan exchanged glances. The Prince lifted the stone and brought it over to Luke. He sat down beside him. 'Eat.'

Luke took the fish and ate. He wiped his mouth with the back of his hand. 'What did I talk about?'

'Anna, Luke. You talked about Anna.'

Shulen came over to them with more fish and sat as well. 'You're cured, I think, Luke. No more blood. It's time to return.'

'To Tamerlane?'

'To Tamerlane. We'll be leaving soon.'

'How soon?'

Shulen shrugged. She gave one of the fish to Mohammed Sultan and her hand stayed on the Prince's arm. 'When they come.'

CHAPTER THIRTY

QARABAGH, SUMMER 1402

It was early evening in the valleys of the Qarabagh and the army was still waiting to move.

Inside Tamerlane's tent, the eagle no longer watched the leopard and the leopard had forgotten its bone. Both of them stared at the man on the bed, the man whose body, yellow in the candlelight, was a mass of suppurating sores and leech-bruises and whose shallow breathing had the rattle of death about it.

Tamerlane was propped up on piled cushions and his eyes were open. He was looking at his grandson, Pir Mohammed, and his heavy lids were blinking from the sting of sweat in his eyes. It was early evening and the tent was suffocatingly hot. On the ground next to the bed were the feathers of different birds and Pir Mohammed was studying them.

'Grandfather, the shaman has been,' he said, shaking his head. 'Shulen told us not to put our trust in him. She said . . .'

Tamerlane slowly raised his hand. 'I know what she said.' He closed his eyes. 'What harm can it do now, Grandson? I am nearly dead.'

Miran Shah had come to the tent earlier in the day, pushing

his way through the guards to stare in horror at what the Lord of the Celestial Conjunction had become. The shaman had entered the tent behind him, a withered, filthy Mongol in a coat of feathers, and Miran Shah had turned to him. 'Bleed him,' he'd whispered. 'Bleed him a lot.'

Now bled, Tamerlane looked weaker than his grandson had yet seen him and could not be far from the end.

'It is for my sins,' he breathed, his eyes screwed shut against the memory of them. 'It is for my sins that they have taken her.'

Pir Mohammed knew whom he meant. 'She will return,' he said quietly.

But Tamerlane was shaking his head slowly, the hollows of his cheeks dark pools below ridges shining with fever. 'It is for my sins.'

The entrance to the ger creaked open and Pir Mohammed turned. His mother was closing the door behind her. She came over to the bed and stood beside her son. Tamerlane's eyes had closed again and he seemed to be sleeping. Pir Mohammed turned to his mother. 'Still no word from the Varangians. We don't even know if they found her.'

Neither of them saw that his eyes had opened again. The old man's brow was furrowed and, with a supreme effort, he raised his head. 'So she doesn't come, after all,' he whispered. 'I am truly cursed.'

Tamerlane closed his eyes and whatever fight had kept him alive thus far seemed to leave him like the blood that had been leeched from his veins. With a deep, cracked sigh, his head sank back into the cushions.

There was conversation outside the ger and an order barked. Pir Mohammed looked up. 'It's Miran Shah. I will go to him.' He rose.

But as the door of the ger opened and the fire in the braziers flared in the draught, it was not his uncle that filled the entrance. It was Luke and beside him was Shulen and she carried the skull of a horse.

'Who let in the shaman?' she asked, throwing the skull to the ground and then her cloak on to the end of the bed. 'And who made this tent so hot?'

Pir Mohammed came forward. 'Temur Gurgan is dying.'

'And you thought a shaman might save him?' Shulen walked over to the bedside. Tamerlane's eyes were still closed and she placed a hand on his forehead. She knelt and put her ear to his chest and a hand to his wrist. She examined the pustulating boils on his chest and arms, each in turn, oblivious to their stench.

Eventually she straightened. 'I don't know if I can save him,' she said. 'The illness is far advanced. I'll do what I can.'

A hand from the bed suddenly grasped her wrist. Tamerlane's eyes were open and they were pleading. 'Save me, Shulen,' he whispered.

Very slowly, one by one, Shulen prised the fingers from her skin. There were red marks where they had sunk into her flesh. She placed his arm gently by his side.

Luke came to the bedside. He knelt beside her and leant close to Tamerlane's ear. 'We have done you some favour, lord,' he said. 'All this time, we have done you favour. Now it is time for you to do us favour.'

Tamerlane closed his eyes again. His breathing was laboured, quickening. 'What do you want?' he rasped.

Luke glanced at Shulen. His hands were shaking below the bed and he clenched them into stillness. 'I want this: if she cures you, we march to Bayezid and when we've destroyed him, you free us Varangians from our oath and let us go home. And

Shulen wants this: to marry Mohammed Sultan, your heir.' Luke heard Khan-zada gasp behind him. He fixed his eyes on the dying man. Temur's breathing was the ebb and flow of tide on shingle. His eyes were dulling. 'All you have to do is nod your head to say that you agree.'

Tamerlane did nothing for a long time, his pale lips pressed together with concentration. Then he let out a long sigh and, almost imperceptibly, nodded.

Shulen stood up. 'Good,' she said. 'Then let's begin.'

Much later, when Tamerlane had swallowed a draught and was sleeping without fever and his breathing had the rhythm of a man who might live again, Khan-zada spoke to Shulen. They were alone in the tent with him. 'You poisoned him.'

It was night and the tent was cooler, only the flames from the braziers lighting the faces of the two women. Shulen was grinding something in a mortar and paused for no more than an instant before continuing. She didn't answer.

Khan-zada took the girl's wrist in her hand, forcing her to turn. 'You poisoned him and then left the camp, knowing when you had to return to give him the antidote. You told the Varangians where to find you.' Khan-zada gripped her wrist tighter. 'Why do you want to marry my son? You don't love him, you love another.'

Then Shulen turned away. 'It is my destiny,' she said softly.

'It is *not* your destiny,' hissed the Princess, squeezing the wrist again. 'Your destiny was to bring Temur to fight Bayezid. This you have done. With poison. You could have killed him!'

The eagle moved on its perch, its claws raking the wood as it lifted its wings, the feathers sighing as they settled. It was staring at them, two unblinking beads of quivering light.

Shulen looked back at the woman. 'Why am I not allowed to find happiness as you did, Khan-zada?' she asked quietly. 'You came down from your father Husayn in Urganch, riding a white camel, so they say. Flowers and carpets were laid down before you on your way to meet Jahangir. You didn't know of love then and you couldn't have known that you would love him. But you learnt to.' She paused. 'Why am I so different?'

'Because you love another.'

'No, I *loved* another, which is why I know what it is to love.' She glanced over at the sleeping mass that was Tamerlane. She lowered her voice. 'Now I love your son.'

Khan-zada began to say something but stopped herself. She shook her head and sighed.

Shulen turned to her. 'I *will* marry him,' she said softly.

Then Khan-zada seemed to crumble. Her shoulders sank and she put her palms to her cheeks and closed her eyes. Her hands were trembling. 'No,' she whispered. 'You can't.'

'But Temur has agreed to it,' said Shulen calmly, frowning. 'Why can't I?'

The two women stared at each other. Then, little by little, the alchemy of souls that had begun in a tower high up in the castle of Alamut finally worked its indefinable magic. A knowledge passed from woman to woman, from mother to daughter. Khan-zada released her arm and looked away.

'So we're the same,' Shulen whispered, already feeling the tears in her eyes. 'We both loved another before.' She paused and looked down at the pestle in her hand. 'You are my mother and Mohammed Sultan is my brother.'

The Princess nodded.

Shulen closed her eyes, letting the meaning seep in. 'Which is why I am here,' she said softly. 'Of course.'

There was silence again between them.

'Why didn't you tell me?'

'Because you might have told Mohammed Sultan.' Khan-zada took her daughter's wrist again. 'And you cannot ever tell him,' she whispered. 'Swear to me that you never will. It would kill him.'

Shulen had turned and walked back to a low divan where she sat. 'My brother . . .' she whispered. Then she looked up. 'But how can I tell him that we cannot marry?'

Khan-zada came to sit beside her. 'You won't have to. Temur will send him ahead to prepare for the attack on Bayezid. He will be away for months. By the time he returns, we will have found a reason for breaking the arrangement.'

Tears now flooded Shulen's cheeks. She leant forward and they fell into her hands. Then she stopped and wiped her eyes on her sleeve. She rose. 'You must make Temur send him away immediately. I cannot lie to him.'

CHAPTER THIRTY-ONE

CONSTANTINOPLE, SUMMER 1402

In the great library in the Blachernae Palace in Constantinople, Plethon was rubbing his eyes. He was seated at a long table on which were the bibles, testaments, uncials and codices that he'd been reading and rereading through the night, checking yet again that the casket held what he thought it held. In front of him was a flattened scroll and in his hand a goose-quill. He was stroking his beard and thinking.

It was, he supposed, nearing dawn and still the drum beat out its dismal tempo as it had since nightfall. He wondered why the Turks hadn't yet attacked. For weeks, they'd been massing their army for the final assault. Listening to the drum, Plethon supposed that this was the night they'd chosen to do it.

Earlier that evening, he'd looked out from the walls across the Lycus Valley, his white toga patched with sweat. Stretched out before him was the Ottoman army, bigger than it had ever been. To his right, it rolled past the Gate of Charisius, past the Blachernae Palace to the banks of the Golden Horn. To his left, it wound its way down to the Sea of Marmara, in whose waters Bayezid's larger bath toys sat at anchor. Great fires were being lit the length of the Turkish lines and battering rams, ballistas, mangonels and scaling platforms hauled forward, their sodden hides slimy as snakeskin. Giant drums beat out a rhythm that went deep into the earth and travelled through the empty mines to rise up the spine of every man who stood on the city walls.

Plethon's eyes had travelled to the top of the Maltepe Hill where he could just see the Sultan's vast tent, a regiment of janissaries standing guard around it.

A voice said: 'That's where he'll watch from.'

A soldier had come to stand beside him. He was a man well into his fifties who, in normal times, would be beyond military service. 'Bloodthirsty bugger.'

'You've seen this before?' asked Plethon, turning to him.

The man nodded. 'Adrianopolis, thirty years ago. His father Murad took the city. As mad a bugger as this one.'

Adrianopolis, now called Edirne. Plethon had been ten when the city had fallen. His father had hidden him in a cellar. 'So what will they do?'

The man grinned, a single tooth pressed against his bottom lip. He'd removed his helmet and streaks of sweat coursed down the deep lines of his face. 'First will come the bashibozouks,' he said. 'They're mad, howling buggers too.' He paused and slapped a fly on his neck. 'Then, when their bodies are piled up against the walls, the janissaries will climb up them to get over the walls and finish us off.' His hand slid horizontally across his neck. 'They'll cut our heads off, that's what they'll do.' He turned and walked on along the ramparts, chuckling to himself.

Now Plethon was seated in the palace library with a letter he'd written on the table before him. The library was a circular room with bookcases spreading out to its perimeter and a long table at its centre. On every shelf was a jewel. The illiterate crusaders had been uninterested in learning when they'd come two centuries earlier and much had survived their onslaught. Now the manuscripts were all gathered in a place deemed safer than most. Here were treasures from Jerusalem, Damascus, Baghdad and many cities besides, probably the greatest amalgamation of human writing outside Cairo. It was to this room that Plethon had welcomed scholars from Florence, Sienna and Ferrara these past years, men of curiosity who'd come to Byzantium to find ancient reason to underpin new thinking.

Plethon was humming quietly to himself and scratching his ear with the end of the goose feather. He stared at the letter. It was written to the only other person in the world who knew what was in the casket at Mistra. He rolled up the vellum, sealed it and looked up at a window, seeing that there was now some light in the sky. Dawn. Surely the Turks must attack now?

The candle flame rose as a draught entered the room and he heard the sound of a door closing and heavy footsteps approaching. The Emperor was standing in front of him wearing armour. He was pale and his eyes were ringed with shadow. He looked exhausted. 'I think you'd better come to the walls,' he said.

Plethon had been expecting this. He'd stated his intention to die defending the city and now he was being summoned to do so. He nodded and rose, placing the scroll in his sleeve. He wondered what he was expected to fight with.

The two men walked in silence from the library and through the halls and corridors of the empty palace, the only sounds the squeak of the marble beneath their feet. There were braziers lit beneath pillars, each creating an island of shifting flame, and

Plethon thought of the fire that would soon consume the city. Would the library survive again? He thought not.

They came to a tower and a spiral staircase that would take them up to the walls. The Emperor stood to one side to let him pass and by the time he'd reached the top and walked out on to the battlements, Plethon was out of breath.

How can I hope to fight the Turks?

Dawn was breaking in the east and the world was strangely silent. He straightened up to look over the walls.

Bayezid's army had vanished. Where yesterday there were men manning the trenches and palisades, now there were none. The siege engines, battering rams, ballistas: all had gone. In the uncertain light of a new day, Plethon could see that the only thing still standing was a solitary tent on the hill of Maltepe and beside it a drum, abandoned.

Plethon looked along the battlements. They were slowly filling with people: soldiers holding their helmets, mothers holding children, priests holding relics that had done their work at last. There was no sound beyond the rustle of the dawn breeze on clothing, a sound that passed through the silent watchers like a sigh.

Then a thousand faces turned from the empty plain and were raised to greet a new sun that was rising behind them; rising over a sea on which no Ottoman galleys floated; rising far in the east where an old man, cured from illness, was at last marching to fight Bayezid.

And with the sun came joy. First one, then ten, then a thousand bells began to peal from the towers of the city's churches, close and far, spreading the news and scattering the silence and causing the people on the walls to blink, then smile, then embrace each other in joy and relief.

Plethon let out a long sigh. He reached into his sleeve and brought out the scroll. He broke the seal, unrolled the paper and read what he'd written. Then he tore it into little pieces which he let drift, like cinders, to the ground below the Christian walls of Constantinople.

PART FOUR

THE BATTLE

CHAPTER THIRTY-TWO

ANKARA, 27 JULY 1402

The army of two hundred thousand that stood beneath the noonday sun was parched. It had stood for over three hours now, row upon row of heavily armoured men motionless beside their horses, the sweat coming off them in rivers. It was an army thinking of water.

A few had fainted, despite the shame, and even a general had fallen in front of his *tumen*. Tamerlane had had the man's head shorn, a dress put on him and rouge painted on his cheeks. Then he'd been made to run barefoot the length of the jeering army. He would open his veins later.

This was an army of many tongues and colours, gathered from the steppes of Turkestan, from Mawarannah, India and Persia. They were armed with the best that money could buy: mail from Georgia, swords from Damascus and bows made from the maple of Kastamonu, their arrow flights feathered by eagles. It was drawn up in eight divisions, each with its *tugh*, or horse-tail standard, at its front. It looked patiently out across an ochre landscape of baked earth and rugged tufts of grass that sagged in the heat like old men's hair. It was a country of snakes and animals that cowered beneath a merciless sun without shade, a land of silence broken only by the wind. But today there was no breeze, only the incessant buzz of flies that added to this army's agony.

Each *tarkhan* would, eventually, have the honour to greet Tamerlane when he chose to inspect the ranks. They were the men deemed bravest in the division, men who'd proved it often on the battlefield, and their rewards were many: a splendid suit of armour, exemption from all taxes, a place of honour at all feasts and access to their leader whenever they wished it. Best of all, they were decreed free of prosecution for any crime up to the ninth time of committing it. Tamerlane had thought of that himself.

Tamerlane had had these reviews before. Many in the army remembered the one out in the frozen wastes far, far to the north when they were chasing Toktamish. It usually meant that the Emperor wanted to reassure himself of his army's discipline at a time when it might be in doubt. Since the forced marches west from Sivas along the Kizilirmak River, there had been grumbling in the ranks. And despite three weeks of siege, the castle of Ankara still hadn't fallen.

Now, while his army awaited him, Tamerlane played chess with a man who didn't speak his language. They were sitting on stools beneath a bright yellow canopy of silk on either side of a giant board on which camels, jornufas, siege engines and a wooden *wazir* joined the usual pieces of the game. Between the two men stood Luke and Khan-zada, there to interpret and admire.

The other man playing was the engineer Benedo Barbi, who'd been summoned from Chios on Luke's advice and presented with an unusual commission. He was wearing a loose cotton shirt open to the waist and white pantaloons against the heat.

His chin was resting on his fist and his face was a mask of concentration.

The engineer shook his head and moved a siege engine. He was not enjoying the game and felt uncomfortable beneath the relentless gaze of the eagle that watched him from its perch.

'You're as bad at this as Sotomayor,' growled Tamerlane, leaning forward to inspect the play. 'I hope your engines work better.'

On his arrival a week before, Barbi had reviewed the siege works at Ankara and recommended the building of long, fire-proofed alleyways that would allow men to get right up to the walls. He had designed giant braziers that could be clamped to the walls so that they became white hot before being cooled by siphons spouting ice-cold vinegar. Then he'd briefed masons on how to split the stones with hammers and chisels so that the whole edifice above would come down. The theory had yet to be tested but Tamerlane had been impressed.

Khan-zada spoke. 'Lord, the army has stood for three hours.'

Tamerlane didn't reply but removed his glasses, wiped them on his caftan, and went back to studying the board.

She tried again. 'Temur Gurgan, will you not go to your soldiers or at least give them water?'

At last he looked up. 'Do I advise you on your scents, Daughter?' he replied. He glanced behind him where the first of the divisions stood no more than fifty paces away. He turned back to her. 'Let me tell you this, woman. Two things bring me victory: cunning and discipline.' He nodded slowly, tapping his temple with his finger. 'Think of Baghdad. How did I win? I made our soldiers attack the walls in the heat of the day because I knew something that they didn't: that the army of Ahmad Jalayrid had its helmets up on sticks! The jackals had gone off to lie in the shade! It was discipline which made them attack in such heat.'

He glanced behind him again, then leant forward as if in conspiracy. 'And these Turks that are coming?' he whispered. 'Their janissaries have discipline, certainly, but the bashibozouks?' He paused and snorted with contempt. 'And if Bayezid had any cunning, he wouldn't have abandoned this position three weeks ago.' He turned to the Italian seated across from him and winked. 'And what of my cunning now, eh?'

He began to speak again but there were horses approaching. Miran Shah had ridden up with a group of shabbily dressed men who dismounted quickly and threw themselves on the ground before him. His son remained standing, clapping his hands to remove the dust. He was dressed in a coat of mail and carried a long, coiled whip. He bowed stiffly. 'Father, your *kourtchi* have returned with news.'

Temur frowned. 'Speak for them.'

Miran Shah cast a look of disdain over the group. 'They report that Bayezid will be here tomorrow,' he said shortly. 'They say that the Sultan has a great army with him and that it has cannon. The Serb Lazarević marches by his side with a strong force of knights and black-steels who have handguns.'

'How big is his army?'

'As big as ours, perhaps bigger,' he replied. 'All of the gazi tribes are with him. And it is rumoured that an army from Cairo is marching to support him.'

Tamerlane nodded. 'Well, certainly the dog has learnt to bark again. He's sent me more letters. He calls me a plague.' He grunted. 'The plague was my friend; it emptied the cities. He is a fool.'

Miran Shah stepped forward. He bent low and whispered

into Tamerlane's ear. 'Father, we should march away while we still can. If we go north, we can escape him.'

Very slowly, Temur looked up at his son. 'What did you say?'

Miran Shah blinked. For the first time he looked uncertain and moved the whip from one hand to the other. 'We can come back with a bigger army, Father,' he said. 'We can return when we know we can defeat him.'

Tamerlane looked at him for a long time. There were muscles moving in his neck. 'Are you one of their kourtchi?' he asked softly. 'Has Bayezid bribed you to say this to me?'

Miran Shah laughed but his eyes shone with fear. 'Father . . .'

But Tamerlane raised his hand to stop him. 'Get out of my sight. You are a cowardly dog and you will not command my left wing as I decreed. You will guard the camp at the rear. Your place is with the women.'

For a moment Miran Shah did nothing but stare, wide-eyed, at his father. Then he glanced venomously at Luke and Khan-zada, turned and walked back to his horse.

When he had ridden away and the kourtchi had been dismissed, Khan-zada knelt before her father-in-law. 'Father,' she murmured, 'Shulen and I will be in that camp.'

But Tamerlane wasn't listening. He shouted at an emir who was standing nearby: 'Where is Prince Mohammed Sultan?'

'He is on his way, lord, as you commanded,' said the man.

Mohammed Sultan had been at Ankara for two weeks, the second spent entirely in the company of the engineer from Chios. Luke had only seen him when they'd discussed sending for Barbi; neither Khan-zada nor Shulen had seen him at all. Now he was before them, his long hair caked in dust, kneeling in front of his grandfather.

Tamerlane looked down on him fondly. 'The Genoese' – he

waved towards Barbi whose name he'd forgotten – 'tells me you and he have done what we agreed.'

Mohammed Sultan nodded. 'We have had the men working day and night to finish it in time.' He glanced over to where that army stood and then up at the sun. 'It is hot, Grandfather.'

Tamerlane scratched his knee and waved the flies away from the chess pieces. He grinned. 'And we will fight tomorrow. Have you heard?'

The Prince looked up. 'I was told by Miran Shah on my way here,' he said. He paused and then said quietly: 'He also told me that you had relieved him of his command.'

'The answer is no.'

Tamerlane picked up a jornufa from the board and banged it down on a different part of the board. 'Check.'

'But who else will command it?'

'General Kurunduk.'

'He is not of your family.'

'He is not my heir. My heir stays by my side. My heir survives me, is that clear?' Tamerlane was frowning now and the stubborn will that had made men march in snow or stand under a midday sun was not to be moved. For a while neither of them spoke. Then Mohammed Sultan changed the subject.

'The Lady Shulen, has she arrived at the camp?'

Luke glanced at Khan-zada, who was looking down at her hands, her shoulders stiff with unease.

'So she is in the camp,' said the Prince. He was frowning slightly. 'Where might I find her, Mother?'

Khan-zada looked up then. 'She doesn't want to see you.'

Mohammed Sultan looked bewildered. 'Of course she wants to see me.' He turned to his grandfather. 'Temur Gurgan has given permission for our marriage.'

Khan-zada began to say something but Temur interrupted. 'I cannot make her see you if she's changed her mind.'

Mohammed Sultan was silent for some time, frowning at the ground. Then he turned to Luke. 'Is this of your doing?' he asked softly. He was nodding slowly, his eyes fixed on Luke. 'Yes, of course. You have decided that you want her after all,' he whispered.

Khan-zada came forward. 'Luke has nothing to do with this.'

She tried to take her son's hand but he snatched it away. He stared at her. 'How could you deny me the same happiness that you had?' he asked. He turned to leave. 'I'm going to find her.'

No one stopped him. Luke and Khan-zada watched him go while Tamerlane rose to his feet. He laughed. 'He'll calm down once we put a Persian whore to him. It's time to dismiss the army. They've stood long enough.'

Bayezid was in an unpredictable mood. Having marched without break from Ankara to Sivas and then back to Ankara, his army was exhausted. And they were thirsty since Tamerlane had poisoned all the wells on their route.

They had finally found a well with fresh water. It was low and there would be little to go round, but it was water. Now the decision had to be made whether to stay the night there and rest the army or push on the few miles to the Cubuk Creek where there would be water in abundance.

In the tent were Bayezid, his three sons, Yakub Bey, Prince Lazarević of Serbia and the general Evrenos Bey, and they were all bent over a map spread out on a table. It was still light outside and the tent door was tied back so that the noise and smells of the vast army were amongst them.

Bayezid had turned to Evrenos Bey. 'What do the scouts say?'

'Temur's army is a mile upstream of the Cubukcay,' said the general, untying the straps of his armour. The tent was hot and the awning admitted no breeze.

'A mile upstream?' said Bayezid delightedly. 'The fool! He could have put his army between us and the river.'

'He chooses to stay on the high ground, lord,' said Lazarević.

Bayezid turned to him. 'Will your men march tonight?'

Lazarević passed a hand through his hair. He was as tired as all of them. 'If it is asked of them, lord. But would it not be better to rest the army here tonight? We can send forward a small force to the river. They can tell us if Temur makes a move. We would be safe here and the men are tired.'

'And he would hardly abandon his high ground to attack us,' said Mehmed. 'I think we should stay here.'

Bayezid turned to his eldest son. 'And you, Prince Suleyman? What would you advise?'

Suleyman was still angry that, against all advice, Bayezid had chosen to abandon his position at Ankara three weeks ago to go chasing after Tamerlane. Now they were back at Ankara with Temur occupying their old position. He bent over the map, running his finger up the line of the Cubuk Creek until it reached the little blocks of wood that were the Mongol army.

'We know this land well, Father, because we have so recently been here,' he said quietly.

There was shocked silence at the insult. But Suleyman went on: 'Temur occupies a good position. But our army has always been victorious when we have defended rather than attacked. It was so at Nicopolis.' He paused and looked round at the other men. Mehmed was watching him intently. 'I think we should wait for him to come to us. Stay where we are and bring water from the Cubukcay. Sooner or later he must attack.'

The Sultan was staring at his son. 'You think we cannot defeat these dogs if we attack them?' he asked quietly.

Suleyman straightened. 'I didn't say that, Father.'

There were veins at Bayezid's temples. He held the side of the table with his fingers pressed hard to the wood, his nails white. His eyes were wide, their pupils vast, and small beads of sweat were gathered on his brow. Suleyman stood very still before him. Little by little, the Sultan gathered himself, exhaling great breaths in the effort. He addressed the men.

'We will rest here the night,' he said. 'Send out a force to the Cubukcay and tell them to warn us if Temur moves so much as a hair of his Mongol arm. We will need that water tomorrow.'

Tomorrow dawned with blood dripping from the heavens.

A small storm in the night had gathered up the ruined crust of this land and hurled it into the sky where it was slowly falling to earth through a sun that had risen like a shield drawn from a furnace. If either army had wanted an omen, then this was the omen they'd feared.

It will be a day of blood.

Luke, Matthew, Nikolas and Arcadius were riding hard, their armour aflame and their long hair streaming behind them. Luke was on Eskalon and far out in front and his shoulders rose and fell as he urged more speed from the horse.

The country south of the fortress of Ankara was formed of low, undulating hills. Its ground was hard and fractured, full of rock and brittle grass and one long sliver of life called the Cubukcay. The creek was away to their right, invisible beneath its steep banks: a single twisting vein within a body exhausted by nature. It was the liquid hope towards which the Ottoman army was marching.

That morning, when Luke had risen, Tamerlane had summoned him to his tent and talked of the Horns of Hattin. It was a place in the Holy Land where, two hundred years past, a crusader army had been defeated by thirst. It was where an invincible army, deprived of water, had sunk to its knees and died in the desert.

'Today we will give them another Hattin,' Tamerlane had whispered, sitting on the side of a bed in which a magnificent creature the colour of ebony still slept. 'Ride out with your Varangians and tell me what you see when they get to the creek.'

And now they were there. The four of them had arrived at the crest of a hill that overlooked the road to the Cubukcay from the east and below them was the Ottoman army. It was in good order, the Serbian heavy cavalry and regiments of sipahis in front, the solid blocks of the janissaries behind and the long tail of the bashibozouks strung out as far as the eye could see. In the early sunshine, the army resembled an endless, jewelled caterpillar flashing its winding way through clouds of dust to the beat of drum and the clash of cymbal. The army was vast.

'When is it to happen?' asked Arcadius.

Luke looked at the sun, measuring the time. 'It's already happened,' he said. 'Watch.'

The army beneath them had broken its line of march and was running towards the riverbank, men dismounting and leaving their horses and racing each other to get to the water. Soldiers were disappearing into the shadow of the creek, their helmets glinting in the sunlight as they tore them off to gather what they could to drink.

Then the silence that had been broken only by the drum and cymbal was filled with shouts of anger and despair, with the cries of men deprived of what they'd been promised.

The creek was dry.

The engineer from Genoa had served Tamerlane well. For a week past the Mongol army had stripped itself to the waist to build the canals, dams and reservoirs that would divert the Cubukcay waters from their natural flow. For a week, Tamerlane's beloved elephants had discarded their castles to haul earth and stones to bring into being his most ambitious piece of cunning yet. The Sultan's army had been led into a trap. It had been given just enough water from the one unpoisoned well to make it come to battle. Now Tamerlane had closed the breach in the dam upstream and the water had stopped.

The Sultan's army would have to fight without water.

Below them was pandemonium. Men were fighting each other to reach the trickle that was still in the creek and the long tail of the army was pressing forward to join the frenzy. Janissaries were beating the bashibozouks back with the flats of their swords, forming lines to prevent them stampeding the men in front. If the drums were still beating, their sound was smothered by the parched cries of desperate men whose throats were swollen with thirst.

Luke turned to his friends. 'We've seen enough,' he said. 'And it isn't pretty. Let's get back to the army.'

They turned and dug their heels into their horses' sides and Luke looked up at the sun.

It will be a day of blood.

CHAPTER THIRTY-THREE

ANKARA, 27 JULY 1402

A mile upstream of the Cubuk Creek, Temur's army was waiting in a giant crescent that filled every part of the landscape. It was drawn up in the same eight divisions that the Emperor had failed to review the previous day, but now there were thirty-two elephants lined up in the middle with towers on their backs and giant scimitars on their tusks. Beside them stood catapults that had been hauled down from the castle and around the base of each machine were what looked like the bloated corpses of goats.

In front of it all was Tamerlane and he was on his knees. Dressed in full armour, he was kissing the carpet beneath him, his old body rising and falling in the rhythm of prayer. He was beneath a canopy of brilliant green silk and, above it, limp in the breathless air, hung his standard: the three circles of the Celestial Conjunction. Not a sound came from the two hundred thousand men waiting behind him.

Luke and the Varangians brought their horses to a stop at what they hoped was the proper distance. Luke looked at the flag and remembered when a black one had been raised outside the walls of Damascus.

Matthew said: 'I think we'll leave you here.' He turned his horse and rode away. Luke watched him go; then he approached Tamerlane.

Tamerlane made three more bows before sitting back on his ankles. He beckoned to Luke. 'The omens are bad,' he growled, signalling for Luke to help him rise. 'The imams didn't like the bloody dawn and the shamans don't care for the goats they've opened.' Now standing, he pushed Luke away and adjusted the sword by his side. He looked down at his hand. 'Still, the ring has clouded so I know they're wrong. What did you see?'

Luke told him all that they'd seen and Tamerlane grinned, his flat face wrinkling in pleasure. 'Fighting each other? Even the janissaries? That's good.' He gestured to the catapults. 'Well, they've worse to come. The first thing we'll throw at them will be goats full of water.' He winked at Luke. 'Your engineer has done well. He may not be able to play chess but he can divert a river. What a game, eh?'

Luke suddenly felt exposed in front of the army. He felt as if a million eyes were watching him talking to the most powerful man on earth. 'Where would you like me to go, lord?' he asked.

Tamerlane shrugged. 'Wherever you like.' He paused. 'No, stand with the gautchin. I may need your riding later.'

Luke bowed and backed away to where Eskalon was waiting. Taking the reins, he led him through a gap in the divisions to where the Emperor's elite stood beside their horses. They were drawn from the forty tribes of Mawarannahr that claimed Chagatai Mongol origin, and they were the best of the best. They were clad in glittering mail and wore domed helmets spouting high plumes of green horsehair. Many wore masks of silver and gold, worked into the features of unearthly creatures: half-Tartar, half-demon. They looked terrifying.

Mounted at their front was Mohammed Sultan, patting his horse's neck and flicking flies from its ears with his mailed fingertips. He had tried to find Shulen but failed. Luke rode up to stand beside him, bowing from the saddle as he approached. They sat there side by side in silence for some time.

It was Luke who broke it. 'Mohammed Sultan,' he said quietly, looking straight to his front, 'you are my friend and I speak only truth to you. Whatever reason Shulen has for not speaking to you has nothing to do with me.'

An hour later Mohammed Sultan still hadn't spoken to Luke and they were standing on either side of Tamerlane who was seated on an old comfortable stallion between the prow and stern of an enormous cushioned saddle. Behind them stood a retinue of emirs and imams, *ming-bashis* and *on-bashis* and standard-bearers carrying a dozen flags and Horsehairs.

They were watching the approach of a dust cloud that covered every inch of the horizon and seemed to shudder to the beat of a distant drum. Already the day was hot and Luke felt himself sealed to his saddle by sweat. His helmet was resting on the pommel before him, his gloves beneath it, and he was trying to remember if he'd seen any other man in the army drink from his water bottle. He put his palm on to the dragon head at his side and withdrew it quickly. It was scalding. But if he was parched, what would the men marching towards him be suffering?

Tamerlane was clearly thinking the same thing. 'When do they come within range of our catapults?' he called over his shoulder.

A ming-bashi rode forward. 'Any time now, lord. They will have their horsemen out in front. You wanted the goats to land among the bashibozouks.'

Tamerlane nodded, chuckling to himself. 'Like rainfall,' he murmured. 'Let us bathe them in a shower of torment.'

Standing slightly behind, Luke had been watching Tamerlane watching his enemy draw closer. He'd seen a man bewitched by the approach of destruction, a man hypnotised by the promise of colossal bloodshed. He'd seen a man who had never lost a battle preparing, at last, to meet another who claimed the same. Both had equal numbers of men but only one had water.

This will be my greatest battle.

Now, emerging from the cloud in front, Luke could see the army they were to do battle with and it was immense. On its left wing rode the Serbian knights, row upon row of heavily armoured cavalry behind their prince in his dazzling white armour, a forest of pennanted lances above them. On its right were the thousands of gazi warriors, the men of the Germiyan and Karamid and Dulkadir tribes, and many others besides. Some wore mail and some the skins of animals but every one of them held a bow in his hand and a quiver of arrows slung by his side. Beside them pranced the high-plumed sipahi regiments and the Kapikulu in their golden and silver mail.

In the centre, behind a screen of bashibozouks, were the regiments of the janissaries, the best fighting men in the world – so it was said – and at their head, resplendent on a huge black stallion, rode Bayezid beneath a tasselled sunshade. The Sultan raised a hand and the cry went up and the whole army came to a staggered halt, the drumbeat halting with it. Then, to a series of commands, the janissaries opened their ranks and men appeared pulling carriages.

Cannon.

Behind him, Luke heard a ripple of unease spread through the Mongol ranks. This was something new.

'Release the goatskins,' growled Tamerlane to Mohammed Sultan. 'Let us give them water.'

There was a shout and suddenly the air was filled with a hundred bloated animals. They flew through the sky, landing in explosions of precious water among the ranks of the bashibozouks. Tamerlane clapped his hands in delight as men scrambled to scoop up something to slake their thirst.

But his delight was short-lived. At a command, the cannon spouted flame and deadlier missiles were flying through the air towards them.

They landed amongst the elephants which reared, trumpeting their fear. Some went down and the rest wheeled round to escape the barrage, their razored tusks slashing the air around them and the castles on their backs lurching giddily, spilling men. There was panic among the horses behind.

Tamerlane was no longer smiling. 'Take the elephants to the rear,' he yelled. 'Quick, before they stampede!'

The Indian mahouts did their best, hauling and beating their charges through the gaps that had opened in the ranks behind, but a second wave of destruction was on its way and soon missiles were landing on the beasts and the men who were scrambling out of their path. The elephants were shrieking in pain and men were going down before them.

'Lord, the screens!' shouted Mohammed Sultan, pulling hard on the reins of his terrified horse.

The screens were already on their way. Walls made of layer upon layer of wicker and mud packed together and covered with animal hides were being carried forward through the army and thrust deep into holes that had been previously dug. They were just in time. More stones were in the sky. The balls smashed against the walls; some flew over the tops to crash into the men behind. Luke looked behind him. He could see the castles atop the elephants swaying their way to the rear while the ranks tried to re-form. The elephants were leaving the battle.

Bayezid has won the first part.

The cannons had stopped firing. The Turks were moving them forward so as to hurl their balls further into the Mongol army. Tamerlane would have to send out something to force them back. He could no longer wait for the Turks to attack him.

But the man in the white armour far off to the right of the Turkish line wasn't going to let Tamerlane seize any advantage. Prince Lazarević of Serbia raised his arm. The sword above it flashed as it caught the sun and the lines of heavy cavalry behind him began to move forward at the trot, their lances held high and their caparisoned horses tossing their heads.

The Serbians were going to charge.

It was a magnificent sight: row upon row of knights in their emblazoned hauberks riding knee-to-knee upon horses twice the size of the Mongols'. The hill seemed to shake as their horses gathered speed, moving from trot to slow canter as the distance closed between them and the wing commanded by Tamerlane's youngest son.

Luke glanced across to where Shahrukh stood in front of his troops. He had been named for the game of chess and it seemed to have shaped his character. Shahrukh was a learned man of great piety, not of destruction. But he was Tamerlane's son and he knew how to fight.

At his signal, horsemen galloped out from the ranks behind him and charged down the hill towards the oncoming knights. Like a flock of birds swooping to take seed off the field, they swarmed down on the wall of advancing metal, loosing volley upon volley of arrows.

In truth, they could do little to slow it, let alone stop it. The big Serbian horses were as armoured as their riders and the arrows bounced off both. A few animals fell but the momentum of the charge continued. The front line of the knights lowered its lances.

Luke glanced over at Tamerlane, who was frowning. The battle was not going to plan. He turned to Luke. 'Go and tell him to charge.'

But the message wasn't needed. Shahrukh had signalled the advance and his troops were already moving down the hill to meet the Serbian knights. Minutes later, the two armies met. The noise was deafening. Fifty thousand men collided and the air rang with the sound of sword hitting sword and animal colliding with animal. It was as if two floodwaters had met, forcing skyward a debris of broken limbs, blood and horseflesh, filling the skies with the sounds of death.

But the Serbs had the weight and the momentum and long, brutal lances which tore through the Mongol ranks and soon the forces of Shahrukh were falling back, men and horses trampled by the hooves of the Serbian destriers. Luke and Mohammed Sultan looked at each other, thinking the same thought.

They could reach the camp. Where Shulen and Khan-zada are.

The Prince was the first to wheel his horse round, digging his heels into the animal's flanks and pulling at the single rein to turn it round. Tamerlane glanced at him, his thick eyebrows arched in surprise. 'Where are you going?'

'To the camp, Grandfather,' shouted Mohammed Sultan over his shoulder. 'To get there before the Serbians do!'

Tamerlane frowned and scratched his beard. Then he shrugged and said calmly to Luke: 'Bring him back. His place is with the army, not the women.'

Suleyman was watching all of this from the back of a skittish destrier whose eyes beneath its face-guard were wild with excitement. Beside him was Yakub in his buff-leather armour. He'd just witnessed the Serbian breakthrough and the Mongol army swinging round to protect its flank.

Suleyman turned to him, his thirst forgotten. 'We should attack now,' he shouted. 'If we can encircle them, then the janissaries can advance to their front to finish them off.'

The gazi looked across to where the tip of Bayezid's sunshade could just be seen above the dust. No rider was on his way to tell them to advance but what the Prince said made sense. Bayezid would win this battle if the momentum was sustained. But there had been no order.

'The Sultan has not told us to go,' he shouted. 'We should await the order. It may be a trap.'

But the Prince was standing up in his stirrups, turning his head from the battle to the Kapikulu behind. His horse was pawing the earth beneath its hooves. 'We'll go,' he said. 'The thunderbolt doesn't know when to strike any more.'

'Lord . . .' Yakub found himself addressing Suleyman's back. 'It could be a trap!'

'A trap?' yelled the Prince, pointing. 'The whole barbarian army has been knocked off balance! How can it be a trap?'

The gazi looked out at the army before them. Mongol divisions were being moved to shore up the open flank. Suleyman was right. He turned back to him. 'It's as we planned?' he shouted. 'You lead with the Kapikulu and I'll bring my gazis up in support?'

Suleyman grinned. 'As we planned, Yakub. Let's show these dogs how a gazi fights!'

When Mohammed Sultan and Luke rode into the Mongol camp, they found a scene of chaos.

There were some tents pitched at its centre and the wagons that carried the army's food and booty were strewn haphazardly around them with no attempt made to form them into a defensive line. Word had arrived of the Serbians' breakthrough and men, women and children were running, panic-stricken, in all directions. The soldiers among them seemed leaderless.

'Where is Miran Shah?' yelled the Prince at an officer whose aventail he'd grabbed from the saddle. The man looked up and recognised him.

'In the tents, lord!' he shouted. 'What should we do?'

Luke had ridden up and reined in Eskalon on the other side of the man. With him were the Varangians whom he'd gathered on his way. He dismounted and took hold of Mohammed Sultan's ankle.

'Get to the tents, lord,' he cried. 'We'll organise the defence.'

The Prince gazed down at Luke for a moment, then nodded and kicked his horse away. Luke turned to the other three. 'Pull the wagons into a line and turn them on their side,' he said. 'And get as many men as you can behind them with plenty of arrows. We don't have much time!'

The Varangians turned and shouted at the soldiers milling around them. The ground beneath them was shaking now and the war cries were getting louder. It was probably too late.

But Tamerlane had forced discipline into these men. With a plan to follow, they could do anything. Within minutes the wagons had been hauled into a line and up-ended, their contents spilling over the ground to leave the pillage of a score of cities glittering amidst the cracked earth. Men were already manning the barricade behind, their bows at the ready and a quiver of arrows by their sides.

The four Varangians had positioned themselves at intervals down the line. Luke ran up to a man who wore the emblems of a ming-bashi. 'Tell them to wait for my command before they fire,' he yelled over the thunder of hooves, now very loud. 'And tell them to shoot at the horses!'

He looked beyond the wagons and saw the Serbian cavalry a hundred paces away. Huge visored knights, their lances levelled for the charge, were galloping towards the wagons as if nothing stood in their way. The grunts of the horses, exhausted by a mile of running, were mixed with the cries of men almost upon their quarry. They looked unstoppable.

'Now!' roared Luke and a thousand arrows crashed into the horses' chests, piercing armour, leather, skin and artery to cause a chaos of falling mounts and knights and broken lances and blood; the sky was filled with the screams of men thrown into the air and hitting the ground in heavy armour. The lines of knights behind had no time to pull in their horses and piled into those in front so that soon the whole scene was a mass of writhing men and animals.

But it was only a temporary reprieve for the Mongols. The knights behind came on, head down through the hail of arrows, trampling their friends to reach the barricade where their armour and maces would give them advantage in the hand-to-hand melee that would follow. Luke looked behind him. There were no more men available.

Where is Mohammed Sultan?

The heir to Tamerlane's throne was inside one of the tents holding a sword to the throat of his uncle.

Miran Shah was lying on the ground amidst the contents of a jug that rolled back and forth by his side. A dagger lay next to it with blood on its blade. The air stank of wine and he was laughing. 'She is my wife,' he was saying, his voice thick with drink. 'I will do with her what I want.'

Mohammed Sultan's arm was trembling. There was a shallow gash on his cheek and a trickle of blood ran from his ear on to his mail. When he spoke, it was in a voice brittle with hatred. 'She is my mother and you will never touch her again.'

Seated on a divan was Khan-zada and next to her was Shulen and they held each other in tight embrace. The older woman's dress was torn and her hair dishevelled. She had a bruise on her temple and bloodied teeth marks on her neck. Her hands clutched at the younger girl's arms, leaving shadows at her fingertips.

'Anyway,' said Miran Shah, attempting to rise to his knees, 'I wasn't going for her. I was trying to be nice to your young slut and she stopped me.'

The Prince pushed the sword so that its tip was lost in his uncle's beard, forcing him back to the ground. His jaw was moving beneath clenched teeth and his eyes were clouded with anger. In a moment his uncle would die.

'Don't.' It was Khan-zada who'd spoken.

'He would have raped her,' breathed her son, pushing Miran Shah's head back to the carpet as he edged the sword tip forward. 'He would have raped Shulen, then killed you.'

'Don't, Mohammed Sultan.' This time it was Shulen who had whispered the words. 'As you love me, let him live.'

The Prince's face became a grimace of pain. 'As I love you?' He turned to her. 'What of your love for *me*? Where is that now, Shulen?'

Miran Shah, drunk as he was, mistook the moment as his opportunity. He grabbed the sword blade in his hand and thrust it away as he rolled to one side, the wine pooling around him. He was within reach of the dagger. But Mohammed Sultan had seen him and his boot stamped down on his arm. There was the crack of bone and Miran Shah howled in pain as the Prince lifted his foot and kicked him hard in the head. His uncle lay unconscious before him.

Glancing back at Shulen, Mohammed Sultan walked over to the door of the tent and looked through it. The clash of sword and mace seemed suddenly much louder. The battle was getting closer.

'You must go,' said Khan-zada. 'We can tie him up. They need you out there. Go.'

The Prince looked at Shulen, who had picked up the dagger and was already cutting rope. 'Not until I know why I am rejected,' he said, walking towards her. 'Not until I hear it from you, Shulen.' He grabbed her arm. There were tears in his eyes as he gazed down into the only face he'd ever loved.

There was a crash of splintered wood outside as a wagon collapsed before the onslaught. A yell of triumph was followed by screams of pain. The Serbs were breaking through.

Khan-zada came up to them. She laid a hand on his arm and said: 'Not now. Now is not the time. We'll talk of this later.'

But Mohammed Sultan was holding Shulen tightly and was oblivious to his mother and the fight outside. His eyes were misted. 'What have I done to deserve this?' he whispered, his brow furrowed with confusion. 'What have I done, Shulen?'

She saw the despair and the pain in the eyes of a man she loved, could have loved properly. She brought him to her, her arms circling his neck, her lips at his ear. 'You've done everything,' she whispered softly. 'You've done everything that a brother should do.'

At first, the word made little impact but Shulen had drawn back and was staring at him in a way that made him recall it. He let go of her arms, shaking his head as if she'd slapped him.

'Brother?' he whispered. '*Brother?*' He took a step backwards, looking wildly from one to the other of the women, a thousand thoughts crowding his mind. He turned to his mother. 'Someone else . . . before Jahangir? You . . .?'

His mother nodded again. 'Yes,' she whispered. 'Shulen is your sister. Now go.'

Outside, the situation was desperate. Luke was using his shield to block the swipes of a huge studded mace swung by a knight whose armour was splattered with filth. His other hand held his dragon sword, poised for the moment to strike. Beside him stood Matthew, axe in one hand and sword in the other.

Mohammed Sultan had emerged from the tent with no helmet and a look of madness on his face. He glanced up and down the barricade. 'Luke!' he yelled, leaping forward with his sword raised above him.

Within seconds the three men were fighting side by side, Luke in the centre. The ground before them was piled with dead and wounded and slippery with their blood.

'Is the battle lost?' yelled the Prince, ramming his pommel into the visor of a knight who'd got too close.

Luke ducked to escape a blow from another mace. He glanced at the Prince. 'I don't know. But your helmet, lord. Where's your helmet?'

Luke was the only one of the three with a shield. He saw that there was something reckless in the way the Prince was fighting. He edged closer to him, ready to give protection should it be needed. He glanced at Matthew. Luke was leaving his friend exposed but what choice did he have? Mohammed Sultan was not acting like one who wanted to survive the battle.

'If the Serbs are at the camp, then the day must be lost,' shouted the Prince. 'Suleyman will have charged from the other side to surround us.'

It seemed likely but it made little difference. They were fighting for their lives.

'Luke,' Mohammed Sultan went on, 'I know now why Shulen . . .' He'd delivered a blow to the neck of a knight and found his mouth suddenly filled with the man's blood. He spat it out and tried again. 'She's my sister.'

'Who is your sister?' panted Luke.

'Shulen. Shulen is my sister.' He parried an axe-swipe and plunged his sword under the cuirass of a knight arching to strike.

The statement was ill timed. Luke heard it and suddenly he was on his knees with blood in his nostrils and stars before his eyes. He'd been struck hard on his helmet. He heard a roar above him as the Prince leapt forward and a scream as his attacker was brought down.

When he could see again, Luke looked up at Mohammed Sultan. He seemed super-human, possessed of the strength of six men. His sword was everywhere, swinging and blocking and finding the gaps in which to thrust. A mound of dead and dying lay around him. But he was beginning to tire.

Luke got to his feet, shaking his head to clear his vision and wiping the blood from his nose. He felt drained of strength. He saw that he, Matthew and Mohammed Sultan were now an island amidst a sea of Serbians. The Mongol line had broken and Temur's men were behind them, falling back on the tents, furiously contesting every inch of the way.

Luke took a deep breath. 'We have to get back!' he yelled into Matthew's ear. 'We're cut off!'

Matthew glanced behind him and nodded. His head was caked in dirt and blood. He grabbed Luke's shield to protect them both from the hail of blows, just in time. A sword came from nowhere and Luke managed to parry it. But he was seeing double and his head was splitting with pain. 'I don't think I can do much more,' he said.

On his other side, Mohammed Sultan was in trouble too. Luke could hear his breathing. It was short and rasping, air drawn through a throat swollen with thirst. He was tiring fast. Luke saw a Serbian in black armour pointing a long tube. His mind flashed back to the kourtchi report in the morning.

The black-steels have handguns.

He wrenched the shield from Matthew. But he was too late. There was a deafening bang and the heir to Tamerlane lay on the ground.

Luke looked down. Mohammed Sultan was quite still. He swayed on his feet and Matthew caught him as he fell. The Serbian knights around them had stopped fighting. They too were in awe of this terrible new weapon. They formed an exhausted ring around Mohammed Sultan, their shoulders rising and falling with fatigue. One of them removed his helmet.

It was Prince Lazarević. He looked at Luke without animosity. 'Give yourself up,' he said in Greek, leaning on his sword, his handsome face streaked black between locks of filthy hair. 'You have fought bravely. Your friend is dead and you are wounded. Don't follow him.'

Luke was staring at the still-smoking weapon. Then at Lazarević.

You don't know who he is.

There was a shout from the Mongol lines behind. The battle in that direction seemed to have stopped as well. A woman riding a big horse was making her way towards them and the Serbians were parting to let her pass. Luke stared in disbelief.

Shulen. Shulen riding Eskalon.

She entered the ring around Mohammed Sultan and stopped the horse before Prince Lazarević. With one fluid movement, she dismounted and passed the reins to Matthew. She looked down at the body and then up at the Serbian Prince.

'He is my brother,' she said simply, her face without emotion. 'Let me take him home.'

Lazarević stared at her and then down at the ground. 'Who is he, lady?'

'He is my brother,' she said again, 'and he deserves better than this for his grave.'

The Serbian Prince stared at her for a long time. Then, very slowly, he nodded. 'Take him.'

It was then that Luke saw Shulen was not alone. Standing unhurt behind her were Arcadius and Nikolas and they stepped forward and gently lifted the body of the prince on to the back of the horse. They held his body in place as Eskalon was led back towards the tents. Matthew came over to Luke. 'You're hurt. You should retire.'

Luke turned to his oldest friend. 'Matthew, the shield . . .'

His friend shook his head. 'It's not important. Leave this battle. You're wounded.'

Luke hardly heard him. Waves of dizziness were sweeping over him and his sight was still blurred. He could only think of how he hadn't protected his best friend with his shield. He saw Shulen walk up to Prince Lazarević and take his mailed hands in hers. He heard her say: 'Wait until we get back to the tents.'

Mongols and Serbians watched her go. Men in bloodstained armour watched a thin girl of mysterious beauty walk back to the tents behind a horse, both picking their careful way through a ground littered with dead.

Matthew took Luke's arm. 'Luke, you're wounded. Stop now.'

There was another bang, the signal for the battle to begin again, and Matthew found himself parrying two blows. Once he'd cleared some ground, he began to push Luke to the rear. A roar came from behind and then Arcadius and Nikolas were beside them, fighting like devils, repelling the Serbs while Luke stumbled back to the tents. He got there in time to see Mohammed Sultan lifted from Eskalon. His eyes were closed and his face very pale. Khan-zada was waiting for him, her face a mask of horror.

Luke turned to Matthew. His head was in agony. He said again, 'Matthew, the shield . . .'

There was something unreadable in Matthew's eyes. 'Luke, we can talk of that later. There is a battle to fight.'

'Is it lost?'

Matthew shrugged. 'I don't know. It looks like Suleyman has charged our left wing with his Kapikulu and the gazi tribes. It looks bad.'

'And Tamerlane?'

'The janissaries were advancing on him behind a swarm of bashibozouks. I don't know if he held.'

Luke looked at the two lines of men before him, embraced in a whirl of weaponry. There were more explosions and more Mongols fell to the earth with holes in their heads. All along the line, the Mongol soldiers were giving way. Inch by inch they were losing ground; it would be only minutes before the Serbians were at the tents.

Matthew said, 'I'm going back to fight. Don't try to follow me.'

Luke opened his mouth but nothing emerged. Then he fell to his knees and vomited. He sank his head in his hands and stared at the ground. It was shaking.

More hooves. More Serbians to finish us off.

He staggered to his feet. He looked towards where the thunder was coming from. It came from behind the knights, from the other side of the low hill on which the camp had been set. It was the thunder of thousands upon thousands of horses and there could be little doubt from which army they came.

'Gazis!' screamed a Mongol to Luke's left.

Luke strained to see above the tide of crests and flailing weaponry.

'Gazis!' The cry was taken up along both lines. The wild men of the steppe were charging to help their Serbian allies.

But the gazis weren't slowing as they approached the rear of the Serbian ranks. With blood-curdling yells, they fell upon the knights and the men-at-arms. The exhausted Serbs tried to turn but it was too late. The horsemen tore into their ranks with their swords whirling above them, mowing them down like ripe wheat and driving them into a mass of bloody chaos. In the crush, the Serbs' handguns were useless and their armour worse. Men fell and couldn't rise, suffocating in their steel beneath the heels of their comrades. It was slaughter.

The Mongols surged forward slashing their way towards these new, unexpected allies, summoning every reserve of strength to win this battle, bellowing with the hope of a new outcome.

At first, it stayed in the balance. The Serbs were well armoured and fought well. But Prince Lazarević's men were tired and they were outnumbered and surrounded. For another hour, they battled with a ferocity that belied their heavy armour. Then quite suddenly it was over. There was no one left to kill.

It was the middle of the day and the relentless heat of the sun bore down upon a camp full of heaped corpses, raising a stench that even the vultures seemed unwilling to approach. All around the tents were bodies twisted into the contortions of death, pile upon pile of men who had risen that morning to see blood in the sky and had watched it flow in rivers on the ground by afternoon.

To one side stood Luke, his helmet thrown to the ground and his face streaked with blood. He was sick from his wound and sick with relief. He heard footsteps approach him and managed to look up. Before him stood the chief of the Germiyans in a deel that still bore the imprint of the armour he'd cast to one side. Its sleeves and neck were spattered with filth and above them the battered face was grinning.

Luke was the first to speak. 'Have we won?'

Yakub nodded. 'I did as I said I would. We followed Suleyman's Kapikulu, then rode across to come up behind the Serbians.' He stepped forward and took Luke's shoulders in his hands. He was frowning. 'But you're hurt.'

Luke shook his head. The pain was unbearable. He said, 'Bayezid?'

'On a hill with his janissaries. Temur has surrounded it.'

'And Suleyman?'

'Fled the field.'

Luke nodded. There was a sound behind him and he remembered something. He turned to find Shulen standing in front of the tent. 'Is he alive?' he asked, dreading the answer. She was wiping her hands on a towel and Luke saw that the blood reached far up her arms.

She nodded. 'But it's bad. We had to remove the stone that was fired into him.' She glanced past him and he knew who she was looking for.

He turned to see Tamerlane approaching on a horse, a cloth held to his face. Next to him rode Pir Mohammed, his head crudely bandaged and his mail slashed in a dozen places. Carried behind them were the Horsehairs of two armies. Tamerlane dismounted stiffly and looked around him, his face devoid of expression. He looked twenty years older. He walked up to Shulen and took her hands. 'Is he inside?' he asked quietly.

'Yes,' she said and turned to open the tent door.

Before he entered, Tamerlane paused and turned about, his old milky eyes settling on Luke. He motioned for him to come forward. When Luke was kneeling in front of him, he placed two hands on his shoulders, bending forward so that their faces were very close.

'Tarkhan,' he said. 'You know what that is, Greek?'

Luke nodded.

'It means', said Tamerlane, 'that you can commit the same crime nine times before I kill you for it.' He paused. 'You are tarkhan now, Greek, and you will sit at my right hand tonight.'

CHAPTER THIRTY-FOUR

ANKARA, 27 JULY 1402

On the evening after the great battle, Luke awoke from the deepest of sleeps to find that he couldn't see. Nor could he move his limbs. In the darkness, every part of him seemed cut or bruised or too painful to lift and, at first, he wondered whether he'd survived the day.

Worst of all was his head, which throbbed with an intensity beyond enduring. Slowly he raised his hands to the bandage around his temples and lowered his fingers to his eyes. Gently, gently he prised them apart.

He was in a tent he knew: Khan-zada's. A woman he didn't know was kneeling next to the bed and behind her stood a steaming copper bath. 'Who are you?' he asked in Turkic.

There was no answer. He repeated the question in Greek.

The woman rose with grace. 'I have been sent by your emperor,' she replied, inclining her head lightly. 'I was part of the Sultan's harem and now it would seem I am part of his.'

Luke looked at her. She was dressed in a long, richly embroidered tunic of the kind worn by the Byzantine nobility. She reminded him of Fiorenza.

Slowly, he raised himself to his elbow. 'What were you sent

to do?' he asked, rubbing his eyes. His throat was dry and his mouth felt lined with dirt and dried blood. His head was breaking apart.

'To wash you, to anoint you with healing oils and to prepare you for the banquet.' There was no emotion in her voice.

'Well, thank you but I can wash myself. Do you have any water to drink?'

The girl turned and came back with a beaker of water and a cup. 'You might as well let me put the oils on you. I'm good at it and you'll feel much better afterwards. Drink.'

In the end, she did it all. Too tired for modesty, Luke allowed himself to be led to the bath and lowered into the hot water and, what with the heat, the oils and the healing caresses, he soon fell asleep again. When he awoke, his head no longer hurt. He moved it cautiously from side to side, his fingers pressed to the bandage. There was a smell all around him, on him. Healing oils. He'd dreamt of Anna. Somehow he felt she was near.

He was lying on the bed dressed in clean linen, his long hair spread either side of him, shining with a colour it hadn't seen in years. The girl was at the other side of the tent, kneeling beside a gorgeous deel suspended from a wooden frame. She was running the embroidered silk through her fingers, admiring it in silence.

She turned. 'Ah, you're awake. That's good because the banquet has already started.'

Luke saw that it was dark outside the tent and that the light came from lanterns with coloured glass. He pointed at the deel. 'Am I to dress in that?'

'Apparently,' she answered. 'I'm told it is the dress given to one who has performed great things: a tarkhan.' She paused and looked at him. 'Did you kill many today?'

Luke began to reply but then remembered something. 'You were in the Sultan's harem?'

She dipped her head.

He propped himself up on his arm. 'Then you must know Anna. Anna Laskaris?' He paused, thinking of something. 'She was with Prince Suleyman.'

'You're Luke?'

Luke nodded. Then he asked: 'Is she here?'

The woman rose, carefully replacing the sleeve she was holding. She came over to the bed and sat beside him. She was smiling and reminded him more and more of Fiorenza. 'She was sent into Constantinople to persuade them to surrender. Which they haven't.'

Luke felt relief flood over him. If Anna was inside Constantinople's walls she was safe for now. 'What is your name?' he asked.

The girl rose. 'My name is Maria. I am from Trebizond.'

Fiorenza. Of course.

'There were three of us,' she continued, 'Anna, me and Angelina, daughter of Sigismund of Hungary. We were friends.'

'What does Anna know of me, Maria?' he asked.

'That you are married to another.'

Luke lay back against the pillows. If Anna had gone into the city, then she'd be there when Luke arrived, released from his oath. He wanted to leave now. Maria went over to the deel and lifted it from its frame. 'Now I will dress you, tarkhan.'

The last thing Maria had done before he left her was to warn Luke not to mix drink with the concoctions he'd been given. But the tent he now entered was thick with the smell of airag.

The tent was, in fact, Bayezid's. It had been pillaged from

the two hundred camels that had carried it from Bursa and erected by the Sultan's eunuch tent-pitchers under the whips of Mongol guards. It was the tent in which Bayezid had planned to toast his greatest victory and was longer than ten galleys parked bow to stern. Inside were monstrous pillars holding up a series of rectangular panels, each with exquisite images of flowers embroidered in gold and silver thread that caught the light of the lanterns hanging along its length. A walkway ran down the centre between two long tables and on it were low braziers burning scented wood. Between them stood pitchers of wine and airag, with lines of jugs by their sides. On the tables were copper basins filled with water, baskets of *naan* and *lavash* and bowls of *torshi*-pickled fruits and vegetables mixed with vinegar and spices.

The Mongol nobility and those that had fought most bravely in the battle sat on either side of the low tables, some using their saddles as back rests. Apart from those serving, there was not a woman among them; Khan-zada and Shulen were elsewhere, celebrating the victory in their own quieter way.

Apart from airag, the smell was of several cooking meats. Great cauldrons of *qorma*, the glutinous stew of horsemeat, mutton, goat and chicken, were placed beside the tables, dumplings bobbing on their surfaces. By their sides sat plates of coloured rice topped with fried raisins and cherries.

At the end of the tent was the high table. It was raised on a dais and had horsetails piled before it, a small mountain of Ottoman and Serbian arms and standards. On the dais sat Tamerlane, with Benedo Barbi on his left. There was an empty space on his right.

You will sit at my right hand tonight.

Luke took a deep breath and began the long journey to the

dais. As he walked, men came and went on either side, some speaking to him, some cheering and some leaning over to slap his back. He was given a cup of wine, then another. His steps became unsteady and he began to stumble. Could he be drunk already? Then someone was speaking his name, someone who was reaching out a hand to help him on to the dais. He looked up and saw the Castilian Sotomayor above him with concern in his eyes.

'Luke?' The voice was far away, then very close. 'You are seated at Tamerlane's right.'

Luke mounted the stage, in wonder that the Spaniard could lift a weight such as his. Then he was clownishly kneeling with his eyes level with the table and saucers of pine nuts, apricots, plums and cherries all around him. A big man across from him was laughing, banging the table with his fist, his head thrown back.

'My jester!' he was roaring, now inside Luke's ear. 'The Greek wants to be jester tonight! Give him bells!'

Instead, the Spaniard raised him and led him around the table to his place beside Tamerlane and set him down upon the cushions.

'Already drunk?' asked the Lord of the Seven Climes, leaning over to him and spilling wine as he did so. His speech was slurred and there was wine running across the table in front of him. 'You should see my cup-bearer.' He stamped his foot. 'Wine!'

A woman appeared before them, naked to the waist. She was tall and fair and her tunic hung about her sides from where it had been ripped from her shoulders. Her face was impassive as she righted Tamerlane's cup and filled it with wine.

'And give him some, you Serbian whore,' growled Tamerlane

as he reached up to fondle her breasts. For a moment, her eyes met Luke's. She moved away.

Tamerlane belched. 'Despina, sister of Lazarević the Serb,' he whispered, wiping his mouth, his fetid breath filling the space between them. 'She'll give me comfort tonight.'

Luke looked after her, seeing the straight, naked back and shoulders of a proud woman walking through hell. He wanted to say something but his voice wouldn't obey him.

'Perhaps I should fuck the bitch on Lazarević's standard,' Tamerlane whispered, pointing to the piled weapons before him. 'Down there, in front of the men.' He tossed back his head to drain the cup and belched again. 'Trouble is, I am old, Greek. Once I would have done it, but now . . .' His forefinger curled before Luke's eye. '. . . the oak won't stay upright. Especially when I drink.'

Sotomayor, seated beside Luke, leant over. He was a clever man, a diplomat, adept at changing subjects. 'Where will you go for your next conquest, lord?' he asked as he poured more wine from the jug he'd taken from Despina. It was the question the whole world wanted an answer to.

'Where will I go?' Tamerlane asked, a malicious grin spreading through his beard. 'Why, Constantinople, of course. Then Castile perhaps. Where would you suggest, Sotomayor?'

The Castilian laughed. 'Constantinople is an empty jewel box and my home beneath your imperial dignity.'

Benedo Barbi spoke from the other side. 'Why not go back to Samarcand, lord? To see to the building.'

Tamerlane roared, throwing his arm around the engineer and pulling him to his breast: 'You could come and help! Ha! What about today, eh, Genoese? My cunning and your science!' He drank more wine, still clutching the Italian. 'Anyway, you're all wrong. I go on a jihad. I need to atone for my sins.'

Suddenly he released Barbi. He looked at the scene around him, then leant very close to him. 'Never hope, Genoese, never hope. I go where I please.' Tamerlane straightened and drained his cup, hammering it on the table for more. 'But Smyrna first. Bayezid couldn't take it. So I will.'

By this time, Luke was feeling strange. The scene before him was unstable. Had he just heard that Tamerlane was planning to march further west? He realised that he was being talked to.

'Tarkhan, I'm asking you. What should I do now?'

Luke took a deep breath, trying to focus. What should he say? What would a tarkhan say? He thought of where Smyrna lay, of where he might be released from his oath, of where Anna might meet him. 'Chios,' he said.

'Chios?' Tamerlane turned to Benedo Barbi. 'He wants me to destroy your island? He's drunker than I thought.'

Luke struggled to bring together a half-formed thought. He turned to Tamerlane and tried to focus. 'No, lord, not destroy. Meet.'

The men around him fell silent, staring at the man on Tamerlane's right.

'Meet,' repeated Luke. 'Meet my emperor there and other Christian kings. Make peace with them.' He paused. 'And release us Varangians from our oath.'

'Why must I make peace with them?'

'To secure your back before you go to China,' said Luke. It was an effort but it was out.

Tamerlane was silent for a while, his big head swaying and an uncertain hand on his beard. 'Well, it's possible,' he said at last. 'Chios is across the sea from Smyrna. I'll need to talk to my heir when he recovers.'

Luke sank back on the cushions. Someone had refilled his cup and he found himself reaching for it. Tamerlane was nodding slowly. Then he looked around him. 'Enough plans!' he shouted, slamming his cup to the table. 'We need entertainment. Bring him in.'

There was so much noise in the tent that it took some time for the instruction to reach the other end. When it had, there were three drumbeats and the conversation stuttered to a halt. Then the drum began again and eight enormous Mongols emerged through the smoke, their muscled bodies straining beneath the weight of a giant cage.

Luke strained his eyes to see what was in it but it was too far away and the wine had made dancers of the people in front of him. He thought of elephants and jornufas and snow leopards and eagles and all the animals that Tamerlane kept to amuse him and tried to imagine what beast was being brought forward to entertain him tonight.

But it wasn't a beast, it was a man. And as the cage came closer, he saw what man it was.

Bayezid.

Lying chained inside the cage was the Sultan Bayezid and he still wore the blood-stained armour in which, on that hill at Ankara, he'd fought to the last beside his janissaries. As the cage approached the dais, the men at the tables on either side began to jeer and laugh and throw bones as if something from the circus was being paraded before them.

When the cage had been set down in front of the piled armour, Tamerlane rose slowly and raised his hand. The tumult stopped. He took his glasses from the table, put them on and peered across the pile of booty at the man before him. Bayezid was lying, face down, the length of the cage, his arms over his head. He might have been asleep were it not for the rise and fall of his shoulders.

'Have you eaten, Bayezid?' It was a growl. Tamerlane reached behind him and came back with a sheaf of papers. He looked at them for a moment and then turned to the cage. 'May I feed you?'

He walked behind Luke and Sotomayor and those seated to their right until he reached the end of the dais. Men came forward to help him climb down from it and once on the ground, he shook them off and limped round to stand next to the cage. He bent over it, speaking down to the back of the Sultan's head. He raised the papers above his head, waving them.

'These are your letters, Bayezid!' he shouted to the hall. 'These are your letters that said you were a ravening beast which would tear the skin from my bones!' He paused and looked down the tent. 'Which beast is now chained inside its cage?'

The tent echoed with the sound of men cheering, banging their knives against their plates and stamping their feet. Tamerlane lifted his other hand for quiet. When it came, he knelt down slowly beside the cage. He began feeding the papers through the bars one by one. 'Eat, you filthy son of a she-pig. Eat your words.'

Bayezid turned inside the cage, his arm pressing down on his head to shut out the shame, his body shaking.

'Eat!' roared Tamerlane, pushing fistfuls of the paper through the bars. 'Where is your pride now, you excrement? Eat!'

Luke saw it all through a prism of merging colour. He saw an old man shaking the bars of a cage in drunken triumph, saw him raise his head and howl something throughout the tent and saw the men at the tables rise as one to lift their cups to the Lord of the Celestial Conjunction, the Conqueror of the World.

Tamerlane.

But there was more than just the cage in front of the dais. There were two women standing behind it. Luke strained to recognise them. Then he did. Zoe and Maria.

Tamerlane saw them too. He staggered back from the cage and called for wine and Despina came forward with the jug, not looking at the man in the cage. Tamerlane lunged at her, taking her by the waist and forcing her round to face Bayezid. He took the jug from her hands and up-ended it into his mouth, throwing it to one side when the last trickles dripped through his beard to the ground.

'I have your whore!' he shouted. 'Look up, Bayezid. See the Serbian Princess naked before me! She'll suck me dry tonight!'

But the Sultan would not look.

For a while, Tamerlane rattled and kicked the cage, hurling abuse through its bars, then he threw Despina to one side, her head hitting the table, and called for more wine. He drank with his legs apart, swaying, then staggered to where the two women stood. He stared at them, his eyes raking their bodies, before grabbing Maria by the arm and dragging her to the front of the cage. He turned to the men at the tables. 'Who will be first?' he yelled, lifting her arm like a prizefighter's. 'I have here a princess from Trebizond. What price to be first, here in this tent?'

Sotomayor said something under his breath and Luke glanced at him. The Castilian was shaking his head, his eyes wide with horror. Luke found himself standing. He leant forward, supporting his swaying body on the table. 'Lord!' he shouted. He wondered whether he, or another, had spoken.

Tamerlane turned. Luke breathed deeply. He'd begun to

sweat. He wiped his forehead with his sleeve. Luke said: 'This woman you gave to me. Is the tarkhan's prize to be auctioned like a cow?'

Tamerlane stared at him, blinking. The tent had fallen silent.

Luke's fists were clenched on the table, keeping him upright. He heard Sotomayor behind him whisper: 'This is good. Keep going.'

Luke sucked in breath. He felt the sweat on his eyelids. Speaking was such an effort. He blinked. 'Was this woman not given to me as tarkhan, lord?'

He heard whispers from the tables and then the thump of a cup on wood, then another and another. Soon the tent was ringing with the banging of cups upon tables. The tarkhan was claiming his prize. Tamerlane looked at the tables and then raised his hand for silence. When he turned back to Luke he was grinning. He bowed giddily, straightened and nodded. 'Tarkhan,' he said quietly, lifting his cup in salute.

Instantly, Sotomayor was on his feet and had run the length of the table to climb from the dais and reach Maria. Amidst the cheering and banging, and with Tamerlane distracted by more wine, he led her down the walkway and out of the tent. There was just Zoe left.

She was dressed in a simple white garment of silk that looked more like a bed-gown than a dress and she was barefoot. The gown was open at the top and the curve of her breasts rose from its top button in two perfect arcs. In the light of the lanterns, her skin was a wash of amber and her hair blacker than panther-pelt; she stood with her head held high and an expression of calm amusement on her face. She was looking straight at Tamerlane and if she was afraid, not one muscle in her body betrayed it.

Tamerlane was leaning against a table, his arms spread out to either side of him like buttresses, and he was watching her through half-closed eyes. He was moving the top half of his body from side to side and every now and then his chin would fall suddenly to his chest. He was breathing heavily through open lips and his brow was beaded with sweat. Despina was kneeling at his feet, her body very still and a wine jug in her hand. She had a gash at her temple and streaks of blood on her cheek and she too was watching Zoe.

'Who are you?' Tamerlane growled.

Zoe tipped her head to one side as if considering the question. Then she smiled. 'Does it matter?'

The two slowly appraised each other and gradually the tent fell silent around them. Men sensed that some new entertainment was imminent and strained their necks to see.

Tamerlane frowned. 'Do you know who *I* am?'

Zoe's head went over to the other shoulder as if these questions were a game to be played. 'Ah, now that does matter,' she said quietly. 'You are Temur, Sword of Islam, Lord of the Celestial Conjunction and master of everyone in this tent, including Bayezid.' She paused and smiled again. 'Including me.'

Then, very slowly, she walked towards Tamerlane, placing each careful foot in front of the other as if stepping on glass. When she reached him, she undid the buttons at her front one by one until the garment fell open. Then she placed two hands on her shoulders, her elbows pointing at Tamerlane, and, with the slightest of movements, pushed the silk away so that the whole dress slithered to the ground. 'Including me.'

She was naked.

Naked except for a cord at her neck from which hung a

pendant nestling within the valley of her breasts. The pendant was of three gold circles joined and it glowed against her satin skin as if painted there.

The Celestial Conjunction. Temur's sign.

Tamerlane stared at it, transfixed, his eyes behind their glasses vast with lust. His hand went to his crotch and stayed there, the palm flat against silk that was moving as it hadn't for months. 'Where did you get that?' he whispered.

'It's my birth-sign,' she said softly. 'And yours.'

Then she walked towards him and knelt at his feet. She took the wine jug from Despina and the cup that had been with it. She poured wine into the cup and rose, offering it to Tamerlane. 'You will need a new cup-bearer, lord,' she said. 'Your last one is hurt.'

Luke watched it all with appalled fascination, hardly daring to breathe. Zoe had decided to survive in the way she did better than any woman in the world. She had decided to seduce the man who ruled the earth.

And it seemed to have worked. Zoe turned slowly, allowing the lantern light to play itself across the curves of her exquisite body, and began to walk towards the dais. Tamerlane followed her in a trance, his lame leg dragging on the floor and one hand still clamped to his crotch. When they got there, she led him round to his place and then sat herself demurely at his feet, the wine jug still in her hand.

She glanced up at Luke and within those dark, dark eyes was a sort of triumph. It was the look that Tamerlane had had above Bayezid's cage, only quieter. It was the look of conquest. Luke stared at her for some time, her face sometimes becoming two. Then he felt a surge of nausea rise from his stomach and knew that, very soon, he would vomit.

He rose to his feet. With one hand on the table, he began to lurch away from Tamerlane and his new pet. He needed air and the fixed certainty of the heavens above to give bearing to the capricious world around him.

I must get outside.

He reached the end of the dais and somehow made it to the ground without falling. He walked in front of Barbi and heard him call his name from somewhere far away and he saw, from the corner of his eye, the figure of Tamerlane reach over the table to him. But he kept walking. He passed vats of stew with eyeless skulls that leered at him and burnt himself on the sides of braziers and crashed into slaves bearing wine. But he kept on walking.

Then he was at the tent's entrance and it was if an island had risen magically from the waves in front of a spent swimmer. He staggered the last few yards and went out into the night and saw that the stars had occupied the teetering earth as well as the heavens. Stretching all around him to the horizon were the fires of an immeasurable army that had won a great battle and was drinking to remember and to forget it.

Luke fell to the ground and rolled over on to his back and took great lungfuls of the dry desert air. He turned his head slowly from side to side, taking in the boundless expanse of the firmament.

Anna, I am coming.

CHAPTER THIRTY-FIVE

ANATOLIA, AUTUMN 1402

It was then that Tamerlane disappeared.

Fifty thousand lay dead on the field of Ankara and long after the crows had picked out their eyes, Tamerlane kept to his tent, refusing access to all but those who provided the necessities for living: food, wine, cool sherbet and water to wash from his body the messy business of love.

Zoe's talented lips and fingers had managed to do what no other woman had in years: to bring Tamerlane to shuddering climax. And she hadn't been permitted to step outside the tent while she could bestow such a blessing. Tamerlane was infatuated.

Bibi Khanum was not summoned from Samarcand, as was the custom, and it was the elephants that carried back the news of her husband's greatest victory, staying on to haul stone for her gigantic mosque. All of them but two.

A message was sent to the army to move to Kutahya and somehow Yakub learnt that he must prepare his palace for Tamerlane's personal use. So the tents were packed up and put on to the wagons, the siege engines hitched to the oxen and the long, long line of Mongol horsemen, their wives, children and slaves behind them, began to snake its way west into the land of the Germiyans.

But if Yakub had thought that his change of sides would spare the fields and villages of his beylik, he was wrong. The Mongols continued their pilgrimage of rape and murder and the horizon that stretched behind this savage army was black with the smoke of its destruction.

Yakub was beside himself with rage. But Tamerlane was still in his tent at Ankara and Shulen had taken Mohammed Sultan into the fortress there, prepared to use every skill she possessed to heal the man she now called brother. Luke, too, had gone there to recover fully from his head wound. Khan-zada went to nurse them both.

Maria had chosen to go with the army. More accurately, she'd chosen to go with the Castilian Sotomayor to whom she'd become attached. Both thought that their chances of reaching Castile together would be higher the closer they got. Meanwhile, she was appointed handmaiden to Zoe.

After a month, Tamerlane emerged from his tent looking happier than he had in years. The pains of age had disappeared and he'd forgotten Shulen and the magic of her lotions. He summoned his courtiers and declared that he would make the journey west to Kutahya by elephant, taking Zoe, her ointments and some poetry along for his entertainment. He set forth in an enormous canopied howdah, reclining with Zoe amidst cushions, porringers of honey and a servant who poured iced sherbet and murmured the sonnets of the Persian Hafiz into his ear. In the second elephant's howdah rode Shahrukh, Pir Mohammed and Tamerlane's grandson Ulugh Beg. The boy was Shahrukh's eight-year-old son and had an interest in astrology; at night, when they camped, he would describe the stars to his grandfather as the old man lay beneath their majesty. Behind the elephants came a jornufa, an ostrich and a cage that contained the Sultan of an empire that no longer existed. Behind them marched a guard of gautchin with three Varangians at their head.

The main army was outside Kutahya and was growing restless. It had secured a great victory, perhaps the greatest ever won, and it wanted to go home. The generals had sent messages to Pir Mohammed urging him to ask his grandfather about his plans. Now the time had come for Pir Mohammed to act.

Zoe was reclining next to Tamerlane on cushions big and soft enough to absorb the elephant's sway. It was a warm day and she wore a thoub of almost transparent cotton. She had a little lectern poised below her breasts from which she was reading aloud from the *Kama Sutra*, her left hand turning the pages. Her right hand was invisible beneath Tamerlane's housecoat. Curtains hung around the howdah and one inside. The servant was, for now, on the other side of this, singing to a stringed instrument.

Tamerlane grunted and lay back against the cushions and Zoe stopped reading and withdrew her hand. It was, she had learnt, a good time to arrange things. 'We have only three Varangians in our party,' she said, discreetly wiping her hand on the curtain. 'I noticed them this morning as we set off. Was there not another?'

Tamerlane's closed eyes formed small arcs of pleasure and he was breathing quickly, his great chest rising to part and close his housecoat. Small beads of sweat teetered on the banks of his forehead before coursing to his beard. He didn't seem to have heard her.

'The Varangians' leader,' she tried again.

'He's at Ankara,' he said. 'With my grandson.' Then he remembered something. 'And his wife.'

'Except that she's not his wife,' Zoe said. 'He lied to you, lord. They both did.'

Tamerlane opened his eyes to watch Zoe pour them both wine from a pitcher held steady in a clever gimbal by her side. He frowned. 'How do you know this?'

The truth was she didn't, for sure. But she'd known Luke from birth and had seen what had happened with Anna. She knew that he and Shulen were a lie.

'I just know, lord.'

Tamerlane took the wine. 'Should I torture the Varangians to tell me the truth?' he asked.

Zoe pretended to consider this. She shook her head. 'No, they've done you no wrong. You should release them from their oaths.'

'And the other?'

'He has lied to you. He should explain himself.'

Tamerlane nodded. 'When he gets here.' He drank. 'He wants me to go to Chios.'

Zoe had suspected this. Indeed, she'd hoped to guide the conversation to this very place, pausing only to secure the Varangians' release. 'It's a good idea, lord. It is an island I have long desired to see.'

Tamerlane's eyes twinkled. His hand pushed aside the lectern and arrived on her breast, squeezing. She gasped convincingly. 'Desired? Would you like it?'

Zoe stretched like a cat. She placed her hand on his, pressing it down. 'I deserve no such thing, lord,' she murmured. 'Anyway, it's not yours to give. Yet.' She moved her hand south.

'No, too soon. I am old.'

'Not so old,' she whispered, turning to his ear. Her hand continued south and its fingers curled around soft flesh. 'You should summon the Varangian to explain himself,' she said again. 'Soon.'

Zoe stroked and pressed and teased and all the while wondered what she was doing. She knew the game her hand played but not her mind. Why did she want Luke back? To share in her triumph? Why had she gone to Allaedin ali-Bey of the Karamanids to get him back for Suleyman? Why had she tried again with the younger di Vetriano, and again with the Mongol envoy? Why had she worked so hard to keep Anna away from him, only arranging for her to go into Constantinople when she'd guessed she might be sent somewhere further?

Her hand rose and dipped in rhythm and her thoughts reached an awful realisation.

I cannot help myself.

The world shifted and her hand lost its grip. Something large had bumped against the side of their elephant. She rolled away and lifted the curtain to see Pir Mohammed leaning out from his howdah.

'Grandfather,' he called over her, 'may I speak with you?'

'Your grandfather is busy,' she said, closing the curtain.

Pir Mohammed tried again. 'Lord, the generals wish to know your plans.'

Zoe glanced at Tamerlane, who was scowling at the wine jug that had left its gimbal and was now resting against his puddled thigh. The servant had dared to draw his curtain and was frantically mopping with his sleeve.

'Your grandson wants to know where we're going, lord,' she said, shooing away the servant and applying her own sleeve to the work. 'Shall I say Chios? Will you meet the Christian powers there?'

Tamerlane grunted and she rose to her knees and lifted the curtain again.

'The Lord of the Seven Climes intends to take Smyrna, as he said he would, then go to Chios. He has reflected on the Varangian's advice and wishes to meet the Emperor Manuel and other Christian kings there. He asks you to arrange it.'

She lowered the curtain too quickly to see the delight on Pir Mohammed's face. They would make peace with the western Kings and then go home. She didn't see the Prince turn to his cousin and say: 'Let's play chess.'

The city of Smyrna was said to be impregnable.

Certainly the defenders thought so. Two hundred Knights Hospitaller under the command of the Aragonese General Iñigo of Alfaro had declined the offer of surrender begged from Tamerlane by his Nestorian advisers. For sixty years their walls had stood firm against every assault by the Turk and they would not open their gates to an illiterate barbarian now. Anyway, they had Greek fire supplied to them by an engineer from Chios who, they'd have been surprised to learn, was somewhere within Tamerlane's army.

It was December and the first snows had fallen on the mountains to the north and the gulf on which the city sat was moiling with wind-clipped waves. It had rained without cease since the army had arrived and the Mongols, miserable, wet and cold, were yearning ever more for home. Their only enjoyment had been the daily spectacle of Bayezid dragged out in his cage to watch them attempt what he'd failed to do: wipe this last Christian outpost from the lands of the Prophet.

The city stood high on a rocky outcrop which extended into the gulf and could only be taken by a two-pronged attack by land and sea. Tamerlane soon saw that the walls were weakest on the seaward side and ordered platforms to be built across the water, supported by sunken columns, so cutting off the city from the shore. Benedo Barbi's covered alleyways, never used at Ankara, were rolled up to the city walls and the fires lit. Meanwhile, the cannon captured from Bayezid were hauled into position on the land side.

After fifteen days, breaches appeared in the walls and they began to fall. The Mongols rushed over them with no thought of mercy in their minds. The men and children of the city were cut down where they stood, the women raped, then slaughtered.

The Hospitallers had sent reinforcements from Rhodes but they'd arrived too late. As the fleet rowed up the gulf, with the city of Smyrna smoking before them, the sky was suddenly filled with comets trailing blood in their wake. A moment later, the two hundred heads of Smyrna's defenders thudded on to the decks around them. The Hospitallers turned about and rowed for home.

Smyrna had fallen.

On Chios, the signori were angry with the Knights.

Dominic de Alamania of their Order had brought his fleet to the island from Rhodes and demanded that the Hospitaller fleet be allowed to revictual there before sailing on to Smyrna. The signori, who now included Dimitri among their number, had had no choice but to agree. So it was in some trepidation that the twelve Genoese and one Greek awaited Tamerlane in the palace of Marchese Longo in the citadel at Chora. The days had been long and nerve-racking and their only relief had been the charm and beauty of their leader's wife and son.

Giovanni Giustiniani Longo was five years old and had his mother's hair. He was tall for his age and would be taller than his father. He was an intelligent child who already spoke three languages, could recite Homer and found amusement in mathematics. And in the hours of pacing the long marble corridors of the palace, the signori would distract themselves by trying to satisfy the boy's endless curiosity.

The signori were further distracted by the arrival on Chios of the Byzantine Emperor Manuel II Palaiologos, the philosopher Plethon and King Sigismund of Hungary, who'd brought Anna Laskaris with him. After delivering her letters, Anna had stayed at Sigismund's court and watched with satisfaction as the letters had done their work: a new crusade had been called with both Popes persuaded to back it.

The King of Hungary, like Manuel, had chosen to obey Tamerlane's summons, the consequences of refusal outweighing the dangers of acceptance. Their arrivals, and the imminent coming of Tamerlane, had brought about the departure of Fiorenza and Giovanni for their home in Sklavia. It was safer for them there, closer to the port of Limenas. They would be missed.

Now Anna was seated on a balcony that overlooked the big throne room, watching the men below wait for Tamerlane to arrive. Manuel stood next to Plethon who stood next to Sigismund of Hungary. Behind were the signori, each trying to forget the stories of horror that had accompanied every move of the man they were about to meet. At their front was the handsome Marchese Giustiniani Longo, a man she'd met only the day before. She wished she'd met his wife as well, to admire her beauty and thank her for the many kindnesses she'd shown to Luke.

At last there were footsteps on the marble outside, quick footsteps that stopped outside the door. There was a long pause and from far away came the sound of something being dragged. Anna felt cold.

Tamerlane. Temur the Lame.

Closer it came, agonisingly slowly. Anna stared at the doors and the Genoese at each other, every man searching for reassurance or just memorising a face they might not see again. The doors were flung open by two soldiers of the gautchin, their pigtails swinging above golden cuirasses as they knelt. As Tamerlane entered, thirty knees hit the marble floor as one. Only the Emperor Manuel and King Sigismund remained standing.

Tamerlane was wearing a tall, pumpkin-domed hat with a heron feather clasped to it and a short-sleeved tunic of brushed silk gathered at the waist by several belts. Above was an overgarment edged in ermine and below short riding boots with mud on them. On his hands were hawking gloves covered with filth. His clothes were wet with rain and the smell of damp came with him.

'You would not kneel?' he asked, approaching the Byzantine Emperor.

Manuel inclined his head. 'We are both emperors, lord. And I am not yet your vassal.'

Tamerlane looked at him for a moment, then glanced at Sigismund, breathing deeply. He was not wearing his glasses and the men before him were vague. He turned to the rest of the room. 'Which of you dogs sent the fleet to relieve the crusaders at Smyrna? I know it sailed from here.'

Marchese Longo answered him. 'The fleet came from Rhodes, lord. It took on provisions at our harbour against our wishes.'

Tamerlane limped over to him. 'Indeed?' he asked, his face bent close to Longo's and his rancid breath between them. 'And you did not think to stop it? Are you not part of the Byzantine Empire which allied itself to me against Bayezid?'

Anna looked down on a room full of men, not one of whom expected to see sunset. The man who had reduced cities to rubble was walking among them talking of betrayal. Tamerlane stepped back from Longo and clapped his hands. There were more footsteps from the corridor and two men came in, each carrying a chair. Tamerlane sat, lifted a hand, and one of the gautchin drew his sword, walked forward, and gave it to him.

Above them, Anna gasped. Zoe had walked into the room. She was dressed as a Mongol princess in a high-collared silk tunic of red, her hair plaited. She looked neither to left nor right but went straight to the other chair and sat down. Tamerlane took her hand.

Anna felt faint. Zoe *here*? She was supposed to be in Edirne, but she was below her holding the hand of a monster. She heard Tamerlane speaking again and forced herself to listen.

'I have heard what Bayezid did after Nicopolis,' he was saying. 'Blind old men with swords.' He paused. 'Thanks to you Italians, I can now see.' He took his glasses from a sleeve and put them on. 'Now, who is to be first?'

Marchese Longo rose to his feet. 'If anyone here is to die, it should be I,' he said quietly. 'I alone bear responsibility for the revictualling of the Hospitaller fleet. The rest are innocent.'

Tamerlane stared at him. Then he leant forward in his chair, still holding Zoe's hand. He said: 'Did you know my mother was a Christian, Genoese? Of the Nestorian persuasion?'

Anna's hands were holding the balcony and they were trembling. This was the man who had had his cavalry ride down Christian children before Damascus when they'd come out to plead for their lives. And beside him sat the most evil woman she knew. She drew back so as not to be seen.

'There is no mercy in Islam,' Tamerlane continued, shaking his head. He brushed dirt from his glove. 'But in Jesus Christ . . .' He leant forward again and blew his nose to the floor through finger and thumb, covering the effect with his boot. He wiped his nose with the back of his hand and clicked his fingers. 'In Jesus Christ there is mercy.' He made the sign of the cross with his gloved hand and frowned. 'Anyway, it pleases me to be merciful. Especially since men from your island have done me some service. The three Varangians who are with me and the engineer are released from their oath.' He let go of Zoe's hand and rose to his feet. 'I have decided to give you the monopoly to sell mastic throughout my empire. So you have it. Get up.'

The signori did nothing at first, too stunned to move. Then, one by one, they rose.

'And alum,' went on Tamerlane. 'You can have that too.'

Longo spoke. 'Lord, your generosity–'

But Tamerlane suddenly wanted to be somewhere else. He leant forward and tapped Longo on the head with his finger. 'Stop. I have honey enough in my tent.' He straightened and addressed the men in the room. 'There is a condition. I give your island to the woman who will be my next wife.' He turned and gestured to Zoe, still seated. 'She knows trade and will be a wise ruler. She will come to rule over you when I am dead.'

The signori exchanged glances but none of them spoke. Was Chios now his island? The Emperor Manuel and Sigismund were still standing. 'What of us, majesty?' asked the Emperor. 'King Sigismund and I have come far to hear your plans. Have you nothing to tell us?'

Tamerlane thought for a while. Then he said to Manuel: 'It pleases me to marry this lady in your Church of Holy Wisdom in the city of Constantinople. I shall enter with a guard and depart when it is over, leaving you in peace. You and Hungary are invited to attend.' He paused and looked around the room. 'In fact you will all come. You can ride with me to Constantinople and get to know your new ruler.' He went over to Zoe and offered her his arm. She rose. 'And after the marriage we will return to Samarcand.'

A little later, after the signori had retired, Manuel remained with Plethon and Anna. Matthew, Nikolas and Arcadius were with them, freed now from Tamerlane's retinue. Their reunion with Anna had been tempered by the news of the wedding in Constantinople.

'He was supposed to stop at Ankara, Plethon,' Manuel was saying. 'We cannot let him enter Constantinople. What has gone wrong?'

Matthew spoke. 'It is the Mamonas girl, majesty. She has bewitched him. He does what she tells him to.'

'Including destroying her own empire?' Manuel's voice was rising.

Plethon shook his head. 'She is ruthless, highness. And she wants more than Chios.'

Anna glanced at the philosopher. 'Perhaps she wants the treasure and Constantinople is her price.'

Plethon said nothing. Manuel had begun to pace. 'So what do we do? Can we defend ourselves? What of Sigismund? Is his crusade credible?'

Anna said: 'It has Medici money and the blessing of two Popes. But it will take too long to come.'

Manuel grunted. 'What about Suleyman? He still has half of Bayezid's army in Rumelia. He could join with a Hungarian army.'

Plethon had already registered his dismay that Manuel had thought to ferry Suleyman's fleeing army across to Europe. That had not been part of his plan. Manuel had wanted another ally should Tamerlane threaten Constantinople but it was hardly likely that Suleyman would find common ground with Sigismund.

Manuel had stopped pacing and was looking out at the evening sky, an eruption of pinks and mauves over the hills to the west. There was a light breeze and his long silver hair moved with it. 'Could we poison him?' he asked. 'That's what stopped them last time: the death of the Khan.'

Matthew spoke again. 'Impossible, highness. Zoe is with him at all times.'

There was silence in the room and the wind played cool fingers over its taut strings. Plethon came and stood behind his emperor. 'There is another way, lord,' he said quietly. 'The Varangians have told me that his grandson, Mohammed Sultan, has influence over him. He was wounded in the battle and rests at Ankara. We could send for him.'

'But why would he come?'

'Because the Varangian Luke Magoris is with him there. They have become friends. He could bring him.'

Manuel considered this. 'But who would go to them?'

Matthew said: 'We would, majesty. The three of us.'

'You?' This was Anna. 'Three fair-haired giants riding through a sea of Mongols? You'd not get past Smyrna. I should go.'

Matthew snorted. 'It's too dangerous.'

Anna turned on him. 'More dangerous than here? How safe will I be on Chios once Zoe knows that I'm here?'

She was right. Zoe's implacable hatred of Anna would seal her death sentence once she'd learnt of her presence.

Nikolas said. 'She could take the paizi. We still have it from the ride to Samarcand. If she was properly disguised, no one would dare stop her. And she'd get new horses at every yam.'

Matthew shot him a glance. But it made sense. Anna had to escape Chios, so she might as well escape to Ankara. She came forward to stand with Plethon, placing her hand on his arm. 'I'm going,' she said quietly.

To her surprise Plethon nodded. Then he took her to one side, out of earshot of the others. 'Yes, you should go.' His voice had dropped to a whisper. 'The ring you gave to Luke: I need it back. If Zoe wants to bargain for the treasure then the ring is an important part of it, you know that.' He looked over her head to make sure they weren't being overheard. 'Perhaps I was wrong, Anna. Perhaps this is the way the treasure is to be used to save the Empire.'

So it was that five days later Anna was looking up at the sandstone walls of Ankara Castle. The sun was setting and the stone above her glowed in the last of the heat, the shadow of her horse stretching out in front like a grave. She had ridden as a boy-messenger, veiled against the dust, and not once had her paizi been questioned. She was on her sixth horse and the animal was tired.

The ride had been uneventful, which had suited a traveller who'd wanted to think. She'd last seen Luke at Kutahya when she'd also met Shulen. That had been at the start of Luke's voyage to Tamerlane, a voyage that must have taken him and Shulen to the very frontiers of life and death, of mutual dependence. Was it so very surprising that they'd fallen in love along the way? But Anna remembered a night in a cave long ago and a promise that had been made.

I will love you wherever you are and wherever I am.

The words had stayed with her through every moment of her life in the harem in Edirne. On the rides with Suleyman, she'd meant to scatter them into the air but they'd always come back to her. Luke might be married to Shulen but he still loved her. She was certain of it.

But she was afraid too, and the closer she got to Ankara, the more afraid she became. What if she was wrong? What if Luke also loved Shulen? Was she going to be humiliated at Ankara? Should she turn back?

She'd not turned back and now it was too late. The vast studded doors were closing behind her and she was inside the castle. She was still veiled and a Mongol officer was approaching her.

'Your message?'

'Is for the eyes of Prince Mohammed Sultan only,' said Anna as she dismounted. She handed her reins to a waiting groom. 'I must take it to him in person.' The paizi around her neck glowed in the waning sunlight.

The man nodded and turned. 'This way.'

They entered the keep and crossed a big hall with a long table in the centre, piled high with food and jugs of wine. There was armour on the walls and crossed weapons. They went through an arch and into a tower and began to climb steps. At last they reached a door and the soldier knocked.

A voice told them to enter. Not Luke's but a woman's. Anna's heart was beating harder than she'd ever known it to do. She took the deepest of breaths and lifted the veil to her eyes. The door opened. Inside were three people, two of them sitting at a table, the other asleep in a large bed. Luke and Shulen were playing chess. Luke was staring at the board while Shulen glanced up.

'A message from Temur Gurgan?'

Anna waited for the soldier to close the door behind her. 'A message for the Varangian,' she said, her voice muffled by the veil and as deep as she could make it. 'For him to read here. I am to know his reply.'

Luke was still staring at the game. He had a castle in one hand that hovered above a knight. Anna saw that there were strange pieces on the board and that it was bigger than ones she'd played on. Luke held up a hand for the letter and Anna looked at the hand. Then she produced one of two letters on her person.

Luke took the scroll, broke the seal and unrolled the vellum. It contained a simple message: 'You promised only to ever remove the ring when you stopped loving me. You wear it still.'

Luke dropped the castle. He turned and rose too quickly and the chair clattered to the ground. 'Anna.'

He ran to her as she pulled down the veil. Then she was within arms that held her so hard that the paizi dug into her breast. 'Stop,' she said. 'The paizi.' She drew away, holding him at arm's length, breathing hard. 'And you are married.'

'Married? To whom?'

Anna looked into a face wide with joy, astonishment, bewilderment. It was a face with no trace of a lie in it. She nearly faltered.

'To her.' She nodded towards the table.

'To Shulen?'

Anna nodded. 'It happened in the caravan. We heard.'

Shulen had risen. She was very different from when Anna had seen her last. Now she was smiling. 'Ah, you heard.' She laughed. 'From Venetians perhaps? Or even from the court of Tamerlane?' She came up to them. 'Anna, I invented the marriage to try and save us from a madman – two madmen.' She pointed towards the bed where Mohammed Sultan lay. 'The only man I have ever come close to marrying lies in that bed.'

Anna nearly sank to her knees with the relief. It was as if a giant vine that had grown around her, that had squeezed the life from her existence, had been cut at its roots. She rose, took a long breath and grasped Shulen's hand. She said: 'Thank you.'

Luke had been watching her throughout the exchange, slowly shaking his head in disbelief. A moment that he'd dreamt of for so long had arrived. He felt weak with joy. But why was she here? And how had she got here? 'Anna . . .'

But she had turned and was walking over to the bed, partly to hide the tears of happiness that were washing her eyes. She stopped and looked down at the sleeping Prince. 'Is he too sick to travel?' she asked.

Shulen followed and stood on the other side of the bed. 'The wound was very deep. He mustn't be moved.'

Luke came to stand next to Anna and took her hand. He looked down at the Prince, whose only movement was the rise and fall of his bandaged chest. 'Where must he travel to?'

Anna said: 'Tamerlane wants to marry Zoe in the Church of Hagia Sophia in Constantinople. Everyone believes that it's an excuse to put the city to the sword. Only Mohammed Sultan can stop him.'

It was said quietly but it caused the man below them to stir. He opened his eyes and blinked twice. He turned his head towards Shulen and took her hand. 'I can be moved,' he said.

Shulen shook her head, kissing each of his fingers as she did so. 'It will kill you.' She looked up at Anna, then Luke. 'There must be another way.'

Anna turned to Luke. 'Plethon wants the ring I gave you. It's possible that Zoe can be persuaded to stop Tamerlane but he needs the ring to do it. Whatever happens with Mohammed Sultan, we must bring the ring to Plethon.'

Luke nodded. 'We should leave immediately, then.' He knelt down so that his head was level with the Prince's. 'And you should obey Shulen. You're too weak to go to Tamerlane.'

Mohammed Sultan nodded slowly. 'I am too weak to go with you but I will come on behind, with Shulen and my mother.' His face wrinkled. Speaking was painful. 'You'll need me.'

Shulen began to say something but stopped herself. The Prince continued: 'Do you remember in the church, when you thought Shulen was Cybele?' The words were slow, mostly breath. He was trying to smile. 'I told you that I'd believed what you'd said about the west, about what was happening there.' He closed his eyes and took several slow breaths. 'Temur must not destroy it.'

Luke remembered something that had been said and not said. The Mongol army would go home on the death of its khan as it always had. But how? He looked down at a face drained of blood, at eyes lying too deep in shadow. He'd come to love this man and he didn't know if he'd see him alive again. Luke nodded, uncertain, if he spoke, whether he would be able to finish a sentence. He bent forward and kissed the forehead, cold as ice. He got to his feet and turned to Anna. 'We should go.'

Anna had ridden five days without sleep and was exhausted beyond reason. But there was no time to sleep now and she had to dig her nails deep into her palms to keep in the saddle. Luke was in front, joined to the back of Eskalon as if the animal were part of him. They hadn't spoken since leaving Ankara and the night was loud beneath her: the pounding of hoof on solid earth, the rhythmic squeak of leather in motion, the staccato panting of an animal doing its best to keep up with one much bigger. She felt so tired.

On the ride to Ankara, the agony of apprehension had kept her awake but now, with the relief of knowing that Luke was unmarried, something had been released and she thought she could sleep for a thousand years. She felt rain on her brow and looked up. The night seemed blacker above her and there was a tension in the air that spoke of storm. She kicked her horse.

The first clap of thunder was not much more than a rumble, the heavens clearing their throat. The second brought her to the ground. It was louder than any she'd ever heard and its effect on her horse was dramatic: it stopped, reared and threw Anna from its back. She landed badly and for a while feared that she'd be trampled. She rolled away and waited for the horse to calm. Then another thunderclap.

'Anna!' Luke had turned Eskalon on the first roar and ridden back. He jumped to the ground and ran to her. 'Are you hurt?'

'Only my pride,' she laughed, the rain splashing her face.

Anything could happen and she didn't care. She was alive and here and so was Luke. And he loved her. 'I'm so tired.'

'Of course.' He looked up. The steppe stretched all around and the rain was drilling into the ground. 'We must find shelter and you must sleep.'

'But . . .'

'No, you must sleep and then we'll go on. There are hills ahead. We can find shelter there.' He lifted her in his arms and walked over to Eskalon. 'We'll ride together.' He put her on to his horse and then went to hers. He gathered its reins and tied them to his saddle. Then he mounted Eskalon behind her. 'Hold on to me.'

And, in a dream, she did. She cradled herself in his arms and felt the warm, strong embrace that she'd felt in a cave on the Goulas of Monemvasia long ago. She wanted so badly to stay awake, to live this moment of pure, rain-soaked joy for eternity. She drifted into sleep thinking of a runaway horse and the moment when he'd held her for the first time. She felt the comfortable rhythm of power beneath her and against her and she fell asleep, smiling.

When she awoke, it was daylight and she was lying on the ground beneath an overhang of rock. She was in dry clothes, warm and covered by blankets. Beside her was Luke. 'How long have I slept?'

He smiled. 'A night. You talked a bit.'

'About you?'

'Mainly me.' He kissed her. 'Others too.' He looked at her for a long time and she looked back. So much time had passed since they'd last met. He dared ask the question. 'Did he hurt you?'

'Suleyman? No. I don't think he would ever hurt me.'

Luke raised himself to his elbow. 'Why didn't he marry you?'

Anna pulled the blanket higher, enjoying the soft wool on her cheek. 'I kept finding reasons for delay. Then I used his seal without his knowledge and Bayezid found out. He forbade the marriage after that.'

'And yet you have your annulment.'

'I have it but don't need it,' she replied. 'Damian's dead. He fell off the Goulas when he was drunk.'

Luke had not heard. He shook his head, surprised at the pain of the news. Flashes of long-ago memory came to him: Damian, Zoe, him on a donkey led by his mother; the three of them looking for kermes outside Monemvasia. They'd been the best of friends once. Then Eskalon had charged and Damian had been in the way and he'd not forgiven Luke or his horse. Now he was dead.

Anna leant forward. She put her hand to his cheek, hoping to draw some of the sorrow. 'We can marry, Luke,' she said softly. 'You are a hero.'

Luke frowned. 'On Chios perhaps. But what will I be when Tamerlane sacks Constantinople?'

Anna said: 'Shulen will bring Mohammed Sultan. He'll stop Tamerlane.'

'No he won't. He didn't stop him at Aleppo or Damascus. Tamerlane cannot be stopped by anyone.'

'Except, perhaps, by Zoe. Show me the ring.'

Luke raised his hand and turned it so that Anna could see the ring. It was of gold and pitted with age, its edges worn. On it was some ancient script.

'It's beautiful,' she murmured. 'What's written on it?'

Luke shrugged. 'I showed it to Ibn Khaldun once. He said it was ancient Hebrew. I don't know what it says. A name perhaps.'

They both examined it in silence. The wind over the steppe made a strange, keening sound as it parted the grass. There was low cloud and the sun was warming some other landscape. Eskalon neighed.

'We should go,' said Luke at last.

Anna leant back and stretched. Then she rolled herself towards him so that they were face to face. She kissed him. 'Not yet, tarkhan.'

CHAPTER THIRTY-SIX

THE ROAD TO CONSTANTINOPLE, AUTUMN 1402

It took Luke and Anna only three days to reach Chios. They rode as hard as the rain and road allowed and stopped only once for Anna to change horses. They spoke little: Anna numb with the pleasure of a recent transaction, Luke thinking hard of how to stop Tamerlane from entering Constantinople. He remembered again and again what Mohammed Sultan had said to him in the church.

The last time that our armies came into Europe, they were stopped by the death of the Khan . . . It might happen again.

But how? Shulen had poisoned him once but she was a long way behind, bringing Mohammed Sultan to his grandfather slowly on a litter. Anyway, Zoe was apparently with Tamerlane every moment of the day and night.

They reached the sea in the evening and commandeered a boat to take them to Chios. And as they crossed the straits, Luke's thoughts turned to something else. He'd been aware of a strange excitement growing alongside his worry, gradually nudging it aside as they got closer to Chios: he was to meet his son. He was about to meet Giovanni on Chios and he felt giddy with yearning.

But it wasn't to be. They arrived late at night at the Giustiniani Palace to be told that Tamerlane had left and that Fiorenza had taken Giovanni to Sklavia and was not expected to return within the week.

So Anna was surprised to wake up the next morning to find a woman of great beauty standing next to her bed holding hands with a boy. She knew immediately who they were.

Fiorenza. Fiorenza and Giovanni.

The woman spoke. 'We are deserted. The men have all left. Luke too.'

Anna looked at the pair. Fiorenza was dressed in a high-collared tunic of brushed silk, cream and without pattern. Her head was uncovered and on her feet were green slippers. The boy was dressed in Genoese miniature: doublet and hose, both in matching blue, and boots of calfskin. He was looking at the floor and his hair was the colour of corn.

Fiorenza spoke again. 'I've been at Sklavia. I came back when I heard that Tamerlane had left. But it seems he's taken my husband with him.' She paused. 'Luke has told me much about you.'

Anna sat up in the bed, studying the woman. 'As I of you. You've been kind to him. Do you know where he's gone?'

Fiorenza produced a scroll. 'I found this in his room.'

It was addressed to Anna. She took the scroll and opened it. Inside was a ring and a message: 'Catch up with Plethon and give this to him but avoid Zoe at all costs. I will join you as soon as I can. I love you.'

She reread the message, certain that someone else had done the same. She looked up to find her hostess guileless and smiling, two dimples bracketing her perfect mouth. She wondered again where Luke had gone. Had he had a message from Shulen? Probably.

Fiorenza turned to her son. 'Giovanni.' The boy lifted his head and Anna's breath left her. A wave of panic surged up her body and she put a hand out to steady herself on the bed. She had to stop herself from crying out.

Luke.

The boy bowed from the waist and straightened up. He smiled. He was Luke. Luke with dimples. There was no doubt. If it wasn't obvious in his size, his hair, his chin, then it shone from his blue, blue eyes.

You are Luke's son.

She was aware that she was staring at the boy but couldn't wrench her eyes away. It was as if Luke was reborn, refashioned in the skin of a child. She wanted to touch him.

'I see you are taken with my son.'

Anna forced herself to look up at Fiorenza.

She knows I know.

Small spots of colour had emerged high in the Princess of Trebizond's cheeks. The dimples had disappeared and there was calculation in her eyes. 'It is possible he reminds you of another?'

Anna felt the blood rush to her face. She knew that she was trembling and cursed the hands that betrayed it. She breathed in. 'I'm sorry.' She put out her hand. 'Giovanni.'

The boy bowed again, still smiling, and took her hand. Fiorenza said: 'I mean to go to my husband. You?'

Anna nodded. 'I'll go to Plethon. And your son?'

Fiorenza paused for a moment. Then she said: 'He will return to Sklavia. There are horses waiting.'

The stench of Smyrna was more than even Tamerlane could stand. The smell of rotting corpses, lifted by fire and autumn wind, penetrated every corner of the citadel so that half of his court performed their duties masked. Tamerlane soon left the city for Constantinople. He travelled by elephant with just Zoe and a servant in his howdah and Pir Mohammed, Sigismund, Manuel and Plethon in the howdah behind. Marchese Longo and the signore rode at the head of a regiment of gautchin that brought up the rear. The army was left to rest in Smyrna and would follow later.

The road had been Byzantine, therefore wide and level, and the ride was comfortable. The summer had extended its reach into autumn and a hot sun turned leaves into fire before they fell from the poplars that lined the road. Beyond the trees were villages without people and fields without livestock. Humanity had disappeared with its food. It was if the last judgement had come and gone without anyone caring to tell the Mongol army. Only the kourtchi, riding ahead, had seen the road into Bursa clogged with people desperate to seek refuge behind the city's walls.

So none saw the passing of this strange calvacade. None saw the two elephants, their mahouts sitting astride painted faces whose steady grins rocked between giant tusks; or the jornufa or ostrich or two donkeys wearing the tall white hats of the janissary corps. None saw the four bullocks that followed, pulling a wagon with a cage upon it in which a clown sat in misery: Bayezid; Yildirim; Sultan of the Ottomans, a man hardly visible through the filth on his bars.

News came from Ankara. Mohammed Sultan would meet his grandfather somewhere along the road to Bursa. For Zoe, this was the first piece of bad news for some time; she'd hoped Mohammed Sultan would be too ill to travel and didn't want his words of reason anywhere near her lover's ear.

Tamerlane had started the journey in the best of spirits. Zoe had used every skill in her repertoire to bring him to grunting ecstasy in the bed of the Grand Master of the Hospitallers. Now he lay against the cushions of the howdah while she read to him, watching the of the young mahout as it swung from side to side with the rhythm of the beast. The music was sweet and the air sweeter than anything he'd breathed in a week. Tamerlane was happy.

Having sent Giovanni to Sklavia, Fiorenza joined the party as it left Manisa. She rode alongside her husband as it passed through Akhisar, barked at by dogs and stared at by cats but otherwise unnoticed. On the third evening, they arrived at the bridge at Sultancayir, just short of the city of Karasi, capital of the beylik of that name, the first neighbour to be annexed by the Ottomans sixty years past. They were two hundred miles from Constantinople. There was a Byzantine castle on a hill there, abandoned by its Turkish sipahi owner, where Tamerlane's guests would be housed for the night. Tamerlane would pitch his tent at the bottom.

Much later, one guest awoke to receive a summons to meet Tamerlane in his tent, alone. Matthew dressed quickly, woke Nikolas to tell him where he was going, and tiptoed from the room. He assumed the summons had something to do with Luke. In the castle stable, he found his horse, saddled it and led it across the sleeping courtyard, through the gate and on to the path outside. He mounted and rode down the hill. He had no difficulty in recognizing Tamerlane's ger. It was the largest and had the flag of the Celestial Conjunction outside, just visible in the moonlight. Two gautchin stood guard on either side of its entrance. They recognised Matthew and lifted the flap for him to enter.

Inside it was dim and very warm and the air smelt of wine. Tamerlane's giant bed, with braziers at each corner, stood in the centre. Veil upon veil of diaphanous material had been ripped from its frame and a copper bath was up-ended at its foot. The remains of a meal were scattered across the carpet. At first Matthew thought that he was alone in the tent. Except for the crackle of fire in the stove, it was entirely quiet. Then he saw a shape move on the bed and his heart missed a beat.

Zoe.

He turned to go.

'It's all right. He's on the floor, too drunk to know anything. I've seen it before.'The words were muffled, as if spoken from below a pillow or from broken lips. It sounded like the voice of one in pain. Something was wrong.

'Are you hurt?' he whispered.

She laughed. There was the brush of fur on fur as she moved. 'Yes, I'm hurt.'

Matthew strained to see. 'Tamerlane?'

He heard slow, careful movement from one finding movement painful. 'I am split and torn and bruised in places I didn't think it possible to hurt.' She paused. 'He is an animal.'

Matthew heard a snore from the far side of the ger, then a grunt, like some beast stirring in its bestial dream. He moved slowly over to the bed. She was lying on a sheet beneath furs and her back was to him. She was probably naked. He said: 'He called for me.'

Zoe sighed. 'He didn't call for you, I did. I wanted to talk to you.'

'Zoe, his guards are outside.'

'No they're not. I told them to go as soon as you arrived. They're getting drunk somewhere.'

Matthew glanced at the tent entrance. 'What did you want to talk about?'

'About Chios,' she said. Her palm patted the bed behind her. 'Sit. We can talk and then you can go.'

Matthew sat.

Zoe turned her head slightly to him. She paused before speaking. 'Temur tells me that Luke saved Mohammed Sultan's life at Ankara. He says they love each other as brothers now. Which is why Luke stayed there instead of coming here.'

Matthew frowned. 'Luke stayed at Ankara because he was too sick to travel.'

'Are you sure? I think Luke has deserted you. He has new friends now.'

Matthew was shaking his head. 'Luke is a Varangian.'

'He's also ambitious. Just look at what he's learnt over the past two years. He's left the rest of you behind.'

Matthew remained silent. He wanted to leave.

'You know that he has Plethon's trust,' went on Zoe, 'particularly in the matter of the treasure. What you don't know is how he's abused that trust. We went into Constantinople, he and I, before Nicopolis, to look for it. He wanted to take it for himself.' She paused and her head turned a little further. 'Just like his grandfather.'

Matthew rose. He'd never believed the story that Luke's grandfather had stolen the treasure. He wouldn't believe it now.

'Sit down, Matthew,' Zoe said quietly. 'I haven't finished.'

He took a deep breath. 'I don't want to hear any more.'

He heard the rustle of sheets as Zoe turned her body. He didn't look round.

'I have a proposition for you, Matthew,' she said. 'Help me rule Chios. I'll need someone to keep all those signori in order, someone strong. You can bring the other two as well. You'll all be rich.'

Matthew exhaled slowly. His mind was churning. 'And Luke?'

'Luke has made other plans. And they don't include you.'

Matthew said: 'Temur won't honour your agreement any more than he has any other. He'll tire of you, Zoe. He might kill you.'

She laughed then. 'I'm sure he might. But I will poison him before that happens. I have good poison from Venice. Look, I have it here. I carry it always.'

Zoe tossed a narrow belt on to the floor. Matthew stooped to pick it up. It had two lumps in the fabric. Two doses of poison; two just to be sure. Matthew stared at it. He wanted to be as far away from this tent as it was possible to be. He had to get out into the air, away from her musk, away from her madness. Away from the monster asleep on the floor. He made to go.

'You'll regret it.' Her voice was calm.

He walked to the door of the tent.

'Did you know that he means to take Constantinople?' she asked. 'How big will the guard he takes inside the city be, do you think? Just his regiment of gautchin? What will he do to the poor citizens when he knows that Manuel ferried Suleyman's army to safety?' Her voice stayed low. 'And what do you think he'll do to Anna when I tell him that she tried to bring a crusade to fight him?' She paused. 'I wouldn't leave, if I were you.'

But Matthew suddenly needed more than air. He pulled aside the tent-flap and stepped into the night.

Outside the tent were four soldiers of the gautchin, their swords drawn.

A mile to the south, Anna was riding towards the bridge at Sultancayir, with her paizi as apparent as she could make it in the moonlight and a ring in her pocket. In her mind was only one thought, one question.

How can he not be Luke's son?

And how could Marchese Longo not see it? Or perhaps he did. Why did Luke do it?

Why did you betray me?

The first campfires of the gautchin appeared on either side of the road and a soldier rose from the sleeping figures. She raised her veil and showed him the paizi and went through. Soon she was climbing the path to the castle. At the top, she dismounted and led her horse under the gate. A Mongol appeared and she showed the paizi. 'The Lord Plethon,' she said.

The servant didn't understand. She managed to convey a toga and length of beard and the man nodded. He led her up some steps and along a passage to a door. He left her.

She pushed the door half open. 'Plethon?' She hoped she sounded less frightened than she was.

Plethon was in bed, reading. 'Come in. Don't worry, Tamerlane is in his tent at the bottom of the hill, with Zoe.'

Anna walked over to the bed and sat down. 'You were awake.'

Plethon put down the book and lifted himself against the pillows. The night was cool and he pulled the blanket up with him. 'I couldn't sleep. I was thinking. And you?'

Anna nodded.

'Of Luke?'

Anna didn't answer. She looked down at her hands, which, she saw, were joined as if in prayer.

'Of a tall boy who looks like Luke?'

Anna looked up. The philosopher's face was quite clear in the moonlight. He was not smiling.

'So it's true?' she whispered.

'You know it's true,' said Plethon. 'You can see it. The question is: why?'

'And do you have the answer?'

He studied her hands, clenched in hope that he might. He shook his head. 'No. Only two people have that.' He looked up at her. 'Where is Luke?'

Anna sighed. She closed her eyes and rocked back on the bed. 'He left me at Chios but didn't say where he'd gone. Probably to Shulen. He gave me this to give to you.'

She took the ring from her pocket and gave it to Plethon. He studied it closely. He said: 'I have been visited by Maria tonight. She is Zoe's handmaiden. She will act as go-between. She told me that she'd seen Zoe meet with someone this evening, someone she recognised. Fiorenza.'

Anna frowned. 'Why would Zoe meet with Fiorenza?'

Plethon shrugged. 'I don't know. But she told me something about Fiorenza. She was the one who fled Trebizond with the Venetian who stole the alum trade from the Genoese.'

Something connected in Anna's brain.

Of course. Fiorenza was Maria's cousin in Trebizond. But why meet Zoe?

'Why is this important, Plethon?'

'Because someone on Chios has been giving Venice information. Could it have been Fiorenza? Has she been betraying her husband to her old Venetian lover?'

The philosopher was shaking his head, lost in the riddle. Anna rose. She was interested in a different betrayal and wanted very much to talk to Fiorenza. 'Where does she sleep?' she asked, moving to the door.

Plethon looked up. 'You may not hear what you want to hear.'

She turned. 'I want the truth, Plethon.'

Not long afterwards, in a room at the other end of the castle, Fiorenza heard a soft knock on her bedroom door. She was lying on a bed wet with her tears. Soldiers of the gautchin had just entered and arrested her husband. She got up from the bed, walked over to the door and opened it. Anna was carrying a candle and its light made Fiorenza's cheeks shine like paint. Her golden hair was disordered, her eyes red, but her back was straight. She was, after all, a princess from Trebizond.

She glanced beyond Anna into the dark corridor. 'It's dangerous for you to be here.'

'It's dangerous to be alive, Fiorenza,' said Anna. 'I must speak with you.'

Fiorenza stepped aside and Anna entered the room. She put the candle on to a table and looked around her. 'Is there somewhere to sit?'

Fiorenza went over to the bed and sat down. The air smelt of must but there was a fire in the grate and the room was warm. She said: 'I know why you've come.' Her face was a mask of misery.

Anna breathed deeply. 'Giovanni is Luke's son.' It was said quietly, not a question.

The Princess was still for a while. Then she dipped her head.

Anna felt numb. There was only one question to ask. 'Why?'

Fiorenza looked away. 'He was forced to. I drugged him.'

She paused for several moments, summoning the words. 'We wanted a child and Longo couldn't. So I used Luke.' Fiorenza turned and there were tears in her eyes. 'He loves you, Anna,' she said quietly. 'I don't think I've ever seen a love like it.'

Anna stared at the woman beside her. This was not the same woman she'd first met four days ago and she had no doubt that she was telling the truth. She closed her eyes, wanting to savour the sweetness of Fiorenza's words, to let them tumble in the whirl of her mind, then come to rest. She opened them again to see that Fiorenza was crying. She took her hand. 'What is it?' she asked softly. 'Where is Longo?'

'You must go.'

'Is it what Zoe said to you?' Anna squeezed her hand. 'I have been with Plethon. We know of your meeting with Zoe. Perhaps we can help.'

Fiorenza shook her head. 'It's too late.'

'What's too late?'

The Princess from Trebizond straightened. She took a handkerchief from her sleeve and brought it to her face, wiping her nose, her eyes. 'I have betrayed my husband. I have betrayed the signori. They've all been arrested.'

Anna took Fiorenza in her arms and held her tightly. 'What have you done, Fiorenza?' she whispered into her hair.

Fiorenza was breathing hard between the sobs. 'I have betrayed the signori to Tamerlane just as I have betrayed them to Venice all these years.'

Anna drew away. 'But why?'

'Because of love,' came the soft answer. 'Because of love for a man called Pavlos Mamonas.' She wiped her eyes with her hand and looked at Anna. 'Love makes you do strange things, but then you know that.'

'You love Pavlos Mamonas?'

'Did love. No longer.'

'So why betray them now?'

Fiorenza screwed her eyes shut, unable to stop the tears, stop the pain. 'Because the man I loved has a daughter who holds my son.' Fiorenza's grip on Anna's hand was tightening. 'She would have killed him if I hadn't confirmed her story.'

'What story?'

'That they sent the Varangian Matthew to kill Tamerlane.'

The shock made Anna start. Matthew sent to kill Tamerlane? It didn't make sense; then it did.

Zoe wants the signori dead before Luke and Mohammed Sultan get here.

Fiorenza opened her eyes. 'They will all die. Tomorrow. All except Longo. I had to . . . for Giovanni.'

Anna had to do something. She released Fiorenza and rose. 'I must return to Plethon.' She paused. 'One thing I don't understand. How could you betray a man like Marchese Longo to Pavlos Mamonas for all that time?'

Fiorenza shook her head slowly. 'I told you. I loved him. I loved him until . . .'

'Until?'

Fiorenza stared at Anna. 'Until Giovanni arrived. Then everything changed. I loved someone else.'

Anna saw the truth set out in all its misery before her. She'd looked for it and there it was. She wanted to ask something else but knew that Fiorenza wasn't listening any more. The Princess was staring into the fire and the embers in her eyes were just one small corner of the hell that burnt all around her.

*

The next morning, the manacled signori filed into the castle hall to find Tamerlane already there and seated in a chair, watching them from beneath a frown deep enough to hide armies. He was not wearing his spectacles. Zoe was sitting on the marble floor beside him, her body resting against his legs, her face expressionless. She wore the simple white caftan of the slave.

Marchese Longo was kneeling next to Dimitri and had just seen the tapestry beside him move. He glanced up. Tamerlane had risen and was walking slowly down the hall towards them, his uneven tread scraping on the marble. He stopped and let out a long sigh.

'You Italians. Always scheming.' He spat on the ground. 'You sent your assassin to kill me in my tent. But he did not find me there, so he tried to rape my bride instead. Do you expect mercy?'

There was shocked silence in the hall. Then Longo spoke. 'Lord, what assassin? We know of no assassin.'

'The Varangian. Is he not one of you?'

Longo was bewildered.

Luke is in Ankara.

'Lord . . .'

But Tamerlane's hand was in the air and two dozen tapestries parted as one to reveal men with bows aimed at the signori's hearts. 'You have betrayed me. All of you.'

A door behind opened and two soldiers came in dragging Matthew between them. He'd been beaten and his face was a mass of blood. They brought him to Tamerlane and pushed him to the floor. Tamerlane took a handful of his hair, forcing his head up. 'Look upon the face of a traitor, Genoese. He was found in my tent last night with poison in his belt. He will die and you will die. It is just.'

Longo had dared to get to his feet. 'Lord, this is madness. We don't even know this man. The Varangian whom we admitted to our campagna is the man called Luke Magoris. This man is a stranger.'

Tamerlane was shaking his head. 'You lie. Someone of your island has told me the truth: that you sent this man to kill me. And your Luke Magoris? I favoured him but it turns out he lied as well. You all lie and you will all die.'

An hour later, Tamerlane was riding towards the bridge, Zoe beside him. The morning was fair and the landscape around as motionless as a theatre set, winter's cold waiting in its wings. The signori walked in chains behind and there were gautchin on either side of them carrying ropes. Behind them marched the rest of Temur's bodyguard but without Varangians at their head.

Arcadius and Nikolas had left earlier to try to intercept Luke and Mohammed Sultan. Matthew hadn't returned from his night meeting with Tamerlane and they'd guessed that he'd gone to Luke.

Last of all came Anna, still disguised as a messenger, hand in hand with Fiorenza, who walked with her head bowed. As Anna made her way to the bridge she was joined by Plethon. After meeting with Fiorenza the night before, Anna had returned to his room to tell him all that she'd heard. But when she'd tried to find him in the morning, he'd gone. Now Plethon was beside her. She wondered if he'd used the ring.

She turned to him. 'Have you seen her?' she whispered.

'Who?'

'Zoe. With the ring.'

Plethon shook his head. 'It's too late for that, I'm afraid.'

Fiorenza stumbled next to her. Anna helped her back to her feet. The Princess hadn't spoken since they'd set out. Anna turned back to Plethon but he'd disappeared.

At the foot of the bridge were four chests, their lids open, with gold coins heaped inside. Tamerlane had decided that the signori would end their lives as they'd led them: with their pockets stuffed with gold. He would take them to the top of the bridge, tie them back to back and then push them into the river. The gold would drag them to the bottom and he'd enjoy watching them struggle against each other before they died.

Especially Longo.

Vaguely, he wondered whether Zoe would allow him some sport with Longo's widow after her husband had died. For Tamerlane, there was entertainment to be had in tears. He dismounted, walked over to the open chests and peered inside. He knelt and plunged his hands into one, lifting them so that the coins ran through his fingers, clinking as they fell. He looked back at Longo. 'I'm going to give you all this,' he said. 'I'm going to share it out amongst you.'

Longo had guessed what was to happen to them. He'd seen the guards with the rope and the furious river below. He'd heard of the many, many ways that this man had devised to kill people and saw the twisted logic of this one. He vaguely wondered how they'd retrieve the gold from the riverbed. He'd not seen his wife and hoped she wouldn't have to witness it.

But she would. When the men in front had stopped, Fiorenza, Anna and Plethon had walked forward, keeping well behind Zoe. They arrived to see Longo and Dimitri tied back to back being dragged up the bridge, Tamerlane following behind.

Fiorenza began to run forward, her hand to her mouth, her

eyes wide with horror. 'Not him!' she cried. 'She said he'd be spared!'

Anna caught her and gripped her arms, turning the woman to face her. 'She lied, Fiorenza. She always lies. She doesn't want *any* of the signori to join her on Chios. But she still has Giovanni. You must control yourself.'

Fiorenza was staring past Anna. 'But . . .'

'You must remain quiet,' said Anna, shaking her. 'If you try to interfere' – she glanced behind her to where Zoe sat on her horse, apparently unaware of their presence – 'your son . . . Longo's son, will die.'

Longo's son. Luke's son.

Fiorenza nodded slowly. She rose to her feet and Anna held on to her, keeping her standing. In front were the signori, chained and guarded, and in front of them was Zoe, looking directly ahead. Beyond was the bridge. It was long and high and they couldn't see over to its other side, but they heard the river below. Swollen by autumn rains, it was deep and fast and full of rocks.

Ahead, Tamerlane was walking up the bridge and looking at the sun, taking pleasure from its warmth upon his face. Perhaps he would stay in this country for a while, enjoy Constantinople with his new wife. Perhaps he'd have two capitals as the Romans once had. He closed his eyes and didn't notice that he was reaching the top. He heard talk in front of him. He opened his eyes to see that the two gautchin and their charges had stopped and were looking over the crest. Tamerlane walked up to them.

In front of him, over the brow of the bridge, was a big horse with a tall, fair man on its back. The man had a bow in his hand and at his side was a sword with a dragon head for a hilt.

Even without his glasses, Tamerlane knew who it was. He threw back his head and laughed. 'Varangian! You are Horatius! Or is it Leonidas? But he had three hundred and you are only one. What is this?'

There was no answer.

'Are you so keen to die?'

Luke lifted the bow. Its arrow was pointing at Tamerlane. Neither of the gautchin on the bridge had bows and they were too far away to reach him with their swords.

'Ah, you will kill me!' The old man clapped his hands. 'But that's suicide for everyone.' He gestured behind him. 'If I die, they all die. The Genoese, your emperor . . . all of them.'

Luke said: 'Bring forward the wife of Lord Longo. Alone.'

Longo, on his knees with Dimitri bound behind him, shouted: 'No!'

Tamerlane laughed. 'You'd have her plead for her husband's life? Why not?' He turned and shouted behind him: 'Have the wife of the Genoese leader come to me. Quickly!'

Anna was still holding Fiorenza by the arm but the next moment the Princess had broken free and was running past the signore, past Zoe, and on to the bridge. For a moment, Zoe looked as if she would follow her. But she reined in her horse and sat perfectly still.

Tamerlane watched Fiorenza come towards him, his hands on his hips. Ahead, Longo had managed to angle his body so that he could see her too. As she approached, Tamerlane turned back to Luke. 'Can she begin?'

Luke stared at Fiorenza. He hadn't seen her for a long time and, if anything, her beauty was greater than ever, perfectly poised between youth and age and seeming to reflect the season around them. Luke spoke to her. 'Lady, I have your son.'

He turned his head and whistled and Giovanni emerged from behind a tree at the bottom of the bridge. The boy ran up to Eskalon and was lifted into the saddle. Luke held him to his front and said: 'He was being held at Sklavia on the orders of Zoe.'

Tamerlane scratched his head. He was frowning. 'Why?'

'To persuade the Princess Fiorenza to lie to you, lord. Did she tell you that the signori sent the Varangian to kill you?'

Tamerlane nodded.

Fiorenza had arrived next to Tamerlane. She seemed composed. She said: 'I lied to you, lord, because Zoe held my son. She said that you'd spare my husband.'

Tamerlane grunted. He said to Luke: 'But what of the poison found on the Varangian?'

Luke had lifted the bow again. 'Zoe's poison was found on him, lord. Poison probably meant for you some day.'

Tamerlane snorted. 'Why would she want the Genoese to die?'

'Because the Genoese stand in her way.' He paused. 'As you will one day.'

Tamerlane looked behind him, down to the bottom of the bridge where Zoe still sat, out of earshot. He stood like that for some time. Then he turned back to Luke. 'But you lied as well, Varangian,' he said. 'You told me you were married to the one who eased my pain.'

'Her name is Shulen, lord.' Luke's hands were steady on the bow and Eskalon stood motionless beneath him. 'And she saved your life.'

'So why did you deny her to me?'

'Because your heir was in love with her. Would you have bedded the one Mohammed Sultan wanted for his wife?'

Tamerlane was silent again, his big head thrust forward in thought, his world suddenly more complicated. He looked up. 'Luke.' It was the first time that Tamerlane had used his name. 'You point an arrow at me to make me release the Genoese, which I will do.' He shouted something to the gautchin, who began to untie Longo and Dimitri. 'But you won't kill me because if you do, there'll be nothing left that you love. Including you.'

Luke said nothing and the arrow remained pointed at Tamerlane's heart. The hand that held the bowstring had begun to tremble.

The last time that they turned back was on the death of the Khan.

Tamerlane continued: 'You can have your signori but you won't save Constantinople. I may not marry her there but then it hardly matters. It was just an excuse to enter. I want to destroy it.' He shrugged. 'It's my way.'

Luke said nothing. He could release the arrow and Constantinople would be saved. But Anna was on the other side of the bridge. His arm began to ache.

Tamerlane had begun to limp slowly towards him. He said: 'I have favoured you, Luke, because you are brave and beloved of my heir. If you stay with me, you can have everything you want. A kingdom? It's yours.' He came on. 'We can conquer the world together.'

Luke said: 'Come no closer, lord. I have already conquered with you. I want no more part in it.'

Tamerlane had stopped. His head was on one side. 'Then I have lost?'

Luke looked beyond Tamerlane and nodded. He lowered the bow and lifted Giovanni to the ground. The boy ran to his mother, soon joined by Longo. Luke kicked Eskalon and came up to Tamerlane. He dismounted. 'We have both lost, lord,' he said quietly. 'Look behind you.'

There was commotion amongst the gautchin at the bottom of the bridge. Some had taken off their helmets and were kneeling on the ground. A deep murmur was spreading through the ranks. Someone was making their way through them. Someone important, someone who could make the gautchin kneel.

Mohammed Sultan.

Tamerlane had turned and was watching the scene before him unfold. In front of him, the ranks of the gautchin had begun to part. By now, every soldier was on his knees, every head bowed, every helmet clutched to a chest. The men's murmur had subsided, leaving only silence in its place. Luke could hear the squeak of wood on stone. Something with wheels was being pulled. Two heads came into view.

Shulen and Khan-zada.

They were dressed for mourning: long, heavy gowns reaching to their feet. Their faces were hooded, hidden. They were walking on either side of a litter being pulled by men.

Tamerlane took a step backwards. He didn't want what these women were here to give him. He didn't want to hear what they had to tell him. He fell to his knees and his head hit the ground in front of him, his hands covering his ears. Luke heard a deep moan.

The wheels stopped but the women kept walking until they were standing over him. Khan-zada knelt and took Tamerlane's shoulders in her hands and raised him from the ground. She brought the terror of the world, sobbing, into her breast.

'He is come,' she whispered.

Tamerlane's great shoulders were heaving with the

fathomless grief rising within him. He hadn't shed tears like this since the death of Jahangir. But he was much older now and it seemed that his ancient frame could no longer contain such sorrow. 'When?' he asked.

'A week past. It was a fever. There was nothing we could do.'

He said: 'It was the journey. I made him do it.'

Khan-zada shook her head. 'It would have happened anyway. It was his time.'

The two women turned and, Tamerlane between them, walked slowly back towards the kneeling gautchin, Luke following behind. As they approached, the ranks opened as men fell back to let them pass. A wagon harnessed to two horses came into view. On one side of it stood Yakub and Anna, on the other Pir Mohammed and Plethon.

The women led Tamerlane up to the wagon and then stepped back. The old man put his hands on its sides and leant over. For a long while he stood there without moving, perhaps without breathing. He looked down upon the man who had been his grandson and his heir and whose goodness was now hidden forever from the world behind closed eyes. He let out a long, agonised groan and Pir Mohammed stepped forward lest he fall. Tamerlane turned to him.

'Grandson, we go home,' he said quietly. 'Tell the generals that the army marches home to Samarcand. The Khan is dead.'

There was movement from within the gautchin and Zoe, no longer mounted, came forward. 'Lord, we have unfinished business here,' she said.

Tamerlane was shaking his head. What other business was there but taking his heir back to Samarcand? He stared at her.

'The Genoese, lord,' she whispered. She removed the phial

of poison from beneath her tunic. 'Remember their plot? They must die as you planned.'

Tamerlane turned to Shulen. He looked bewildered, lost. Shulen said: 'I have your glasses, Temur Gurgan. To help you see.' She proffered them.

The old man took the glasses and put them on. He was fumbling as old men do. 'What would you have me see, Shulen?' he asked.

'I would have you see your friends, lord.' She paused. 'And your enemies.'

Zoe stepped forward. 'Temur Gurgan doesn't need your glasses to see treason when it is before him,' she said. 'You have killed his heir as you planned to kill him.'

Shulen looked at Zoe for a while. They were so alike: both dark, both clever. Both strong. 'He needs them', she said quietly, 'to see you better.'

But Tamerlane wanted to see someone else. He looked down at his heir and reached down and parted his hair, leaving his hand resting on Mohammed Sultan's cold forehead. He looked back at Shulen and there was mist on his glasses. Gently, she removed them and wiped them clean on her sleeve. She put them back on to his nose. 'Temur Gurgan, I could not have killed Mohammed Sultan,' she said softly.

Zoe said: 'No? You've been nursing him since the battle. You needed something to stop Temur Gurgan from taking Constantinople. You killed his heir and brought him here.'

Khan-zada had come forward to stand next to her daughter, taking her hand. She said: 'Father, Shulen was Mohammed Sultan's sister. She loved him as a brother. She would not have killed him.' She paused and looked at Yakub. 'Temur Gurgan, you must know that I loved another before Jahangir. Our child was Shulen.'

Tamerlane stared at her, his mouth open. 'You loved another before Jahangir?'

She lowered her head. 'As I learnt to love your son, lord,' she said softly.

'Who was he?'

Yakub said: 'It was I, lord.'

Tamerlane was shaking his head, his mind exhausted by revelation. He suddenly wanted very much to be in a tent in a garden outside Samarcand. But a realisation was slowly taking shape. He turned to Shulen. 'You are of Genghis's line,' he said quietly. 'If you are daughter to Khan-zada, then you are of the blood.'

There was noise behind them. They turned and saw that Zoe was pushing her way back through the ranks from which she'd just emerged. Men were rising to let her pass. They looked towards Tamerlane.

He saw her and said: 'Let her go.'

Luke looked at Tamerlane as he watched her leave. His eyes, enormous in their magnification, were old and tired and full of grief. But they were no longer mad. Luke looked at Tamerlane and knew that he was now free, that Constantinople would remain free. Zoe had known it too and Luke knew that she wouldn't come back.

CHAPTER THIRTY-SEVEN

CONSTANTINOPLE, WINTER 1402

The city of Constantinople did play host to a marriage, but this one did not include a single Mongol amongst its congregation. In fact, the only trace of Tamerlane was in the dress of the bridegroom, who'd added some tarkhan dash to his Varangian dress in the form of a five-circled brooch, his parting gift from the Lord of the Celestial Conjunction. The city had been saved and it seemed only fitting that it should celebrate the wedding of the man who many saw as its saviour.

And celebrate it planned to do. The monks of the great Church of Holy Wisdom swept away all signs of supplication and set themselves to turning the church into a place of festival. The patterned marble floor was polished, the mosaics repaired and Barbi was once again summoned to pitch angels into the firmament. The Emperor wanted a spectacle worthy of the hour and the city frothed with excitement as the hour drew near.

In truth, Luke and Anna would rather have been married in the cathedral in Mistra than the Hagia Sophia. But Plethon had spoken of the importance of ceremony and civic pride and Luke had nodded and smiled and kissed Anna again. They were to marry and the *where* was unimportant. The *when*, however, was. Something had happened on that night ride from Ankara and quite soon its consequence would begin to show, no matter how loose the marriage gown.

Anna had told Luke on their arrival in Constantinople as they'd waited for their audience with the Emperor.

'You're sure?' he'd whispered, unable to hide the excitement in his voice and cursing the echo of the marbled antechamber.

'Of course I'm sure. Why else am I eating like Eskalon?'

Luke had nodded. 'And your freckles show. You look happy.'

The Empress had guessed at once. Helena Dragaš had looked at the bloom of pregnancy in a dozen mirrors and knew the signs. She'd come to the rescue. 'They should marry immediately,' she'd decreed as the couple stood before her. 'Or the people will forget.'

When the day arrived, a winter sun shone down on the capital of Byzantium. It was a kind sun that bathed everything in a general, mellow light, hiding the patches and fraying of its battered cathedral. Luke and Anna stood in its narthex, awaiting the entrance of the imperial couple, Luke dressed in the ceremonial armour of the Varangian Guard and Anna in a long white tunic of crushed silk embroidered with gold thread. Her red hair, littered with tiny flowers, swept past her shoulders in brilliant sheen. Matthew, still bruised, stood behind them in the dress of the *Akolouthos*, Luke having insisted his friend be given nothing less than the highest Varangian title there was. Next to him stood Shulen, handmaiden to Anna, also in white but without decoration, flowers or any flush of fertility; she would rejoin Tamerlane later. Behind them all stood Luke's three Varangian friends. Arcadius held a cushion on which rested Luke's dragon sword.

Trumpets sounded and they looked across the square to see the imperial party approach. The procession was led by six Varangians of Constantinople, axes on shoulders and eyes straight ahead until curiosity to see their new Akolouthos got the better of them. Then came a frieze of priests, court pages and high officials, the churchmen with their forked beards, stiff hats and long white robes spattered with crosses, the courtiers in towering, elaborate headwear, brocaded skirts and soft boots. There was the Master of Horse, the Megas Doux in his paper-boat hat, the Grand Vestarios and the Candidatoi with their golden wands. This was Byzantium, faded but fine.

At last the Emperor Manuel II Palaiologos appeared with his wife on his arm, the imperial family behind. The Emperor and Empress wore the same: the imperial *mitra* with its curtain of jewels above long white robes sewn with double-headed eagles and fringed with ermine. They looked ethereal.

The procession swept solemnly into the church and only the Empress Helena cast a smile and a wink at Anna as she passed.

There was a clearing of throat and they looked up to see the Patriarch in a vestment that seemed too heavy for his frame. He was telling them to exchange rings in a voice that quivered to find volume. Then he turned and led them into the church.

It seemed that the whole of Constantinople had come to see them married. Thousands sat in the nave and many more stood behind, and those that were not inside the church filled the square outside. Walking slowly, Luke looked up and remembered what the Emperor Justinian had said when first he saw the finished glory of the Hagia Sophia:

Solomon, I have outdone thee.

Despite age and pillage, the church was still a thing of splendour. The walls glittered with mosaics of the Holy Family, saints and emperors: arch-browed, straight-nosed, their heads buckled with diadems. They walked beneath heaven's aristocracy, beneath archangels and six-winged cherubs, the vast dome above seeming to float on a halo of light that came in through the windows ringing its base.

Then they were in front of a table of green and white marble on which were set two golden crowns. Beside it sat the Emperor and Empress on backless thrones and on either side of them, straight-backed and solemn, sat their mothers: Rachel and Maria. Luke bowed to them and, rising, saw beyond them Marchese Longo, Fiorenza and Giovanni, seated with the rest of the signori. Beside them sat Plethon, Omar, Yakub and Benedo Barbi.

The Patriarch lifted each of the crowns and placed them on their heads. Then he offered them a chalice of sweet Malvasia wine to share. Luke looked over its rim at his bride and his face creased into a smile.

At last.

Psalms and incense rose around them in scented litany as they walked three times around the table, each holding a candle. The cathedral echoed with holy chant and the saints looked down on it all, moving to the rhythms of light that cascaded from a million tiny tiles. Heaven was inside the Church of Holy Wisdom and its glory touched everything and everyone within it.

At last it was over and the Patriarch was telling them to leave. They turned and walked back to the narthex, their crowns heavy on their heads. Outside, the winter sunshine, soft as spun syrup, made them blink. The crowds in the square cheered and waved and threw their hats in the air. They were joined on the steps by the imperial family, the Despot and Despoena, their mothers and friends. A shower of rose petals, somehow preserved, was released from the windows above. A trumpet sounded from the waters of the Propontis and twenty thousand heads turned to see the twelve triremes of the imperial navy bedecked in bunting, their oars lifted in salute. Beside them were twelve round ships flying the flag of Chios, rocking like tipsy monks in the winter swell. A cannon sounded, then another. The crowd roared its approval and more hats went into the air. The Empire was delivered from Tamerlane and its saviour was before them with his bride. Byzantium was still Christian.

There was a flutter of wings and they looked up to see doves rising into the sun, tiny olive branches tied to their feet.

The Emperor laughed. 'It's to celebrate the peace treaty with Suleyman,' he said. 'He's given us back Thessaloniki.'

Luke knew this but perhaps the mothers didn't. Ferried to safety, the heir to Bayezid had established himself at Edirne and seemed keen to make peace. Thessaloniki, second jewel in Byzantium's crown, had been returned.

Plethon stood beside the Emperor. 'Suleyman's still dangerous, majesty,' he said. 'He's just buying some time.'

The Empress smiled and pressed his arm. 'Tush, philosopher. Be merry like the crowd. We are delivered. Look.' She was pointing towards the hippodrome where a single horse stood on a plinth. 'Now, *that* is a wedding gift.'

It was Luke's gift to the city. The four horses of the hippodrome had gone to Venice two hundred years earlier so Luke had replaced them with Eskalon, carved in Chios as the quartet had been centuries ago. The bronze horse shone like a god.

Luke turned to his wife and raising her crown with one finger, kissed her on the lips.

EPILOGUE

MISTRA, CHRISTMAS 1402

The snow was falling thickly on the hill of Mistra and the little courtyard of the Peribleptos Monastery was deep with it. It was the hour before dawn on Christmas Day and the monks were sleeping in, having enjoyed their annual holy supper the night before. With twelve dishes for the twelve apostles, and straw beneath the table for when the baby saviour chose to come, it had been more fun than last year. The Turks had been defeated and Mistra was still free. They'd even drunk wine.

For the three people in the crypt below the monastery church, the padded silence of snow and sleeping monks was welcome. Although Varangians kept guard at the doors and windows, what they had before them could never be revealed to anyone. For two of them, it was known. For the other, it was a revelation.

Luke, Anna and Plethon were kneeling by the side of an open casket and none of them had spoken for several minutes. Beside them was an empty grave with earth piled to one side. There were torches on the walls and their light made a nativity of the scene. It was very cold and a night creature howled from deep inside the woods beyond the city walls.

This seemed to stir Plethon. 'We should replace the ring now and bury the casket. It's nearly dawn.'

Luke nodded. What he'd just seen was beyond comprehension. He leant forward and placed the ring in the casket. Then he took Anna's hand and found it trembling either from the cold or something else. 'When do you think we'll need it?' he asked, his voice a whisper.

Plethon rubbed his eyes. The casket always made him so tired. 'Soon. Bayezid might be beaten but Suleyman lives on. And he still has a powerful army. We don't have much time.'

Luke knew this to be true, just as he knew that the next part of Plethon's plan would be played out in the west: in Italy. They'd talked long about Popes and Medicis and the union of Churches. Soon he'd have to go there, but not yet. He'd been appointed Protostrator of Mistra, the youngest yet. And the Protostrator's new wife was with child, a brother or sister for Giovanni. No one would stop him being in Mistra for the birth.

He let go of Anna's hand and, very slowly, closed the casket's lid.

HISTORICAL NOTE

The Mistra Chronicles take place in the late fourteenth and early fifteenth centuries, the decades leading up to the fall of the Constantinople in 1453. It was a time of colliding empires: the Ming in China, the Timurid in central Asia, the Mamluk in Egypt and Syria, the Ottoman in Turkey and the Balkans, and what was left of the Empire of Byzantium: Constantinople and the Greek Peloponnese, where *The Mistra Chronicles* begin and end.

The Byzantine Empire had once been one of the greatest powers on earth. Its citizens had always called themselves Rhomaioi, never Byzantine, because they saw themselves as directly descended from Romulus and Remus (or Aeneas who himself was Greek). They were right. The Empire had once been the right-hand half of the Roman Empire, the part not overrun by the barbarians in the fifth century, and its capital was Constantinople, founded by the Emperor Constantine in AD 324.

The Empire had waxed and waned in the thousand years leading up the start of our story. Under the Emperor Justinian in the sixth century, it had recovered much of the western half of the Empire. But his successor Maurice fought a twenty-year war of attrition against his eastern neighbours, the Sassanids of Persia, so that the Byzantines were in no shape to withstand the Arab invasions that swept out of Saudi Arabia after the death of Mohammed in 632. But the walls of Constantinople, greatest in the world, had held, helped by the Byzantine secret weapon of 'Greek fire'. This was a liquid that, when spouted from a siphon and ignited, could burn on water. How it was made was a state secret known only to the Emperor and a few others and it was particularly lethal against besieging ships. It wasn't until the thirteenth century that Constantinople's walls were finally breached by an entirely unexpected enemy: the Christian Fourth Crusade.

This was a story of pride, greed and ignorance, and led to one of the worst cultural rapes in history. The aged Doge Dandolo of Venice had agreed to build ships to carry the crusade to Egypt. But when the crusaders couldn't pay for them, he did a deal: take back the city of Zara for Venice and the debt would be repaid. But once the crusaders had a taste for pillage, they found the offer of 200,000 marks to help the son of the deposed Emperor of Byzantium recover his throne impossible to resist. They put Alexios Angelos back on the throne and waited outside Constantinople to be paid. After a year, they stormed it, led over the walls by the blind nonagenarian Doge. Only fifty years later was the city recovered by the Byzantines and by then, most of its riches were in Venice.

So by the end of the fourteenth century, the Byzantine Empire had no money, no army, no navy and precious little territory. Constantinople was a city of fields and ruined palaces and its population had sunk to just fifty thousand. Meanwhile, a Turkic tribe from the Anatolian steppe had conquered most of its neighbouring tribes and crossed over to Europe in 1354. The Ottoman Sultan Bayezid, fourth in the line of Osman, had, by 1400, swept up to the Danube and as far south as the Peloponnese, thus surrounding Constantinople. In 1396, the West had sent a crusade to the aid of the city, an army that 'could hold up the sky with its lances'. But the chivalry of Europe had jousted and feasted its way to the Danube only to be annihilated at the field of Nicopolis. Now Bayezid boasted that he would 'water his horses at the altar of St Peter's in Rome' and it seemed that he might. The rebirth of wealth and culture that was taking place among the city states of Italy, the movement we know as 'the Renaissance', which would lead to the Ages of Discovery and Enlightenment and ultimately secure western global dominance, was under threat. All that stood in Bayezid's way were the walls of Byzantium.

In contrast to Constantinople, by 1400 the Byzantine Despotate of Mistra in the Greek Peloponnese was thriving. 'Despot' has bad connotations but the rulers of this tiny kingdom were usually the brothers or sons of the reigning Emperor and were good, cultured men. The Despotate had two main cities: Mistra, built in the twelfth century near the ancient site of Sparta, and Monemvasia. They were very different. Mistra was the home of the court and government, run by the Protostrator, a sort of prime minister. It was a place of music, culture and courtly love, a sort of Camelot. Monemvasia, meanwhile, was a rich seaport on the trade route between Venice and the east. Its main export was Malvasia wine, an expensive, sweet wine much favoured in the courts of Europe. In England, they called it Malmsey and the Duke of Clarence was said to have drowned in a butt of it. Monemvasia was ruled by an Archon, subservient to the Despot in Mistra but often in rebellion. In my *Chronicles*, the families of Laskaris and Mamonas hold the offices of Protostrator and Archon as indeed they did at the time. You can still visit the ruined Laskaris House in Mistra. Perhaps its most famous citizen, from early in the fifteenth century, was the philosopher Plethon, a disciple of Plato and a man of eccentric views, who advocated the return to a Hellenic, even Spartan, model of society.

With or without help from their Spartan past, the Byzantines were no match for the vast forces that the Ottomans had at their disposal. Not only could Bayezid call on the Anatolian gazi tribes with their lethal composite bows, but the conquered Serbs provided him with heavy cavalry. The Ottomans also had the Devshirme, introduced by Bayezid's father Murad I, by which Christian boys were forcibly taken from the villages of Eastern Europe to be trained as janissaries, the elite slave soldiers of the Ottoman army.

What Bayezid didn't have yet, however, were cannon large enough to bring down the walls of Constantinople. Invented centuries before in China, these weapons had first appeared on the battlefields of Europe at the siege of Algeciras in the Iberian peninsula. Two English knights brought the technology back with them and cannon were used, with only modest success, at the Battle of Crécy in 1346. By 1400, there was an arms race to develop cannon big enough to make city walls redundant. They were ultimately to be used to devastating effect by Mehmed II in the siege of Constantinople in 1453.

By the time of these *Chronicles*, the Byzantines' own elite force was mostly memory. The Varangian Guard had once been the finest fighting unit in the world, famed for their use of axes. They had come from England, Anglo-Saxon refugees from the Norman Conquest in 1066, to place themselves at the service of the Emperor of Miklagard (Byzantium). They'd grown rich in his service, having the privilege of filling their helmets with gold on the death of an emperor. By 1400, however, they had almost ceased to exist.

But what the Byzantines lacked in armies, they more than made up for in diplomacy. Their cousins, the Komnenoi of the tiny Empire of Trebizond, had after all survived for centuries by marrying off their beautiful princesses to local warlords. Manuel II Palaiologos of Byzantium, however, had two better plans for survival. The first was to bring a monster even greater than Bayezid west to fight him: Tamerlane.

Tamerlane, or Temur-e-leng (Timur the Lame), was a Mongol warlord of unreliable descent who'd been made lame while horse-rustling as a young man. By 1400, he had conquered most of Central Asia with a savagery not even matched by his predecessor Genghis Khan. Having united the tribes and kingdoms of his home Chagatai Khanate, his horde swept down the superhighway of the steppe to lay waste to everything as far as Anatolia, where he came up against the Empire of Bayezid. On the way he had levelled Aleppo, Antioch, Delhi, Herat, Kabul and countless other cities, building his trademark towers of skulls among their ruins to spread terror before him. In twenty short years, it is estimated that he accounted for some 5 per cent of the world's population. His greatest desecration may have been the destruction of the beautiful Umayyad Mosque in Damascus, one of Islam's noblest buildings.

But Manuel's problem was that Tamerlane didn't really want to come west. He had two obsessions: making his capital of Samarcand into the greatest city on earth, and reuniting the four khanates created by the sons and grandsons of Genghis Khan. By 1400, he'd conquered three of them: the Khanates of Chagatai, Persia and the Golden Horde of the north, and only the greatest remained: China, the former Empire of Kublai

Khan now ruled by an ambitious new dynasty: the Ming.

As for Samarcand, by 1400 it certainly had some of the biggest buildings on earth and its suburbs were named after other great cities to prove that it was the greatest of them all. But such was the fear inspired in the architects by Tamerlane to make them build faster, many of the mosques and palaces were built without proper foundations and fell down soon after he died.

To build Samarcand Tamerlane needed booty, and there was far more booty in the east than the west. Why was this? In large part it was due to the Silk Road (not called so then) that stretched six thousand miles from Chang'an in China to Constantinople. It was a trade route like no other, with caravanserai every twenty miles, which was the distance a camel could walk in a day. It was also a sort of internet along which new ideas and new inventions could travel. Great cities like Palmyra and Tabriz sprang up along it, made rich by the taxation of trade. In 1400, the annual revenues of the city of Tabriz exceeded those of the King of France.

Manuel's second plan was to bring another crusade from the west. But there was a problem. Since 1054, the Western Catholic and Eastern Orthodox Churches had been in schism and the Pope would not give his blessing to any more crusades until the schism had been ended. Worse still, the Western Catholic Church was itself in schism and two Popes, one in Rome and the other in Avignon, were at each other's throats.

In *The Mistra Chronicles*, I use some artistic licence to describe the way that Plethon (who was in fact instrumental in ending the East–West schism) makes an ally of the powerful Florentine banking family of Medici to further this end. In this book, he meets Giovanni de' Medici, the founder of the bank. In future books, his son Cosimo will become crucial in unifying the Churches. In fact, Manuel spent the years 1398–1400 touring the courts of Europe trying to gain support, and money, for the Byzantine cause. He was even entertained by the English King Henry VI at Eltham Palace, but no funds were made available.

So this is the historical context and the narrative of *The Mistra Chronicles*: a once-great empire on its knees with two plans for its survival, one facing east, the other west. How it happened is part-fact, part-fiction.

This second book in the series, *The Towers of Samarcand*, includes some interesting historical characters that are worthy of further description. In the Byzantine camp, the Emperor Manuel, his wife Helena Dragaš and his brother Theodore, Despot of Mistra, were all brilliant, cultured people determined to do what they could to save their empire. Plethon was very much as described, an eccentric thinker of genius who didn't have much time for organised religion.

In the Ottoman camp, Bayezid is depicted in the book as past his best. Certainly he'd been a man of rapid and unexpected conquest in his youth, earning for himself the name of Yildirim, or 'Thunderbolt'. His heir Suleyman was a good soldier but, after the Battle of Ankara, became debauched. Suleyman's brother Mehmed was the clever one who ultimately triumphed in the civil war that engulfed the Empire after the death of Bayezid. Bayezid's mother, the Valide Sultan Gülçiçek, certainly existed, although whether she was quite as nasty as depicted in the book is a matter for conjecture. The Valide Sultan, mother of the ruling Sultan, was always a very powerful figure whose power held sway far beyond the harem walls.

Tamerlane was an odd mixture of psychopathic cruelty and cultural sensibility. He was a brilliant strategist who rarely lost a battle and the stories of his military ruses described in this book are all true. He was intelligent, could speak several languages, and did invent a new version of chess. His son Miran Shah was as mad as depicted and lacked any of his father's genius. Miran Shah's wife Khan-zada was said to be beautiful and brave and did warn Tamerlane of his son's intrigues against him. Tamerlane's grandson and heir, Mohammed Sultan, known as a paragon of virtue, did die from his wounds after Ankara. Much of the description of the extraordinary court of Tamerlane, including the feast on the plain of Kanigil (which happened in 1404, rather than 1399 in this book), comes from the diaries of the Castilian envoy, Ruy González de Clavijo, who arrived at Samarcand with the Ambassador Sotomayor. His diaries describe Angelina of Hungary and Maria from Trebizond, both captured on the field of Ankara. They are an entertaining read.

I have been inaccurate as to the timing of the Chinese Emperor's death to fit in with the narrative. In fact the Hongwu Emperor, the first of the astonishing Ming Dynasty, died in 1398, three years before I describe.

One of the more intriguing characters in the book is the historian Ibn Khaldun. He led a strange and peripatetic life, including holding the position of Kadi to the Mamluk Sultan, before he sat down to write his extraordinary histories. The story of him being lowered from the walls of Damascus to meet Tamerlane is entirely true, as was his success in securing the release of his compatriots in the city.

Yakub II of the Germiyans existed and his capital was Kutahya in the Anatolian steppe. He hated Bayezid, who had imprisoned him for three years in the castle of Ipsala after annexing his beylik, only slightly less than he hated Allaedin ali-Bey of the neighbouring Karamanid tribe, which had yet to fall beneath the Ottoman yoke.

King Giorgi of Georgia also existed and Tamerlane's campaign into Georgia took place as described, although it wasn't led by Mohammed Sultan. The story of the baskets lowered to smoke out King Giorgi's army in the caves of Vardzia is completely true as is the story of his escape with Prince Tahir.

Little is known about Qara Yusuf of the Qara Qoyunlu (or Black Sheep) tribe who had his capital in Tabriz. The Black Sheep formed a buffer state between the Ottoman and Timurid Empires and Qara Yusuf tried desperately to play one power off against the other. Amazingly, he survived to die in 1420.

Another fascinating character was Hasan-i Sabah, founder of the assassin cult. He was a brilliant mathematician, astronomer and alchemist who, in the late eleventh century, gathered a following of fanatical Ismai'li diehards who were prepared to die for the Shia cause, their main targets being the ruling Sunni Seljuk Turks of Persia. He captured the impregnable stronghold of Alamut in the Alburz Mountains and used it to send forth his assassins to do their work. It is said that they would first be drugged with hashish, then led into a garden where they would awake to beautiful women. Then they were told that they were in paradise and could only return having performed their deed.

Apart from the wily Doge Venier of Venice, the main Italian of the book is the Genoese Marchese Giustiniani Longo, Lord of Chios. By the end of the fourteenth century, Venice was pulling ahead of its fierce trade rivals, the Genoese. The two republics had gone to war in 1378 and a Genoese fleet had actually entered the Venetian lagoon, briefly occupying the island of Choggia. But Venice had won the war and, at this time, was busy trying to prise as much territory and trade as it could from Genoa. Chios was one of the few Mediterranean islands still controlled by the Genoese, most of their colonies now being in the Black Sea. It was held under a long lease from the Byzantine Empire by a joint stock company, the Mahona, which was the first of its kind and a forerunner of the England's East India Company. The Mahona had been formed in the mid-fourteenth century by twelve Genoese families under the collective name of Giustiniani in deference to the great Byzantine Emperor Justinian. Its purpose was to exploit the trade of alum, mined in neighbouring Phocaea on the Turkish mainland, which was the valuable substance used to fix dye in clothing. Its other purpose was to trade mastic and it is entirely true that Chios produced a kind of mastic found nowhere else in the world. Mastic was used as a breath freshener, a wound sealant, an embalmer and, in India at least, a filler for tooth cavities. At the time of this book, the Genoese had already begun to build extraordinary maze-like villages in the south of the island to protect their workforce from Turkish corsairs. The 'Mastic Villages' of Chios can still be visited today.

The book reaches its climax with the extraordinary battle of Ankara, one of the greatest and most important battles ever fought in history. The story of the interchange of slanderous letters between Tamerlane and Bayezid is well documented, as is the way that Tamerlane persuaded Bayezid to abandon his position in front of the fortress to follow him around Anatolia in a wild goose chase. The diversion of the Cubuk Creek by Tamerlane did happen and Bayezid's army was forced to fight without water. Most telling for the outcome of the battle, however, was the defection of the gazi tribes to Tamerlane at the height of the battle. Afterwards, Bayezid was placed inside a cage for Tamerlane to gloat over. Bayezid died of the shame a year after the battle.

Whether or not Tamerlane intended to march on Constantinople after Ankara is unknown, although he did take Smyrna from the Hospitallers and the story of the defenders' heads being hurled from the battlements to land on the decks of the relieving Hospitaller fleet is true.

What is also true is that the only time a Mongol horde had turned back from invasion of Europe before was on the death of the Khan. This was Ögedei Khan, third son of Genghis, who gave permission for his sons Kadan and Güyük to conquer all the way to the 'Great Sea' or the Atlantic Ocean. They were on the point of taking Vienna in 1241 when the death of their father forced their recall to Karakorum to crown his successor. The Mongols never again reached further west.

So, by the end of *The Towers of Samarcand*, Tamerlane has gone home and Constantinople is still free. The first of Manuel's plans has worked but Bayezid's son, Suleyman, unwisely ferried to Europe in Byzantine ships, has lived to fight another day. The next book will see Luke and the Varangians continue their mission to secure the future of the beleaguered Byzantine Empire.

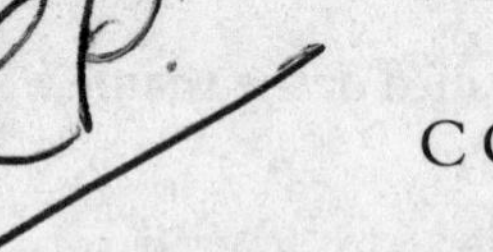

COMING SOON

More memorable heroes, epic history and the Varangian treasure finally revealed as

THE MISTRA CHRONICLES

continue in

THE LION OF MISTRA

PUBLISHED JULY 2015

www.heronbooks.co.uk